# PROTOKOL

## A Novel of International Intrigue

**Eugene Golub**

and Quinton Skinner

Alliance Press, Inc.
Chicago, Illinois

Published by Alliance Press, Inc.
Chicago, IL 60611
alliancepress@goco.com

Library of Congress Cataloging-in-Publication Data
Golub, Eugene.
        Protokol: a novel of international intrigue / Eugene Golub and Quinton Skinner.–Chicago, IL: Alliance Press, Inc. 2002.

        p.     ;     cm.

        ISBN 0-9719259-0-9

1. Espionage-Fiction. 2. Mystery-Fiction. 2. Spy stories. I. Title.

PS3607.O583 P76        2002              2002104049
813.6                          -dc21              CIP

06  05  04  03  02  •  5  4  3  2  1

Cover design by Kelli Leader
Book design by Katherine Hyde

*Printed in the United States*

# PROTOKOL

This book is dedicated to all my colleagues,
and in particular to the forward-looking
men and women of Central and Eastern Europe
who embraced a vision of reform
and free-market economies to the benefit
of their countries and the world.

To my wife Hanna, you are the best

Thank you, Tricia

# Contents

# Part One

# *The Secret*

# Chapter One

*February 16, 1998. 8:20 a.m.*
*St. Petersburg, Russia.*

THE MORNING AIR CARRIED A CHILL WIND and dry flakes of snow onto the city. Soldiers, roused hours before sunrise, fell into lines and cleared away the snowfall with old metal shovels that scraped and clattered on the pockmarked sidewalks.

Traffic had just begun to thicken; cars wove carefully through a web of deep potholes capable of easily snapping a Volga or Lada's axle. Headlights poked through the gloom and illuminated the lower facades of palaces that had once belonged to royalty in the time of the czars. Now many of the palaces had fallen into neglect, their luxurious colors faded and their edifices crumbling in the harsh northern climate.

Lights flickered on in the huge Soviet-era apartment buildings that ringed the city. There, families shared bathrooms and kitchens; the shoddy standards of the defunct regime had left the citizenry in

3

homes that literally crumbled away beneath their feet. Cold drafts blew through cracks in the walls, and the electricity sparkled and failed without warning.

The sun rose above the horizon and flickered upon the frozen canals that ran through the city like arteries through an aged and tired heart. The splendor of the Winter Palace was illuminated over the banks of the River Neva. The city was almost fully awake now, the smell of car exhaust and smoke starting to fill the air. This was Peter the Great's city, his gateway to Europe. Now the past mingled uncertainly with the present, as though each era of history struggled unsuccessfully to come to the fore, erasing all others.

People emerged from the depths of the Metro, where subway lines were dug deep into the solid earth beneath the sandy topsoil. Their long coats and scarves were tight around their necks, their heads covered in fur hats, their expressions tight against the cold and the uncertainty of Russian life.

A crowd ascended the stairs near the Metro station by the Cathedral of Our Lady of Kazan. A young child laughed as she reached the snow-covered sidewalk, her hand enveloped in her mother's. The sound pealed in the subdued quiet. A man carrying a briefcase containing only his lunch heard her, also an elderly *babushka* carrying a plastic bag like a treasured possession. Everyone who heard the child smiled and turned, seeking out her face. The child's glee spread for a second then disappeared as the people of St. Petersburg returned to their lives and worries.

---

ALEXEI SOKOLOV LEANED BACK against the headrest of his new Volvo sedan and held his cellular phone tight against his ear. He was in the passenger seat and watched as his driver, Fyodor, expertly drove into the city.

"*Dobroye utro,*" he said. "Good morning. This is Sokolov. Is Anatoly in the office yet?"

"Good morning, sir," said the receptionist at GlobusBank. "No. Mister Dorokhin has not arrived."

Sokolov checked his watch. It was almost eight-thirty in the morning. Anatoly, his deputy at GlobusBank, should have arrived a half-hour ago. There was a meeting starting at nine with officials from the European Development Bank regarding financing for the renovation of a historical building on Nevsky Prospect in the heart of St. Petersburg. The building had been vacant for forty years, and GlobusBank was entering into a partnership with an American development group, Olen Europe, to do a historical renovation. Sokolov needed a last-minute report from Anatoly on the current status of GlobusBank's projection with the addition of the Value Added Tax in response to the Duma's new tax laws.

"I'll be there shortly," Sokolov said, letting his annoyance bleed into his voice. "Tell Anatoly to call me on my cellular phone if he gets there in the next few minutes."

"Yes, sir," the secretary said.

Sokolov closed his eyes and felt the motion of the car as his driver accelerated into the central city. There were always problems. He should have fired Anatoly months ago.

"Is anything the matter?" asked a soft voice from the back seat.

Sokolov turned in his seat and looked back at his wife. Masha was more beautiful at thirty-eight than she had been twenty years before, when they met at the university. Her long hair was black, her eyes a sparkling green. Though she had had two children, she maintained a youthful vitality.

"The usual, darling," Sokolov said, forcing a smile. "Incompetence and laziness."

"You are hard on them," she replied with a sympathetic smile.

The car slowed, and Sokolov turned to look. Traffic was crawling alongside one of the city's canals. Sokolov took a deep breath. Masha could always calm him with a word, a gesture. She understood him better than anyone.

He was forty-one now, and he had lived in St. Petersburg all his life. So much had changed since he was a young boy in the Pioneers and the Komsomol. He and Masha had once shared a small apartment in the city, where they lived on her schoolteacher's wages and his salary as a bureaucrat in the City Property Committee.

In the short time since the dissolving of the Soviet Union, old roles had fallen away with new ones created out of fresh cloth. Sokolov had been well-placed in the city government when a series of private banks were founded in Russia. Within five years he had become the president of the St. Petersburg branch of GlobusBank—which was operated and owned out of Moscow by one of the country's new elite billionaires. Sokolov's new position had brought him money and prestige. He now oversaw an operation that functioned on the profit motive, a new idea for a citizenry that had previously lived under central government control in a command economy. Some people had fallen into obscurity and poverty when the change came and were unable to adapt their ways and seize new opportunities. Sokolov had not been one of them.

Sokolov's driver cursed under his breath as he pulled into the heavy traffic on Nevsky Prospect, the city's most renowned central street. St. Petersburg had been designed long before the invention of the car. Traffic was congested and harried, and driving there required a daunting combination of skilled reflexes and aggression.

He turned around to look at Masha. "So, you are going shopping after you drop me off at the office?"

Masha nodded yes. "Could you please stop by the athletic sports store?" he asked. "They should have that new pair of Nike running shoes I ordered."

"I'll remember," Masha said with a small smile.

"Also, look for that mathematics computer program for the children," he added. "I want Dmitri and Mila staying ahead of their classmates."

"I'll buy the software," Masha replied. "But good luck getting Dmitri to use it. All he wants to do is draw and paint."

Sokolov snorted with good-natured derision. "I want my children to have the tools for success," he said. "Drawing is well and good. But business puts food on the table and a roof over our head."

Masha gave him the same indulgent look she always had, ever since their college days. Sokolov felt she both agreed with him and humored him as though he were still an opinionated young man.

"That look of yours," he said, reaching back to brush his fingers under her chin. "You know I am right. I am always right."

"Of course you are, darling," she said, laughing softly.

Sokolov turned around again. The traffic had ground to a halt. He enjoyed sparring with Masha, but he *was* right. New opportunities were appearing all over Russia. But it took energy and creativity, along with a solid education, to meet them. His son, Dmitri, was a smart boy. But this was not the time for drawing and playing with clay. Those who did not participate in the new economy would be lost.

"What is this?" Fyodor said under his breath.

Traffic was moving around them and coursing down Nevsky toward the winding Neva River. Their Volvo remained stopped. A black Mercedes was stopped in front of them and blocked the way.

Sokolov checked his watch. "Go around," he ordered Fyodor. "The fool must have broken down. Come on, I can't be late."

Fyodor threw the car in reverse and looked in the mirror.

"Come on," Sokolov demanded. "What's the matter?"

He turned around and looked out the back window. He saw what was keeping Fyodor from pulling away: A second car, also a Mercedes, was stopped behind them. They were blocked from the front and also from the back.

Masha saw the look in her husband's eyes. "What is it? What's happening?"

Sokolov turned and saw three young men getting out of the car in front. They were all stocky, their hair cut short, their faces impassive as they walked around to the Volvo's passenger side.

Each one reached into his coat.

Sokolov saw flashes of metal.

"Get down!" he cried out to Masha, straining against his seat belt. Beside him, Fyodor opened his own door and dropped out of the car onto the pavement.

Sokolov heard the sound of glass breaking. It was his window.

Alexei Sokolov heard a series of harsh cracks, sounds that seemed to come from someplace far away. He felt a terrible pain in the center of his body that radiated outward. *I'm being shot.* He saw a flash of color, a roar, then nothing at all as his world turned to black.

*February 16, 1998. 9:00 a.m.*
*Chicago.*

DAVID OLEN PAGED THROUGH a stack of documents on his white marble desk and scanned through rows and columns of numbers and technical notations. He focused his attention keenly on the details of the current land purchase with which his company was involved. A laptop computer was open on his desk; it had idled to display a screen saver showing the Olen and Company logo tracing an elliptical path. From the telephone's speaker came the sound of voices.

"The thing is, Ray," said a man's voice from the speaker, "I can't tell from their attorneys' comments to the purchase contract whether they included the long, narrow parcel on the north side of the survey."

"Well, Phil, if you look at page five—"

"I'm *looking* at page five, and there's nothing—"

"You'll see a reference to each parcel in the title policy."

"Oh, I see." A pause. "But where is this parcel marked? Maybe I'm going blind in my old age," Phil said with a chuckle.

David ran his hand lightly along the smooth line of his clean-shaven cheek and looked out the window at the far end of his spacious corner office. He was up on the twenty-fifth floor, seemingly almost level with the low curtain of overcast that pressed down on the city of Chicago and extended out to the horizon. Downtown skyscrapers lined up one after another, their windows reflecting the passing clouds. A spot of sunlight appeared, brightening the sky for less than a minute until it disappeared into the wintry gloom.

"Here's the issue," said a voice from the speakerphone. "Olen and Company isn't interested in this deal unless that adjacent lot is included, even though there is a utility easement. We'll need every F.A.R. foot possible in order to justify the land price."

The persistent voice negotiating on David Olen's behalf was that of Phil Hernandez, an attorney representing Olen and Company, David's real-estate investment and development company. The conference call that morning was about a fairly straightforward land purchase. But as in any deal, no matter how seemingly simple, there were always issues that required debate, compromise, and ultimately concessions from both sides of the transaction. It was the nature of business.

David leaned back in his black leather ergonomic desk chair and stretched with a quiet sigh. He stifled a yawn and reached for a coffee cup resting on a coaster next to an array of stacked files.

"I'm correct about this, right, David?" asked Phil. His sonorous voice and clipped diction were deeply familiar to David.

David had been silent for the past ten minutes and had been listening carefully to the half-dozen men on the line who were negotiating the sale and purchase. There were attorneys and managers who worked for his company, as well as their counterparts representing the firm selling the land parcel. Now there was silence on the line as all parties waited for David's input; they knew that he could make or break the deal as he wished.

A small smile played at the corners of David's lips. "Of course you're right, Phil," he said. "We definitely need that strip to do the deal. And that's why we're all here on the phone this morning, right? We want to make it happen. I assume everyone is in agreement on that point."

Several voices murmured their assent. "Then that's what we're going to do," David continued. "Let's cut the bullshit, and let's do the deal. The narrow parcel on the north end of the survey: It has to be included for us to buy the property. Otherwise let's just forget it, and we can all go on our way."

A moment of silence. David heard whispers, papers shuffling. Finally one of the seller's representatives said: "I guess we can live with that. It's up to us to straighten out the easement language; it's tricky, but we'll get it covered. What's the next point?"

"Excellent," Phil said. "The next issue is the environmental report. We can't work the deal with the existing zoning. And we'll have to go for a P.U.D. When we apply for a Planned Unit Development, the environmental report is going to have to stand up to the city's engineers and attorneys. So we won't close until our guys are satisfied that it's pristine clean."

David sipped his coffee and allowed himself the luxury of relaxing for a moment. He had been involved in real-estate development for close to thirty years, since he was in his twenties. These meetings were always the same—he could have written a script of what happened each time. All parties put their demands and concerns on the table to be worked through slowly and laboriously.

It was nothing like the movies, where business deals were all about winning and losing and screwing the other guy with a dramatic flourish. It was instead all about knowing what you wanted, what you were willing to give, and how far you were willing to go in the spirit of compromise. Some developers considered their work to be an expression of their vigor and *machismo*, each new development an extension of their ability to affect and shape the world. There was some truth in this; David wouldn't deny it, but the reality was more subtle. He was proud of his accomplishments, proud of being a self-made man. But his success had been about more than willpower and drive. He had also always been a student of people and human behavior. In the business world he was successful because he worked at understanding people's motivations—and what made them feel like winners or losers. He strove for an understanding of what motivated people, what they wanted, and how they viewed the world.

David caught his reflection in his office window, his form shaded against the backdrop of office towers across Michigan Avenue. His height was a little above average, just under six feet. His build was slim but still muscular. His hair, just beginning to gray at the temples, framed a face with thin lips, a straight nose, and sparkling brown eyes under a broad, lined forehead. With each year that had passed in his thirties and forties, he had seen more and more of his father in himself. Now he had just celebrated his fifty-fifth birthday and had marked the occasion the next morning by running his customary six miles on the West Bank Club track. After that he had played twenty minutes of one-on-one basketball with Gabe Wolf, an old friend and prominent Chicago attorney. It had been a close game, and David won with an off-balance jump shot to make the score 22-20. It had been a hell of an effort—his moves on the court didn't come as easily as they had thirty years ago.

David stood up and stretched his legs and forced his mind to return to the business meeting.

"OK, Phil," said one of the attorneys representing the seller. "When we talked about that opinion letter you said—"

"I *know* what we said, and it's what we're going to do," Phil interrupted. "Come on, how many times have you dealt with us? When we say something's going to happen, you can take it to the bank. Olen and Company isn't exactly a fly-by-night operation, you know."

David smiled. Phil Hernandez had graduated from the University of Chicago School of Law ten years before; now he was the rising

11

star at Parson, Freeman, and Wiley, the most prestigious real-estate law firm in Chicago. David had done business with Phil's senior partner, Tom Parson, for twenty-two years. Phil was a sharp negotiator: aggressive, quick, demanding, yet always honest.

The coffee had gone cold; David replaced the cup on its coaster. It was almost eleven in the morning, and he had two more calls much like this one planned for the afternoon. In the interim he had a lunch scheduled with Jay Dawkins, a VP in the Olen and Company acquisitions group. David wondered whether they would have time to go eat at the new French restaurant across the street, in the 404 Building owned by Olen and Company, or whether they would have to order in sandwiches and eat in the office—which was, more often than not, David's custom.

Thirty years was a long time to do anything, but by changing his professional focus, David had managed to retain his interest in and intensity for the business. Most of Olen and Company's domestic operations were now handled by Gary Ballard, an intelligent man with a kind heart. This morning David sat in on this call only because Gary was on a week's vacation in the Caribbean with his family.

David built Olen and Company from the ground up; now it was one of the leaders in the industry. David had started as a young architect with ambition. He had a knack for working in the real world and had taken advantage of some strong political connections. In the past few years David had started to focus almost entirely on Olen Europe—the branch of his business that he had founded in the seventies and that now had operations in Poland, the Czech Republic, Hungary, and Russia.

David now listened to the negotiations on the speakerphone with only half an ear. His thoughts returned to Eastern Europe, as they had so many times in the past twenty-four years. Could it possibly have been that long since . . .

Today Jason Rudas headed Olen Europe's business in Central and

Eastern Europe; he was a younger man who had proved himself to David many times over. He had earned David's total confidence, and they fostered a warm relationship that had become almost familial. Jason had an architectural degree from the University of Illinois, as well as a Wharton MBA. He acted as David's emissary, with decision-making power and David's total trust. Today he was in Warsaw at the monthly construction meeting for the company's newest office tower.

Which was a story in and of itself, David thought. Jason was meeting with Andrzej Kapinski, a Pole David had known since the seventies, when they were both drawn into . . . what would David call it if he had been pressed to explain in that moment? Words such as *conspiracy* and *cabal* had become almost corny and quaint at the end of this century. They were the stuff of TV shows and movies. But no other words would do.

"Thirteen," Phil said, his voice cold and efficient. "We've talked about this before, so we should be able to—"

Down on the street below, David saw cars and city buses moving slowly through the heavy traffic on Michigan Ave. A light afternoon drizzle had turned into freezing rain, the sky gray and bleak. David imagined he could feel the cold on the lake shore even in his warm office. On the sidewalks umbrellas moved and jostled against each other like balloons too heavy to take flight.

He turned to face his desk and tried to listen more closely to the deal being made. He would want to give Gary a complete report when he got back from St. Kitts.

On the credenza behind David's desk were more than a hundred tombstone ads encased in blocks of Lucite: Each one commemorated the completion of an Olen and Company or Olen Europe acquisition or construction project. Each symbolized months and years of negotiation, hard work, and follow-through. David ran a hand through his hair and looked at the rows of these souvenirs. Voices still crackled from the speakerphone.

"All right, fourteen," Phil said, tireless as always. "What we need to discuss here is the cost—"

David shook his head slightly, as though disagreeing with an unspoken objection. The reason he gave the world for having stepped back from his domestic business was the array of opportunities he had created in Europe. But there was more.

Europe gnawed at David Olen, its history insinuating itself into his consciousness during every hour of the day. David had shifted most of his attention to Olen Europe's business because of the challenge of adding value to the rebuilding post-Soviet economies. He also savored the task of adapting to new ways of doing business there, the chance to learn new ways of doing business after decades of mastering those at home. But there was more in his mind than buildings, projects, deals.

David Olen's personal history was intertwined with that of the world during the past quarter-century—a fact that he rarely allowed himself to speak aloud, not even to those closest to him. He had seen and done things never heard about or printed in newspapers. He knew a hidden history that would have shocked any student of world affairs or politics. This was his secret that he at once cherished and wished he could forget.

*Wouldn't it be something to be able to tell someone?*

"What are you doing?" whispered a voice from behind him. "Talking to yourself again?"

David turned, pulled out of his reverie. In his office doorway was Cynthia Barry, David's secretary, assistant, and confidant of more than twenty-five years. Originally from England, she had maintained her British accent after living more than half her life in the United States. Tall, her brown hair cut in a smart style that accentuated her striking eyes, she displayed a hint of concern mingled with her typically amused expression. She glanced at the speakerphone as she crossed to David's desk.

"Moving on to 17C," Phil Hernandez said. "We need to review the seller's warranties."

"What is it?" David spoke in a whisper that matched Cynthia's, both keeping their voices low so as not to interrupt the conference call.

"A call from St. Petersburg," Cynthia replied. "Terry James. He said it was urgent, and he sounded really upset."

David shared with Cynthia an intimacy based on mutual trust. Cynthia always knew when a matter was important enough to warrant interrupting David; her judgment was impeccable.

Terry was a young American in his early thirties. He was Olen Europe's manager on a complicated historic renovation project in St. Petersburg, Russia. He was serious and conscientious—and if he had left an urgent message, David knew it needed his immediate attention.

David whispered his thanks to Cynthia and waited until she had left and closed the door behind her before speaking.

"Phil, guys, listen. This is David," he said as soon as there was a momentary lull in the negotiation.

"Yeah, David," Phil replied. "What's up?"

"I just got a call that I have to return," David said. "Phil, you'll handle this without me?"

A pause. Phil had only a couple of times before conducted negotiations on behalf of Olen and Company without Gary or David physically present or at least listening in.

"Of course," Phil said. "If we can't hook up again before we're finished here, I'll try to get in touch with you before the end of the day."

"Great," David said. "I have faith in everyone that this will all work out. We're interested in purchasing the property, so let's make this deal happen. Agreed?"

"Got it," Phil answered. The seller's representatives said their farewells. David disconnected the call, filling the room with sudden silence.

David buzzed Cynthia on the intercom and asked her to place a call to Olen Europe's St. Petersburg office. International connections to Russia were unpredictable, and while David waited, he went through a mental list of all the things that might have gone wrong.

The project was a costly and ambitious renovation of a historic building on Nevsky Prospect, the famous main thoroughfare of St. Petersburg since Czarist days. The structure was originally built in the 1730s and had been totally abandoned and vacant for the past forty years. The agreement with the Turkish contractor was almost in place, but numerous issues kept coming up. The St. Petersburg Historic Preservation Council was giving David's team a hard time with expensive historic-reconstruction specifications that threatened to push the project over budget—everything from demands for historically accurate marble in the stairwells to matching the original window frame design. With each push upward in the project's budget, David had started to foresee problems with financing.

The financing itself was a complicated arrangement with the European Development Bank, the St. Petersburg branch of Moscow's GlobusBank (a frequent partner of Olen Europe's), and a syndication of U.S. banks. The Russian equity partner was the Krassnaya Corporation, a former Soviet military contractor that was now involved in everything from oil rigs to real-estate development to boutique retail operations. Like most development projects, it was a complicated web that could fall apart if any strand was broken.

David felt a personal stake in the project—a certainty that Olen Europe was going to create something truly unique on Nevsky Prospect that hopefully would contribute to the slow but general restoration of the former Russian capitol. But business was business, David reminded himself. He was committed to the project and, for the moment, he had to deal with the problems as they arose.

"Terry's on the line," Cynthia said over the intercom.

"Thanks," David replied. He pushed the button on his phone that put the call on the speaker.

"David?" Terry asked. His voice was youthful, carrying the intonation and inflection of his New England upbringing. He would be sitting at his desk in the small, cramped fourth-floor apartment that served as Olen Europe's St. Petersburg headquarters, numerous framed photos of his wife and infant son on the shelf behind him.

"Yeah, Terry. What's going on?"

David heard Terry sigh and then pause.

"I've been making calls all afternoon and trying to figure out what the hell happened," Terry said. "No one from GlobusBank even got in touch with us. We had to hear about it on television."

"Slow down, slow down," David said. Terry was talking in a clipped staccato. "You had to hear about what on television?"

"Alexei Sokolov," Terry said.

"What about him?" David asked, his pulse rising.

"You don't know?" Terry asked. "God, I'm sorry. I thought some-one already called you. David, Alexei Sokolov was killed this morn-ing on Nevsky Prospect."

"Killed . . ." David's voice trailed off. "Jesus."

"He was shot in his car on the way to work," Terry said, his voice flat. "There was more than one shooter. They didn't shoot the driver or Sokolov's wife."

"His wife was in the car?"

"Yeah, but I hear she's all right," Terry said. "I mean, given the circumstances."

David brought Alexei Sokolov into focus in his memory. Young, intelligent, intense. David had developed a good rapport with Sokolov in the brief time he had spent with the St. Petersburg head officer of GlobusBank; he had sensed that Sokolov was someone with integrity and that he was loyal to his Moscow superior, Vladimir Borchenko. Sokolov had been popular with the St. Petersburg office of Olen Europe and had become a social acquaintance of Terry James.

"How are you handling this?" David asked. "You sound a little strung out."

"It was a professional hit," Terry replied, tightness creeping into his voice. "They killed him in broad daylight, and then they left the guns at the scene. They shot a banker to death in front of a crowded street full of people, and then they were so arrogant they left the guns on the hood of the car for the police to find."

Post-Soviet Russia wasn't the gun-slinging Wild West the American media made it out to be—at least David didn't think so. But it was a chaotic place and a difficult country in which to live, especially for American sensibilities. The Soviet Union had fallen apart less than a decade before, and Russia was still struggling from month to month to build a sustainable society. The Russian Mafia was real, and it did what it wanted to do. Including murdering those who stood in its way.

"So it was a Mafia killing; that's what you're telling me," David said. "But Sokolov was clean, wasn't he? He was a legitimate banker. There's no reason anyone would want to kill him."

"I don't understand it," Terry conceded. "And the police don't have any suspects. At least that's what they're saying in the media."

"Who have you talked to?" David asked.

"I made a lot of calls as soon as I heard," Terry answered. "The local GlobusBank office is in a state of shock. Popovich and his people at Krassnaya are really shook up. We'll keep in touch with them over the next couple of days."

"Good, good," David said absently, his mind churning.

"And I got a call from Vladimir Borchenko really early," Terry added. "In fact, he was the first one to call us."

"How did he sound?" David asked.

"The same as always," Terry said. "He didn't really sound upset if that's what you mean. But Vladimir's always in control of his emotions. If anything, I'd say he sounded annoyed. He wanted to know whether I'd heard anything here on the ground in St. Petersburg that he might have missed in Moscow."

David said nothing in return; instead, he pictured Borchenko.

He'd known the Russian since 1974—the year that changed David's life.

"I didn't say anything, but Vladimir asking me for information is a real joke," Terry added. "I mean, isn't Vladimir involved with everything that happens in Russia, one way or the other? It's like we say here in the office: 'All roads lead to Vladimir Borchenko.'"

David let the comment pass. Terry had a habit of talking too much when he was upset. David knew how much Vladimir impressed and intimidated those who came into contact with him. David's employees in Russia expressed this through joking about Vladimir's refined manners and deliberate way of speaking—and by speculating that Vladimir's elaborate web of connections and influence couldn't have been developed through honest means. They couldn't possibly know Vladimir Borchenko's real story, how much the shadowy Russian had accomplished.

"I'll call Vladimir," David said.

"It might sound heartless, but we also need to look at this from a business perspective," Terry said. "Sokolov was a key link between our financing structure and the city government here."

"GlobusBank will still be on board," David said. "Borchenko won't withdraw his support."

"I understand," Terry said. "But Sokolov was really keyed in to the local players. And he was on our side. Things can only be more difficult without him."

If Terry's assessment was correct, then this was something to be concerned about. Doing business in Russia required cultivating connections and relationships in order to sort through the labyrinth of what seemed, at times, to be a confounding mix of regulations and lawlessness.

"I'll fly over right away," David said. He had scheduled a trip for later in the month, but his itinerary would have to be pushed forward. "Find out where the funeral is. Cynthia will get in touch and tell you which flight I'm on."

Terry had lived in Russia for four years with his wife, and they had had a son a year before. Terry was a good project manager; he had potential to grow in the company. David also knew that Terry had been through a lot of turbulence recently on the Nevsky project and was under a lot of stress. David could tell from this conversation that Sokolov's murder had hit him hard.

"I know this is a major blow, Terry," David said. "I appreciate the fact that you were friends with Sokolov. Let Cynthia know if you need anything, and I'll see you soon."

"It's just . . . a shock."

"It's a fucking tragedy," David said. He remembered hearing his people in St. Petersburg talk about Alexei Sokolov. They said he doted on his wife and talked about his children in glowing terms. Now his family had lost him forever.

After saying goodbye to Terry, David pressed a button to terminate the call. He sat silently behind his desk and looked out at the gathering gloom of early afternoon. A gust of wind blew outside, and raindrops splashed against the window.

David had yet to psychologically process the full ramifications of Sokolov's murder. That would take time. For now he let his mind focus on other considerations.

Such as the fact that Sokolov was, in a sense, more than just a banker. He was the employee and emissary of Vladimir Borchenko—one of the wealthiest and most powerful men in Russia. David knew that Vladimir's influence extended upward into Russia's government and downward into the organized crime that controlled segments of the country's society and economy. The parties responsible for murdering Sokolov had to know about Borchenko—and had to realize that their action represented a slap in the face to a man no one in Russia dared alienate.

David reached out for the phone then paused.

In all the time David had known Vladimir, the Russian had never seemed to lose control, had never been without information or a plan of action. David needed to get the full story from Vladimir.

In Vladimir Borchenko's world, nothing was ever as it seemed on the surface. Vladimir always had another card available for him to play if a situation threatened to spin out of his control.

David took his hand off the phone. He would wait until he saw Vladimir face-to-face in Moscow. That was how it had always been: old friends shaking hands, looking each other in the eye, and doing business based on trust and mutual respect.

After all, Vladimir Borchenko was the only man who knew all of David Olen's secrets. But then, didn't that make sense? Vladimir knew everybody's secrets.

# Chapter Two

*February 16, 1998. 3:04 p.m.*
*Warsaw, Poland.*

THEY STEPPED ONTO THE CONSTRUCTION ELEVATOR one at a time. First two young Polish engineers in suits and overcoats from Andrzej Kapinski's office. Then Kapinski himself, squinting into the rising wind, followed by the Austrian construction crew foreman—the only one of them not wearing a tie. The last to get on was Jason Rudas, who tapped his shoe on the hard ground for good luck before stepping onto the steel platform.

The elevator was latticed at the top and walled in at the sides, which afforded a view obstructed by steel mesh. It was attached to one edge of the skyscraper's skeleton by what looked like little more than a two-foot-thick metallic structure that ran up the side of the building.

The construction elevator operator closed the gate behind them. From somewhere to Jason's left, there was a mechanical groan; the elevator lifted with a jerk.

They rose. Ten stories up. Twelve. Fifteen. When Jason turned his head, he saw Warsaw down below, a view looking down on the rebuilt Stare Miasto, the Old City. The perspective grew broader and more impressive with every floor they climbed.

Jason was the first out of the elevator after the foreman, and he stepped onto the bare concrete slab of the Warsaw Commerce Center's thirty-second story. He looked around the exposed concrete columns that extended like individual spears holding up the massive concrete structure and grimaced when a cold wind hit his face. There was no exterior wall here encircling the floor. There was only open air and a spectacular view of the Polish capital city. Two floors below, the Austrian contractor's crew was installing the curtain wall.

"Damned cold," said Andrzej Kapinski as he joined Jason. They walked slowly along the perimeter of the floor, the other men following. They were only a couple of meters from the edge, where only a thin yellow nylon cord stood between them and a fatal drop to the street below.

"Reminds me of Chicago," Jason said, looking out at the overcast sky and twilight of a winter afternoon in Poland.

"Perhaps that's why I liked living there," Andy Kapinski said with a laugh.

They moved in a semi-circle around the floor then headed back to the center. In the wind-swept emptiness Jason imagined how this floor would look in about six months—filled with desks, computers, work stations.

"Well," he said, "let's go have a look at the curtain-wall installation."

The group descended an interior concrete stairwell, their steps illuminated by the foreman's battery-powered lantern. They walked carefully down five flights to the twenty-seventh floor, where a team of workmen was working on the glass panels that comprised the building's exterior wall. When they were finished, the building would appear from a distance as a giant reflective pane of glass, its color changing with the sun, the clouds, the time of day and season—like a kaleidoscope shifting through the spectrum.

Jason was a step behind Andy; he watched the Pole's thin frame shift beneath his expensive charcoal cashmere overcoat. Andrzej Kapinski's manner typified to Jason what he considered the mournful, doleful mien of native Poles. Jason imagined that the country's history of suffering under oppression—at the hands of Nazi Germany during World War II, followed by political and military occupation by the Soviet Union—had imprinted itself upon its people and had left them with a distinctive, soulful quality.

Andy's salt-and-pepper hair was cropped neatly against his temples, and he walked with a cautious though spirited step. He was always impeccably groomed, even walking through the chaotic jumble of a construction site. There was also something defiant in his manner that Jason struggled and failed to define.

Andrzej Kapinski was an entrepreneur, a deal-maker in the privatizing economy of post-Communist Poland. He was the owner of one of the largest architectural and engineering companies in the city of Warsaw. In the '70s, Jason knew, Andy had worked as an architect for Olen and Company in Chicago. He had been described to Jason as a quiet, introverted political refugee who spent his days working alone at a drafting table. Something happened after that, and David and Andy started to travel to Poland together. Within a couple of years Olen and Co. had a new corporate entity, Olen Europe, and Andy Kapinski was transferred to work in the country he had fled only a decade before. By the mid-'90s, Andy had struck out on his own and had become one of the most prominent businessmen in Warsaw.

Jason had once asked David Olen how Olen Europe had started and how it was that David only in his thirties had been allowed to do business in the Soviet Bloc when many American businesses were kept out. David had shrugged, looked away. *You know, right place at the right time,* David had said. *I was able to fill a need.*

There were a lot of mysteries surrounding David Olen. Andrzej Kapinski's rise to prominence was only one of them. Olen had long-standing connections that he had forged more than a decade before the fall of the Iron Curtain, an advantage shared by few Western businessmen. Jason had long ago given up trying to find out how his employer had cultivated these contacts and knew that he would receive explanations that were elusive and insubstantial.

David Olen had the right to keep aspects of his life private if that was what he wanted, thought Jason. David had mentored and promoted his career, and as a result Jason had advanced to a level of achievement that few men his age shared. Jason had two more years before he turned forty, and already he was the Managing Director for the most prominent American developer in the region.

"Come over here," Kapinski called out in his Polish-accented English. "What are you doing, anyway? Daydreaming?"

Jason stood watching a team of workmen in the final stages of connecting the curtain wall to the concrete slabs and columns of the building's exterior.

"Just watching the process, Andy," Jason said. He used the Americanized nickname that David Olen had tagged onto Andrzej Kapinski. It was a name to which Kapinski answered only when David or one of his American colleagues addressed him.

Jason moved closer to the lightly tinted green window of the curtain wall and was pleased to see how it cut out the glare of sunlight now that the clouds had parted outside.

"It looks good," Andy said with satisfaction.

Jason trained his eye on the seal where the curtain wall met the building's exterior supports. The original curtain-wall testing, conducted in Miami, had failed; there had been a problem in the interior-window seal connecting the individual plates. It had been a factory problem that would have resulted in leakage into the building's interior. Jason had taken charge of confronting the contractor and making arrangements to straighten out the problem—though negotiations on the local level had started to stall until Andy stepped in and placated the local faction of the contracting team.

"The contractor surprised me on this one," Jason said. "He took care of it really quickly."

"What did I tell you?" Andy smiled. "No problem." He started to walk away; Andy couldn't pass up the chance, in his egocentric way, to subtly mention that he had been instrumental in getting everyone on board to take care of the problem.

Jason followed Andy to the middle of the floor, to the openings for the four elevators in the high-rise core.

"Quite a drop, eh?" Andy asked, looking down the elevator core.

"Only if you fall in," Jason answered, standing close to the edge and allowing the toe of his shoe to slip out over the edge.

Jason and Andy shared a quiet laugh. Andy's light, almost grayish eyes lit up with good humor. Andy Kapinski was known throughout Warsaw as a sharp, sometimes ruthless businessman, but Jason also knew him as a decent person with a deep sense of honor. David Olen had instilled in Jason from the beginning that strength of character would help him rise above in business.

Jason walked slowly to the end of the core and examined the rough-ins for the framing that would become the finished elevator doors.

"I know I'm just eyeballing it," Jason said to Andy, "but have you had a look at this framing? Aren't they supposed to be cut back above the opening so the granite can extend above the frame to the ceiling?"

Andy stuffed his hands in his overcoat. "What do you mean?" he asked, motioning for the foreman to join them.

"This looks like only about eight feet," Jason said. He formed in his mind the prints for that section of the building. His memory was just short of photographic, a trait that had resulted in his grammar school sending him for a series of neuropsychiatric tests when he was a child.

"And what is it supposed to be?" Andy asked.

Jason took a step back; in his mind's eye he added drywall to what he saw. "Three-and-a-half meters," he replied. "I'm almost certain." Jason was always converting the feet and inches he saw in his mind's eye into the European metric system.

A cloud passed over Andy's features. As the local partner, much of the day-to-day construction supervision fell to him and his staff.

"What do you think?" he asked the foreman.

The foreman, who struck Jason as shy but intelligent, had been following their conversation. "It may be," he said.

"We should look at the section plans for verification when we get down," Andy said. "This will have to be dealt with right away if there's a mistake."

"It's not that big a deal," Jason said. "But if it's wrong, we'll have to change the detail in the field when the marble is applied. We need to resolve this as soon as possible."

They walked back toward the construction elevator. Andy took a cigarette out of his coat pocket, sighed wearily, and lit it with a silver lighter. They were protected from the wind by the curtain-wall installation though a chill still infused the building. Andy exhaled a cloud of smoke, and an instant later, a cellular phone rang. Jason, Andy, and one of Andy's men all reached for their pockets simultaneously. Andy pulled out his phone, looked at it, shook his head. His employee did the same.

"It's for you," Andy said, a slight ironic smile on his face at the moment of confusion technology had created.

Jason took a few steps across the concrete slab, switched on the phone, and pulled his scarf tight around his neck. A blast of cold air reached him as he said hello.

"Jason, it's me," said a woman's voice on the line.

"Cynthia, what's up?"

"David's on the line for you."

Jason turned from the elevator core and walked toward the far end of the floor, away from Andy and the other men.

28

"Jason, are you there?" asked David through a fine hiss of static.

"I'm here with Andy in the building," Jason said. "Something's come up involving—"

"Listen," David interrupted. "I'm catching a flight to Warsaw this afternoon, and then I'm going to connect through to St. Petersburg as soon as I can. I need to get to Moscow after that. I'm going to need you to come with me."

Jason took a deep breath. He had rarely heard David sound so serious.

"Alexei Sokolov was murdered in his car on Nevsky Prospect," said David. He then described the assassination.

"Shit," Jason whispered.

"Is your Russian visa current?" David asked.

"Yeah, no problem there." Jason said. "Are you flying LOT direct?" "Yeah. I had Cynthia book us on the afternoon LOT flight to St. Petersburg." He paused. "You know, this is a little bit of a delicate situation. Terry sounded shook up. We both need to be there to support the office, and then I'm going to see Vladimir in person."

"Do they know who did it?" Jason asked. He shivered in the cold. "Sounds like a Mafia hit to me."

"I know," David agreed. "But why?"

"He was clean as far as I know," Jason said.

"I thought so, too," said David. "But who knows?"

Jason thought he heard a slight note of ambiguity in David's voice just then. David had seen a lot in his life. He had gone from hanging out on street corners on Chicago's West Side in the '50s to dining with European royalty in the '90s. He tended to view everyone with a sort of cautious detachment. He had said to Jason: *Sometimes what you see isn't what you get. Your instincts about people are what really matter.* The question: What were David's instincts telling him about Alexei Sokolov?

"The only factor that comes to mind is Sokolov's attitude toward privatization," David said. "There are a lot of guys on the take in

Russia, but he wasn't one of them. Borchenko left him on a pretty long leash in terms of investing GlobusBank's money. He had a lot of discretion, and he pretty much aligned himself with pro-market forces rather than the old *apparatchik* mentality that's led to a lot of the corruption over there."

"So maybe he got in someone's way—" Jason began.

"It's just a thought," David interjected. "Look, let's get to St. Petersburg, find out about the funeral, then see how we're going to pick up the pieces on the Nevsky project."

"Right," Jason replied, feeling numb. There had been assassinations in Russia before involving businessmen, but never someone he knew.

Jason stepped to the window. Less than half a mile away loomed the monolithic wedding-cake style of the Palace of Culture, a copy of the seven sister buildings in Moscow and a pure example of Stalinist architecture. It was a giant monstrosity built as a "gift" by the Soviets for the Polish people. It dominated Warsaw as the largest and tallest building in the city. During Communist times, it had been a reminder of Poland's place in the Soviet empire; now, it was a reminder of how much had changed in such a short time.

"I'll see you tomorrow morning, your time," David said. "Have Deren meet me at the airport, and then you and I can have a couple of hours together before our flight. And say hello to Andy for me."

Jason snapped shut the almost-weightless GSM telephone, a cellular phone that worked on global satellite links, and replaced it in his coat pocket. He stared out at the city below, the murky smudge of the horizon. When he joined Andy again, an animated discussion was taking place in Polish between him and one of his associates.

"What is it?" Andy asked when he saw Jason's expression.

"That was David," Jason said. "One of our banking associates in St. Petersburg was assassinated. David's coming here in the morning; then, we're heading to Russia."

Andy folded his arms and looked down at the concrete floor and shook his head. "Terrible," he said. "Was it someone you knew well?"

Jason nodded.

"I'm sorry to hear it," Andy said in a soft voice, his gaze fixed in the near distance. For a moment Jason forgot his own feelings and looked at Andy, sensing that he was staring off into a past of his own suffering and pain that perhaps only another Pole would comprehend.

Andy and Jason went back to the construction elevator without exchanging another word; the shadow of death had driven Andy Kapinski and Jason Rudas into the privacy of their thoughts.

---

DAVID OLEN HUNG UP HIS PHONE on his desk. He had to get home, pack a bag, and say goodbye to Annia, his wife. She wouldn't be happy that his trip to Russia had been moved up unexpectedly.

He needed to get his thoughts in order before he reached Russia. He didn't know why Sokolov was murdered or who had wanted him dead. Surely Vladimir Borchenko would know. Perhaps what frightened David the most was the notion that Vladimir would be unable to explain what was happening.

Vladimir Borchenko. History circled the man. His father had been a diplomat in the Soviet Union, and Vladimir had been around the Russian black market since his days at Moscow State University in the '50s. Now he was a banker and industrialist, one of the wealthiest men in Russia. But in the twenty-four years he had known Borchenko, David had never been able to take his measure.

He did know a very important fact—one that ensured that nothing around Vladimir was ever as it seemed.

Vladimir Borchenko, along with a handful of other men, was responsible for secret events after World War II that affected the history of the world. And David had been involved—reluctantly at first, but then wholeheartedly.

It was a fact that would never go away—no matter how much David Olen might have wished it would.


*February 16, 1998. 5:10 p.m.*
*Moscow.*

VLADIMIR BORCHENKO glided through the streets in the back seat of his black Mercedes 600. Looking out his window, he saw people walking through the rain in Arbat square. The winter had stripped the trees of their leaves, and a deep chill had descended over Moscow.

The car was warm. He lit a cigarette and leaned back against the plush seat. Inside he felt a rage growing that frightened him.

The cellular telephone at his hand rang. He ignored it for a moment while he watched an elderly woman crossing the street and clutching a plastic bag to her chest. She wore a heavy wrap around her head, her face frozen into an unreadable expression. What hardships had that old woman seen, he wondered.

When the phone had rung five times, he picked it up. The car lurched into motion through the intersection, his driver steering expertly through traffic.

"Yes?" he asked.

"I have Maxim Belarin for you," said Tatiana, his office receptionist.

Vladimir paused. "Put him on."

He picked up his cigarette and took a deep drag as he waited for the call to be transferred. Belarin. Of course.

"Hello, Maxim."

"*Dobre dyen*," said a man's baritone, a hard voice that had deepened over the years. "How are you, Vladimir?"

He did not reply.

"Well, in any event," Belarin said, obviously rebuffed by Vladimir's silence, "I need to speak with you immediately. Perhaps—"

"I have nothing to say to you," Vladimir replied.

"I cannot believe that," Belarin said with what, for him, passed for drollness. "Surely you have some comment on the tragic loss of your associate in St. Petersburg."

The drizzle outside had solidified into sleet; Vladimir's driver paused at an intersection as the traffic began to stack up.

"What are you saying?" Vladimir asked.

"It is a shame that a young man like Sokolov had to die," Belarin replied.

"You—"

"My hands are clean," Belarin interrupted. "Your stubbornness is to blame. All I have asked from you is your assurance that the group I represent will have an unimpeded path to purchasing MosElectric. There has been no question about my intentions, Vladimir." Vladimir's body tightened; he fought off a crazy urge to throw the phone out the window, to find Belarin and strangle him.

"I do what I want," he said instead. "I don't answer for my actions to fools and assholes. You qualify as both."

Belarin laughed, a cold glacial sound, a rumbling deep in the former KGB colonel's diaphragm.

"I knew you would be defiant," Belarin said. "I had no idea you would be reckless as well."

"I haven't decided what to do about the acquisition of that business," Vladimir said. "You will find out when I do."

"Vladimir," Belarin said, a tone of sadness in his voice. "It is a shame to have our relationship sink to this level after all we have been through together."

"We have no relationship," Vladimir said.

"I am giving you so many chances," Belarin continued. "Do you think I would be so lenient with just anyone? I look back on our years together with fondness. To think of all we accomplished . . . and now we are still here, the lords of Russia. It almost makes me nostalgic."

"How dare you?" Vladimir yelled. He glanced up at the partition between himself and his driver, made sure he couldn't be heard. "You are a coward. Striking at me through my innocent employees."

"You won't have to worry about your employees any more," Belarin said. "The time for warnings is nearly past."

Vladimir breathed heavily, his chest feeling hot and tight. Belarin was a snake, a lethal predator. Taking a life meant nothing to him.

"To hell with you," Vladimir said. "I would advise you to reconsider your plans. Don't get in my way."

"That's a good one," Belarin said, laughing impudently. "Are you threatening me? You never were one for dirty work, Vladimir. You give orders; you manipulate. You never had the guts to take affairs into your own hands."

Vladimir held the phone close to his ear. His anger was nestled deep in his gut, a seething core he had never felt before. Mingled there was also a hint of fear. Belarin was capable of anything. Vladimir sensed that Belarin was toying with him, that the full dimensions of what he wished to accomplish had yet to become clear.

"We'll see," he said, keeping his voice cold as steel.

"We shall indeed," Belarin said. "It was nice speaking with you, Vladimir Dmitrievich."

"I cannot say the same," Vladimir said, disconnecting the phone.

He looked out the window at the mud-streaked city he had called home all his life. Moscow. Vladimir Borchenko had spent a lifetime working to rule it. And now this bastard from the past was threatening his authority, his power.

The sleet was falling harder now, coating the street signs with a thin sheen of ice.

For an instant Vladimir wondered if Belarin had been right. Vladimir had never done the dirty work; it was true. He had always had Belarin and men like him for that. But times had changed. Vladimir was a businessman, a leader of finance and industry.

But he was more than that. So many things had occurred in the past. He and Belarin were among the few men left who knew the truth of the past half-century. And he had seen Belarin at work, and he knew what Belarin was capable of.

Now Vladimir Borchenko stood in the way of Maxim Belarin's latest ambition.

# Chapter Three

*February 16, 1998. 9:12 p.m.*
*Moscow.*

VLADIMIR BORCHENKO PACED SLOWLY across the expanse of
his private office. It was a contemporary space with polished
wooden floors and a hand-woven carpet in tasteful, subdued
colors. One wall was floor-to-ceiling glass; on the others hung his art,
his passion, including pieces by Rothko and a Kandinsky. Each painting hung under custom-designed lights that dimmed and brightened
as the light in the room shifted and kept the art always under perfect
illumination.

Outside his window, evening traffic crawled slowly on packed
Tverskaya Street. The sky was dark. The people on the streets wore
heavy coats and fur hats. Pedestrians walked past glowing shop windows displaying expensive brand-name goods: Calvin Klein, Cartier,
Armani, Reebok. Few Muscovites could afford such temptations. A
designer dress might cost six months' salary for a clerk or a life's

savings for a pensioner. Yet there was a growing elite who could pay for Western luxuries—because they were thriving in the new Russian economy.

Vladimir recalled a time when those same shop windows were darkened and featureless, when people had to stand in lines for as long as an entire day for a small sack of potatoes or a cut of fatty, stringy beef. In those days there had been another elite—the Communist Party. The streets bore little traffic then; their only drivers had been the well-connected in their Russian Zil limousines. They had shopped at special stores unavailable to the masses, where produce, meats, and liquor were available at a price.

Many members of this communist elite had made the change to the new system and had grown wealthy by virtue of their connections and influence. But not all members of the new ruling elite were former communists. There were entrepreneurial tycoons, as well as outright criminals. Vladimir knew them all, understood them, strove to manipulate them.

He was glad the days of communist rule were gone. True, Vladimir had benefited from the days of the command economy. He had thrived in the black market since his college days, when he affiliated himself with the post-War Chechen network of smugglers and put himself in a position to supply the needs of a restless communist ruling class in Moscow. His late father, formerly the Soviet ambassador to Poland, had mentored Vladimir in how to work within the system, how to skirt the rules without landing in a Siberian labor camp.

But Vladimir's father had been, at heart, a functionary—an *apparatchik* in his own fashion, a product of the power structure in which he came to prominence. Vladimir had always harbored greater ideas. He had always possessed the ability to look beyond the particular circumstances of the moment into all the possible futures that might come to be. He had thought about the illogical inconsistencies within the Soviet system; along with a friend and fellow visionary, he had tried to imagine Russia once the Soviet system was reformed. He had pictured a society full of limitless opportunities for men of means and ambition—men like himself.

It had been less than a decade since Mikhail Sergeivich Gorbachev had resigned and turned over the Soviet empire's nuclear codes to his old comrade and new nemesis Boris Yeltsin. In the intervening years, Borchenko's vision had been proved right. He had become one of the wealthiest men in Russia—because of Yeltsin's reforms and privatization.

When the Soviet Union was disbanded, Russia found itself cash-poor, struggling to turn its centralized command economy into some variant of an open-market system. Few understood the daunting complexity of the task. During Soviet times, *Gosplan*, the central economic planning agency in Moscow, had sent each state enterprise a detailed program for the coming year. A factory would receive its directive in the form of documents as thick as telephone books. It would delineate each economic function for the business—including the prices at which it would buy its raw materials from other state-run enterprises. As a result, nothing was priced according to its worth or demand. Factories churned out products that no one bought or used. Goods were made with shoddy standards in order to meet Moscow-mandated quotas. In time the system began to sag under its own weight.

The new Russian government inherited this economic disarray and immediately felt the pressure of creating a viable system. Western economists arrived—at the same time as foreign-aid packages—advocating "shock therapy" or removing price controls and privatizing the state economy in order to "correct" the economy.

The Russian government had little hard currency, but it was in possession of the vast resources that had been centralized by the Soviets—from petroleum and mineral deposits to power-generation utilities and huge manufacturing monopolies. These assets became "privatized," an ambiguous process in which individuals and groups—inevitably, often men who had been prominent and well-connected as communists—put together financing to buy large sectors of Russia's national wealth in exchange for the cash the government needed to survive from month to month. Overnight the system produced some of the richest people in the world.

The entire process occurred in a country in which few comprehended the workings of a market economy or even private ownership of goods and services. It happened quickly, with little comment at the time. And there was no reversing it, unless another revolution took place—and who had the heart for another?

Borchenko owned interests in Russian oil, metals, real estate, and communications through his private GlobusBank. He had become one of the "oligarchs" described in the world media. He didn't know precisely what he was worth in American dollars. Two billion. Maybe three. He personally oversaw the construction of his office building—where his bank occupied the top six of twenty-eight floors—a new, modern addition to the city, with state-of-the-art telecommunication capacities. The building stood on a premiere Moscow site where a Soviet institute had faltered, no longer functioning in the new Russian economy.

It was a shame, in a sense, that few of Vladimir's associates had possessed the foresight to anticipate what would happen in the early '90s. Their vision had been incomplete, and they had failed to take advantage. Take Mikhail Sergeivich himself. He could have had so much, accomplished so much more than he had.

But Vladimir's old friend Mikhail Gorbachev had wanted only to reform the communist system. True, the reforms he envisioned for the future of the Soviet Union were considered drastic and radical, but they remained mere reforms of a system that had rotted out and failed to keep the faith of those who lived under it. Mikhail Sergeivich had been the last to understand that the old system was beyond reform. He had failed to foresee what would happen the moment millions living under communist rule were allowed a faint crack of light under the door of oppression.

Vladimir smiled at the thought of his old friend. Mikhail Gorbachev was often in Moscow, at his institute, though they rarely saw each other. Each was a reminder to the other of the past, of deals made and compromises struck. Vladimir also sensed that his presence made Mikhail Sergeivich somehow uneasy . . . whether as a result of jealousy, or perhaps resentment, he couldn't say. Theirs had been a genuine friendship, forged through the decades, albeit one that was undeniably improbable from the start. Vladimir had been the sophisticated Moscow counterpoint to Mikhail's naive country boy. The contrast between them defined their relationship and never vanished, not even when Mikhail rose to the Politburo and beyond. The very thought of Mikhail now made Vladimir's heart swell with love—the affection of one brother for another. Yet it wasn't unheard of for brothers to lose their common connection and become estranged.

Perhaps it was just another of history's jokes. Mikhail gave meaningless speeches to fawning Americans for pocket change while Vladimir regularly reaped millions of dollars with well-timed transactions.

Vladimir sighed. It was no wonder so much of his attention had been focused on the past recently. *Belarin*. He was out there somewhere, in the city framed by Vladimir's office window. The KGB colonel, the bastard.

Vladimir picked up the phone and dialed a St. Petersburg extension. "Donolov," he said to the man who answered. "Tell me, what do you hear about Sokolov? What are people saying? Was it the Mafia?"

Vladimir listened to the man on the line and shook his head impatiently.

"Of course it's all speculation; that doesn't make it meaningless," Vladimir said. "Someone had Alexei Petrovich killed. We all know that. I want to find out who."

Although Vladimir knew the answer already, he also wanted to

41

know what the business community in St. Petersburg was saying. Sokolov had been a GlobusBank employee—as such, he had been protected by Vladimir Borchenko's intangible presence. Now Vladimir feared that his intimidating influence might be weakened by the killing.

Vladimir was speaking to Igor Donolov, a director at Petrobank, a small St. Petersburg bank that was nonetheless ingrained in the city's financial and political life. Donolov cleared his throat, obviously uncomfortable with the direction this conversation was taking.

Borchenko pictured Donolov in his mind's eye—short, thinning hair, quick, nervous gestures like a bird. Vladimir had made an informal associate of Donolov five years before. Their arrangement was straightforward: Borchenko supplemented Donolov's income with cash, and in return Donolov supplied Borchenko with any information he might have gained from inside or outside his bank.

"You sound nervous to me, Igor Konstantinovich," Borchenko observed. He made his voice soothing to relax the tremulous man.

"Sokolov's death has been a shock," Donolov admitted. "There seems to be no reason for it."

"We are all saddened here," Vladimir said. "We will all miss him. But we have to move on, as well. Alexei would have wished it. Now you should tell me everything you have heard—"

"I think . . ." Donolov paused. "I think I should be careful now who I speak with."

"Careful?" Vladimir repeated. "For what reason? Surely you are not afraid of me?"

"No, no," Donolov said quickly. "I did not say that." Vladimir thought. Donolov was scared. Sokolov's assassination represented the presence of the Mafia in St. Petersburg's streets, and this had made him feel unsafe and insecure. Perhaps he feared Vladimir now as well. Vladimir shook his head. He had always hated cowardice.

"Very well," he said. "Igor Konstantinovich, it saddens me to hear suspicion in the voice of such a trusted associate as yourself."

"No, no," Donolov said again. "It is just that . . . Sokolov worked in banking. I work in banking. You see? We are all frightened. And the fact that he worked for you . . ."

And there it was. This is what worried Donolov the most. Sokolov had worked under Vladimir Borchenko's protective umbrella, and still he had been shot with impunity. Donolov thought that Vladimir was slipping. Perhaps he was already thinking about shifting his alliances.

Belarin was responsible for this. Vladimir gripped the telephone so tightly that his hand began to throb.

"I plan to travel to St. Petersburg within the month," Vladimir said. "I will arrange to meet with you. As always, I will bring a token of my gratitude for your willingness to discuss current events with me." In crude terms, an envelope full of American dollars.

Donolov thanked Vladimir and hung up, sounding relieved to be concluding the conversation. Vladimir allowed himself a deep sigh as he walked slowly to the leather sofa that faced the window. He took a cigarette from his silver engraved Asprey case, lit it, dragged hard, and exhaled a cloud of smoke.

The city outside lay under dark of night. Klieg lights shone on buildings and exposed the city's regal architecture; the ornate facades had been sandblasted clean a few years before for the 850th anniversary of Moscow's existence. Vladimir had lived in this magnificent city all his life; now, at the end of the millennium, he thought he had never seen it look so splendid.

Vladimir put the cigarette down in a silver ashtray and stretched his arms toward the ceiling. He was sixty-eight years old now, but he worked harder and thought faster than men half his age. He liked to eat and drink, but he had gained very little weight with age; his six-foot-two frame was still wiry and athletic. His hair had turned almost entirely white, but it still framed his face with a thick mane above his high forehead.

All the secrets, the lies, the decades of scheming. He had always known that some aspect of what he had done would come back to haunt him. But Belarin . . .

As if on cue, a flash of pain tore through his guts. He grimaced and put a hand on his belly. His ulcer.

No man who triumphed in the world was without enemies. They accumulated through the years like trophies, Vladimir thought, spilling over until there was no longer a way to count them all. Enemies in business, in politics. From the past and from the present. His eyes darted across the room to a mirrored inset bar stocked with liquor. Beneath the bar was a ledge set flush against the dark wood, almost invisible. Atop the ledge was a Beretta pistol, loaded and ready to fire. It was another sign of how much things had changed. During the worst of Soviet times, Vladimir had never felt compelled to carry a gun.

He took another drag on his cigarette. There was a knock on his office door. He tensed, listened. He had thought his staff was gone for the day.

"Who is it?" he called out, stubbing the cigarette. Despite himself, a burst of adrenaline gripped his chest. Surely Belarin wouldn't try to kill him in his own office.

"I hope I'm not disturbing you," said a young woman after opening the door. "I knew you were still here. I want to talk through a couple of things before tomorrow morning's meeting."

Vladimir smiled, his tension dissolving. "Natasha," he said. "I should have known it would be you, working late. Why haven't you gone home?"

Natasha Alyeva shifted a stack of files from one arm to the other. She was only thirty, but already she was the head analyst at GlobusBank. She had been educated at Moscow State University and the London School of Economics and was one of the new breed of young Russian businesspeople—those who had grown up with *bizniss*, the Western-style concept of competition and drive. Natasha

44

Alyeva epitomized the best of the new generation: She was educated, cultivated, professional.

"I wanted to finish the evaluation analysis of MosElectric before the status meeting in the morning," she replied.

Natasha sat down in a comfortable armchair in front of Vladimir's desk, her traditional place whenever she and her employer were brainstorming. Vladimir came around to his side of the desk, sat back in his chair, and lit a new cigarette.

"What do you think?" he asked her. "Is MosElectric worth our time?"

She paused to choose her words carefully. Natasha's jet-black hair was styled in a short cut that framed her translucent blue eyes. She was tall and thin, her face open and expressive. Vladimir wondered if she was truly aware how different she was from the women of his generation. She was driven, hard-working, diligent, her manner straightforward and confident like a Westerner.

"It's worth our time," she said. "I've had my team examine the MosElectric privatization in exhaustive detail. *Pro forma* analysis leads me to believe this is something we should take to our major investors."

Vladimir folded his arms, nodded with approval. MosElectric was a major state-owned utility company that served more than a thousand square kilometers within and to the west of Moscow. It was scheduled to be privatized at some point in the next year; it was a deal that might net millions for investors. GlobusBank was in a position to put together the capital to acquire a substantial interest in the shares of MosElectric.

But it wasn't as simple as that, a fact that burned in Vladimir Borchenko's mind. Because of Maxim Belarin, the old ghost from the past who now served in Russia's *duma*, the national legislature.

Natasha leaned forward in her chair. "We should determine who our competitors might be and how serious they are," she continued. "Our bank has experience with public utilities going private. But so do other groups. The bidding might go as high as $500 million."

Vladimir knew who their main competition would be, but he decided not to share the information with Natasha. How could he explain his connection to Belarin without telling her about Mikhail Sergeivich, about the deal they had made, about the American David Olen? And there was another factor—Belarin's bid for MosElectric, and subsequently greater things, was being bankrolled by some of the most dangerous crime figures in Russia. Vladimir worried that this fact might scare away Natasha, who was schooled in legitimate business. Vladimir knew he didn't want to lose her as GlobusBank's head financial analyst.

"What are the drawbacks?" he asked her, feeling his pulse quicken. *Damn it*, he thought. Nothing was going to frighten him away from pursuing his business interests.

"We're going to have to cut the workforce almost in half," she said, motioning to her written report, where all her assertions would be carefully articulated and evenly substantiated. "The company management has been elected by the workers' council. They're going to be very fearful of change."

"They always are," Vladimir replied.

"Precisely." Natasha allowed a faint smile to show. "But these things can be dealt with. In the long run, in the right hands, this company will be very profitable."

Vladimir stubbed out his cigarette and picked up her report. "I'll read this before tomorrow's meeting," he promised.

"And now I will go home," Natasha said with a tinkling laugh, standing up.

"Good, good, you work too much," Vladimir said affectionately.

Natasha gathered her things and snapped shut her leather brief-case. It was past nine o'clock.

"How is your mother?" Vladimir asked as he walked her to the door.

Natasha was a curious young woman, Vladimir thought. She was beautiful, cultured, earned a very generous salary on par with

Western standards—yet she lived alone in a small apartment and spent most of her evenings visiting her parents in their small *dacha* outside the city. Her father was a retired Soviet naval officer, and her mother suffered from emphysema. Vladimir had never met them, though he had seen a picture of her mother on her desk.

From time to time Natasha brought a date to GlobusBank social affairs—usually a good-looking, self-confident young businessman—but Natasha never seemed overly interested in him, and by the next banquet or acquisition party, there would be a different one. Vladimir sensed that she was too self-possessed, too reserved, to give herself to anyone. He thought it was a shame. More than once he had been tempted to take her aside, tell her to seize her youth while there was time, to make the most of her life, and to find a lasting love.

"My mother's condition is the same," she said in a tight voice. "Thank you for asking."

Vladimir put his hand lightly on her elbow. "Please tell me if there is any way I can help," he said, his standard offer.

"Of course," Natasha replied. "Thank you."

A slight movement in the corridor caught Vladimir's eye; he moved past Natasha into the hallway.

"Is someone there?" he called out loudly.

"Vladimir Dmitrievich," said a baritone voice.

"Nikolai," Vladimir said, finding himself face-to-face with a much larger, younger man. "I didn't know you were here."

Nikolai Petrov shrugged his powerful shoulders, his impassive expression unchanged. "I was driving to a dinner meeting," he said. "I came up to see if there was any word about Sokolov."

Vladimir looked into the younger man's eyes. Nikolai Petrov was Vladimir's eyes and ears in Moscow, his most trusted employee alongside Natasha Alyeva. Nikolai had just turned thirty-five. He had a powerful wrestler's build and a square jaw that might have once stared out from a Soviet propaganda poster glorifying the hearty stock of the Russian peasantry.

"Nothing much," Vladimir lied. He hadn't told Nikolai about Belarin; he wasn't sure how to frame the situation.

Vladimir knew that many in his organization distrusted Nikolai—especially those, such as Natasha, who had been educated in the university and had never had to make a deal on the streets. They didn't understand Nikolai and the debt the young man felt he owed Vladimir Borchenko.

---

SIX YEARS BEFORE, Vladimir met Nikolai. At the time, Nikolai was working for Oleg Graskov, a St. Petersburg businessman who was Vladimir's chief rival in a competitive negotiation to buy a TV station. Nikolai was a rough-mannered, muscular young man with an intangible quality about him, a presence. Intelligence shone in his eyes. He was a quick thinker, Vladimir thought, his wit honed on the streets.

Nikolai Petrov was the product of the criminal streets of post-Soviet Russia. And Vladimir, for all his power, lacked a viable and trustworthy connection to those same streets. It had been decades since he had done deals on his own behalf with Chechen smugglers and renegade army officers. The new breed of young Russian criminal was virtually unknown to him. Vladimir stole Nikolai away from Graskov by hiring him during their first meeting.

---

"NOTHING NEW has been learned about Sokolov," Vladimir said to Nikolai. "But come in. Natasha was just explaining to me that we should pursue the MosElectric deal."

Nikolai unbuttoned his overcoat and revealed a dark suit and silk Hermes tie with a splash of red. He nodded hello to Natasha, his gaze lingering for a moment until both seemed uncomfortable and looked away.

"Good evening," Nikolai said to her, his voice cold and defensive.

"Nikolai," she replied, a look of distaste crossing her mouth.

Vladimir watched them, tried to read the depths of the discord between these two. It was easy to understand. Natasha was a university-educated financial analyst, the product of a prominent military family. Nikolai was GlobusBank's "Director of Special Projects," and his job was as nebulous and unformed as his background. He was a negotiator, a representative, an enforcer—whatever the situation dictated. Nikolai came from an alcohol-ravaged family full of ignorance and brutality; Natasha was the product of the best teachers, an educated family, the brightest opportunities. It was no wonder they clashed.

"I spoke with Donolov at Petersburg Bank," Vladimir said to Nikolai.

"And?" Nikolai asked, his interest evident.

"Nothing." Vladimir sighed. "Perhaps we will have to wait until the police have investigated. Perhaps you can speak to people you know in St. Petersburg?"

"Of course," Nikolai said. "I've already made calls. I'll follow up in the morning."

"You will both excuse me," Natasha said, buttoning her coat. "I was just leaving."

"Of course, of course," Vladimir said. "We will see you in the morning. Please give my warm regards to your parents."

Natasha thanked Borchenko and left without a word for Nikolai, who shrugged when they were alone and went to the bar on the other side of the room.

"Want something?" he asked Vladimir.

"Glenlivet," Vladimir replied.

Nikolai filled two glasses and brought them to the desk. After they clinked glasses and toasted, he asked, "So Natasha's group recommends going after MosElectric?"

"That's right," Vladimir replied.

Nikolai nodded, seemingly deep in thought. For all their

differences, Natasha and Nikolai always listened carefully to each other's opinions.

"It's the kind of deal Sokolov would have been interested in," Nikolai volunteered.

Vladimir sipped his scotch, lit a fresh cigarette. "And why is that?" he asked.

Nikolai leveled his gaze at his employer. "It's a large utility going public," he said. "There's a lot of room for corruption and inside deals. Sokolov was always singing the praises of the free markets, of doing things the Western way. Of not letting old cronies and crime bosses run the country. Surely you recall."

Vladimir smiled warily. "I recall Alexei Sokolov talking a lot about the way our country should go," he said. "And I recall more than once telling him to look out for GlobusBank's interests first."

"Which he did," Nikolai said. He looked into the amber liquor as though it were a crystal ball.

"So what are you saying?" Vladimir asked. He knew Nikolai's propensity for elliptical thinking and speech. The young man was preoccupied with something.

"That I don't know the whole story about Sokolov and MosElectric," Nikolai said.

Vladimir stroked his cheek. "Go on."

"First of all, you haven't asked me to investigate the competition for the MosElectric bidding. By now you should have done that. We need to know who we're up against, what their weaknesses and strengths might be—the kind of things that don't show up on Natasha's *pro formas*."

Vladimir took a drag on his cigarette. Nikolai continued to impress him.

"Which means you know who the competition is," Nikolai observed. "But you haven't told me. Why is this?"

"It's complicated," Vladimir said in a tone that implied he wouldn't be questioned much longer.

"All right," Nikolai said, lowering his voice. He finished his drink, took it to the bar, refreshed it.

"But you're right," Vladimir said when he returned. "We have competition. They are motivated and might be dangerous. I don't want to say more until I know what I want to do," Vladimir told the younger man. "When I do, you will be the first person I speak with. Does this satisfy you?"

Nikolai allowed only an equanimous expression to show. "I only want to do my job," he said. "I hope you will trust me soon with what you know."

Vladimir turned away from his young associate's intense expression. His instinct told him to confide in Nikolai, to tell him about Belarin. But where would he stop? Could he ever share the entire story?

"It's terrible, what happened to Sokolov," Nikolai said, a non sequitur that indicated his curiosity was far from satisfied.

Vladimir nodded in agreement, thinking that the younger Nikolai Petrov could have been capable of such a crime.

"Where are you going for dinner?" Vladimir asked.

"*Glazour.*"

"Very nice," Vladimir replied. "I hope that you are not dining alone."

"I am not," Nikolai said. His mouth remained a tight line; he obviously felt rebuffed that Vladimir was keeping information from him.

An instant later the phone rang on Vladimir's desk; he held up his hand for Nikolai to wait while he answered it.

"Vladimir, it's David," said the familiar and warm voice on the line. "I'm catching a flight to Warsaw this afternoon, and then I'm coming to Russia. Do you have a minute to talk?"

"David," Vladimir replied, breaking into a smile. "Of course I do. Can you hold for just a moment?"

Nikolai took his empty glass to the sink by the bar; Vladimir pressed the "hold" button on the phone.

"David Olen?" Nikolai asked, buttoning his coat.

Vladimir nodded. "We'll talk first thing in the morning, before the staff meeting," Vladimir said. "I'll explain the MosElectric situation in greater detail for you then."

Vladimir watched his young associate turn to leave. A year ago Nikolai would not have shown his irritation over not knowing every aspect of a business situation. Something had changed, and it showed in Nikolai's attitude and actions. He felt a sense of privilege and importance.

Perhaps one day, Vladimir mused, Nikolai might decide he no longer needed Vladimir Borchenko. And at that point Vladimir would no longer be able to trust him.

"*Dasvidanya,*" Vladimir said as Nikolai left. He swiveled around in his chair without waiting for a reply.

But before he picked up the phone, he glanced over his shoulder to make sure Nikolai was gone. A half-hour ago, when Nikolai had been in the hall—had he been eavesdropping on Vladimir and Natasha?

*So this is what it has come to.* Vladimir shook his head. Seeing enemies everywhere. Distrusting those closest to him.

# Chapter Four

*February 16, 1998. 12:10 p.m.*
*Chicago.*

D AVID," SAID VLADIMIR WHEN HE RETURNED to the line. "You
are in Chicago? What time is it there?"

"Around noon," David replied. "I knew I'd reach you in
the office, even this late. I didn't even bother trying to reach you at
home." With the phone in one hand, some clothes in his other, he
walked back and forth from his closet to his bed while he packed a
garment bag for his trip. The bedroom he shared with Annia in their
spacious high-rise apartment in downtown Chicago had a view of
Lake Michigan as did most every room. Annia had done the apartment in simple, elegant decor.

Vladimir laughed. "David, how long have you known me? I am
always working. You know that."

For David as well as for Borchenko, life and work were intertwined.

"I heard that you spoke with Terry James this morning," David said. "I'm really sorry about Sokolov."

A beat of silence. "As am I," Vladimir replied.

"I'll be in Warsaw tomorrow morning, and then St. Petersburg in the evening. I'm going to check up on the Nevsky project; then, I'll be coming to Moscow. We should meet then."

"Of course," Vladimir said. "As soon as you arrive."

For a moment they were both silent. David closed his eyes and, for an instant, allowed his mind to drift. He had known Borchenko for a quarter-century. In that time they had become close friends, comrades.

---

DAVID OLEN MET Vladimir Borchenko for the first time in 1974 when he was thirty-one. David had flown to Warsaw on a connecting flight from Paris. Though the distance between the NATO countries of the west and the Soviet Bloc nations could be bridged by a two-hour plane flight, the psychological gap between the two was effectively millions of miles. David had traveled overseas and knew how to handle himself in a foreign country. Still, he had to admit to himself that he had felt a twinge of apprehension when the plane landed in Soviet-dominated territory.

His first impression of Poland felt like a dulled blow to his senses. The airport was drab gray, dilapidated, the passport-control agents rude and openly suspicious. Few times before had David felt like such a conspicuous foreigner. He was made to wait while his bags were emptied and searched. Soldiers stood by holding rifles, their eyes sullen beneath uniform hats.

A car and driver were there to meet David. He didn't know who had arranged the pick-up. Maybe the CIA agent who had arranged for him to travel to Poland or perhaps the man David had been sent to meet. Somehow it didn't seem to matter. David sat in the back of the car and nearly choked on the smell of gasoline. He increasingly wondered whether he would ever see his home again.

As he entered the city, David watched grim Soviet cement-gray apartment buildings pass by the window, one after another along the roadside. Even from a distance they looked like tenements; their weather-beaten facades and square edges were seemingly designed to repress individuality, joy, expression. The buses belched dirty diesel smoke into the air. People walked the streets with dour, downcast expressions. Their body language suggested a deep sense of defeat or resignation. The storefronts on Jerozolimskie Street, one of the main thoroughfares, were barren and dark. Long lines spilled out onto the sidewalks outside the few shops that seemed to be open.

David felt the place's oppressiveness like an invisible hand pressing down upon him. He wondered how the Poles were able to bear it. The country had been geographically subject to the military ambitions of Russia and Germany for centuries, and it suffered whenever either entertained imperial aspirations. Twenty years before, the Germans had nearly reduced Warsaw to the rubble; after the war, Poland was assigned to the Soviet political sphere with no pretense that the country could ever look ahead to self-determination. Poland's government officials were puppets who implemented Moscow's demands, and the free world might as well have been on another planet. Even the nation's strong faith in Catholicism—one of the main currents in its history—was under attack by the Communist regime.

David's car drove past the towering Palace of Culture, the great symbol of Soviet occupation. The huge Stalinist-style building narrowed upward from its sprawling base until it terminated in a single spire that seemed high enough to pierce the clouds. Atop the point was a red Soviet star. The building dominated Warsaw like a mythological colossus, rising up from the flat landscape to dominate every view of the city.

The driver pulled up to a building's front entrance and sat there, saying nothing. After nearly a minute David realized that they were in front of the Europejski Hotel. David got out of the car and pulled his suitcase out of the back seat. He leaned forward to thank the driver but the car pulled away, leaving him alone in a damp drizzle.

When he was alone inside his room, he allowed himself a deep sigh, felt the tension that wound his body like a coiled spring. He dropped his bags on the bed and looked around. The room was shit. A single bed without a headboard was jammed into the corner. The walls had cracks in the plaster and were painted in a nauseating green color. There was no air conditioner, no television, a phone that looked as though it was probably thirty years old. The fixtures in the bathroom were stained and cracked. When David opened the window, flakes of paint fell from the casement.

"Well, I didn't come for the amenities," David said to the empty room. "Good thing."

He washed his face with cold water—the hot-water tap didn't work. Then he paced the room a few times, stretched his arms, tried to come back to life after so many hours spent in airplanes and cars.

If he hadn't been so frightened, he might have laughed out loud. A month before, he had been secure in his life back home in Chicago with his up and coming business. Things were going well. Then he had got a call from his boyhood friend, Carl Becker. A couple of days later, he was being interviewed by a CIA agent.

*The CIA*. And they weren't playing games. David had figured this out from his first meeting with Jim Allen. David had been dragged into something he barely understood, told only the bare minimum that he needed to know; then, he had been sent beyond the Iron Curtain. He hoped he wasn't being used as a pawn or that some lunatic in the CIA might consider him expendable. He also hoped that he wasn't going to be arrested as a spy.

"What the fuck am I doing here?" he whispered to himself. Jim Allen had warned him that the hotel room would almost certainly be bugged.

David's visa said that he was in Poland as a real-estate developer. He was supposed to conduct preliminary site inspections on a series of industrial plants that his company was being contracted to build. He was supposed to meet a COMECON official from Moscow named Vladimir Borchenko.

A couple of weeks before, David had never heard of COMECON, the Council for Mutual Economic Assistance, the region's economic agency overseeing commerce between the Soviet Union and its satellites. Borchenko, whoever he was, would be in charge of the proposed industrial development from the Soviet end. But Borchenko was also involved in something else, something more. Something that the CIA hadn't been willing to share with David. He had been told only that Borchenko knew why David was being sent, that he would hopefully explain everything David needed to know.

David looked at his watch. He had barely slept the night before and had tossed and turned uneasily. But it was time. He could rest later.

He stood in front of the hazy mirror next to the dresser; the metal around the glass was tarnished and coming apart from the frame. He stared into his own eyes in the reflection, willed his breathing to slow and his hands to remain still at his side. Then he put on his suit jacket, flipped off the light, and went out into the hall.

He had memorized the instructions he had been given. He walked down the long empty corridor until he reached a set of stairs. He went up two flights until he reached the fifth floor then emerged into another empty hall. It seemed as though the place was empty of guests.

David followed the hallway until he reached a set of chipped wooden double doors. He pushed his way through and suddenly found himself in the din of the hotel's laundry facility. There were three women folding linens on a long table; none of them looked up when David stepped inside. An older woman in a dirty smock stood in front of a huge steel washing machine. She looked up at David with a momentary curiosity then looked away again. David walked past them without a word of greeting and stepped through a parted woolen curtain that led to a small dark passageway, the linoleum beneath his feet a bad imitation of oak flooring.

At the end of the hall was an open door. David stepped through it; he squinted when sunlight hit his eyes. Improbably, he found himself in a little stucco sunroom; louvered windows were open to the fresh air of the day and the muffled sounds of traffic on the street below.

There was a table in the corner, beneath the window. A man sat there alone, his long legs crossed and smoking a cigarette. He stood up and extended his hand.

"Vladimir Borchenko," he said in a firm but warm voice. "It is a pleasure to meet you, Mister Olen."

David returned the Russian's firm grip, tried to return his smile.

"Come, sit," Borchenko said. "We have much to discuss."

Vladimir offered David a French cigarette from an open package next to a ceramic ashtray.

"No, thanks," David said. "I just quit a few months ago."

"I see," Vladimir said, raising an eyebrow.

David sat down and exhaled slowly. Borchenko wasn't what he had expected. The Russian was relaxed, with an open manner. He wore a fashionable business suit, like a Westerner rather than the locals David had seen in Warsaw. His eyes were piercing, his gaze direct.

"Let's talk," David said. "Maybe you can tell me why I'm here."

―――――――――――――――

"So you'll be here in Moscow in forty-eight hours," Vladimir said, his voice still deep and clear after twenty-five years.

David willed his mind back to the present. He zipped his garment bag closed and sat down on his bed.

"It will be good to see you again; it's been too long," Vladimir continued. "Unfortunately, the circumstances could be better. We have matters to discuss."

"Sokolov?" David asked.

"Yes, and more," Vladimir replied.

"I see." David resisted the urge to press Vladimir.

"How is Annia?" Vladimir asked, his voice suddenly turning warm. "And Monica?"

"Just great," David said.

"How long ago was it that you and Annia adopted your daughter?"

"Nine years," David replied. "She's almost ten now."

"I have heard that is a wonderful age," Vladimir said. "I hope you're finding time to enjoy your daughter."

David was silent. Vladimir had been married once, years before, a subject that he was rarely willing to discuss. His wife had died before they could have children.

"I'm loving it," David said.

"I worked so much when I was younger," Vladimir said. "Often there wasn't time for personal matters."

"You still work hard," David said. "And so do I. But we're smarter now. We know how to pace ourselves. Not so much wasted energy."

"Ah, yes, but you're still younger than me," Vladimir said.

David laughed. "I always will be."

"I wonder," Vladimir mused. "Lately I have been thinking of the past."

"Why is that?"

A few beats of silence. "So many things have happened," Vladimir said. "And it seems like it will never end."

"But it's over," David said quickly. "I mean, look at Poland, Russia. It worked. Look at everything that's happening today. It's all because of what we were able to—"

"But it never ends for *us*," Vladimir interrupted.

A weariness had crept into Vladimir's voice, a note that he had never heard before. David frowned. *It never ends.* How many times had he entertained that very notion? But why was Vladimir bringing it up now and in such a desultory tone?

"We succeeded," Vladimir continued. "But we should have known that some actions continue to reverberate far into the future. Once the bottle is open, the genie does not want to return."

"What do you—"

"Come see me in Moscow, David," Vladimir said. "We can talk then."

David heard a click and then a dial tone. He hung up the phone. *It never ends.*

He picked up his bag and carried it into the living room where Annia sat on the floor doing a puzzle with Monica. Annia was a beautiful blond-haired Polish woman he had met in Warsaw twenty-two years ago while there on business.

Their adopted daughter, Monica, now almost ten, was thriving. She was a treasure that David had never expected to discover. Together, Annia and Monica were his joy.

Annia turned to David, saw his luggage, and tilted her head questioningly to the side. David could read her expressions. This one said she wasn't happy. He had told her about Sokolov's murder, and it scared her. She knew much of his secret life but at times he withheld details of his clandestine business and thought the less she knew, the safer she'd be and the less she'd worry.

David caressed Annia's face. "I'm sorry, love."

"I don't want you missing out on Monica's precious early years," she said quietly, her English beautifully accented with her native Polish language.

"Believe me, neither do I. I'll be home soon." David scooped Monica up and sat her on his lap. He tickled her, and she laughed. Then she threw her arms around her daddy's neck.

Annia, who gave him strength, and sweet Monica, who made him feel so young again—they meant the world to David. No, he promised himself, he would not let things from his past interfere with his present anymore.

# Chapter Five

*February 16, 1998. 3:03 p.m.*
*The Vatican.*

INSIDE THE FOURTH FLOOR of the Vatican's Apostolic Palace, the Bolivian Bishop Jorge Ramirez clasped his hands together and looked down at the floor. His head was swimming. He hadn't felt such a disorienting rush of excitement since he was a child looking up at the altar in his village during Mass. The altar of Ramirez's childhood had been made of simple wood, the same as the huge crucifix that had hung above it.

Bishop Ramirez looked up, feeling better now. He allowed his eyes to take in every detail of the pope's private chapel, where Ramirez and a small group of Latin American bishops and cardinals had been invited for a private Mass with the Holy Father himself. The altar faced the wall; it was designed in the days when priests performed Mass with their backs to the congregation. Above it was a bronze statue of the crucified Jesus. The ceiling was a mosaic of colored glass through which the light of afternoon shone.

And there, less than ten feet away, was the Holy Father himself.

Bishop Ramirez let his eyes linger on the pontiff, who was hunched over slightly at the waist, his eyes closed as he waited for the ceremony to begin. John Paul II led a billion people. He was a man of celebrated religious fervor—and of renowned personal charisma. The former priest Karol Wojtyla, the first non-Italian pope in nearly 500 years, had dominated the history of his time like few other men of God. Now he was almost eighty years old, but his frame still seemed infused with an incomprehensible authority and power.

Ramirez glanced around. He had known some of the other bishops and cardinals before this pilgrimage; others he had met only since his arrival in Rome. They were all, like him, dressed in golden robes and red and purple *zucchettos*, or skullcaps. Though they were all awed in the pontiff's presence, the aged pope's serene presence seemed to calm them, to fill their movements with grace.

The Mass began. Two priests stood to either side of the Holy Father and helped him to his feet. Ramirez's heart quickened. There was no organ, no choir, no music. They were alone with the Pontiff in his most private sanctuary.

Cardinal Fernando Garcia of Rio began the Mass after receiving a small nod from the pope. Ramirez felt an energy in his body like a jolt of electricity as the Mass began. He couldn't keep his eyes off John Paul, who was a couple of meters away; Ramirez could see his face in profile.

*Let us proclaim the mystery of the faith.* Cardinal Garcia's voice was joined by that of the other bishops and cardinals.

The pope's eyes were focused in the middle distance as he sat at the head of the aisle in a cushioned bronze chair. His hands shook slightly. He seemed to Ramirez to be conserving his energy; his lips moved slightly slower than the vocal liturgy of the Mass.

What power the man seemed to have. More than once John Paul had made Bishop Ramirez contemplate the concept whether the spirit of a century, through God's will, could move through a man and use him to transform the world. If it were so, then Karol Wojtyla was that man.

*Lord, remember your church throughout the world.* Ramirez heard the voices echo in the small chapel.

It was time for Holy Communion. Ramirez glanced up at the young priest from Argentina who had been chosen to hand out the Eucharist. Then he looked back at the pope.

And realized that something was wrong.

John Paul gripped the arms of his chair, and his eyes widened. Ramirez hoped that the moment would pass, but then he realized that his fellow clergy had noticed the same. The room fell into a sudden silence as the last prayers faded from earshot.

The pope leaned back in his chair then pitched forward as though someone was pulling at him.

Ramirez gasped. The room fell into stunned silence. The two young priests at the Holy Father's side knelt over him and spoke in hushed but insistent whispers.

The pontiff's eyes bulged. He seemed to be fighting for breath. A third priest stepped forward and motioned for the visitors to the Vatican to step back.

The young priests raised John Paul to his feet then half-carried him to a small door leading out of the chamber. He was gone in a moment; it left the room in shocked silence.

Bishop Jorge Ramirez put his hands to his face and felt the warm tears that were coursing from his eyes. He looked around. The pope had been taken away without a word of explanation.

"What are we going to do?" asked Cardinal Garcia.

No one answered him. No one knew. When the Holy Father had left the chapel, it was as though he had taken the collective spirit of the gathering with him. Now there was another question, one that they dared not ask aloud but that burned in all their hearts: Had they just witnessed the pontiff's final moments?

Ramirez knelt down on the hard floor, his eyes closed, and began to pray.

*February 16, 1998. 5:19 p.m.*
*Washington, D.C.*

CONGRESSMAN CARL BECKER walked slowly from the committee meeting room in the House, enjoying the tranquillity of the hallway outside. It had been a hell of a session in there.

Becker had been in Congress for twenty years, and he had finally reached one of his long-term goals, becoming the chairman of the Foreign Relations Committee. For the past six months he had been at the forefront of efforts to appropriate low-interest government loans and outright aid for Eastern Europe.

In typical congressional fashion, this attempt had been dragged down by Becker's political rivals. Many congressmen claimed they would never be able to sell aid to Eastern Europe to their constituents, not in a time of government belt-tightening and campaign promises to cut taxes. They feared that their opponents in the next election would pounce on them if they voted for aid to the region.

It was typical politics, self-serving and shortsighted. Carl Becker didn't support aid to Eastern Europe because he was a nice guy. His aid proposal was based on hard, straightforward world politics. Some of the former Soviet countries were doing all right, but not all. They needed help developing a financial infrastructure to complement their nascent democracies. If things went to hell over there, the whole world might get dragged into the mess. But if they had food, jobs, and shelter, then they would have a better chance of pulling through—and there would be a hell of a lot less possibility for civil unrest. Becker would probably win in the end; he usually did. But it would take a lot of negotiating, promising, and cajoling to get the aid passed.

He got onto the elevator and pressed the button for the fourth floor. His mind wandered to the pile of message slips he knew would be waiting for him when he got back to his office.

Politics was a sort of family business for Carl Becker. He was the son of a Chicago alderman who had himself risen to serve two terms in the Illinois legislature. After the Vietnam War, Carl had utilized his family's connections and clout, and his own knowledge of how the political system worked, to win a seat in the Illinois House. He had eventually won his seat in the U.S. House on the second try. Now he was fifty-five, and he had held onto his seat for almost twenty years. He wasn't one of the flashy ideologues fighting for a few seconds on the network news. Instead he was a deal-maker, a power broker who worked behind the scenes to get the job done. Younger congressmen might have called him a dinosaur—behind his back, at least—but few of them were willing to take him on on the House floor.

Coretta Young, Becker's secretary, sat behind her desk when he stepped into the office. She was absorbed in Becker's appointment book and traced a line down the page with her finger. A stout black woman in her forties, she wore a telephone headset.

Carl Becker went into his office, closed the door behind him, allowed himself the luxury of a deep breath and a sigh. The Committee Meetings always drained his energy. What he needed was a walk outside, in the brisk air, to bring him back to life. Too bad there was no time.

Becker recalled the voices in the Committee room, the arguments against aid to Eastern Europe. Many of them remembered him as the staunch anti-communist. They used this impression to dismiss him at times, as though he still viewed the world from the anachronistic perspective of a Cold Warrior.

More than once during that morning's session Becker had wanted to take over the meeting, grab the microphone, and say: "Look, you know we need to keep these countries stable. They're selling nuclear technology left and right to wild-card countries; we've got terrorists eyeing half the conspicuous targets in the U.S.; we've got our own allies making deals behind our backs. Let's cut the bullshit; pass the aid; get this mess in order before it blows up on us. Let's make a difference while we still can." But that wasn't the way the game was played. Becker had decades of solid contacts within the U.S. intelligence apparatus, and he knew the way things really worked in the world. Yet he couldn't share a fraction of what he knew. And what he was allowed to say no one wanted to hear.

He poured himself a cup of black coffee from the pot that Coretta kept hot for him throughout the day. He loosened his tie, took off his jacket, and sat down at his desk.

Becker put on his reading glasses and scanned the printout of his phone messages. More than three-dozen calls this morning. Representative Alomar from New Mexico, probably wanting to talk about his education bill. Mike Johnson from Maine, probably some hunting-and-fishing bullshit. He checked a few that he intended to call before that afternoon's session, ignored the rest. Becker reached for the phone, ready to start calling, when he saw a name that stood out from the others on the list.

*Ricardo Pilletta.*

Becker looked at it again, convincing himself that he had read the name correctly.

"Shit," he muttered quietly in the silence of his office.

It was a name that belonged to no one. The number left on the message was also fictitious.

The message was a code and an old one. It had been established in the '70s, back when Becker had been contacted by the CIA when he was working as an attorney. Because of some indiscretions when he was in the Army, back in the early days of the Vietnam War, he found himself dragged into something so vast that even now he barely understood it. A message from Ricardo Pilletta meant that the CIA needed to speak with Carl Becker immediately.

Becker put down the phone and rubbed his cheek. His mind flashed on his childhood friend David Olen. Did David know about this?

He picked up the phone again and dialed a number that he had committed to memory more than two decades ago.

He listened to the phone ring. It had been about ten years since they had contacted him this way. Becker felt the back of his neck growing cold and moist.

"Falcon Enterprises," said a woman's voice on the line.

"Ricardo Pilletta," Becker said.

A pause. "One moment, please," said the woman.

The line went silent. Becker turned in his chair and looked out the window at the chilly Washington noontime. He had been a patriot. He had always done as they asked. And now he was sure, more than ever, that they would never leave him alone.

# Chapter Six

*February 17, 1998. 7:20 a.m.*
*Over Poland.*

T HE BOEING 767 FLYING UNDER THE REGISTRY of Polish LOT Airlines soared over the water-drenched peninsulas of the German Baltic coastline; the flight pattern turned slightly southeast and the chaotic, scrubby farmland of Central Europe appeared. In contrast to the regulated quilt-like grids and irrigation circles of American farmland seen from the sky, here in Poland the agricultural plots were small and fragmented, broken down into irregular shapes that seemed to follow no consistent logic. This chaos was a result of the fact that farm ownership in Poland had remained in private hands even during the communist era; each family-owned plot had been broken down into smaller parcels as it was passed down to subsequent generations until large farms eventually transformed into collections of adjacent odd-shaped plots.

Within a half-hour, the plane banked steeply then began to

descend. David Olen checked his seatbelt and brought his seat upright. The Boeing, a 767-400 leased by LOT, had a different feel for the passenger than the old Soviet TU-144s that David had flown many times coming in to Warsaw. The ride felt smoother; the interior was more comfortable. David looked out the window. After the plane descended from the typical low ceiling of a gray late-winter morning, David saw the runway appear under the wing. The plane landed with only a slight jostle.

David picked up his bags from the baggage carousel, walked to the clean, well-lit passport-control line. After waiting only a few minutes, David presented his passport to a uniformed young man who stamped it and waved him past.

*Incredible*, David thought. The change never ceased to amaze him. When he first came to Eastern Europe in the '70s, entering and leaving Poland was an arduous nightmare of surly customs agents and intimidating soldiers. In just a few short years, Poland had completely changed its face to the world.

David spotted Deren, his local driver, at the back of the arrivals area as his eyes scanned the crowd. Deren smiled with recognition when he saw David.

Deren was a stocky man with black hair and a thick mustache whom David had found nine years ago.

Back then, Deren had the only air-conditioned car, a small Mercedes, for hire in Warsaw. God only knew how he was able to get such a prized possession. David offered him employment, Deren accepted, and he was put on Olen Europe's full-time payroll. David didn't believe in unnecessary luxuries, but having a car and driver in Warsaw was now a necessity.

Deren tipped his hat and took David's bags. "Good morning," he said in heavily accented English.

"*Dzien dobry*," David said in return, patting the man on the shoulder. They walked out of the terminal into the gray morning. The sky was overcast, the trees around the airport bare of leaves.

David sank into the back seat as Deren pulled onto the main road leading into the city.

"*Corpo?*" he asked in his deep voice.

"Where is Jason Rudas?" asked David. "At the office?"

"*Nie*, at Pan, Kapinski's office," Deren said.

"Let's go to Kapinski's office," David replied.

Deren merged into traffic and picked up speed. Like seemingly every driver in Poland, he drove as fast as he possibly could—never slowing unless to avoid a collision.

"Deren, please," David said. "Slower. *Wolniej. Prosze.*"

The car slowed slightly—Deren's concession to David's request. They drove along a tree-lined boulevard that hadn't existed four or five years before. In long rows on one side of the road were huge Soviet-era apartment blocks, the monumental sameness of their appearance broken up only by the occasional painted balcony. The apartments were monolithic concrete hulks, all suffering from decay and dilapidation because of the poor standards of their construction. David had been inside them, seen the peeling walls, the crumbling plaster, the lights flickering from inadequate electrical systems. It would take decades of work before much of the city's commercial and residential space could even approach Western standards.

Yet a few years ago this well-paved road hadn't been there, nor had the trees and grass that had been planted to provide arriving visitors in the city with a favorable impression. The city might take a generation to rise out of the conditions the Soviets had left it in, but the improvements and upgrades were well on their way. People were improving their lives, ridding themselves of more than forty years of communist oppression.

David thought of his younger colleague, Jason Rudas. Though separated in age by more than a few years, they had shared an easygoing rapport since the day they met. Jason had been working for a competing firm, and David had met him during a negotiating session on a downtown-Chicago construction project. Jason had received an architecture degree and worked locally for a couple of years before going back to Northwestern to get an MBA with an emphasis on international business. When David met him, Jason had been out of school for a little more than a year. After being around him for an afternoon, David had invited him out to dinner. Before the evening was finished, David had offered the younger man a position with Olen Europe.

On the surface the two men were quite different. David was relaxed, almost irreverent in his manner. Jason was serious almost to the point of seeming stern, though he was capable of quick flashes of dry, intelligent humor. Both men shared a passion for their work, and both found fulfillment in making deals and seeing through major projects. Jason, like David, was capable of long days of work and intense mental focus. In his off time Jason practiced martial arts, but he was also willing to play a round of golf with David when they had a free afternoon.

If David had one criticism of Jason, it was that he was almost too focused and intense; he was a workaholic. He was so effective, smart, and trustworthy that he had essentially become David's partner in Olen Europe. But David suspected Jason used his work as a "great escape," a way of avoiding those parts of his life he was afraid to deal with.

Jason was good-looking and cultivated. He dated a lot yet never saw the same woman more than once or twice. David felt that Jason had built a wall around himself that no woman could break through. It was a subject that David had broached only once, after a long day of work and a few drinks in a quiet restaurant. Jason had said to David, "I'm going to settle down in a year or so, as soon as I meet the right woman." But that time never arrived.

The streets were crowded with pedestrians. Young people in business clothes. Middle-aged men and women raising their faces to a patch of sunlight through the cloud cover. The city had been moribund and depressing a decade ago, but now it was bustling and alive. There was a palpable sense in the air that something was happening, some progress was being made. Such a sense of optimism would have been almost unimaginable before the fall of the Soviet Union.

Deren slowed as they reached an intersection on *Ulica Foksal*. There was no place to park—there never was in Warsaw—so Deren eased the Mercedes over the curb.

David hopped out of the car before Deren could come around and open the door for him.

Andrzej Kapinski's company office was on the fourth floor of a building that had been constructed in the early 1950s. David glanced next door and saw that a new American software company had just opened an office in a small two-story building; it was obviously trying to get a piece of the exploding Polish market. He crossed the street against the traffic and stepped inside the six-story building.

Kapinski's offices were marked only by a small plaque beside a plain wooden door; inside was a well-lit reception area with an attractive, young Polish receptionist who greeted David. He toted his briefcase to the work area where some of his local staff were officed during the construction of the newest high-rise in the center of town.

A chorus of male voices called out David's name when he stepped into the office. Three younger men who were sitting at a round table piled with papers and coffee cups stood and greeted David.

First he shook hands with Roger Wolf, the project manager for the high-rise tower, a young man in his middle thirties with curly hair parted in the middle and a compact wrestler's build. Next was Mike Roth, a consultant recently recruited by Olen Europe from a U.S. developer working in Moscow. Finally David shook hands and clapped Jason Rudas on the shoulder. Jason was wearing a sport coat and wool turtleneck; his expression was as focused and serious as always.

Roger Wolf had grown up in Milwaukee and gone to the University of Chicago, where he stayed on to get his MBA. He was incredibly detail-oriented, and he was capable of juggling the countless factors involved in managing a large-scale construction project. He could switch from providing input on the selection of electrical fixtures, to coordinating construction draws, to dealing with the lender supervisors—all in the space of an hour. He had innate good sense and an ability to make things happen. He had started out on local projects for Olen and Co. then moved to Warsaw with his wife more than a year ago.

"How's Chloe?" David asked Roger.

"Fine, thanks," Roger replied. "We leased a nice flat. She won't drive the roads, though. The Polish drivers are too crazy."

David looked at Jason. "See what I'm saying?" he asked. "I wouldn't drive here on a bet."

"Depends on the bet," Jason said, deadpan.

Jason brought a pot of fresh coffee to the table; all four men sat down, and David poured himself a cup from the steaming carafe.

"I heard what happened in St. Petersburg," Roger said.

"It's a real tragedy," David said, looking down at his coffee. He didn't feel like discussing Sokolov, not until he had a chance to speak with Jason in private.

Sensing this, Jason said: "Mike was just telling us about his meeting with the two architectural groups who want to do the verification and permit work for the Jerozolimskie site. Mike, now that David's here, maybe you can start at the beginning."

David put on his reading glasses and glanced down at the photocopied report that had been placed at his seat at the table.

Mike Roth cleared his throat and gathered his thoughts. He was a paunchy man of about forty, his sandy hair receding at the temples. He had a slightly nervous manner, which David chalked up to his role as an interim consultant who was effectively auditioning for a full-time job on the Olen Europe staff. Mike had been brought in to get the development process off the ground for a land parcel that Olen Europe had recently leased from the city; it was a quarter-mile from the center of town, a very appealing piece of real estate where the company wanted to build two mid-rise office buildings.

"Well, I've talked to both the Kapinski team and the WCR team," Mike began. "And I'll say right off the top that I think WCR is a far more impressive architectural group. They have local knowledge of politics in the Gmina Centrum district, where the site is located. And their approach to the design was interesting and well thought-out. Very professional and sharp."

David crossed his arms and leaned back a little. Kapinski Export, of course, was Andy's company. Andy, who David had known since the early '70s, who had been integral to David getting involved in the region in the first place. Andy was now a developer on his own and was Olen Europe's primary Warsaw partner. He also ran Kapinski Export, an architectural and engineering company.

"WCR sat down with me and outlined their strategy," Mike continued. "They had a lot of quality things to say about their local contacts, in terms of permits and authorization."

"Which is also one of Andy Kapinski's strengths," Jason interjected.

David looked at Roger. "Is Andy here in the office today?" he asked, nodding toward the half-open door.

"Not that I know of," Roger replied. Nonetheless, he got up and closed the door.

"I know you guys are dependent on Kapinski locally," Mike said. "And I know he goes way back with you, David. I don't want to step on any toes here, but—"

"Don't worry about anyone's toes," David said. "Just tell me what you think."

Mike took a deep breath. "I think Kapinski and his people don't have their shit together. They weren't fully prepared when I came to meet with them. Then Andy himself came in half an hour late and treated me like I was something he found on the bottom of his shoe."

"Andy has a way of doing that," Roger offered.

David smiled, said nothing. It wasn't the first time his people had complained about Andy. Andy, once shy almost to the point of invisibility, now could be imperious and rude—especially to people he didn't consider important. But Andy always delivered in the big picture, and David knew he could trust him implicitly.

Jason caught David's eye and seemed to understand something that didn't need to be said aloud. "What about the bids, Mike?" he asked. "Kapinski versus WCR?"

"WCR is higher," Mike said.

"By about twenty percent," Roger added. His eyes were focused in the middle distance. As always, he was calculating. His mind never seemed to rest.

"But part of that is style," said Mike. "Kapinski will probably cost the same. In the end they'll probably hit us with extra design fees and call it necessary to get the building permits."

"Fair enough," David said. "But what about permits and authorizations? This isn't back home. The District can make it hard for us to ever get a shovel into the ground."

"I'm aware of that," Mike said, a little defensively.

"Where have you worked before?" David asked.

"Moscow for the past four years, the Czech Republic before that."

David nodded appreciatively. "OK, then you know the score. The trick on these projects is getting permission just to break ground."

"And one of the first things Andy Kapinski said—when he was damned good and ready to talk to me—was that this was one of the main things he can bring to the table." Mike tapped a pencil nervously on his knee as he spoke. "He knows who to talk to. He's the inside guy."

"And he's right," David agreed. "He's done it a million times in the past. The Warsaw Center of Commerce is a good example."

"He also has strong connections with Polish subcontractors," Jason offered.

"Sure, but WCR is also a local company—" Mike said.

"But they haven't got Andy's track record," Roger interrupted.

Mike Roth sighed. "Let me be straight here," he said. "I think Andy exaggerates his level of local influence. I think WCR can get the job done just as well as he can. The difference is that they would get us enrolled in the process. We can cultivate our own contacts, get our own ground forces. Everyone knows we're tied to Andy. I suggest that we use this project to help us establish our own contacts in the District."

Jason raised his eyebrows and leaned forward in his chair. David could see that what Mike had said interested him greatly.

"There's one major problem as far as I'm concerned," David said. "We've been working with Andy for a long time. It would be a major statement to cut him out now."

Mike held his hands up. "I can't help that," he said. "I was hired to render my opinion after receiving the responses to our proposal requests. That's all I'm doing."

David glanced over at Roger. "There's a lot of truth in what he's saying," the younger man uttered.

"Well, it would be an unpopular move," David said.

"I'm not here to win any popularity contests," replied Mike.

David laughed softly. "I get what you're telling me," he said. "But there are a lot of factors here. A lot of sensitivities."

"I understand that," said Mike. "I know you have a lot of factors to weigh on the managerial side. Look, I know I'm new here. My opinion is that of someone who's trying to get the lay of the land."

"And you're doing a good job," Jason said. "That's what makes your opinion valuable to us."

Mike nodded, accepting the compliment.

---

MORE DISCUSSION and a half-hour later, David rubbed his eyes and took a sip of his coffee, which had turned cold. He suddenly felt weary and drained. It might have been the long overnight flight from Chicago or this conversation with his young associates. Or it might have been the weight of the past pressing down upon him.

"All right, so maybe you feel you're locked in to doing business with Kapinski," Mike Roth said, tapping his pen on his knee in a jerky rhythm. "But maybe you can use WCR as a wedge. You could try to pin Kapinski down on a fee structure or else get assurances of specific services. You know, play one against the other."

"The real question is who we want to use," Jason said. "We negotiate everything else after that."

David smiled. He would have said the same thing as Jason, in basically the same words.

"I like the fact that you're willing to tell us things we don't want to hear," David said to Mike.

"But Andy's your guy," Mike said, sounding a bit defeated.

"It's not that simple," replied David. "There are other factors at play here."

David glanced over at Jason, who returned his look with a flash of inquisitiveness. David had expressed this sentiment many times in the past to Jason. He knew rumors circulated about how Olen Europe got started in the '70s, how the company was able to grow into a powerful entity in communist countries. Stories that included the KGB, CIA, FBI, David being a spy. Seemingly far-fetched stories that, in reality, weren't all that far from the unbelievable truth. Jason had never asked for the real story—perhaps because he sensed that David would never share it with him.

David knew that Jason had a hard time living with this. Jason was curious, with a searching intellect. Eventually he would want to know what brought David Olen to Eastern Europe, how he had managed to thrive there, and eventually David might decide to tell him.

# Part Two

# *The Deal*

# Chapter Seven

IT HAD BEEN A HOT CHICAGO SUMMER. Heat rose in waves off the downtown sidewalks. The Watergate hearings and the threat of impeachment for President Nixon were all over the television. Cynicism and distrust were the messages of the day.

David walked slowly from City Hall to his office, his shirt clinging to his back from sweat.

There was a message from Carl Becker waiting for him at his desk, which was nothing unusual. David had known Carl since they were in the same Chicago elementary school class. They were born the same year, lived in the same neighborhood. By the time they were in high school, they were inseparable best friends, and they eventually served together during the Vietnam War.

Carl and David had chased after the same girls, smoked their first cigarettes and took their first drinks together. They hung out on the same street corner night after night in front of a delicatessen, pitched pennies, talked up the neighborhood girls, tried to get into trouble. In the summer they spent the afternoons at North Avenue Beach. When it rained they went to the BBR, the Boy's Brotherhood Republic. They played basketball in the gym, learned how to box, sparred until one of them had a split lip or a bloody nose.

When they were a little older, they spent their nights in the Hamlin billiards room and shot pool for money and played short cards in the back room. David and Carl had felt the invincibility of youth.

David's father immigrated from Russia in the '30s. His mother was born in Chicago, after her parents immigrated from Riga, Latvia. David used to listen to his father speaking Russian to his friends as they sat in the kitchen and drank tea from a glass, but he never was taught the language. David's father was sharp and intense, although he lacked schooling and could read and write English only enough to get by. He bootstrapped himself into a small textile business and was always able to provide the family the essentials of life and sometimes a little extra. More and more David felt the pull of the outside world beyond the walls of his family apartment. He had a burning sense that there was *something* going on out there—some action, he would have called it then. Whatever it was, he had to be a part of it.

Carl Becker's family was more affluent than David's. Carl's father Daniel was an alderman, part of the old-school Democratic machine in Chicago. The patronage system ruled local political life with a per-vasive heaviness that bordered on oppression. Each alderman had precinct captains who worked under him. If you were an ordinary person, you went to the precinct captain when you needed a driver's license, or needed a ticket fixed, or when you were in a dispute with your landlord. The precinct captain on David's block was a painting contractor named Julius Pine. Julius ruled over a three-block radius on behalf of Daniel Becker. When election day came, Julius paid David to drive people to the polls to vote for a straight Democratic ticket. Anyone who could walk was expected to vote—and vote the right way, or else they might find themselves out of luck the next time they needed a favor.

Carl and David grew up in a neighborhood in which local politics reigned supreme. Every favor granted became a marker that would be cashed in later. Instead of dealing with the city government, the people on the block dealt with Julius. David grew up seeing firsthand the way politics and power worked. Carl learned these lessons directly from his father, and when he began his political career, he knew the system, the way deals were made, the way things got done. When they talked to each other, they spoke the same language—and they both understood the realities of the world.

David had been able to use inroads from Carl's political connections to build his own business. As a result, David owed much of his success to Carl, and they remained close friends.

But there was something unusual about this message: its urgency. *Meet me at the Shore Club at one o'clock this afternoon. It's extremely important that we talk right away.*

Carl had never before broken into David's schedule in this way, without checking to see if he was free. David looked at his watch. He had about half an hour to get over to the Shore Club and see what the hell was on Carl's mind.

The Shore Club was a meeting place for Jewish businessmen in Chicago. It was softly lit and comfortable, with a number of fine dining rooms and numerous private rooms for business meetings that required privacy. Carl was waiting for David in the lobby; the first thing David noticed was the way Carl looked around as they shook hands, as though he anticipated seeing someone else.

"Expecting someone?" David asked.

"Maybe," Carl said evasively.

The club steward, an older man named Charles who had worked there as long as anyone could remember, greeted David and Carl with a friendly smile.

"Two for lunch?" he asked.

"Make that three," Carl said. "I'm expecting a third party."

"Who?" David asked.

"I'll tell you in a minute," Carl answered, following Charles through a portico into the library lounge.

They sat on opposite sides of an intimate table covered in white linen. David noticed that Carl's face was flushed, his eyes darting nervously. His forehead creased with worry as he ordered a Chivas Regal from the hostess and took out a pack of cigarettes.

"What're you having?" Carl asked.

"Just a Coke," David said.

"You might want something stronger," Carl said.

David shook his head no and said: "I have meetings this afternoon. I don't want to—"

David stopped when he saw the grave seriousness of his old friend's expression. With a small shrug, he looked up at the hostess and said, "All right, bring me a Chivas."

They sat in silence until their drinks arrived. Carl lit up a cigarette, offered one to David.

"No, thanks," David said. "You know I just quit."

Carl smiled and put the pack in his pocket. "I'm glad you did," he said. "You'll live longer. I just hope you stay quit after we talk today."

Carl took a long drink of his scotch, draining the glass. He was working at Samuels and Croft, a politically connected law firm in Chicago with a branch office in Washington, and lately he had been talking about going into politics. As the years went by, David thought that Carl resembled his father more and more.

"All right," David asked. "What's this about? What's so terrible that it's going to make me start smoking again?"

"First, how are you, buddy?" Carl asked, almost apologetic.

David looked at the pack of cigarettes, marshaling all his will not to light one. He knew this lunch wasn't about the current state of David's emotions.

"Cut the shit," David said. "What's going on?"

Carl looked down at the table then up into David's eyes. "We have a problem."

"So we have a problem," David replied. "So what? We'll fix it. Haven't we always taken care of each other?"

"We have," Carl agreed. He took a long drag on his cigarette, let the smoke curl around his face. "But this one is different. It's bigger."

"In what way?" David asked.

"We've been sucked into something," Carl explained. "And I don't think we have a choice in the matter. It goes back to 'Nam, when my dad got us out of trouble."

David took a sip of his drink, felt the warm liquid running down his throat.

"What are you saying?" David asked. "Are we being blackmailed?"

"That's one way of looking at it," Carl said with a bitter tone.

"Who?" David asked.

Carl paused, looked around the room. The afternoon lunch crowd had filled the place, though there was a generous distance between tables that enabled private conversation.

"The CIA," Carl replied.

"Is this a fucking joke?" David asked. "This isn't funny."

"The CIA got in touch with me a couple of days ago," Carl said. His voice was flat, his expression serious. "Guy named Jim Allen. Real straight-looking Captain America type, you know what I mean?"

David pressed his hands against the damp wood on either side of his glass. His ears rang with disbelief.

"Turns out this guy knows all about Sagami Depot," Carl said. "And he threatened to go public, to open the issue and take down a lot of people. I started to tell him to go fuck himself, but it was no use. This guy was serious. He's going to use the quartermaster thing against us unless we do what he says."

David leaned back against his seat and closed his eyes. Memories from ten years ago came flooding back to him. Was it possible that mistakes made when he was only twenty-one could have such dire consequences?

*1964.*
*Sagami Depot; Sagamihara, Japan.*

DAVID OLEN AND CARL BECKER were sent overseas in 1964, during the early days of the Vietnam War. Less than a year had gone by since President Kennedy had been assassinated. It was the end of "Camelot," and the whole tone of the nation had changed. There was talk that Lyndon Johnson was planning to send in more troops to Vietnam and that the war was really going to escalate. They had been deathly afraid that they might be drafted for front-line combat, so Carl's father, Daniel, had arranged to have his son and his son's best friend stationed in Sagamihara, Japan, about forty kilometers from Tokyo at the U.S. Army General Supply Depot, often called Sagami Depot. It had taken a lot of political clout, the calling in of a lot of markers, to make it happen, but the end result was that the young men were hundreds of miles from the bloodshed of war. They were given desk jobs at the Supply Depot, where they could push paper until their duty was over. The Depot stored and supplied equipment designated for special approved projects as well as critical medical supplies.

They were young men, away from home for the first time. Tokyo soon became their personal playground. They bought a motorcycle together and sped through the streets with little regard for the locals. They met young Japanese women in bars and impressed them with stories of American life—mostly made up. Decades later David Olen still winced at the memory of how cocky and naive he and Carl had been. They shirked their military duties and figured that the same political clout that had gotten them their jobs would protect them. During work hours, they raced through Sagamihara, drunk on cheap stuff moving through here, David. Some of it disappears before it gets on the boat for Sagami Depot. One can do a lot with creative book-keeping."

David glanced at his own face in the mirror; it was pasty white, his expression shocked fear.

"You could go to jail for this," he hissed at Carl.

"Relax," Carl said. "Look, do you think I cooked up something this big on my own? I'm smart, but I'm not a mastermind."

"Then who—" David stopped himself. He pictured Daniel Becker in his study in Chicago; he was always talking on the phone when he was home, always making a deal with someone.

"It's not just my dad," Carl said. He waved to the bartender for another beer. "There are guys in Washington involved, congressmen. Maybe even a Senator for all I know. I just sign off on the paperwork they send, make sure things are working, and keep my trap shut. They're the ones who are really operating the scam. I just get some spending money, some booze. I have to be cool about it, anyway. People'd get suspicious if they saw me wearing a gold watch all of a sudden."

"Shit, Carl," David said. He took a deep breath as he fought con-flicting reactions in his mind. This was incredible, and David was pissed at himself that he hadn't caught on to it sooner. On the other hand, he was appalled. This was theft, plain and simple.

"Don't look at me like that," Carl said. "The plan is airtight. As long as nobody rocks the boat, we'll be fine. We have guys in Tokyo who are in on it."

"We?" David asked. "I just found out about it."

"You're in this with me," Carl said. "You have been since day one."

"No, no," David said. "I haven't—"

"You didn't complain when we used connections to get you over here with me, did you?" Carl asked. "And look at that form. What's the other signature there on the bottom?"

David held the piece of paper up to the light in the dim, smoky bar. His signature was there, a couple of lines below Carl's.

"I get shit to sign all the time," David said. "You know how it is. I don't even look at all of it."

Carl shrugged. "I know," he said. "But it doesn't look good."

David stuffed the paper in his pocket, turned around to face his friend. He felt his face turning flushed red.

"I didn't ask to be in on this," he said to Carl.

Carl gave a thin smile. "I didn't either, not really," he explained. "But don't sweat it, buddy. We're in this together. We get a little more free booze, a little more spending money. All you have to do is look the other way."

David felt the requisition order burning in his pocket, as though it were a hot coal rather than a thin sheet of duplicate paper. He relaxed, let his body slump on the barstool. His father had passed away suddenly three months into his stay, and David would have to help support his mother when he got back to the States. He could use the extra money, he rationalized. Besides, what choice did he have, really?

In the next couple of months, nothing changed outwardly. David and Carl turned in their usual lackluster performance at the Depot. David noticed another purchase order discrepancy. Now he was stuck, and he had to go along. Late at night, he and Carl would divvy up their payment for helping the scam move forward: cartons of Camels, bottles of Johnny Walker, a few frozen Japanese steaks that they paid the company cook to grill for them. They had no idea how much the masterminds behind the plot were taking in, and neither cared much—as long as they had spending money for the bars and enough money to keep their motorcycle gassed up. Finally David made enough money to buy a motorcycle of his own, so he and Carl no longer needed to share one. The war escalated in Vietnam, but it seemed so far away that it might have been a dream.

One afternoon David sat in the office. He had just plugged in the would happen next. His father had died, so he was responsible for taking care of his mother. He was accountable to more than himself, and he burned with fear and regret at the idea that this episode might haunt him later.

Daniel Becker picked them up at the airport with a cold, unflinching expression. He walked them to the car, asked them how their flight had gone. All the way home he said nothing, instead staring at the back of his driver's head as they made their way back into Chicago. David looked out the window at the city that had always been his home, his happiness dulled by a restless anxiety that seemed to color his every sense.

When they reached the Becker house, Daniel took them into his study. The alderman was imposing, with broad shoulders and graying black hair cropped close to his scalp. He wore a suit with his shirt collar buttoned up to the neck at all times, even in the privacy of his own home. He lit a cigar and sat down behind his mahogany desk and left the boys standing on the other side.

"You fucked up," he announced, the first words he had spoken directly to them since the airport. "You fucked up as bad as you possibly could have. We had a nice little thing going over there, and you threw it in the toilet. Do you boys understand what I'm telling you? You got stupid."

"Yes, sir," Carl and David said, almost in unison.

Daniel Becker examined the end of his cigar, which smelled musty and sweet in the closed air of his office.

"I had to call in a lot of favors to get you boys out of there without handcuffs on your wrists," he said. "I had to call in more favors than you could even imagine. I had to make a lot of promises that're going to be hell to keep."

"I'm sorry," Carl said. David could sense his friend's body trembling.

"You ought to be sorry," Daniel Becker said to his son. "You had to fucking talk, didn't you? You had to be a big shot to try to get some pussy. I heard what happened. If you'd kept your mouth shut, we wouldn't be here crying about it right now."

David stayed silent, even though he knew that Army intelligence had found cracks in the scam that they were already investigating. Carl's bragging had hastened a downfall that might have come anyway, but David knew better than to bring up this point to Daniel.

"We will never speak about this matter again," Daniel Becker announced, looking from one young man's face to the next. "Is that understood?"

"Yes, sir."

"If the press ever got their hands on this one, a lot of heads would roll," Daniel said. The alderman seemed, for a second, genuinely frightened by the thought. "It would be one fucking scandal. So we're forgetting about it here and now. Everyone is."

Daniel let his gaze settle on David until it was obvious that he expected a reply.

"I understand," David said.

"You'd damn well better," Daniel replied. "This is a lesson for you two. Don't waste it."

When David walked out the front gate of the Becker house, headed back to his own home for the first time in a year, he felt as though he had been transformed into a new person. He hoisted his Army bag onto his shoulder and walked slowly. He saw the corner store where he used to hang out; the Boy's Brotherhood Republic; the unimposing, orthodox synagogue in the middle of the block between three-story walk-up apartment buildings—as though he was seeing them for the first time.

He knew nothing would ever be the same. He had sat there being interrogated by Colonel Caldwell in Japan and said nothing. He could have spoken up about the Congressmen on the take, about the whispers of a Senator, and how it all came back to Daniel Becker. But he hadn't.

Political life in Chicago worked on the marker system. You do talk to you so soon. We have to get started on this thing. We need to start cooperating."

David felt overheated even in the air-conditioned club. All around them businessmen were talking, laughing, drinking. They were making deals and blowing off steam. Something inside David recognized that his life was changed forever the moment he walked into the club that afternoon. He yearned for his old life, just an hour ago, before he had been drawn into whatever the hell this was.

"Everything you've said to me has been totally crazy," he said to Carl, letting out his anger. "I don't want to get into this. I don't need or want this."

Carl tossed a burnt-out match into the crimson blown-glass ashtray that sat by his hand.

"David, you can get pissed off at me if it makes you feel better," he said. "You can yell and scream if that helps."

"You know, Sagami Depot was ten years—"

"Yeah, and it hasn't gone away," Carl interrupted. "You don't need this; I don't need this. My father doesn't need it, either. But we're all sucked into this, all three of us. And if I'm in this, you are, too. It's as simple as that, David. I'm sorry. But that's reality."

Carl's words broke through David's rage. He exhaled and leaned back in his chair, feeling suddenly exhausted.

"That's reality," David repeated sarcastically. "I should have known that one of these days . . ."

David stopped speaking when he saw Carl stiffen and look over his shoulder. Involuntarily, David jerked around. A tall man was talking to Charles in the dining room doorway. Charles pointed at their table, and the man started walking toward them.

"What's going on?" David asked.

Carl didn't answer. Instead he looked down at his burning cigarette until the man reached their table. David knew Carl well enough to see that his old friend was trying not to let on how angry he was.

"Hello, Mr. Becker," the tall man said, extending his hand. "Good to see you again."

Carl didn't get up. He reached out and shook the man's hand and made a show of his reluctance to observe even the most minimal social rituals of politeness.

David stood. The man was six feet tall, solidly built, wearing a plain brown suit. His features were chiseled, all-American. His dark hair was cut short, and although he was large, he carried himself with an ease and grace that said this was a man who knew what he wanted and got it. David noticed he wore a wedding band, and for a second he wondered who this guy might be married to. What sorts of secrets must he hold from her?

"David Olen?" the man asked. He smiled then shook David's hand and looked directly into his eyes. "I'm Jim Allen. It's a pleasure to meet you."

They sat down. David waved for the hostess, who took Allen's order of a club soda.

"You've had time to talk?" Allen asked Carl.

Carl shook his head. "We've been talking. Not that any of this shit makes sense, but yes. We've certainly been talking."

Allen was sitting next to David, on his side of the table. The CIA agent gave off a stony calmness, but David could also tell that Allen was intense and determined. Even if he hadn't sensed this, he could have seen the effect that Allen was having on the normally unflappable Carl.

"First of all," Allen said to David, "I'm sorry I had to approach you in this manner. Eventually you'll probably understand that these kinds of operations require a certain amount of aggressiveness in terms of timing." He spoke so softly that David and Carl had to strain to hear him—but with an intensity and authority that gave them both a chill.

David nodded. He could hardly believe he was sitting next to a CIA agent exerting powerful leverage over his and Carl's lives.

"How much have you told him?" Allen asked Carl.

"Well, I got through the part about you having us by the balls," Carl said in a cold voice.

"Fine," Allen said, no emotion in his voice.

David took another sip of his drink. He couldn't believe that Carl hadn't told him Allen was coming to lunch, but perhaps that was why Carl had been so nervous. Maybe he hadn't known for sure.

"This isn't an ambush; you have to believe me," Carl said, almost reading David's mind. "I told him where and when we were meeting. But he wouldn't say whether or not he was coming."

"I had to clear my schedule," Allen said, ignoring Carl's tone of voice. "But this was important enough to merit a flight to Chicago."

David put his hands flat on the tablecloth. "Something is going on between Russia, the Vatican, and Poland; I know that much from Carl," David said. He let out a nervous, little laugh. "All right, I'll play along. What does it have to do with me?"

"We need you to travel to Poland," Allen said.

"Poland?" David asked, surprised. "Why me?"

"Because of your real-estate development experience."

"But I haven't been in business all that long," David said. "I have no experience working in Poland. There must be others who have more—"

"I'm aware of that. But you're young, bright, aggressive. You'll catch on fast. The CIA has put together some industrial contacts for you there," Allen explained in a low voice. "You're going to meet a COMECON official in Warsaw who has a lot of the answers. We've been in touch with him in secret, and he's willing to exchange help for information."

"Industrial contacts?" David asked.

"Here's what I'm bringing to the table," said Allen. "We're offering to get you started in business in Eastern Europe. You'll be one of a handful of Westerners permitted to do business there."

"What's COMECON?" David asked, intrigued despite the anxiety that gnawed at him.

"It's the economic governing administration for the countries controlled by the Soviet Union," Allen said. "The man you're meeting is named Vladimir Borchenko. He's absolutely crucial to the operation we're investigating."

"What is this guy Borchenko supposed to be up to?"

Jim Allen folded his hands on the table and looked into David's eyes. "That's your job—finding out."

"Again, why me?" David said. "Don't you have professionals for this?"

"We do," Allen agreed. "But Borchenko doesn't want to talk to an intelligence professional. I've looked into your background. I think you can handle yourself with Borchenko. And the contacts we've arranged for you are very real. This is a chance to expand your business operations in a very profitable way."

David finished his drink and savored the smoky flavor of the scotch. Now he understood why Carl had started drinking so early in the day. His mind reeled against the surreal quality of what was happening as he replayed everything Carl had told him.

"I don't know about this business with Andy Kapinski. He's my employee. That doesn't mean I can get him involved."

"Don't worry about that," Allen said. "Kapinski is no problem. He has some discrepancies in his immigration status."

"Jesus," David said. "He's an immigrant. Does that mean he should be blackmailed?"

David looked up at Carl and searched for help. Carl frowned sadly.

"David, the world works the way it works," Carl said. He motioned to the waiter for more drinks. "I didn't make it that way. I didn't make the rules."

"I go over there and talk to this Borchenko. He tells me what he tells me. I come back and share it with you, and then that's it, right? Then I'm finished?"

Allen was silent for a moment when the waiter arrived with the drinks and put them on fresh napkins and emptied Carl's ashtray.

"Would you gentlemen like lunch?" the waiter asked. He nodded at their unopened menus.

"Nothing for me," David said. "I'm not hungry."

"Bring me a club sandwich," Carl said. "And some fries."

"Nothing, thanks," Allen said. "I have to be heading back to Washington in a few minutes."

David shook his head when the waiter walked away and looked at Carl. "You could eat a five-course meal in the middle of a hurricane," he said.

Carl smiled bitterly. "Have to keep my strength up."

"So anyway, I'm in, and then I'm out, right?" David turned to Jim Allen. "One conversation about whatever, I file a report or get debriefed or whatever it is you do, and then I go home, and we all forget about it. Do I have the right idea?"

Carl sipped his drink and looked away.

Jim Allen didn't reply. He stared stone-faced straight at David.

"I said, do I have the right idea?" David asked.

Carl shrugged. "They have us," he said.

"And what does that mean?"

"We're not setting up these business contacts for you as a sham," Allen explained. "Let me reiterate: This is for real. If you play it right, you could do a lot of business. You could become a very rich young man."

"But that assumes I want to do business in the Soviet Bloc," David said. "And I know you aren't setting this up out of the generosity of your heart. You're going to expect something in return." David shook his head. "No, I don't think so. I'm not your man. I don't know anything about the Soviet Union. I don't want to get involved."

Jim Allen smiled at David, a phony, creepy smile, then said, "I'm afraid it doesn't matter what you want," in his soft but somber voice. "We can make life very unpleasant for you. If your little Army exploits become known, you can say goodbye to your business, your freedom, life as you know it."

"You're threatening me?" asked David incredulously.

"Just be grateful that they saw fit to sweeten the pot for you," Carl said. "You know what I'm getting out of this deal? I'm getting to keep my good name. That's it."

David finished his second drink in a single gulp. He felt as though, at any moment, Carl might start laughing and tell him this had all been a put-on, that Jim Allen was an actor he had hired to play an elaborate practical joke.

But this was no joke.

Jim Allen stood up, glanced around the room. He seemed satisfied, ready to leave. David also stood.

"Thanks for your time," Allen said. "Sorry I can't stay, but it was important for me to meet you in person. I'll be in touch in the next couple of days. I'm sure you understand that you're to speak with no one about this."

"Who the hell would believe me?" David asked.

Allen shook David's hand then smiled that scary smile of his. "You won't be sorry." He shook Carl's hand then turned and walked out of the club. David and Carl sat down again, avoiding looking at each other.

"The CIA," David whispered. "Who'd have thought?"

"Who'd have thought?" Carl repeated, lifting his glass in an ironic toast.

When David went back to his office later in the afternoon, he canceled all his appointments and meetings. He went down the long corridor to the section of his offices where the architects and draftsmen worked. Andy Kapinski's drawing table was in a partitioned area, where a design team was putting together a mixed-use high-rise plan for a Kansas City developer.

David knocked on the cubicle wall as he entered. Andy looked up from his work, his eyes furtive. He was a thin young man, with a hesitation in his manner and speech that David guessed was a result of his difficult life. His hair was streaked with gray, which made him look older than he was.

"Yes, David?" asked Andy, putting down his pencil, looking up from the drafting table.

"I just got contacted by the government," David told him.

Andy shook his head, the blood rushing to his face. He said nothing, but his chin dropped to his chest. He obviously understood that whatever peace he had found was about to be taken away from him.

# Chapter Eight

*February 17, 1998. 2:29 p.m.*
*Over Poland.*

IN THE HALF-FULL BUSINESS-CLASS SECTION of the LOT Airlines 737, passengers leaned back in their comfortable seats and examined their dinner menus printed in both Polish and English. David Olen finished his glass of water, unbuckled his seat belt, walked across the aisle, and sat in the empty seat next to Jason Rudas.

"What are you looking at?" David asked Jason.

Jason tipped the stapled document so David could see. "Mike Roth's report, comparing Kapinski and WCR."

"He has some good points," David said. He leaned the seat back and calculated in his mind. It was four in the afternoon. Nine in the morning in Chicago. Six in the evening in St. Petersburg.

"He does have some good points," Jason said. "He also has an attitude."

"That's not always a negative," David offered.

"Sometimes it's what we want," Jason agreed. "But I think he's letting his personal impressions color his judgment."

"You mean he let Andy piss him off, so he doesn't want to work with him?" David asked. "Could be."

"Wouldn't be the first time," David said.

The two men sat together in silence for a moment, lulled by the sound of the plane's engines. The craft had reached cruising altitude, and flight attendants were circulating and taking dinner orders.

"Now we have a chance to talk about Sokolov," David said.

Jason put Mike Roth's report away in a folder and tucked it in his briefcase on the floor. "I noticed you didn't want to talk about it in front of the guys," he said. "Are you worried they're going to get scared about doing business over there?"

"No, it's not that," David said. "Mike lived in Moscow for four years, anyway. He knows things have happened."

Jason sipped his cup of coffee. "But this one is weird," he said. "I really don't think we're going to find out that Sokolov was involved in anything dirty."

"That's what I keep hearing," David said. "The guy was clean all the way through. Which might have been his problem."

"You mean he got in someone's way?"

"It makes sense," David said. "You know how things can get in Russia. It's the old *apparatchik* mentality, the Mafia way of life. Sokolov was a reformer."

"But he worked for Vladimir Borchenko," Jason said. "That makes it a little different."

It sure as hell did. David still couldn't figure it out. Vladimir wasn't directly involved in the Mafia—at least he didn't think he was. He always assumed Vladimir was above all that. But he was one of the major players in the entire country. Killing Sokolov would be viewed as a slap in Vladimir's face.

"I don't think it's going to affect the Nevsky deal," Jason said.

"The Nevsky property is ready for development, and it's in GlobusBank's interests to go through with it as planned, no matter who replaces Sokolov."

"Who do you think's going to replace him?" David asked.

Jason paused for a moment and thought. David knew that Jason had already considered the question, that he would be at least a couple of moves ahead. It was important to know who would be sent to St. Petersburg to replace Sokolov because Olen Europe would be dealing with him for the next couple of years.

"Fyodorov," Jason said. "Or maybe Gukassov."

Both men worked in the St. Petersburg office of GlobusBank. Fyodorov was a young man a lot like Sokolov: energetic, educated, forward-thinking. Gukassov was more of a product of the old system, a man in his late fifties who had a reputation for being methodical and levelheaded. David thought Olen Europe would have no problem dealing with either one, though neither was as respected as Sokolov had been.

"Have you talked to Vladimir?" Jason asked.

David nodded. "But not in depth. I'm waiting until we can talk face-to-face in Moscow."

David shifted in the seat and unbuttoned his wool cardigan sweater. He turned and saw that Jason was staring at him.

"What's your gut feeling?" Jason asked.

Jason was very smart, and he was also intuitive. He obviously felt that the truth of Sokolov's death would be found through Vladimir Borchenko.

"You know Vladimir," David said. "I won't know what he's thinking until I talk to him."

"It was obviously a Mafia hit," Jason said. He creased his brow. "Which is what puzzles me. Vladimir doesn't deal with the Mafia; I'm sure of it. Of course, he has Nikolai Petrov to take care of that."

Nikolai Petrov was a thug, as far as David was concerned. He had met his type plenty of times in Chicago. It didn't matter how expensive his suit was or what circles he moved in—he would always have that violent predatory instinct lying just below the surface of his actions. Vladimir thought he needed Nikolai; he had said as much to David. But David wasn't as sure. Employing someone such as Nikolai was bound to come back and haunt Vladimir.

"Well, maybe you're on to something," David said.

"About Nikolai?" Jason asked.

David didn't reply. Nikolai Petrov seemed to be just the kind of street criminal who perpetrated crimes like the hit on Sokolov. David wondered if Vladimir should be watching his back. David saw the flight attendant approach, ready to take his dinner order. At that moment he realized that he had lost his appetite.

*February 17, 1998. 1:20 p.m.*
*Washington, D.C.*

CARL BECKER STOPPED in front of a door marked *Falcon Enterprises*. There was a small intercom box at eye level next to the door. He pressed a button and waited.

"Falcon Enterprises," said a young woman's voice, the same as the one he'd heard on the phone when he called.

"I'm here for an eleven o'clock appointment," Becker said.

"Who are you here to see, sir?"

"Ricardo Pilletta."

A long pause, almost enough to convince Becker that he had made some kind of mistake. But that was impossible. The instructions he had been given were precise.

The door buzzed; Becker heard the lock click. He opened the door and went inside.

The lobby of Falcon Enterprises looked as though it had been decorated from a cheap furniture store's going-out-of-business sale.

Behind a desk was a young woman with red hair who was wearing a telephone headset. "Have a seat," she said, smiling. She turned and focused her attention on her glowing computer screen.

Becker sat down and looked over the magazines fanned out on the coffee table. *Time, Newsweek,* both more than six months old. There was *Highlights for Children* next to a copy of *Soldier of Fortune.* Nice to see the CIA still had a sense of humor, however twisted.

An unmarked door at the far side of the reception area opened. Out stepped a short man with a receding hairline and wire-rimmed glasses. He wore a pair of casual slacks and a dress shirt with the sleeves rolled up.

"Good morning," he said, spotting Becker. They shook hands. "It's really great of you to come on such short notice. Janine, hold my calls, will you?"

The receptionist looked up, flashed a smile at Carl Becker. "Of course," she said.

Becker followed the man into a fluorescent-lit corridor. They walked past a couple of closed office doors and into a small office. The man indicated a cheap folding chair in front of a desk.

The desk seemed to sag under the weight of huge piles of seemingly disorganized papers. A computer was turned on but relegated to a corner of the work space amid a pile of hard-bound books.

"So you're Ricardo Pilletta?" Becker asked the man.

He laughed, shook his head. "I guess I am now," he said, self-deprecating. "My real name is Thomas Gleason, Congressman Becker. I apologize for contacting you in such a cloak-and-dagger fashion, but I feel it's imperative that I don't leave a trail with my current activities."

Gleason's casual manner seemed to harden instantly. He looked around the room for a moment, as though trying to recall something, then fixed his gaze again on Becker.

*Who was this guy?* Becker felt almost offended by Gleason's youth. He couldn't have been older than thirty, thirty-three, tops.

"I know I'm young," Gleason said, as though having read Becker's mind. "Try not to let it bother you. What's important is that I worked under Jim Allen as soon as I finished my agency training. He was my mentor."

Gleason chewed his lip, looked serious. "Jim Allen recruited me right out of Stanford. Damn, it was sad about his cancer. He was a brilliant agent. It's a shame no one really knows about him outside of agency circles."

Carl Becker thought that the real story was considerably more complicated. Jim Allen had used whatever means were at his disposal in order to pursue America's interest—including, in the case of Becker and David Olen, what amounted to blackmail.

"Obviously you know how Allen used to contact me," Becker said. "The Pilletta alias. It always struck me as paranoid."

"I don't think so," Gleason said with a slight patronizing edge. "People never connected him with you or David Olen, did they? The real story of what happened has never been made public. Don't you think Allen's security measures had something to do with that?"

Becker folded his arms and sensed that he had to be careful what he said next. He didn't like this kid, nor did he trust him. Becker had been contacted out of the blue by using an old code to arrange a meeting, but how was he to know whether Gleason had ever really worked with Jim Allen? For all Becker knew, this could be some kind of expedition fishing for information.

"I know what you must be thinking," Gleason said. He folded his hands into a cat's cradle. "This is all pretty sudden. And we're already touching on some pretty compromising information."

"I don't feel in the least bit compromised," Becker said. He wondered suddenly whether he should stand up and walk out.

"Good," Gleason said. "Because officially the deal in Europe never happened. And the United States was never involved."

*The deal.* Becker hadn't heard it referred to in that way in years.

"If you say so," Becker said, suddenly irritated.

"Every presidential administration from 1974 to the present has plausible deniability in terms of the European activity between Poland, the Vatican, and the Soviet Union," Gleason continued. "Jim Allen filed only the most oblique reports."

"You're starting to make some very dangerous statements," Becker said. "Tell me what you want, or I'm leaving."

"I'm not trying to antagonize you," Gleason said. "It's simply important that you understand—I have total knowledge of all of Jim Allen's agency activities. I gained access to his files, and I've been waiting for the proper moment to act on what they contained."

"You—"

"I know how he got you and David Olen involved," Gleason said. "I know about what happened at Sagami Depot."

Becker looked into Gleason's eyeglasses and fought a sudden urge to leap across the desk and smash them into the younger man's face. One damned mistake, one series of bad judgments, and still Becker was paying.

"I have a lot of admiration for you and David Olen," Gleason said. "It's a shame it was all a secret. Olen's name should be in the history books."

"David Olen is my oldest friend," Becker said. "I don't appreciate your throwing his name in my face. I don't appreciate your bringing up ancient history as a way of making veiled threats. And, most of all, I don't appreciate the fact that I don't really know who you are or what you're about. I'm starting to believe you don't even really understand what you're alluding to. Just because you say you've read a file—"

"Jim Allen contacted you and persuaded you to enlist your friend David Olen in 1974," Gleason broke in. "The CIA had gathered intelligence about financial transactions moving between Moscow, the Vatican, and Warsaw—something very irregular in those days. A couple of field agents verified a trail leading to Vladimir Borchenko, a COMECON official based in Moscow."

Carl Becker sat up straighter in his chair and became transfixed by hearing Gleason describe events that had happened when he was a younger man.

"This was dropped in Jim Allen's lap and then officially forgotten," Gleason said. "But Allen had contacts in the KGB. Have I made any errors so far?"

If he wanted to draw this out, then fine. "No," Becker said. "You're right. It was the Cold War. The KGB and the CIA were two sides of the same coin. Sometimes they exchanged information."

"Allen was able to make contact with Borchenko through KGB channels," Gleason continued, obviously enjoying himself. "Borchenko had contacts in the KGB that were keeping him out of trouble. And when Allen contacted Borchenko, the Russian suggested that the CIA send someone over to speak with him. Not an intelligence agent, he said, but a businessman. He wanted to talk business."

"Vladimir Borchenko has always been a businessman at heart," Becker said. "I'm sure you know where he is today."

"At the top of Russia's financial pyramid," Gleason said. "Still sitting pretty."

"All right," Becker said. "You know what you're talking about. I believe you worked with Jim Allen. But I haven't been involved with any aspect of the deal in years."

Gleason got up from his chair with a hard sigh that indicated he was out of shape, almost breathless.

"Want a cup?" he asked Becker, pouring a cup of coffee from a blackened pot sitting on a credenza behind the desk.

Becker shook his head.

"What David Olen stepped into after that first meeting with Borchenko was nothing short of amazing," Gleason said.

"I agree," Becker said. "It was incredible. And the world never knew."

"It never will know, hopefully," Gleason said. "Too many lines

were crossed. First of all, we'd have to explain why the CIA was indi-
rectly sponsoring an American businessman doing deals with Soviets
and the Vatican. It would take a lot of explaining."

"Which isn't why you called me here today," Becker said.

Gleason pushed his glasses off his nose, rubbed his eyes, and
yawned. It seemed incredible that this kid possessed all the knowledge that Jim Allen had accumulated over the years. Jim Allen had
struck Becker as straight-laced and pompous the first time he met
him, but later he realized that the CIA agent was keenly intelligent,
shrewd, and always totally convinced of the propriety of his actions.

Whereas this Gleason was . . . a lightweight, Becker thought. It was
the only word that fit.

"How often do you talk to David Olen?" Gleason asked.

Carl Becker started to speak then paused. It felt strange to be back
in these treacherous waters where he had to watch everything he
said even to an agent of his own government. And stranger still to be
talking about *the deal* again, after so many years of silence spent
wishing he could share his secret with someone who understood.

"We still speak," Becker said. "Not as much as we used to. When
we both lived in Chicago, we talked every day."

"Do you still talk about what happened?" Gleason asked, inching
forward a fraction in his chair. "You know, go over old times?"

"Not really," Becker replied, which was the truth. They never
talked about that aspect of the past because they had already learned
how phones could be tapped, how eavesdroppers could put secrets
to use. But there was something deeper at play; neither friend
wanted to talk about the past because of a shared, unspoken desire
to forget about it.

"David Olen did really well for himself, didn't he?" Gleason asked
with an icy smile. "He took the ball and ran with it, didn't he? Not
bad. Serve your country and get richer than sin."

"What are you trying to suggest?" Becker asked.

"Nothing much," said Gleason. "I contacted you before Olen for a few reasons. First, you're here in town. Second, I wanted to hear from you whether Olen still talks to you about the old contacts. I would be interested to know whether he's still profiting from them."

"I don't like your tone," Becker said. "I don't care for you talking about my friend that way, and I don't like being questioned like some fucking asshole. You're playing games with a United States congressman, you punk."

Gleason's smile broadened. "That's your second speech this morning, Congressman," he said. "You don't like my style. Fine. But I'm Jim Allen's heir in the CIA, and you have to deal with me. I think we're at a turning point and—"

"What kind of turning point?" Becker interrupted.

"We know that the pope is ill again," Gleason replied. "He collapsed during an official function. The Vatican is keeping it quiet for the moment, but it doesn't look like he's going to make it this time."

"He's very old," Becker replied. "It would be a shame, but you can't say it would be unexpected."

"Not like the last one," Gleason said, a tone of suggestion creeping into his voice.

Carl Becker closed his eyes for a second. He felt so tired. It had been years since he had dealt with Jim Allen and this entire insane enterprise. They had taken his secrets and turned them against him. They had filled him with new secrets and pledged him to secrecy. And now it was starting again.

"The last one," Becker repeated.

"In 1978," Gleason said. "Luciani. The Venetian."

Outside the window, Becker could see, a couple of young women were talking next to a minivan. Life went on while inside he was discussing the secret history of the world with some upstart spy.

"I have an idea of something I want to accomplish," Gleason said. "I can't take complete credit for it. It's just an update on an old theme. And I'll need your help and David Olen's."

The winter sun was breaking through the clouds and playing on the branches of the evergreens. Carl Becker fixed his gaze out the window. He knew that he could do nothing to stop Gleason from talking.

"Olen didn't tell you everything, did he?" Gleason asked.

"I don't know," Becker said. "I believe what he told me. Listen, it was all so long ago. I thought we did our part, paid for our mistakes."

Gleason chuckled. "It'll be over when I say it's over. Even Olen doesn't know everything. Let me tell you a few things, play a little connect-the-dots. I think it'll help you understand where I'm going with this."

---

CARL RUSHED BACK to his office. He hurried past Coretta and waved her off when she tried to tell him something. "Not now, Coretta. No calls. No interruptions."

He closed his door and locked it, something he hadn't done in years. He picked up his phone and dialed David Olen's office number in Chicago.

"David Olen's office," answered Cynthia.

"It's Carl Becker. David, please. It's urgent."

"Oh, hello. It's Cynthia. I'm afraid David is out of the country on business."

"Find him for me. Now. This is really important," he said gruffly.

"Is there anything I can help you with?

"I wish, Cynthia, but no. I need David. I'm at my office, and I'll be home this evening. He can call at any hour." Carl hung up his phone. All those anxious feelings he hadn't had to deal with for years were bubbling back up to the surface. He slid open his desk drawer and pulled out a bottle of Tums from the back. He popped a few into his mouth.

"Damn," he said aloud. Now he'd have to wait for David to be located, and that could take hours.

# Chapter Nine

*February 17, 1998. 9:09 p.m.*
*St. Petersburg.*

AVID OLEN AND JASON RUDAS arrived in St. Petersburg and walked down the drab hallway leading into the airport terminal. They had a long wait until a uniformed official finally showed up to get them through customs.

Russia was a country of endless inconveniences and minor slights. The Soviet system had bred cynicism and inefficiency. Daily life in Russia often seemed to be composed of a series of small cruelties, and waiting endlessly in lines was the norm.

After they had gone through passport control and customs, they picked up their bags from a battered baggage carousel and walked together into the main terminal.

"There's Yevgeny," Jason said, pointing.

Yevgeny Passorov, Olen Europe's full-time St. Petersburg driver, was about forty years old, though he looked about ten years older by

Western standards. He was slim, and his lank brown hair was combed over his forehead. His cheeks were sunken, and he wore a permanent expression of suspicion that was often mistaken for hostility.

They stepped out into the night; the air was crisp, and their breath turned to clouds of vapor in the air. As they walked to the parking lot, David looked around them. As always, the airport doors were surrounded by a group of men, all smoking, all wearing black leather jackets and fur hats. They eyed every new arrival with inquisitive stares. Though they looked intimidating, they actually were making themselves available for rides into the city, a way of earning cash. Many of them were associated with the Mafia, which more and more claimed a percentage of business in all walks of life, but for the most part, they were harmlessly trying to earn a little extra cash with their cars.

David and Jason exchanged pleasantries with Yevgeny as the Russian hoisted their bags into the trunk of his small BMW, which was wedged into a tiny parking space next to an old rusted Russian truck, a heap of a vehicle with a missing fender-panel and decades worth of road-sand and grime caked onto every available surface. As David opened his car door, he sniffed the air. Eastern European cities had a particular smell of pollution, an odor of chemicals mixed with the exhaust emissions from inefficient and ill-maintained cars.

Yevgeny pulled a cigarette from his coat pocket as soon as they were all in the car.

"*Nyet*, Yevgeny," David said, pointing to the cigarette. "*Pazhahl-stah*. Not when I'm in the car."

Yevgeny glanced in the mirror and, with a shrug, carefully put away the cigarette. He pulled out onto the main road leading into the city.

As David's mind drifted, the thoughts in the back of his mind came into clearer focus. This trip had been necessitated by a terrible event, Sokolov's assassination, and now that he had arrived in Russia, David felt a foreboding that he had kept at bay until that moment. He wondered whether Vladimir Borchenko was hiding something. Vladimir had emphasized their meeting in Moscow in less than thirty-six hours, and David now realized that—in true Borchenko style—the Russian must have had some revelation he wanted to make in person.

David glanced over at Jason, who yawned and rubbed his eyes. Sokolov being murdered had business ramifications for Olen Europe and, ultimately, Jason would have to take care of that. But Jason had no idea about the web of connections between Borchenko, Sokolov's employer, and David. Jason was better off not knowing.

No one in David's world—with the exception of Vladimir Borchenko—knew the full scope of what they had been involved in. Carl Becker knew some of the vague outlines yet few of the details. Kapinski knew some of it, and so did David's wife, Annia. None of them knew about more than the small part with which they had been involved. It was safer that way. Jim Allen at the CIA had stressed that knowledge could be dangerous and that sometimes the best way to protect people was to insulate them from the truth. Once something was learned, it was impossible to ever go back to not knowing.

"Oh, shit," Jason said, snapping David out of his reverie.

Yevgeny slowed the BMW and veered toward a traffic island between the lanes of highway traffic. David saw flakes of snow swirling in the car's headlights.

David looked out the window and saw a police car had pulled them over. Now the car was parked behind them, and two uniformed officers stepped out. The younger of the two circled the car on the passenger side; he was holding a semiautomatic rifle and wincing into the cold breeze.

"Has to be a random stop," David said quietly.

"Hope so," Jason said, under his breath.

The older of the two officers tapped on Yevgeny's window with a gloved knuckle. Yevgeny lowered the automatic window.

David saw the two officers sporadically illuminated by the

headlights of passing cars. Both wore overcoats and Russian fur hats. The older officer wore a sidearm on a strap outside his coat; unlike his young partner, he kept his weapon holstered as he leaned forward into the window and said something to Yevgeny in a rough voice. After a brief negotiation Yevgeny produced a plastic satchel from underneath his seat then handed the policeman a small bundle of documents.

David didn't notice the other officer moving closer until he heard a loud rapping on his window that made him jerk in his seat with shock. He opened his window and squinted into the beam of a flashlight. The young officer moved the light onto Jason's face and then their belongings. As he moved, the barrel of his gun shifted and for an instant pointed directly into David's face. He felt himself wince and instinctively turn away. The kid on the other end of the gun looked curious, maybe a little out of his depth. For a very long moment David hoped that nothing jostled his trigger finger.

Yevgeny and the officer exchanged a few more words. They sounded like they were having an argument, but to David's ears native Russians always did. The older officer handed Yevgeny his papers, shone his flashlight around the front seat, then walked away.

Yevgeny, his shoulders slumped, started the car. They had been pulled over by the police for no reason, and no reason was required. Russia had been a police state under the Soviets, and such things didn't change overnight. If Yevgeny had been in a hurry, he could have slipped the policeman some cash with his bundle of papers. It was a typical shakedown. The police had pulled over Olen Europe's company BMW because it looked affluent. Yevgeny, being either prideful or stubborn, hadn't played the game and refused to offer a bribe to expedite the process.

"Business as usual," Jason said to David as they sped up again on the highway.

David watched Yevgeny's eyes in the rearview mirror and looked for some sign of emotion or reaction. He saw nothing. They drove on through the slush and neared the city.

"Grand Hotel?" Yevgeny asked, his eyes on the road.

"*Da*," David replied. "The Grand Hotel Europe."

Outside the ubiquitous Soviet apartment blocks nestled in the snowy landscape, huge anonymous structures that each housed hundreds of occupants. David shifted in his seat as they passed the arched monument commemorating the spot where the Red Army stopped Hitler's troops during the catastrophic Siege of Leningrad. A few moments later they drove past a huge statue of Lenin pointing into the darkness, as though peering into a future that never came to pass.

When they reached the city center, they drove slowly on roads alongside one of St. Petersburg's many canals. Yevgeny swerved from side to side, careful to avoid one of the myriad potholes capable of wrecking the car's suspension.

"It was right around here," David said to Jason as they approached Nevsky Prospect, the city's famous main street.

"It was broad daylight, wasn't it?" Jason asked.

David nodded, trying to picture Alexei Sokolov's violent death. It happened in the morning, when the day was full of promise and possibility. As he looked out at the street at night, David pictured Nevsky by day: the wide thoroughfare bustling with traffic, the ornate building facades four and five stories tall above the sidewalks, the pedestrian traffic bustling in and out of the subways. And there in the middle of it all, Sokolov was shot to death.

Yevgeny turned on the windshield wipers, which smeared heavy clots of snow across their field of vision. It was snowing harder now, obscuring the relatively few cars that were out on the street.

"You can barely see our site through the snow," Jason said.

David turned around, tried to cast out the image of Alexei Sokolov dying on Nevsky in front of hundreds of people. He looked instead to where Jason was pointing, farther up in the distance on Nevsky, toward a group of buildings that Olen Europe was renovating in financial collaboration with a consortium headed by GlobusBank. The four structures were arranged in a square around a central courtyard; although they had once served as cells for Orthodox priests in the eighteenth century, they had been neglected for decades and had fallen into severe disrepair.

Across the street was *Gostinny Dvor*, the "merchant's yard," a two-story mall of individual shops that had once been the Soviet state department store. It had since been renovated, and its upper floor contained shops that sold Western designer clothes. On the first floor were shops that sold clothing and various sundries, along with a bustling video arcade. During the day, the marketplace would be vibrantly alive with shoppers and browsers.

Yevgeny turned onto the short street that connected Nevsky with Arts Square and found a parking space in front of their hotel. He hopped out of the car and unloaded their bags while Jason and David paused on the street. David looked up at the facade of their hotel then across the street, where another of St. Petersburg's palaces had been turned into living and commercial space. Much of the city had originally been built as palaces for the Russian royal families, with elaborate stonework and ornate architectural details. Many of these palaces occupied entire city blocks.

At times St. Petersburg felt like a city whose best days were two hundred years ago. Sea air from the Gulf of Finland, along with industrial pollution, had eroded and dirtied the regal architecture. A lack of money combined with government apathy under the Soviet system had left buildings' interiors battered and decaying. It would take a lot of money to rebuild St. Petersburg into a modern city— money that, for the moment, wasn't available.

But David hoped that businessmen like him could change the equation. The new Russia needed residential and commercial space of a much higher standard than what was currently available.

Although there was ample motivation in St. Petersburg, it needed wherewithal and financial bite. It needed cash and Western expertise, and it filled David with optimism to think that he was making a contribution.

Jason and David stepped through the metal detector inside the hotel entrance and then into the lobby. They checked in, said goodnight in the elevator.

David unpacked his garment bag. He hung his suits in the stylish armoire that was among the new furnishings designed specifically for the five-star hotel.

He sat down heavily on the bed and flipped on the TV set. CNN came on—in English. It was incredible. Ted Turner should have won the Nobel Prize. Without CNN, what might have happened in Tiannanmen, in Moscow, in Iraq, in Somalia? What would have been allowed to occur without the watching eye of the new world media? And now there was BBC Sky and NBC Europe, broadcasting in English to a global audience.

David's interest perked up when he saw file footage of the pope on the TV screen. He turned up the volume. The pope was rumored to be seriously ill, although the Vatican refused to confirm or deny the information. David looked at the aged features of the man he had met in Poland almost a quarter-century before, saw the charisma and intelligence still present in Wojtyla's fatigued expression. He idly wondered what John Paul II's death might mean in the Vatican. Did any part of the old cabal still exist, and wouldn't there be another similar power play to elect the next Pontiff?

David turned down the sound. He didn't have to worry about that anymore. He picked up the GSM phone and dialed a long series of numbers to get an international connection. It was midnight in Russia, three in the afternoon in Chicago. As the phone began to ring, he imagined his home full of afternoon light coming from the windows overlooking the lake.

"My darling," answered a warm voice.

Annia always knew when he was calling from overseas—the phone rang a slightly different way that she could detect.

"Annia," David said, smiling. "I'm in St. Petersburg."

*June 1974.*
*Warsaw.*

WHEN DAVID SAT DOWN with Vladimir Borchenko for the first time, he felt as though an electrical current was moving through him. Anxiety seemed to clip his every breath short. He heard a noise outside the door of the little stucco room and reflexively grabbed the edge of the table.

"Don't worry," Vladimir said, relaxed. "We're alone here."

Vladimir took a languid drag on his cigarette and exhaled slowly. His dark eyes were sharp and observant and, though he exuded calm, he sat up straight in his chair, his long legs crossed at the knee.

"Don't worry," David said with a nervous laugh. "I don't even know if I should be here talking with you."

Vladimir shrugged. "But you are here," he said. "For whatever reason, you are taking the risk."

David wasn't sure which was greater, the risk of being there with Vladimir or not going along with Jim Allen and his "deal." "There are a lot of factors at play."

David assumed their conversation was being monitored. Jim Allen had warned him about that.

"You are a successful American businessman. Quite young." Vladimir cocked his head slightly, looked at David with something like admiration. "You live in a world of risks. You deal with the unknown by using your instincts. So tell me. What are your instincts telling you about this situation?"

David said nothing for a moment. Vladimir Borchenko was obviously very intelligent—and superbly confident. He had the air of someone who never took chances until he had factored in all fore-seeable outcomes.

"That you think you're in control of it," David replied. "And that I hope you're right."

Vladimir laughed. His eyes brightened, which made him appear more youthful and innocent than David could have imagined.

"You know about my background," David said. "What do you want with me?"

Vladimir lifted a black briefcase from the floor and put it on the table. "We should have some tea and biscuits," he announced.

"Sure," David said. Borchenko left the room with a few long strides. *What if I ran for it right now?* David asked himself. *What information would I have for the CIA? Nothing.*

He looked across the table at the briefcase Borchenko had left there. For an instant he was tempted to open it, see what was inside. But David stopped himself. *Don't do anything foolish.*

Vladimir returned five minutes later with a small silver tray bearing a pot of tea and a little dish of dry cookies.

"Sorry about the quality," he said with a sniff. "It's the best they have here."

Vladimir poured two cups of tea, put in tablespoonfuls of jam in what David would later learn was the Russian style. As he pushed David's cup across the table, he looked up.

"How many American companies have been allowed to enter into contracts with the Polish government?" he asked. "Very few. You will soon be in very select company."

"Be that as it may," David said, keeping his voice noncommittal.

The Russian conformed to none of David's preconceptions. His manners and aristocratic air seemed steeped in refinement. His thick black wavy hair swept across his head in a European-looking style, his fingernails were trimmed and groomed, and his suit hung perfectly on his athletic frame. He was by no means the stocky, grumbling, badly dressed stereotype of a Soviet *apparatchik*.

125

"OK, you don't want to talk. I understand." Vladimir gestured around the small porch. "But there is no one else here. No one will hear what we say."

"How can I believe you?" David asked.

Vladimir's features clouded. "I am the one who is making deals with the CIA," he said. "I think I have sufficiently compromised myself. But I will tell you something I know. There are no listening devices here in this room, but there are some in your room. Say nothing there you do not wish to be heard."

"All right," David said, suppressing an involuntary chill.

"And do not speak freely in public," Vladimir added. "There will be agents following you and listening. I will be able to obtain safe times and places in which we can meet, but I cannot guarantee your privacy when we are apart."

David mulled over what he was hearing. Borchenko must have had contacts within the KGB; how else could he have been in contact with the CIA, and how else could he be meeting with an American in Warsaw? Obviously Borchenko had very highly placed contacts within the Soviet government.

"OK, and one other thing," Vladimir said. "I will be debriefed by the KGB after every time I meet with you. I will supply them with a few nuggets to keep them interested. For instance, I will say that you had critical comments about socialism. I will say that you asked about the workers' rights in the factories you plan to build. That will ring of authenticity to them, and they will stop there."

"All right," David said. "Tell me about these industrial sites."

"As a COMECON executive official for Poland, I would like you to consider the following," Vladimir said.

Vladimir's lips turned down in a small frown of concentration as he opened his briefcase and produced a thick stack of folders. Each was labeled with Cyrillic letters that David assumed were the COMECON designation heading.

"Here is the preliminary information about the potential sites," he said to David. "These files are for your use. They contain information about previous land use, utility capabilities, highway access. You'll find regional maps and construction specifications. It is assumed that you will be asked to share this information with your government, and that is fine. There is no sensitive information here."

David opened the first file. It showed a map of an area outside of Warsaw, followed by general specifications for an industrial site.

"Why me?" David asked, looking up from the file.

"As a COMECON official, I recognized the need for an American builder on these projects," Vladimir said, his mouth an impassive straight line. "An infusion of your know-how and capital might be beneficial to the region. Hopefully you will do a good job. Because I will eventually be in a position in which I will have to defend my choice."

David tapped the stack of files with his index finger.

"I can do this," he said. "But so could a lot of other American builders. You haven't answered my question. Why me?"

"I don't know precisely how it happened," Vladimir said, holding his empty palms upward. "I was in contact with the CIA; I asked for a successful businessman who could be persuaded to help me. In exchange I would give this businessman information that, I think, would make the CIA happy. Apparently you were someone they thought they could persuade."

David thought back to his youth, to his indiscretion during the Vietnam War. He thought of his old friend Carl Becker, how it was almost unbelievable that he would find himself in this position after so many years.

"Come on, David," Vladimir said, sipping his tea. "You look so serious."

"This *is* serious," David said. "What about the Vatican and Russia? What is it that I've come here to—"

Vladimir held up a hand for silence. He glanced at the closed doorway, as though there were limits to the security he could provide.

"Later," Vladimir said. "For now we are an American builder and a COMECON official having a meeting. You know, everything aside, this is going to be a great business deal for you."

David rubbed his cheek. He hadn't really considered it, but he was in fact being handed what could turn out to be a lucrative opportunity.

"There's got to be a catch," David said.

"A catch?" Vladimir replied.

"You know, a drawback," David said. "No one ever gives something for nothing, not like this."

Vladimir smiled. He lit another cigarette.

"Of course, you are right," he said. "But you might also enjoy the other aspect of the deal we are making here today."

David put his hands on the table. Vladimir Borchenko obviously relished the fact that this was his world, that he controlled the moment. And, although he couldn't have said why, David was starting to feel as though he could trust the Russian.

"Is that what we're doing here?" David asked. "Making a deal?"

Vladimir's cigarette was tucked between his first and second fingers. He was about to bring it to his lips when the door leading inside opened with a creak. A young blonde woman wearing a black apron and holding a broom seemed surprised to see Vladimir and David.

"So the plant workers are used to a great deal of discipline," Vladimir said. He glanced in the direction of the young woman.

David paused then understood.

"I hope they can be taught some degree of flexibility," he said. "That is the hallmark of a good worker—it doesn't matter what kind of work or what country you're talking about."

Vladimir looked up at the young woman, who was still in the doorway. She smiled shyly and sheepishly backed out, closing the door loudly behind her. Vladimir held up a hand for silence, and then, after thirty seconds, he relaxed again.

"KGB?" David asked in a quiet voice.

"Who knows?" Vladimir asked with a grin. "Could be. I don't know them all."

"We were talking about making deals before she opened that door," David said. "That's something that makes sense to me. Making deals. Getting things done. But I need to know what we're—"

"I can see I'm talking to the right person," Vladimir interrupted. "Wait until the morning. Then you will understand more."

"The morning? But—"

"I have to leave you for now." Vladimir nodded at the pile of files. "I trust those will keep you busy."

David nodded, saying nothing more. He would learn what Borchenko was willing to tell him when the Russian was ready. He could see even then that this was how things were going to be.


*February 17, 1998. 10:34 p.m.*
*St. Petersburg.*

"How are you, darling?" Annia asked David.

He looked up at the television. CNN was showing American sports highlights. It was hard to be interested in the Bulls now that Michael Jordan had retired.

"Pretty good," he said. "We just landed about an hour ago."

"And how is Jason?"

"He's real good. We're going to . . . you know, look into the Sokolov thing."

David heard noise in the background, a young child's high and insistent voice.

"Monica wants to talk to you," Annia said with a tone of playful exasperation.

"Put her on," David said, smiling through his fatigue.

A rustling on the line. "Daddy?" asked a young voice.

"Yes, sweetie," David said. "How are you?"

"I'm good." A pause. Monica was sounding more adult by the day. "Mommy and me watched a movie."

David leaned back on his bed, adjusted the pillows. "A movie?" he asked. "Which one?"

"It was *The Lion King*," Monica said. "I've seen it before, you know. But not lately."

"How about that part where the lions fight each other?" David asked. "That always scares me."

"Not me," Monica said proudly. "You know, I don't really get scared of kid's movies, Daddy. Not anymore."

David heard Annia's voice in the background. "I have to give the phone back to Mommy," Monica said. "I checked off my calendar this morning. You've been gone for two days. That means you'll be coming home in another eight days."

"That's right, sweetheart," David said. He and Annia had worked out a method for making Monica comfortable with David's absences during his hectic traveling schedule; when he was away, Monica marked off the days with smiling-face stickers and counted off the days until his return. It was a way of keeping them connected.

"OK, Daddy." A pause, as though she was searching for the right words. "I'll be looking forward to seeing you."

"Me, too," David said.

"So are you staying out of trouble?" asked Annia in a firm voice when she was back on the line.

"Of course," David said. He knew what his wife had on her mind; the news of Sokolov's killing had unnerved her.

"Have you found anything out about the murder?" Annia asked.

"I will in the morning," David replied. "I'm sick over it. It's not easy to deal with."

A moment of silence. "Did you see Andy Kapinski?" she asked.

"No, he wasn't in the office when I was in Warsaw," David replied. "Jason saw him, though, on the new construction site. Said he looked good."

"Have you heard the news about Father Wojtyla?" Annia asked.

"I did," David answered. "Looks like he might be seriously ill."

Neither said anything for a moment. David pictured his wife in their apartment. Her blond hair was shorter than when he had met her in Warsaw in the mid-'70s; it framed a face that was even more beautiful than it had been more than twenty years ago. Few who knew her now knew the details of her history, how she had been a respected children's author in Soviet-dominated Poland and how she had used her position to work against the communist regime.

And there were few people in David's office who knew the complete story of Annia's childhood, that she had grown up in a Polish orphanage. The orphanage was visited often by a young priest named Father Wojtyla, a kind man who gave of his time, his heart, and his energy to the children. Andrzej Kapinski had also grown up in that orphanage and, though he was five years older than Annia, he had taken care of her as though she were his own sister. They had maintained a special, close relationship over the years.

"Be careful, David," Annia said. "Monica and I love you."

"I love you, too," David said. "Can't wait to see you."

David put down the phone, switched off the lights, and settled in bed under the down comforter. It would be hard to sleep that night. He knew that his mind would race with memories.

St. Petersburg fell silent beneath the winter snow. David thought about the city outside. The palaces and monuments were like mute reminders of Russia's long history, the wars, the suffering, the revolution. He tried to picture what the city had been like when Czar Nicholas was forced to abdicate, when the reign of the Romanovs was ended and the strange historical experiment of communism begun.

It felt like he had been asleep for only a couple of minutes when his phone rang. It was his morning wake-up call.

# Chapter Ten

*February 18, 1998. 8:15 a.m.*
*St. Petersburg.*

DAVID AND JASON MET AT EIGHT in their hotel lobby then walked to the office of Olen Europe in an old palace perched close to a canal, a long five-story building with a stone facade and painted a fading yellow. A travel office was set up on the bottom floor, its bright green awnings lending a splash of color to the overall dinginess of the streetfront.

The office was formerly a five-room apartment, with a small bathroom and smaller kitchen area. It looked like anything but the headquarters of a branch of an international development company. It was atrocious by Western standards, though David kept reminding himself, by local standards it was excellent. Though it had been dismal and depressing when they first moved in, they had installed all-new partitioning and painted the walls white. The electrical supply was steady, and they had satellite connections that made international calling and faxing reasonably reliable.

As they entered, someone called out. "David!" It was Terry James who came out in his shirtsleeves and shook David's hand with warmth.

"Good to see you, Terry," David said. "I wish it was under better circumstances."

Behind Terry was Olga, a middle-aged woman with a deceptively severe appearance who worked as an office assistant and document translator. She had been a schoolteacher but had quit after her state wages became too little to live on. She now earned twice as much working in the private sector.

"Mister Olen," she said with a smile as they shook hands. "You had a good trip?"

"Very good, thank you," David told her.

"David, it's good to see you," said a tall, shy young man who emerged from the next room with a sheepish grin. Yuri Tetrov was, to David's thinking, an exemplar of the new young Russian. He had studied English at St. Petersburg University and now applied his language skills by working on Olen Europe's project-management team as a liaison between the city bureaucracy and the contractors.

"Yuri, how are Lena and the kids?" David asked, returning his warm handshake.

"Very well, thank you," said Yuri.

Terry James clapped his hands together quietly. "We've cleared out space in the conference room," he said.

"Good," Jason said, coming out of the back of the office in time to hear what Terry was saying. "We need to talk."

As they moved to the conference room, David asked Terry, "What's the latest with Sokolov?"

Terry James sighed and looked down at his folded hands. David could see the strain in the younger man's features.

"We went to the memorial service yesterday," Terry said.

"Yesterday?" David asked, shocked.

"His family wanted to do it right away," Terry replied.

"Was Vladimir there?" David asked.

Terry shook his head. "It was too short notice," he said. "I heard that Vladimir gave Sokolov's family a generous gift earmarked for his children's education."

"What was the service like?" Jason asked. He poured himself a cup of coffee and listened intently.

"Lots of people," Yuri said. "From GlobusBank, from the city government, from other institutions. Sokolov was very well-liked."

"Olen Europe extended condolences to the family," Terry added. "And passed on condolences on your behalf."

David nodded.

"What about the police investigation?" Jason asked.

"There were two killers," Terry said. "The police have sketches from witness accounts. They're supposed to print them in the paper tomorrow."

"Is there any talk of suspects?" Jason asked.

Terry shrugged. "Nothing in particular. They looked like thugs; that's all I heard. Hired killers. And the way they left their guns at the scene is a Mafia trademark."

They paused for a moment, each lost in contemplation. Through the open door they could hear Olga speaking Russian on the telephone.

"The city has announced a reward for information leading to an arrest," Yuri added.

"Really?" asked David. "How much?"

"A hundred grand," Terry said. "The last thing they need is another unsolved killing."

Yuri cleared his throat and looked around the table. "My brother-in-law is a reporter," he said. "I spoke with him this morning—on the condition that I keep the information a secret until it is printed."

"It won't leave this room," David assured him.

"Obviously the suspicion is that Sokolov's assassination is linked to organized crime," Yuri said. "A member of the city finance office says that Sokolov mentioned being threatened last week outside the GlobusBank offices."

"Threatened?" Jason asked, his expression darkening. "Over what?"

"That's not so clear," Yuri answered. "But it seemed to have something to do with GlobusBank business. And Vladimir Borchenko's name was apparently mentioned."

David rested his chin on the tip of his fingers as he listened. GlobusBank business. Vladimir Borchenko. But GlobusBank was Vladimir's, and the two were synonymous.

"Anything else?" David asked.

"There's going to be a lot of finger-pointing," Yuri said. "The Federal Security Service. The city police. The Duma. With something so high-profile, there are going to be politicians trying to milk political mileage out of it."

"Why Sokolov?" David asked. "Let's say this source with the city government is right, that Sokolov was threatened and that it had to do with GlobusBank business. Why single out Sokolov?"

"Sokolov was aligned locally with the reformers," Terry said. "He tried to see that privatization buy-outs were done on the level. He was squeaky clean as far as bank business went. And he had Borchenko's approval behind him, so he carried a lot of clout."

"Could someone get killed because they're aligned with reform?" David asked.

Yuri took a deep breath. "You have the government; you have organized crime," he said. "Sometimes it is hard to tell the two apart. Sokolov had control of a lot of money, and he had the final sign-offs on all of GlobusBank's St. Petersburg transactions. Someone might have been pissed off at him because he didn't cooperate."

"So he might have said 'no' to the wrong people," David mused aloud.

"It could be complicated," Yuri added. "Depending on who's

136

responsible, it might not be in the Duma or the police's best interests to find out the truth."

David shook his head. "Well, I can't believe that," he said.

"I only tell you what I've heard," Yuri said with a shrug. "I don't know what the truth might be. There's a Russian proverb: Wait forty years before making a judgment about what happened in a complicated matter such as this."

"I wish we all had that kind of time," David said.

"What about Vladimir Borchenko?" Jason asked. His face was a mask of concentration. "He was mentioned in connection with this threat against Sokolov, right? Well, if it was GlobusBank business, and for the sake of argument, let's say it involved Vladimir, then why not simply go after Vladimir? Why kill the managing director of his St. Petersburg branch?"

"Vladimir Borchenko is one of the most powerful men in Russia," Yuri said. "It might not be so easy."

"Easy to get him, you mean?" Jason asked. "So they might go after Sokolov instead?"

David looked around the room. Everyone seemed to mull over what Jason had said. Then, one by one, they turned and looked at David.

"Maybe we'll never know what happened," David said. "But I'm talking to Borchenko tomorrow. That might clear a few things up."

For about fifteen seconds no one said anything. Finally Jason broke the silence.

"What about GlobusBank?" he asked. "Have they appointed anyone to take over the St. Petersburg branch?"

"Not yet," Terry replied. "Supposedly they will within the week. They're waiting for Borchenko to give approval from a short list of candidates . . ."

As Terry James spoke, David felt his mind wandering. Everything came back to Borchenko. All the answers, all the plans, he was always at the center of everything. It never changed.

*February 18, 1998. 10:45 a.m.*
*Moscow.*

VLADIMIR BORCHENKO LIT a French cigarette as he stepped out of his black Mercedes limousine parked behind the Beklemishev Tower, the high tower that marked a corner of the Kremlin ramparts. He cupped a hand over the cigarette to protect it from the icy drizzle that had begun to fall. As he walked, he looked out over Red Square; apparently, the weather had scared off most of the tourists. Only a few stragglers walked across the brick expanse, their faces cast down to avoid the wind.

He glanced back over his shoulder. His driver was still in the car, the engine's exhaust forming a cloud of vapor behind the tailpipe. And standing a few meters from the car, watching Vladimir's every move, was one of Vladimir's security officers. His name was Valery, and his scowl at the moment indicated his displeasure over having to stay back and watch his employer from a distance. But Vladimir had wanted it this way—it would be a sign of weakness at the moment to be seen in public with a bodyguard.

Bogomolov was waiting in a stone portal at the foot of St. Basil's Cathedral. Vladimir looked up at the eight spire-like structures arrayed around the ninth, tallest church. Even in the cloudy gloom the churches' colorful domes brightened the visual landscape. Vladimir let his eyes feast for a moment on the forest greens, the weathered ochre of the exterior brick walls. The Cathedral was a national symbol of Russia in the West, always appearing in documentaries and news footage. Though it was perhaps a cliched image, Vladimir thought, it still had much to recommend it.

"Vladimir Dmitrievich," said Bogomolov when Vladimir joined him beneath the portal. The two men shared an embrace.

Bogomolov was short and stout, with the red cheeks and broken blood vessels of a lifelong heavy drinker. Though it was cold out, he wore only a suit and a silk scarf knotted around his neck.

"Arkady Petrovich," Vladimir said. "Thank you for coming out in this rotten weather to speak with me."

Bogomolov shrugged. "You said it was important." He looked around him at the weathered brick. "I just wish you didn't want to meet at this fucking monstrosity."

Vladimir laughed, offered Bogomolov a cigarette from his silver case, lit it for him.

"We're more likely to be spotted at a restaurant or a club than at a tourist attraction," Vladimir said. "Anyway, what do you have against this Cathedral? Don't you have a sense of humor?"

Bogomolov shook his head, puffed on his cigarette. He looked out over Red Square and squinted as if he were trying to spot someone there.

"And why don't you want to see me in public, Vladimir?" he asked. "Am I such an embarrassment?"

"Completely," Vladimir replied. "I don't think that my reputation could survive an association with the likes of you."

Bogomolov looked up at Vladimir and, with a raspy cough, exploded with laughter. Vladimir had known Arkady Bogomolov for more than twenty years, since the latter was the manager of a state distribution center during a time in which Vladimir had wished to obtain a supply of imported liquor for his black-market business. They had struck up a partnership and a friendship of sorts and toasted over scotch and cognac whenever they had arranged a new purchase.

Bogomolov had been trained as an accountant and, though he looked fat and guileless, he was in fact intelligent and sharply opportunistic. Eight years before, he had come to Vladimir asking for help finding a job in the new market economy. Vladimir had supplied a couple of government contacts and, within a few years, Bogomolov had risen to a central management position in an economic planning ministry of the national government. He had become a bureaucrat, albeit an important one, and he was keenly aware of the debt he owed to Vladimir Borchenko.

"Seriously, Vladimir," Bogomolov said, his smile disappearing. "Why do we have to meet out here? It's not the old days. Come into my office; we can have some tea, maybe a little shot of something. Let's be civilized."

Vladimir lit a fresh cigarette and looked out over Red Square. He could see the curious squat structure of Lenin's tomb, and the revived face of the GUM department store.

"It's known as caution, Arkady," Vladimir said, already growing tired of Bogomolov's perennial propensity for complaint.

"All right, so we are cautious," Bogomolov said. "Now what can I do for you, Vladimir? I am at your service as always."

"I am having a problem with Maxim Belarin," Vladimir said. He exhaled smoke and waited for his words to sink in.

"Belarin, that asshole," Bogomolov said with a harsh laugh. "His mentality is back with the dinosaurs. He gets elected to the national Duma, and he acts like he's still a colonel in the KGB."

A white police car drove slowly to the edge of the square and stopped. Vladimir watched it as he smoked.

"I need to know about his interest in MosElectric," Vladimir said.

"Well, I haven't been associated with that one," Bogomolov said. "The bastards have stuck me dealing with Siberian rail. They must think I give a shit about a bunch of snowbirds."

"I know that Belarin is interested in MosElectric," Vladimir said, ignoring Bogomolov's comment. "But I need to find out who's behind his investment group."

Bogomolov threw his cigarette down on the ground, crushed it hard with his boot. He looked up at Vladimir with sudden recognition.

"You want to buy MosElectric?" he asked.

"I might," Vladimir replied. He looked around him until he saw, loitering near the Kremlin wall, the imposing figure of Valery.

"Well, watch out for Belarin," Bogomolov said. "He's a fucking crook. Well, who isn't these days? But he's worse than most. He's been asking around about MosElectric ever since it was first discussed as a potential privatization."

"There's no way Belarin has the capital," Vladimir said.

"Of course not," Bogomolov said, blinking as though the thought was too ridiculous to consider. "But the people he's with do."

"Who are they?" Vladimir asked.

"We don't have the details on his bid, but Belarin has made it known that he expects to be the buyer. He's said coming up with the capital is no problem. I've heard names," Bogomolov said. "Palchikoff, Solovyov, Barinov."

"Gangsters," Vladimir said.

"Damned right." Bogomolov snorted. "They put up the money: Belarin supplies the government contacts and the legitimacy. I mean, I've been willing to cut a deal or two in my life, but this is too much. And the thing is—he'll probably put in the winning bid. Unless you do."

"There is—" Vladimir paused, thinking of Sokolov. "There is resistance to my getting involved in the bidding."

"I'll bet." Bogomolov made a motion with his hand as though he was smoking, a signal that he wanted another cigarette. Vladimir opened the case, held it out.

"Belarin is a prick," Vladimir said. "I've known him for a long time. I hate to see him get what he wants—especially when it conflicts with my own interests. I wanted to see if he really had a legitimate chance at buying MosElectric."

"From everything I've heard, it sounds like he does," Bogomolov said.

Vladimir stared out into the drizzle then checked his watch. "I've kept you long enough," he said. He held out a small folded envelope and pressed it into Bogomolov's hand. "Please, take this."

Bogomolov put the cash in his pocket without looking at it. Vladimir knew he didn't have to tell his old associate that he was to speak to no one about this conversation.

"One thing," Bogomolov said as Vladimir began to step out of the alcove. He hunched his shoulders, which made his suit look tight against his belly.

"Yes?" Vladimir said, half-expecting to be asked for a favor.

"Be careful," Bogomolov said. "Belarin is a prick, but he's also dangerous. And now he's with some of the real scumbags of Moscow. Take care of yourself. He'd like a couple more chances to embarrass you."

Vladimir gave a nod and a small smile before he turned and walked toward the Kremlin. He cast his eyes down and shoved his hands deep in his overcoat pockets as his thoughts went back to his past.

When Vladimir went to Moscow State University, he began to do business with his father's help. First he started to sell pencils made by the Western manufacturer Eberhard Faber, far superior to Soviet pencils that constantly smudged and broke. From there he moved on to cigarettes, liquor, nylon stockings, petrol—commodities hard to get in the command economy, but ones that the sons and daughters of the Soviet elite were willing to pay for in cash.

Vladimir had been making deals all his adult life, in one fashion or another. It was a logical progression to move from small-time black-market deals to a larger smuggling operation. And after the Soviet state fell apart, Vladimir had been in perfect position to take advantage of the wholesale sell-off of the state's assets. He became one of a handful of men who effectively owned and exploited the country, and he owed the foundations of his success to two men: his father and Mikhail Sergeivich Gorbachev, his college comrade whose vision of a reformed communist state had made possible the strange exploitative capitalism that had arisen from the wreckage of the Soviet Union.

*February 18, 1998. 12:15 p.m.*
*Moscow.*

THE DINING ROOM of Moscow's Metropol Hotel featured an immense stained-glass ceiling that intermingled sky blue with tints of golden yellow and imperial red. Lavish metal detailing ringed the ceiling line, reflecting light from crystal chandeliers. The tables were covered in spotless white linen, the plush chairs upholstered in deep burgundy mohair. In the center of the room was a small marble fountain of undulating water from which emerged a cherubic golden figure.

Nikolai Petrov leaned back and swirled the cognac in his glass and let its rich aroma waft up to his nose. Across from him was a man in an Italian suit, his hair combed back from his pale, puffy face. They had both lit cigars, and the smoke curled up into the air.

"Alexsandr," Nikolai said through a forced smile. "We've been talking for half an hour. I hate to be so blunt, but you've told me nothing. Is that what has become of our friendship?"

"Our friendship," Alexsandr said with a quiet laugh. "I will be blunt as well. Our friendship was a long time ago. Now, you buy me drinks every couple of months. We smoke your cigars. And you try to get information from me. Is that a friendship?"

Nikolai had met Alexsandr when they were both in their teens. They became part of a disorganized gang of young street criminals and then both graduated to a Moscow crime syndicate when they were barely twenty. Now Nikolai worked for Vladimir Borchenko while Alexsandr had become one of the flashy criminals who looked out at the city from behind the tinted windows of their imported German automobiles. Nikolai counted Alexsandr among his best contacts within Russia's underworld, although increasingly both had sensed that they had lost the connection they had made when they were still adolescents stealing cigarettes and getting drunk together in city parks.

"I don't mean to insult you," Nikolai said sincerely. "What about last summer, when I gave you a chance to become involved in that GlobusBank investment in Finland? Do you remember that?"

Alexsandr's face showed no expression.

"Well, you would have made a hundred-thousand dollars if you would have listened to me," Nikolai continued. "For doing nothing. So it's not true that I no longer do anything for you."

Nikolai shook his head and was vaguely embarrassed by how his anger had flared. He took a drink of his cognac and looked away. He hated the way his old friends looked at him, as though he had gone soft by working for a banker. Most of them were too stupid, too limited to know that Vladimir Borchenko had more real power than almost anyone in the country.

Or so Nikolai had thought. Now Sokolov was dead in St. Petersburg, and it seemed as though Vladimir intended to do nothing about it. Vladimir was hiding something from him as well. He could sense it.

"All right," Alexsandr said, puffing on his cigar. "Perhaps I was out of line to speak to you in that manner."

"We both have stressful occupations," Nikolai offered with a sly smile. Alexsandr nodded and grinned, finished off his drink.

"You speak the truth," he replied.

"I have another financial opportunity for you if you're willing to listen this time," Nikolai said to his old friend.

"What kind?" Alexsandr asked.

"Currency speculation," Nikolai said. "In a few months the bank will net millions. If you want to invest a few dollars, I can see that you get a nice profit."

Alexsandr thought for a moment and chewed on the tip of his cigar. He wore a thick ring around his finger studded with a set of diamonds.

"Call me," Alexsandr finally said. "This time I will listen."

"Good, you are a very smart man." Nikolai smiled, finished his drink. "Now, tell me what you have heard that I might be interested in."

"I heard that you wear a dress and high heels," Alexsandr said, giggling.

"You're drunk," Nikolai said.

Alexsandr folded his hands on the table. "Maybe," he said. "But if you haven't heard what's happening, then you're more out of touch than I thought."

"What do you mean?"

"Some of the biggest bosses in the city are going against Vladimir over this privatization deal," Alexsandr said. "Surely you—"

"Of course," Nikolai interrupted. "I had hoped you could tell me if anyone plans any drastic action against him."

"I don't know," Alexsandr said. "They might. Now you tell me— why does Borchenko want to fuck the bosses like Solovyov? He has enough; he doesn't need to cross them."

"Vladimir does what he wants," Nikolai said. "He's been around a lot longer than Solovyov or anyone else."

Alexsandr didn't reply; instead, he folded his arms, leaned back in his chair, and stared at Nikolai for almost a full minute.

"What?" Nikolai finally asked.

"You're right. Borchenko's been around longer," Alexsandr said slowly. "That's why he doesn't get grouped in with the Mafia bosses—he's too powerful, too rich. But even he should be careful who he messes with."

"Who says that?" Nikolai asked.

"Anyone with a brain in their head," Alexsandr replied. His mouth curled into a sly smile. "Tell me, Nikolai, honestly: What are your plans for the future? You work for Borchenko; surely, you have your eye on the chair in his office."

"What do you mean?" Nikolai asked.

"Don't play dumb," Alexsandr said. "You know what I mean."

Nikolai thought for a moment. "Perhaps," he said, quietly.

"Vladimir won't rule forever," Alexsandr suggested. "Even the communists had to hand over their power."

Nikolai didn't reply. Instead he thought about what his old friend had said. It was true. Vladimir Borchenko wouldn't be around forever.

# Chapter Eleven

*February 18, 1998. 12:34 p.m.*
*St. Petersburg.*

AVID AND JASON ENTERED THE NEVSKY SITE through a side door that had once been used as a kitchen entrance for the monastic community that had lived inside the main building. From the moment they stepped inside, their ears rang with the din of power tools and loud voices echoing down long brick-and-stone corridors and high ceilings.

"We'll all put these on," Yuri said, taking hard hats from the Russian foreman, a thin man with gaunt dark features and callused hands. Yuri's own hard hat had the contractor's logo in large letters. Jason had brought his own from the site offices. David took one of the hard hats and adjusted the plastic band before putting it on.

David looked down the long hallway that ran nearly the entire length of the first floor of the main building. The old walls had been stripped down to raw brick, exposing two-hundred-year-old masonry. The walls themselves were nearly a meter-and-a-half thick, exposed by new-punched openings to accommodate circulation for the new floor plan. The floors were chipped, damaged wood, covered with a thick coat of dust and debris.

The foreman began speaking to Yuri in Russian as they walked deeper into the darkened building, the corridor lit by electric bulbs strung along the wall. Yuri translated to the Americans as they went.

"The crew has been working hard to stay on schedule," Yuri said. "He says the local crew and the Turkish contractor are pleased with their wages and that they are grateful how quickly their requests for additional workers and equipment have been met."

"Well, that's doing business with Americans," David said in a low voice only Jason could hear. "You get one-tenth the bullshit and ten times the results."

Jason smiled and adjusted his hard hat. "Can we go to the atrium area?" he asked Yuri.

Yuri spoke in Russian to the foreman, who nodded and gestured for them to follow.

They walked down a side passage until they emerged in an open area surrounded on all four sides by building facades. Here was the central courtyard of the restoration project. Once the four buildings were renovated internally, they would then be united by this central atrium, where the original buildings' facades would be reproduced in a frame of a well-designed contemporary curtain wall. The open space above them would be enclosed by a glass roof, creating a temperature-controlled public space that would bring together the classic and modern elements of the project.

For now the atrium was still an abstraction rather than a reality. Windows gaped open in all four buildings; the ground beneath their feet was little more than a plot of rocky dirt. An area was marked off that would one day be a fountain; for now there was just a circle of weeds.

David walked a few steps behind the group, ran his hand along exposed masonry that had been mortared two hundred years ago by craftsmen who had long since disappeared from memory. He imagined his own Russian ancestors; it was even possible that someone named Olenchik had worked on one of the grand palaces in St. Petersburg and left the imprint of his craft just as David would leave the buildings he was instrumental in creating.

Crews of men were working in side chambers off the hallway and stripping the walls and floor so that the restoration work could begin. At the end of the hallway, the sound of machines and power tools grew even louder. David stepped carefully around a metal scaffolding and into the area that would hold the new elevator core.

The workers wore dirty coveralls, frayed jackets, caps instead of hard hats. Both their clothing and exposed skin were coated with gray dust, lending them a dull, monochromatic appearance. Yuri and the foreman stopped to talk to a crew that was tearing a thick section of plaster away from the wall. Another team was repairing a section of two-hundred-and-fifty-year-old wooden structural beam supports. A third was working with a pneumatic nail gun that emitted harsh bursts of compressed air.

"This will be completed by the end of the week," Yuri translated. "Then they will begin work on the second floor, which should take about three weeks to complete."

"Are these the same guys who'll be working on plaster and finishing when we get to stage two?" Jason asked, sliding around a pile of debris to get a closer look at the work on the wall.

"We have a couple of other bidders," Terry said. "But we're probably going to stick with these guys."

"They look like they're doing a good job," Jason said approvingly.

"They've been reliable," Terry said. "The work has been good so far."

"Tell the foreman that," Jason said to Yuri.

Yuri spoke in rapid-fire Russian to the foreman, who smiled and nodded at the Americans.

David stepped away toward a section of wall that was ready for a fresh plaster coating, situated next to one of the main openings that connected this site to the adjacent building. One problem had arisen. Three of the four buildings had been constructed at the same level; their floors corresponded and could be linked seamlessly. But this fourth building didn't match up; its floor levels were about eighteen inches lower than the others. People walking from one room to the next in the new offices would have to step up or down nine inches. It was a relatively minor detail, but it would have to be dealt with perfectly to attain the seamless feel that was essential to the new design.

A couple of workmen paused from what they were doing and looked up at David with curiosity. David nodded at them and looked up to envision the finished ceiling height. As soon as the nearest workman paused from his work, chiseling away at a stubborn section of old plaster, David heard a familiar electronic chirping.

He looked at Jason and Terry, both of whom pulled their cellular phones out of their pockets and then shook their heads.

"Must be mine." David switched on his phone and said hello. In the same instant someone turned on a loud power tool just a couple of feet away. The noise was so loud David could feel it in the back of his neck.

"Sorry, hold on a minute," David said. "I can't hear a thing."

He moved past a pile of debris, his hand over his nose to keep from breathing too much dust, then through a doorway into a small empty chamber. Once he was around the corner, the thick brick walls absorbed some of the construction noise.

"Yes, this is David," he said. "Are you still there?"

"This is Edward in Moscow, David. Can you hear me now?"

"Yes," David said. He put his free hand over his ear and turned his body away from the construction noise. "Edward, how are you doing?"

Edward Preston worked as a project manager in Olen Europe's Moscow office. He had worked for David for almost ten years.

150

"I'm OK," he said. "Where are you, anyway?"

David looked around. The little room's walls had been exposed to dull, chipped masonry. The flooring had been damaged and broken, exposing dirt underneath. The single dirty electric bulb hung on a wall bracket almost created more shadows than light.

"I'm at the Ritz, where else?" David said, laughing. "No, I'm at the Nevsky site with the guys."

"How does it look?" Edward asked.

"You can imagine," David replied. "Things are going according to plan—it's a total mess."

"Well, listen David, I need to talk to you for a second."

"It can't wait until I get in Moscow tomorrow?" David asked.

"Not really," Edward paused. "We're just about ready to submit our proposal for the MosElectric building."

"Right," David said. MosElectric, a major Russian utility company, was taking proposals and bids for a huge centralized office tower they planned to build in Moscow. Olen Europe was by no means assured of winning the competition, but if it did, it would be the largest construction project the company had attempted in Russia.

"Well, you know the company's in play. Right?"

"I do," David said. "That's part of the contingency for the project. We have to see whether privatization is going to affect the company's need for the building. But we're pretty sure it won't, right?"

"Pretty sure," Edward said.

"So what's the problem?" David asked.

"I was just talking with Natasha Alyeva over at GlobusBank," Edward said. "Did you know Vladimir Borchenko's considering bidding for the company?"

David processed this for a moment. "But GlobusBank is one of our main financial partners on the building proposal," David said. "This doesn't necessarily create a conflict, but—"

"But it might," Edward said, finishing David's thought.

"This is the first I've heard of it," David said. "But it isn't completely out of character. Vladimir doesn't always keep everyone appraised of his intentions. Even when he has a responsibility to do so."

"I figured you'd want to know about this," Edward said. "I mean, I assumed you hadn't . . . about . . ."

Edward's voice became hard to hear over the sound of a piece of heavy machinery in the next room. David pressed the phone tighter against his ear.

"Sorry," he said. "What was that?"

"I assumed you hadn't heard about it, but I wanted to be sure," Edward said. "To tell you the truth, I thought Natasha Alyeva was acting a little strange about the MosElectric privatization."

"Strange?" David asked. "How?"

"She sounded kind of evasive at first," Edward said. "Then she apologized. She said that something was going on around the MosElectric deal, that Vladimir had some kind of agenda that he wasn't sharing with her."

"She told you this?" David asked.

"Well, in passing, really," Edward said. "Do you know Natasha?"

"Not well," David replied.

"Well, she's incredibly sharp," Edward told him. "She's at the top of her field. It really pisses her off how Borchenko keeps her out of the loop sometimes."

"Well, that's Vladimir."

"That's what I told her," Edward said. "Anyway, I thought you'd want to know as soon as possible. It probably won't affect the MosElectric building. But forewarned is forearmed and all of that."

"Thanks, Edward," David said. "I'll see you tomorrow."

David switched off the phone and put it back in his coat pocket. He stepped back into the open area just as Jason reached the doorway.

"I was coming to look for you," Jason said.

"That was Edward," David said. "Did you know GlobusBank is considering bidding for MosElectric?"

Jason's eyebrows raised. "No."

"Well, that's what the call was about." David leaned closer to Jason to be heard over the work. "I was planning to talk to Vladimir tomorrow anyway. This'll be another item on the agenda."

Jason shook his head. "More surprises," he said. "Still, this doesn't necessarily affect the proposal."

"We'll wait and see," David replied. He thought for a moment. "You know what? I need some air. I'm going for a walk."

"Want some company?" Jason asked, mildly surprised.

"No, thanks," David replied. "I'll see you back at the hotel. I need to sort through a few things."

"I'll finish up here with Terry and Yuri," Jason said.

"Thanks." David walked slowly down the hallway that led outside. He barely noticed the work going on around him or the brief curious stares of the work crew. His thoughts were preoccupied with Vladimir Borchenko, with everything that had happened in the past and the dawning sense that new mysteries were unfolding in the present.

David let the rhythm of his stride settle his mind. At the edge of his consciousness was the apprehension that something was going on with Vladimir Borchenko in Moscow, some line of events that connected Alexei Sokolov with Natasha Alyeva's concerns about the prospective MosElectric privatization bid. If anyone had asked him, David would have been unable to explain why he was making this connection in his mind. Perhaps it was simply because he had known Vladimir for so long that he had developed a sense for when the Russian was involved in something eventful.

In the diffused sunlight, exhaust trailed behind cars like fast-moving clouds. St. Petersburg was nearly as far north in latitude as Anchorage, Alaska, and in the winter the daylight was weak, and the horizon began to darken in the early afternoon. As David walked, he watched the lengthening shadows on the Neva embankments.

David squinted into the snow, which was falling heavier now. To the north was a residential district. David had driven through that neighborhood, a trip that had depressed him. People there lived in communal apartments, where two or three families shared a single bathroom and kitchen. It was hard for working people to pay even the minimal rent and still afford food in the current economic climate, and everyday life pressed down on ordinary Russians in a way that most Americans would have found difficult to understand.

He paused across the road from the Winter Palace, the home of the czars from Peter the Great to Nicholas II, the last of the Romanov dynasty. David let his eyes wander over the exquisite green baroque facade, the cornices and windows in white and gold, the statuary looking down like otherworldly sentinels. A busload of tourists disembarked in front of the palace and headed inside to view the Hermitage's seemingly infinite art collection. The children in the group paused outside and looked up at the winter palace; they were stunned into impressed immobility just as David was.

A cold wind swept over the river and blew snow. David shivered, shoved his gloved hands deep into his coat pockets. He felt the familiar contour of his GSM phone there and briefly considered calling home. But it was probably too early in Chicago. Instead he walked on, a solitary figure by the river, his thoughts drifting.

*June 1974.*
*Warsaw.*

THE MORNING AFTER HE MET Vladimir Borchenko for the first time, David had stepped out of his hotel into the warm Warsaw morning. A long black Zil limousine was waiting for him at the curb.

"Good morning," Vladimir said, stepping out of the car to shake David's hand and usher him into the plush interior of the car.

"Did you have breakfast?" Vladimir asked once they were moving.

"In a manner of speaking," David replied. He had been able to get a bowl of thick, tasteless oatmeal, a couple of slices of dried-out toast, and a cup of lukewarm tea in the hotel dining room.

154

Vladimir sat with his back to the driver, in the seat facing David. He took a piece of fruit out of a paper bag and began peeling it with a knife from his jacket pocket. The movements of his hands were deft and precise. He sliced the fruit and handed a piece to David.

"These pears were grown in Greece," Vladimir said, popping a piece into his mouth.

"Delicious," David said.

Vladimir nodded in agreement. "And very hard to get in this part of the world," he added. "The general rule of life here is scarcity. No matter how well the nation might be doing, the individual has to live with rationing, long lines, shortages. And never, never, is there any assurance that it will ever get any better."

Vladimir looked into David eyes as though searching for evidence that he had made himself understood.

"You are a Western businessman," Vladimir said. "Your mentality is different. If there is a shortage, you try to find a way to meet it in a way that also enables you to make a profit."

"That's simply logical," David said.

Vladimir snapped his fingers. "To you," he said. "To you it is logical. But not for people living under communism. They grumble. They complain. If they have connections, they buy what they want on the black market. But no one is permitted to talk about making a change."

David glanced past Vladimir's shoulder at the driver, who kept his eyes on the road and appeared uninterested with anything happening in the back seat.

"Is that what this is about?" David asked Vladimir. "Is that why I'm here? You're interested in doing some kind of business?"

Vladimir's eyes gleamed. "You could say that," he replied. "But for now I beg your indulgence. I wish to share my secrets with you a little at a time."

David accepted another slice of pear but said nothing in reply. Vladimir looked out the window as they reached the outskirts of the city, a vague expression of disapproval on his face.

"At least tell me where we're going," David said.

"Krakow," Vladimir replied brightly. "You know this place?"

"It's a point on a map," David replied. "That's all I know."

"It's the best of Polish culture," Vladimir said. "And it will be important to us. We have an important associate who spends a good deal of time there."

"Who?" asked David.

"The plans I devised with COMECON will require you to travel a lot," Vladimir said, brushing off David's question. "In addition to the Warsaw industrial site, you have been granted permission to build a food-processing plant just outside Krakow. It will be necessary for you to travel there on business at regular intervals. We will have a look at the site; then, I will make some important introductions for you."

David could tell that Vladimir was going to dispense information at his leisure and that questioning him further would serve no purpose. He looked out the window at the landscape passing by. They had left the city for the countryside. From the road David could see farms that seemed to be entrenched in poverty; the old wooden houses were drab and small, and a hunch-shouldered old man was plowing a field by hand.

"Poland has only had Communism since the war," Vladimir said, looking out the window. "About thirty years, as opposed to almost sixty in Russia."

"What's the difference?" David asked.

Vladimir gestured out at a farm that they were quickly passing. Rows of crops were arranged in haphazard angles, forming a chaotic sort of patchwork.

"The state owns all the land in Russia," Vladimir said. "Here individual citizens still own their farms. But look at the plots. They have been split up over generations until they look like this."

David loosened his tie a little, forced himself to take a deep breath. Borchenko was willing to talk about anything other than the substance of why David was in Poland. David felt a sudden wave of panic. What was he doing there? What if he were arrested and thrown in jail? Would the CIA try to get him out, or would he be an embarrassment from which they would try to distance themselves? He knew nothing about Borchenko. What he did know could be pure fiction. Maybe he was a KGB operative trying to entrap David somehow, or maybe he was trying to get information about the United States. David could be mistaken for a spy, he could be . . .

*Enough,* David told himself. He forced himself to look calm and composed, not wanting Borchenko to see his anxiety.

Vladimir leaned forward and opened a small built-in cabinet at his feet. Inside were bottles of scotch, vodka, water.

"It will be a couple of hours before we reach Krakow," Vladimir said. "Would you like something to drink?"

"Water, please," David replied.

Vladimir served David a small cup of water then downed a shot of scotch. When he had closed up the cabinet he lit a cigarette, leaned back, and looked at David with an expression that mixed expectation with sympathy.

"You are able to deal with uncertainty and ambiguous circumstances," he finally declared. "That's very good. These are skills that you will need."

David waited before speaking. He was feeling calmer, but spikes of fear and anger moved through his system. At the moment he wanted nothing more than to grab Borchenko by the throat and make him explain everything.

"We will have a chance to talk privately later," Vladimir said, glancing over his shoulder at the driver. "It won't be long before I've shared what you need to know."

"That's very reassuring," David said in an icy tone that made Vladimir's eyes widen before he broke into a friendly grin. Despite himself, David found himself returning the smile. Through the worry and doubt, David found himself beginning to like the imposing Russian.

After what seemed like a moment later, David opened his eyes with a start. He looked out at the gray, monotonous landscape and blinked away a haze of confusion.

"You were sleeping," Vladimir said. He was smoking and leaning back in his seat with his long legs crossed.

"Jet lag," David mumbled.

"Look out there," Vladimir said.

Their limousine had slowed down on the two-lane highway. David craned his neck to see what was happening. Blocking the way was a caravan of three wooden carts laden with vegetables. As they slowly passed, David saw cabbage, carrots, beets. A family ranging from small children to an elderly woman walked behind and alongside the horse-drawn carts. One by one, they looked inquisitively at the black car then cast their eyes down as though afraid to let their attention linger.

"There is your shining face of communism," Vladimir said. He puffed on his cigarette and shook his head as he looked out at the family with clinical fascination. "Peasants dragging their wares to the market. And they are the fortunate ones. In my country the farms were collectivized under Stalin. It was insanity. The whole agricultural system was damaged almost beyond repair. These peasants might be poor, but at least here the state doesn't confiscate their crops in exchange for the security of a one-room shack and a meal-ration card. And they don't have some idiot bureaucrat in Moscow who tells them what they can and can't grow and how much they need to produce whether it rains or there's a drought."

Vladimir's voice rose with venom as he spoke, as though he relished criticizing the Soviet system. He gestured with his cigarette, his eyes shining with intelligence and defiance. David wondered whether the driver was listening, whether Vladimir was courting trouble.

"Organization, distribution, rational planning," Vladimir continued, tapping his finger on the seat with each item. "Supply and demand. These do not have to be impossibilities. These are not insurmountable problems. But the Soviet system cannot make them happen. Do you follow me?"

"I agree based on what I've seen."

"A cautious answer," Vladimir said appreciatively. "You are still waiting to see what happens. Good. But do me a favor. Remember the sight of those peasants dragging their vegetables to the market. Remember that miserable hotel breakfast you had this morning."

"Why?"

"At some point in the future, these experiences will help you understand what I am going to tell you," Vladimir explained.

"I don't follow," David said. "Are you concerned about the farmers? Is that what you're getting at?"

Vladimir laughed loudly, as though he had never heard such an absurdity.

"Of course not," he said. Then he paused. "But I have an associate in Russia who is. He is an agricultural specialist in the government. He is someone who you will have to meet."

"Is he here in Poland?" David asked.

"No," Vladimir replied. "I meant when you come to the Soviet Union."

The limousine's tires made a rhythmic slapping as they drove over a rough patch of road. David took another deep breath and fought off the urge to ask Vladimir for one of his cigarettes.

"Change is the basis of everything that you are involved with here and in the Soviet Union," Vladimir said in a quiet voice.

"I didn't know I was involved in anything in the Soviet Union."

"You will be," Vladimir said. "But first you have to understand the sort of change that I am talking about."

"And what's that?" David asked.

"For me, it all comes to one word," Vladimir explained. "*Profit*. A society in which a motivated man can do business and make a profit."

"I don't understand," David said. "I don't know much about Poland or the USSR. But one thing I *do* know is that there's basically no profit incentive. It's a command economy; the government controls every aspect of production and distribution. If you want to change *that*, you're talking about changing the very basis of the society."

Vladimir folded his arms, looked out the window. For an instant he seemed agitated, as though he was fighting with himself over how much to divulge, what to say.

"Perhaps that is precisely what I mean," he said to David before lapsing into moody silence.

A couple of minutes later, Vladimir's attention was solidly focused on the landscape outside. He leaned close to the window and said something in Russian to their driver. The car slowed to a crawl, and they pulled as far to the edge of the road as they could to allow traffic to pass.

"There," Vladimir said. He pointed at an expanse of water-inundated, scrubby land. High grass ringed a couple of tiny wooden shacks in the near distance; a couple of wild rabbits ran through the wet marsh.

"What is this?" David asked.

"This is the site of the food-processing plant." Vladimir waited a second. "Have you inspected it to your satisfaction?"

"Have I . . . I'm going to need a lot more than a five-second drive-by."

"That's why you'll have to return," Vladimir said.

David sighed. "All right. I've seen it."

Vladimir turned around and barked an order to the driver, who pulled back onto the road and accelerated.

"Good," Vladimir said with a surprisingly mischievous smile. "Now that we have that out of the way, we can get down to business."

# Chapter Twelve

VLADIMIR BORCHENKO STOOD WITH HIS ARMS FOLDED in front of the main picture window of his Moscow penthouse apartment. He watched the afternoon traffic on the streets below. The sky was heavy and dark, and droplets of rain spattered against the pane of glass. He ran his hand along the white window sash, which had been redone as part of the remodeling of this old building that Vladimir owned. He occupied half of the top floor and rented out the stories below to those members of Moscow's new elite who were capable of paying extremely high rents.

He hummed an old tune from his childhood, one of the old Russian folk melodies his mother used to sing to him as, she had said, an "antidote" to the marching songs he learned as a young man in the Octobrists, then the Young Pioneers. The sound of his voice seemed to dissipate into the empty silence of his home.

He turned away from the window and crossed the polished wood floor with slow steps. He stopped in front of the fireplace. On the mantel was a framed photograph that had been taken twenty years before.

She had been tall, as tall as Vladimir. She stared straight into the camera, almost defiant, her beautiful features ringed in light-brown hair. She wore a stylish dress that Vladimir had bought her on a trip to Paris, and in the picture Vladimir could just see her calves and the gentle slope where her knee disappeared under the fabric. Behind her was the sea, the aquamarine tint of water reflecting sunlight. Vladimir was standing beside her in the picture; he was almost fifty years old then. She would have been about thirty-eight or -nine, just a couple of years after her retirement from the ballet.

"Sonia," Vladimir said to himself, looking into her eyes in the photograph.

They had been married almost ten years when the photograph was taken while on a holiday in the Crimea. He had never spent as much time with her as he wanted to. He was always traveling and shuttling back and forth to Poland and occasionally to the West. He had been consumed with the plan he and his college friend Mikhail Gorbachev had hatched together, and as the plan began to succeed and grow in scope, it had taken over the lives of all involved: Mikhail himself, Vladimir, David Olen.

Sonia died of cancer in 1987. She never lived to see the end of the Soviet Union. She had been ill for years, almost as long as Vladimir could remember. She had been frail and weak when they first married. He had known she wasn't well, and he had known that they would never be able to have children. But he had loved her so much that none of it mattered. He had treated every minute he spent with her as though it had been stolen from a greedy and spiteful owner. And then she died and left him alone in the world.

*Damn this melancholy,* Vladimir said to himself, turning away from the photograph after a final longing look. He went to the mahogany bar in the corner and poured himself a short snifter of cognac then returned to his desk. His bright desk lamp shone down on a stack of newspapers and framed them in a cone of luminescence.

The headlines were phrased differently in each, but the story was the same: *Belarin Said to Consider Presidency; Belarin Speaks on Candidacy; Presidential Run Strong Possibility for Maxim Belarin.*

Vladimir spread the newspapers out on the desk. There was a picture of Belarin: stocky, squinting with distrust, his cheap suit ill-fitting over his barrel chest and belly.

"Belarin," Vladimir said, spitting out the name.

Vladimir took a sip of cognac and ran his hand through his hair. He was beginning to understand. Maxim Belarin, Duma member and former KGB officer, had announced that he was considering running for president in next year's Russian presidential elections.

The question: Who cared? Belarin was an old *apparatchik*. As far as Vladimir was concerned, he was also an idiot. But Belarin was prominent in all the newspapers. That meant Belarin had support— the kind of money and influence it would take to get his name and face in the media.

Support from where? Vladimir looked down at Belarin's picture and smiled. Support from the gangsters. From Palchikoff. Barinov. Solovyov. The same gangsters Belarin was trying to help acquire MosElectric.

Vladimir pondered the thought of Maxim Belarin as president of Russia. It was chilling. What had Belarin ever stood for; what had he believed in? Personal gain, power, ruthlessness. Belarin was corrupt and amoral. He cared for no one but himself. And if the stories of Belarin's notorious KGB interrogations were true, he was also a sadist.

*Belarin Said to Consider Presidency.* Vladimir read the headline again, twice more. Maxim Belarin wanted to run the country. He wanted to have access to the codes that controlled the nuclear bombs. He wanted power over the army, the police. It would be a disaster.

Buying MosElectric was the first, most vital link in the chain. Vladimir intuitively understood this as complete fact. And he also knew that he was standing in Belarin's way. This is why Sokolov had died.

There was another way in which Vladimir could impede Maxim Belarin's attempt to gain power. Vladimir had known Belarin for more than thirty years. He knew Maxim's secrets—because they were intertwined with his own. And, although he had loathed the man for many years, Vladimir knew that Belarin was extremely dangerous. Vladimir knew well that Belarin himself had killed.

Vladimir went back to the window and looked at his watch. It was dark outside. He decided he would return to the office, work a few more hours before eating dinner. He would need something to take his mind off the events that were swirling around him. David Olen was arriving in the morning, and Vladimir wondered what exactly he would tell his old comrade.

He finished the cognac, left the glass on the bar. There was another story in the papers: Pope John Paul II was ailing. Surely David Olen knew nothing of how this pope had come to power. As far as David was concerned, the drama of their conspiracy had ended with what Vladimir knew was only the first intermission. Vladimir had done David a favor. Some information was better left unknown.

Vladimir turned off the light. His thoughts drifted again to David Olen. Vladimir wondered how often David thought about the past, about the days when they first met and Vladimir shared the scope of the plan. The world had been so different in those days. Sonia had been alive. Belarin had been a minor annoyance. And Vladimir had been deeply pleased, and so optimistic, to have met a kindred spirit in David Olen.


*June 1974.*
*Krakow, Poland.*

BY THE TIME THEY REACHED KRAKOW, Vladimir had forced himself to stay quiet for a while. It wasn't like him to talk so much to a stranger, to expose his innermost thoughts in this fashion. He feared saying too much too soon. David Olen had to be slowly introduced to his and Mikhail's plan. Vladimir had to watch Olen carefully to see if the American understood and was worthy of the task. And Vladimir had to be sure he could trust David Olen.

The driver slowed as they entered the city, where medieval stone walls and buildings gave way to new, Soviet-era construction.

"So hopefully this is the part where you start explaining to me what's going on," David Olen said, his tone dry.

Vladimir smiled. Olen was intelligent, with a sense of humor and a soulful manner. Vladimir liked him, a fact that he tried not to let cloud his judgment or his powers of observation.

"We're going to a church," he replied to Olen.

"A church?" David repeated. He blinked, as though not sure whether he was being put on.

"Think about it," Vladimir said. "You're going to a Catholic church with a Soviet atheist. That should give you something to remember."

David smiled, shaking his head slightly but saying nothing. Vladimir could tell that the American was impatient with Vladimir's secrecy. Probably he was anxious and uncertain. Vladimir realized that he would have felt the same if he were in David Olen's position.

Vladimir had contacts throughout the Soviet military, police, and intelligence communities—through his own doing and through Mikhail's growing influence. Only a very small handful had an inkling that Mikhail and Vladimir were doing anything more elaborate than a traditional Soviet-style operation of patronage and influence-building. Which was how Vladimir and Mikhail Gorbachev were able to operate below the radar of the state security apparatus and to stay out of prison.

Just a couple of months before, Vladimir had met secretly with one of his top contacts in the KGB, an ambitious officer named Maxim Belarin. Vladimir didn't trust Belarin, and he didn't like him, but Belarin knew too much for Vladimir to sever their connection.

That day Belarin had brought Vladimir some valuable information: Through an information exchange with a CIA operative stationed in Paris, Belarin had learned that Western intelligence agents knew about a connection between the Vatican, Moscow, and Poland. The CIA apparently knew that COMECON industrial manager Vladimir Borchenko was integral to this so-far tenuous connection.

Belarin was a bastard, but he had served a very useful function so far for Vladimir: He had kept the KGB from troubling him or Mikhail. Now the information that Belarin was providing—about the CIA beginning to learn about Vladimir's activities—was extremely troubling. Vladimir had spoken with Mikhail, and both agreed that they couldn't simply ignore the news and wait for it to go away. If the CIA subsequently decided to investigate Borchenko, it might learn too much, and this information might find its way back to the Soviet Union. Their plans could be ruined.

Vladimir had come up with a solution: Use Belarin to contact the CIA, and have the Americans send an operative to Warsaw. They could meet, exchange information. The CIA wouldn't want to get in Vladimir's way; after all, didn't they also want the Soviet system to fall away and be replaced with something new.

The idea had continued to develop in Vladimir's mind. An information exchange might help keep their plan secret, but why stop there? This was an opportunity. Lately their activity had grown in scope. It was almost more than Vladimir could handle. And wouldn't it help to have someone involved who could travel freely in the West?

Through a series of scrambled communiqués, with Belarin's help, Vladimir had learned that the CIA liked the way he was thinking. Vladimir began to communicate with an agent named Jim Allen. Vladimir offered to provide a cover story if they sent a businessman rather than an intelligence agent. To Vladimir's surprise, Jim Allen agreed. Weeks later David Olen arrived. Vladimir didn't know how they had found him or how they had selected him. But he knew that

Olen was compromised somehow, that the American intelligence agency had power over him.

"We'll stop here," Vladimir said to the driver.

The car slowed, and Vladimir motioned for David to get out. They walked together on a cobblestone sidewalk under the shadow of deciduous trees. In the distance were medieval turrets and churches looming up over the treeline as reminders of the ancient past.

"I had no idea this city was so old," David said.

"It's a thousand years old," Vladimir replied. "The Nazis were planning to destroy it, but they ran out of time when the war went against them. Pollution from the new steelworks is eating away at everything, but at least it will take longer than the Germans' tanks would have."

When they turned the corner, they stood before the imposing stone palace of the Archbishop of Poland. It always reminded Vladimir of an outpost in the new world, a remnant of ancient faith that would probably be left behind in mankind's future. Vladimir Borchenko didn't care for religion; he didn't recognize its insights. But he respected its power over populations and knew that some men of God were as formidable and driven as believers in any political ideology.

He and David were escorted to the second floor by a young priest. They walked into a large sunlit office where the windows opened to the suddenly warm afternoon. Paintings of religious subjects adorned the walls; a large table with four matching wooden chairs occupied the center of the room. The young priest announced Vladimir and David to two men. They were dressed in clerical robes and were huddled together by a window. They were deep in conversation.

"I hope we are not late," Vladimir said in Polish.

The two priests stopped talking and looked up. The older of the two was slightly stooped, and his collar showed a spot of empty darkness between the cloth and his neck. His face was lined with age, though his eyes were sharp and piercing.

167

The younger man was in his mid-fifties. He looked strong, athletic. He stood up very straight, with a dignity and presence that seemed somehow to fill up all the empty space around him.

"Cardinal Litwinski, Cardinal Karol Wojtyla," Vladimir said. In Polish, he said: "Thank you for meeting with me this afternoon. As I mentioned, I have someone that I would like you to meet. This is David Olen. He is an American and speaks only English."

David stood watching this exchange with a look of extreme confusion. He paused, obviously unsure how to approach two cardinals of the Catholic Church. He recovered himself, however, and respectfully offered his hand to each. They shook and nodded greetings. Vladimir carefully watched David Olen's reaction to meeting Wojtyla for the first time; the Polish cardinal was possessed with a strong magnetism and sense of personal power. Vladimir saw David's eyes flash with recognition of this as the two men shook hands.

"You are from Chicago," Wojtyla said in English. As always, his eyes seemed ablaze with intelligence and compassion.

"Yes," Olen replied.

"There are many Poles there," Litwinski, Wojtyla's mentor, observed. He talked in fractured English but spoke as though for Wojtyla's benefit and reminded the younger man of a fact he should bear in mind. "And there is a very strong Archdiocese in Chicago."

Litwinski looked at David expectantly.

"Yes, you're right," David said quickly.

"And are the people of Chicago aware of the plight of the Polish population?" Wojtyla asked. His hands were clasped peacefully in front of him, though the force of his presence made David involuntarily take a half-step back.

Vladimir was almost ready to intervene and step into the momentary void of silence between the cardinal and the American businessman, but then David Olen recovered himself.

David replied: "I cannot speak for everyone in my country. And I'm not Catholic. But are Americans aware that people in Poland are living under Soviet domination? Yes. They are. And I also think it's safe to say we're well aware that the Polish people want to be free of political domination."

Olen spoke with a conviction, which, Vladimir could see, impressed Wojtyla. The younger cardinal's thin lips curled into a relaxed smile, and he gave a small nod of satisfaction. Litwinski looked at Olen with a penetrating expression, also pleased with what he was hearing.

"I would like to speak with Mr. Olen alone before our lunch," Vladimir interjected. "I hope you won't find my request rude, but we have had little time together, and I think our friend may have some questions for me. We will need only a few minutes."

Cardinal Litwinski nodded, glanced at the clock on the wall. "We will meet in the dining room in a half hour," he said.

"You can stay here," Wojtyla offered. "Cardinal Litwinski and I will move to my office."

"Thank you," Vladimir said with a slight bow.

He waited until they were alone in the room and motioned toward an empty chair. David sat down with an expression of equal parts expectation and irritation.

"The CIA sent you here because it knows something is happening," Vladimir began. He remained standing, his hands on the back of a wooden chair across the table from David's. "And it knows that I am in the middle of it."

"You're not telling me anything I don't know," David replied. He sat in his chair at an angle, as though ready to spring out.

"That was a good answer, the one you gave Wojtyla," Vladimir said. "You'll find that he is very single-minded about liberating his people. The idea drives nearly everything he does."

"I wasn't trying to give an answer that pleased anyone," David replied crossly. "I told him the truth. The Soviet Union is controlling Eastern Europe by force, against its will, and that's wrong. I was merely speaking honestly."

"So you are an American patriot?" Vladimir asked.

David pushed himself slightly away from the table. "I don't know what you're getting at," he said. "There's a saying in America: 'My country, right or wrong.'"

"Is that what you believe?"

"No, I don't," David explained. "I believe right and wrong are bigger concepts than a single country. But I also believe that America, however flawed, has been a historical force for personal freedom and opportunity. I'm willing to do my part to keep it that way. So maybe that makes me a patriot. I suspect it does."

"Freedom and opportunity," Vladimir repeated. "We think alike."

David looked around the simple room, at the bookcase and the small religious statues inset into tiny alcoves.

"Do we have privacy here?" he asked.

"We can talk," Vladimir answered. "No one is listening."

"Then tell me what's going on," David said. "With all respect, Vladimir, that's not a request."

David Olen remained seated, though his eyes flashed with frustration that, Vladimir could now see, had reached a limit. The American's cheeks were flushed.

"I attended Moscow State University," Vladimir said. "As the son of a diplomat, I was admitted to the finest university in the country automatically—my application was nothing but a formality. And there I met someone who was very different from me. A young man from a village in the countryside, someone just as comfortable on a combine as in the classroom."

Olen leaned forward and put his hands on the table. He started to say something but stopped, apparently realizing that he was closer to the answers he demanded.

"He was named Mikhail Sergeivich Gorbachev," Vladimir continued. "He was different from everyone else. More intelligent, harder working, more driven. He was also extremely political. His grandfather had been repressed for speaking out against government policies. As a result he was very wary, but after we became friends, he began to confide in me. He had ideas about reforming our country—solid ideas, pragmatic, grounded in political reality. I was very impressed, to say the least."

Vladimir watched the American digest what he was hearing.

"We talked together," Vladimir added. "I had some ideas of my own. We decided that our ideas could work. And I knew that Gorbachev was destined for greatness somehow, some way. Ever since I saw him take the lead in our political study sessions. He is a born leader."

"Where is he now?" Olen asked.

"He is the Communist Party leader of the Stavropol region of Russia," Vladimir replied. "He is moving up through the system. He has powerful allies and a mentor in Moscow. We feel that, within the end of the decade, he might be called for membership in the Politburo."

Outside the window the sky had lightened; the pale sky filtered through the tall trees.

"Who is 'we'?" David asked. "You and your friend Mikhail? That's what this is all about?"

Vladimir said nothing for the moment; instead, he waited for the ambiance of the room to creep into David's consciousness, the fact that they were in the palace of the Catholic Church.

"This thing has to be bigger than you and your friend's ideas," David said. "Those two cardinals are in on it. There's a bigger scope."

"Mikhail and I had big ideas," Vladimir said, picking up his thread of thought. "But we were just students. Mikhail Gorbachev was poor, an ambitious nobody. My father was a diplomat, so I had privileges. But I had no pretensions that I would ever rise to a high leadership position in the Soviet Union."

Vladimir still stood on the other side of the table. He felt his heart beat heavy in his chest, the ends of his fingers tingling. He had never before tried to explain the total scope of the plan, the deal that he and Mikhail had instigated. To speak it aloud was like uttering the words of a spell that might unleash terrible dangers.

"You were young idealists," David said. "You wanted to make a difference."

"Mikhail is the idealist," Vladimir said.

"Fine, fine, and you're the pragmatist; I get it," David said. "And you had this plan, but you didn't have the means to make it happen. So the two of you needed to find support from somewhere. You needed help."

Vladimir nodded. He could see David Olen's mind working, his businessman's instincts grasping the practical dimensions of what he was hearing.

"You needed to put together a group of some kind," David said. "A pooling of resources for a common goal."

They had nearly taken up the half-hour Litwinski had allotted them. Vladimir hoped they would be left alone a few minutes longer. He sensed that Olen was beginning to grasp what he was hearing, and a sense of pride over what he had accomplished began to fill him as he anticipated the American making the larger connections.

"And who would help us?" Vladimir asked, excitement creeping into his voice. "There were not many like-minded individuals at Moscow State—these were the final days of Stalin, you realize. So we asked: Who stood to gain the most from reforming the Soviet Union?"

"Depends on what kind of reform," David said. "The first to benefit would be all the Soviet citizens, obviously. But they're living in a police state; what can they do to change their lives?"

Vladimir leaned against the chair and listened intently.

"But if we're talking about large-scale political reform, the next to benefit would be the countries of Eastern Europe," David said. He looked up, into Vladimir's eyes. "The millions of people living under Soviet political and military domination."

Vladimir smiled with pleasure though, when he spoke, lowered his voice a fraction. Part of him felt this was moving too fast, wished that he had time to step back and consider what he was doing.

"Poland was a natural choice," he said. "I traveled here often with my father on his diplomatic assignments."

The air in the room seemed stifling and still. A heavy silence enveloped both men. David's expression turned grave as he instinctively understood the import of what he was being told.

"Poland is a Catholic country," Vladimir added. "Very much at odds with atheistic communism. We decided to find someone in the Polish Church who also had vision, drive, and ambition. Someone with whom we could . . ."

Vladimir paused, looking for the correct expression in English.

"Someone you could make a deal with," David said.

"Precisely."

David Olen got up form the table and walked slowly over to the window and paused for a moment to glance at the titles on the bookshelf. He folded his arms behind his back and looked down on the street below through the antique window. Vladimir remained where he was, knowing that soon they would have to join Wojtyla and Litwinski. He had an ulterior motive for wishing to continue this conversation where they were: His KGB contacts had told him that the Archbishop's Palace in Krakow was one area in which the local police had definitely not placed listening devices.

Suddenly Olen turned from the window and walked across the room to Vladimir. His expression was conflicted.

"What if I don't want to know about all of this?" he said, almost whispering. "Maybe it's all bullshit. Maybe I should go ask those two cardinals if you're telling me the truth."

"If you wish," Vladimir said with a shrug. "But there's no real hurry. You'll have plenty of dealings with them in the future. Especially Wojtyla. He's a remarkable man. I'm sure you noticed."

David rubbed his eyes. "All right, you made a deal with him and Litwinski," David said. "For what? How are they helping you?"

"Money," Vladimir said. "Through them we've accessed a faction at the Vatican that is sympathetic to our goals."

"How does money help you?" David asked. "You can't just buy a seat on the Politburo."

"Of course we can't," Vladimir replied. "But money makes things happen. The region of Russia that Mikhail controls, for instance, has recently enjoyed a great deal of agricultural success. Why? Because farm implements are being repaired, new machines are arriving, and advanced seed strains from the West are being quietly introduced. As a result, Mikhail's standing in the Party is growing every year. This would be impossible without outside support."

"And that's going to get your friend on the Politburo?" David asked, still skeptical.

"There are other factors," Vladimir explained. "Mikhail and I have made political accommodations throughout the country. And Mikhail is a shrewd man who knows how to make allies for himself. Stavropol is a picturesque region. Mikhail has overseen the construction of a very comfortable resort there—"

"With the money you've gotten through this alliance?" David asked.

"In part," Vladimir said. "The resort is very popular with high-placed Party members, many of whom have illicit appetites. Sometimes they come to the countryside, relax, and compromise themselves. Mikhail has been effective in gathering proof of their indiscretions."

"I guess that's a pretty good bargaining tool," David said.

"Among others," Vladimir answered. "You see, David, we are very serious. This is not a fantasy."

"What about the Church?" David asked. "What's in it for these cardinals? Aren't they running a risk—wouldn't it be a scandal if anyone found out they're dealing with Soviets?"

"They run a serious risk," Vladimir said. "But it is worth it for them, especially for Wojtyla. They want Poland to move toward independence and religious freedom. Which will happen when Mikhail is in the Politburo and he is in a position to influence policy."

David Olen stared into Vladimir's eyes; both men stood facing each other, neither moving.

"What's in it for you?" David asked.

"The future," Vladimir replied with hesitating. "Mikhail envisions economic reform. I see a future in which I can do business and make a profit, outside the control of the state."

A small smile appeared on David's face, almost as though he finally appreciated the audacity of the plan Vladimir and Mikhail had crafted and honed together in their university dormitory almost twenty years before.

"I understand your motivation," David said. "What about everyone else? Do they really think there's a chance that—"

"Litwinski is old, but don't underestimate him," Vladimir said. "He has plans of his own. He wants to engineer Wojtyla's rise to the papacy."

"That's ridiculous," David said. "The pope's Italian. The pope's always Italian. Nothing's going to change that."

"Our group has allies in the Vatican," Vladimir replied. "We are very well organized. Nothing is certain, but there will probably be a Papal election before the end of the decade. When that occurs, we will have a group in place that will try to influence the selection of the next pope."

There was a quiet knock at the door; a middle-aged nun opened the door quietly and stuck her head inside, her eyes wide with curiosity about these strange visitors.

"A few moments more," Vladimir whispered to her in Polish. "Please extend our apologies to Cardinal Litwinski. We won't be long."

The nun nodded, glanced at David Olen, then quietly closed the door. When Vladimir met David's eyes, he saw that the American was shaken to his core.

"A few days ago, I would have said you were crazy if I'd heard any part of this," David said.

"But now . . ."

"But now . . . here I am." David shook his head; in that instant, Vladimir could see that David wished he had never come to Poland, never heard of this audacious plan.

"Do you want to know what I want from you?" Vladimir asked.

David looked up, almost surprised. "I suppose so," he said.

"I have practical needs," Vladimir explained. "We have brought together a number of people in Moscow, in Poland, and in the Vatican. Although we may have different reasons, we are working toward similar goals. Because of the nature of what we are doing, we cannot share our plans with anyone outside of a small, trusted circle."

"You'd be thrown in jail," David said.

"Precisely. Our group is small; our scope is ambitious. As a result, at times our organization can become a bit overwhelmed."

David thought for a moment. "There's only one way I can look at this thing," he said. "It's a deal, like a business deal. You have a group of parties who share a common goal, and you're bringing various assets to the table in order to make it happen."

"That's perfect," Vladimir replied. "And now the deal has grown in scope. It is accelerating to a new level, and we require the involvement of a new party in order to make the deal continue to work."

"And that's me," David said quietly, almost funereal.

"I need a diplomat," Vladimir explained. "Someone who can move between the Vatican, Poland, and the Soviet Union. I need a broker, a businessman with businessmen's instincts."

"Why a businessman?" David asked.

"Because we're dealing with money," Vladimir said. "I think we could start to receive funds from the Chicago Archdiocese; you could facilitate that. And we are receiving funds from a bishop in the Vatican Bank, an American who has proven difficult to deal with.

176

Think of what you could achieve, David. You can expand your business into Eastern Europe, and at the same time you can affect the course of history. And through your newfound contacts in the CIA, you can ensure for us that there will be no interference from the United States."

David was silent for almost a full minute, his chin cradled in his hands. Vladimir walked to the window and looked down on the street and square outside. Two armed soldiers walked slowly, smoking cigarettes and talking, neither probably older than twenty.

"This is too big," David said in a quiet voice, almost to himself. "Someone's going to get killed. You can't grab that kind of power without stepping on someone along the way."

Vladimir walked over to David, looked into his eyes. "The way the Soviets have stepped on millions in Hungary, in Czechoslovakia? The way the communists have stepped on countless victims in their own country? Would you let that go unchecked? Don't you want to be part of a force that resists these transgressions?"

"You don't care about that," David said evenly. "You want to make money."

"Are you frightened?" Vladimir asked. "Scared for your own skin?"

"Don't try to manipulate me," David said, anger flaring. But of course he was scared. He was terrified. This so-called "deal" was huge. There were so many implications.

"You can't walk away now," Vladimir said as if reading his mind. "If I understand anything about you, I know that you can't back out of an opportunity of this magnitude."

They stared at each other, both of their emotions boiling beneath the surface. Vladimir could hear his own pulse beating in his ears.

There was another quiet knock at the door. The same nun stepped in and looked expectant.

"We are coming," Vladimir said to her. "I apologize for our tardiness."

He patted David Olen on the back. "Come, let's talk with your new friends," he said. "I'm sure you will find them very interesting. And they will want to hear about your new role in our enterprise."

Vladimir held his breath for a moment as he waited for David's response. But then David stepped toward the door with purpose in his stride. Vladimir allowed himself to breathe then. He had done it. David Olen had become part of the deal.

---

THE FIRST FEW TIMES David returned home from his business in Poland with Vladimir Borchenko, David would stop in Washington to be debriefed by Jim Allen. Later, when David had earned Allen's trust, they would communicate briefly through a secure phone line.

The routine was always the same. At the airport a car would be waiting for David and would then take him to the same nondescript office building in central Washington. David would take the elevator to the fifth floor and walk into a drab, unassuming reception area.

Jim Allen would emerge from his inner office with his usual grim expression and a handshake. His black hair, always looking as if it had just been cut, had started graying at the temples. He wore dark suits, solid-color ties, and carried himself with the erect formality of a career military officer.

"Have a seat," Allen said, motioning to the chair in front of his desk.

David did as Jim Allen asked, his eyes wandering over the family photos on the plain metal desk. A pretty wife and three children: two boys and a girl. In the pictures Jim Allen always wore the same expression of pride mixed with a sort of cool restraint.

"What do you have for me?" Jim Allen asked, getting right to business. He listened intently as David relayed the details of his latest trip. Allen nodded, obviously pleased with David's information. David's discomfort would increase throughout the meeting.

When they were finished, Jim would always stand and say, "As usual you'll commit nothing to paper and speak about this to no one." He walked David to the door and always said, "This meeting never took place."

David felt intimidated in Jim Allen's presence. It was nothing in particular that Allen said or did, simply David's strong sense that he was in deep waters that men such as Allen knew how to navigate far better than he did.

They met a total of perhaps twenty times in the '70s. Each time, David would try to get a sense of who Jim Allen really was. The man was an enigma, though cracks in his bland exterior would surface occasionally. The diploma on his wall was from Georgetown, and once in the middle of a debriefing, the two men started a spontaneous conversation about college basketball teams and the NCAA tournament. Once David found Allen tanned and relaxed, a fact that seemed to embarrass the CIA agent when he admitted that he had taken his family to Disneyland for a summer holiday.

David knew that Jim Allen had contacts in the KGB, that they enjoyed a reciprocal relationship based on the sharing of selected information. David was never entirely certain what information Allen shared with his own government or precisely to whom he reported. Allen operated under a deep cover, ensuring plausible deniability for each successive presidential administration under which he worked.

Once, in the late seventies, a few years before Allen's untimely death from cancer, the two men sat looking at a packet of photographs David had shot in Poland. Allen stopped and looked hard at a picture of Vladimir. Borchenko was standing on a street in Warsaw and was dressed in a long black overcoat. He looked into David's camera lens with an expression of total self-assurance.

"History is going to forget about this guy," Allen said quietly, almost to himself. "Sometimes I think that's too bad."

"Why is that?" David asked, taken aback by Allen's uncharacteristically relaxed tone.

"Just look at him," Allen said. "He looks like he rules the world. A week with Borchenko would teach someone more about the way the world works than six months with the president."

"I guess you're right," David said.

"Back to work," he said, shaking his head over his own digression. It was probably the only time David ever saw Jim Allen let down his guard, even for an instant.

# Chapter Thirteen

*February 18, 1998. 5:10 p.m.*
*St. Petersburg.*

WITH LATE AFTERNOON IN ST. PETERSBURG, winter darkness descended over the city; a light mist of snow fell over the streets, and car headlights formed dim cones of illumination that barely cut through the gloom. David Olen sat alone at the desk in his hotel room and looked over the latest construction costs on the Nevsky project. He looked up with a start when he heard a loud knocking at the door.

Jason Rudas stood holding his briefcase in the hallway, his overcoat draped over his arm. David gestured for him to come in.

"I just got off the phone with Edward in Moscow," Jason said.

"Anything I need to know about?"

Jason shrugged. "I wanted to see if there was anything new on MosElectric," he said. "Edward's heard rumors that there might be competitive bidding in the privatization."

"Vladimir doesn't have it locked up?" David asked.

"Doesn't sound like it." Jason looked out the window and watched the snow falling. "I wonder what he's up to."

"Making a profit," David replied. "If you ever want to understand Vladimir's motivation, the profit incentive is always right at the surface."

David picked up the remote control and flipped on CNN in English. There was a story, complete with footage, about a miner's strike in Romania.

"Have you heard anything more about the pope?" David asked.

"Nothing new," Jason said.

"He's not really that old," David mused. "It's a shame he's had all those health problems. Still, he's been one of the longest-reigning popes of the past couple centuries."

David glanced over at Jason; the younger man regarded him with a fixed, impassive expression.

"What did Edward have to say about the MosElectric construction project?" David asked.

"We're definitely in the running," Jason said with a small smile. "Edward's getting optimistic. You know how he is."

Olen Europe had made a presentation the month before to key decision-makers within MosElectric and flew them to Warsaw to meet Roger Wolf and Mike Roth and the rest of the team. They had shown off the high-rise project Olen Europe had completed in Warsaw, as well as the one currently under construction. The MosElectric representatives had been leaning toward the Harmon company, one of Olen Europe's main competitors in the region, but the demonstration had put Olen firmly in the running for the contract.

"We're drafting the letter of intent," Jason added. "The whole thing should start to shake out in the next week or so."

David thought for a moment about the scope of the project. It would be a massive project in scale; the end result would be one of Moscow's largest office towers.

"You know," he said, "this would be one of those jobs where the good news would be getting a letter of intent signed—"

"And the bad news would also be getting a letter of intent signed," Jason said with a laugh, finishing David's thought for him. "Because then all the shit would really start."

David laughed aloud, was about to add a thought when he glanced at the television. He grabbed the remote control and turned up the volume.

"I know that guy," he said.

On the screen was a stocky, balding man in a black suit. He was walking in the middle of a group of reporters with microphones through the long corridor of what looked like a government office. He was talking in Russian in a deep voice punctuated with mirthless laughter.

"—Maxim Belarin today elaborated on his intention to run in Russia's presidential elections next year. In a style typical of his blunt, populist approach, the former KGB officer and current member of the Russian Duma stated that 'The people are tired of Russia's being America's doormat.' He added that 'A firm hand is required for Russia to resume its place among the great nations, and to hell with anyone who tries to stand in the way.'"

"You know him?" Jason asked. "He looks like a nut to me. How'd you meet him?"

"Through Vladimir," David mumbled vaguely. "Some dinner or something a long time ago. I remember his face."

The TV report ended. A moment later the news shifted to Britain, where there was a suspected reoccurrence of mad cow disease.

"So was this guy KGB when you met him?" Jason asked.

David looked up at his colleague, who wore an expression of curiosity.

"I'm not sure," David replied. "It was quite a while ago."

A flash of disappointment flashed across Jason's face, so quickly that someone who didn't know him wouldn't have noticed it. Over the years Jason had grown more and more frustrated with David's unwillingness to talk about his past. It was an emotion that Jason tried to mask but one David could detect.

"Anyway," Jason continued, "I wonder if this guy is going to have a chance to win. A crackpot like that is the last person this country needs as a president."

"It depends on who might be supporting him," David said. "I'll remember to ask Vladimir. He probably knows the story behind the story."

"Doesn't he always?" Jason said.

"Where are we going to dinner tonight?" David asked. He flipped off the television and started straightening papers on his desk.

"A place pretty close to here," Jason said. "Terry picked it out. It's an old nineteenth-century merchant's house that's been restored in the past couple of years. They serve a real traditional Russian dinner: caviar, vodka, the works. And there's a private casino on the top floor."

"Sounds like fun," David said. "Are you planning to do any gambling?"

Jason smiled. "You know I never gamble."

"And you know I do," David said. "It proves you're smarter than me."

"And in the morning we're leaving for Moscow," Jason said. "The bad news is that we couldn't get a Transaero flight. We'll be taking domestic Aeroflot."

David groaned. That meant they would be flying on the domestic branch of the Russian national airline, with its notoriously bad service and aged fleet of planes.

A moment later the telephone on the desk began to ring. David picked up and heard a familiar voice say hello.

"Cynthia," David said brightly. "Hold on a second. Jason's here."

"I'm going to work out in the hotel gym before dinner," Jason said, gathering his things. "Say hello for me."

David waved goodbye to Jason and waited for him to quietly leave and close the door behind him.

"You're in early," David said to Cynthia when he was alone.

"I wanted to get a few things done before it gets hectic around here."

"Good idea," David said.

"Anyway, I'm calling because you have an urgent message." David heard the sound of Cynthia flipping through sheets of paper. "Well, actually, it was two messages. Carl Becker. He called yesterday and again today. He sounded upset and said it was very important that he speak with you. ASAP."

David shifted the phone to his other ear. Carl. He wondered what possible reason would require Carl to talk to him immediately.

"I told him you were out of the country, but he said he needed to talk to you anyway," Cynthia said. "He said to call him at home or at his congressional office. Any time day or night."

"Did he say what this was about?"

"He said it was old business," Cynthia told him. Cynthia had worked for David for more than a quarter-century, almost since the beginning of David's involvement with Vladimir Borchenko and the CIA. But David had shielded Cynthia from the knowledge of his activities, and she had always understood that certain questions would never be answered.

"Well, you know Carl," David said. "Everything's always an emergency."

"That's true," Cynthia said with a knowing laugh. "Anyway, it seemed like a message you should get right away. Otherwise, how are things in sunny Russia?"

"Oh, you know. Sandy beaches and drinks with little umbrellas in them," David joked.

"I'm so jealous," Cynthia said.

"Seriously, though, it looks like we have a better shot at the MosElectric development than we thought."

"Really?" Cynthia said. "That's great."

They chatted a few minutes more and got up to date on a few matters that required David's attention.

After they hung up, David looked at his watch and dialed Carl's number at home.

# Chapter Fourteen

*February 18, 1998. 5:30 p.m.*
*St. Petersburg.*

H ello," said a sleepy female voice.

"Gail, this is David Olen. Sorry, it sounds like I woke you up," David apologized. "I got an urgent message from Carl."

"David," said Carl's wife, her voice happy with recognition. "Don't worry about it; I was just sitting here in bed watching television. Carl's up already. I know he really wants to talk to you. Hold on a minute; I'll get him for you."

"Thanks, Gail," David said. "And I really am sorry about calling so early."

"Oh, stop it," Gail said.

A moment later a familiar voice came on the line. "David?"

"Carl, it's me," David replied.

"I'm glad one of us finally caught the other," Carl Becker said. "I have some news for you about our old business." He paused, then said, "The deal."

*The deal.* David took a deep breath. "What's going on?"

"I was just contacted by someone inside the agency," Carl said. "A young guy. He said that he's taken over all of Jim Allen's work. He had access to all Allen's old secret case files and everything."

There was a gravity in Carl's voice that David rarely heard.

"So he's in the know?" David asked. "About everything?"

"Don't ask me how it happened," Carl replied. "When Jim Allen died, I thought the knowledge of our activities died with him. But this kid is starting up a new splinter group within the agency. He's working on general guidelines, without specific oversight, so his superiors can maintain plausible deniability."

"Allen did the same thing," David pointed out.

"Well, this kid is no Jim Allen," Carl said.

"You keep calling him a kid," David pointed out. "How old is he?"

"Thirty, maybe," Carl said. "His name is Gleason. Thomas Gleason. And I don't like him one fucking bit. Maybe I never wanted to get dragged into anything involving the agency, but at least Jim Allen was a total pro when it came to his work. This kid, he's getting mixed up in old business that was going on when he was in grade school. And I'm pretty sure he's out of his league."

"Ah, shit," David whispered. He began pacing his room.

"And I'm sure you understand the timing on this thing," Carl added. "It has to do with our old Polish friend."

David understood instantly. The pope, ailing in the Vatican.

"Are you still there?" Carl asked. "You just got quiet."

"I'm here. I'm thinking." David sat down on the bed. "What does this kid want to do? Is he trying to draw you back into something?"

"Draw me into it?" Carl repeated. "What, are you shitting me? I'm already in it, whether I like it or not. He made that pretty damn clear to me. The past isn't going to go away, David."

"All right, don't get excited," David said. "It won't do anybody any good if you start freaking out."

"Look, David," Carl said with a sigh. "There's something else. The kid told me a bunch of shit I didn't know about. You know, my involvement in the deal pretty much ended after I brought you in. They were finished with me after that, other than a few House Committee issues that I was in agreement with, anyway. I was briefed on the general outline of things—or so I thought."

"I told you as much as I could over the years," David said, lowering his voice. "There were some things you didn't need to know."

"I realize that, and I know you were trying to protect me," Carl said. "But I'm not sure if even you're aware of everything."

David paused. "Maybe I'm not," he said. "Maybe I need to know what you're talking about before I can say."

"I don't know how secure this phone is," Carl's voice rose a tone, his stress almost palpable. "But Gleason basically wants to continue the deal somehow. He wants to influence what's going on in Rome, especially when our old friend passes away."

"Screw him; let him try," David said. "We don't need to—"

"He's got me by the balls." Carl laughed weakly. "You, too. Why do you think I needed to talk to you? He wants me to bring you in. I can't have the press finding out what happened in Sagami, David. Even now it would kill me politically. I've been trying to think of a way out. But listen, the kid wants to see if there's a way to reestablish some of the old financial pipelines in order to influence the politics in Rome.

"Are you there?" Carl asked.

"Yeah," David said.

"Are you seeing your guy in Moscow?" Carl asked. "Borchenko?"

"Yeah, first thing," David replied. "But what am I supposed to do, drag him into all this crap without any support or verification?"

"We're in deeper than even you might realize," Carl said. "We can't talk about it now. Maybe Borchenko will know what I mean."

"This is bullshit, Carl! How am I supposed to ask him if I don't know what the fuck I'm asking about?" David yelled.

"Look, this Gleason has got a lot of compromising information on both of us. He could be dangerous."

"But what am—" David said before he heard a click and then nothing. He'd been cut off. "Shit!" he muttered as he dialed the operator and had her try Carl's number again.

"I'm sorry, sir, that number is busy," the operator said. "You'll have to try again later."

David pulled out his cell phone and tried Carl's number himself a few more times, but, not surprisingly, he got a busy signal. Could someone have been listening in at Carl's end? Or was it simply a bad Russian connection? In any case, the conclusion of his conversation with Carl Becker would have to wait.

There was nothing David could do for now. Carl had said that someone from the CIA wanted to start meddling in matters that had been left untouched for a decade or more. The very idea made David clench his fists in fear of what might happen.

*When am I ever going to be done with this?* he asked himself.

David had always hungered for the deal, for the negotiation, for the moment when talk turned into agreement and action. He was addicted to the thrill of the moment. But he no longer wanted to deal with CIA agents or conspirators with global dreams. He wanted to put his energy into his business and spend his every free moment with his family.

He wanted out.

*February 18, 1998. 6:30 p.m.*
*Moscow.*

VLADIMIR BORCHENKO SAT at his steel-and-glass desk in the living room of his penthouse apartment. He held up his hand to the young woman he had just brought home after a dinner in one of Moscow's finest restaurants and signaled her to be quiet. She frowned, and Vladimir motioned to the bar on the other side of the room. She busied herself mixing a drink with a look of rapt concentration.

"This is Borchenko," he said, answering the phone.

"This is Sergei downstairs. Sorry to disturb you." Sergei was the head of the security team for Vladimir's building. He was a former member of an elite military unit, a man who rarely spoke. He had seen Vladimir coming home with the girl, which probably accounted for his apology.

"It's all right, Sergei. What is it?"

"You have a visitor," Sergei said. "Are you expecting Mr. Maxim Belarin?"

Vladimir paused. He felt a clenching sensation in his stomach.

"He says you have business with him," Sergei said in a cold tone. "He is in the lobby with two bodyguards. Do you want me to let them in?"

Vladimir watched the girl wander across the room to look at pictures on the wall. She was slender and pretty, about twenty-five. There were few nights when Vladimir felt sufficiently free of the past to enjoy a woman's company.

"Send him up," Vladimir said.

"Yes, sir," Sergei said.

"My driver is waiting outside," Vladimir added. "I am sending my friend down, the young woman you saw me with tonight. Please escort her to my car and tell the driver to take her anyplace she needs to go."

Vladimir hung up the phone. The girl had been listening.

"You're kicking me out?" she asked.

"Yelena. I apologize, but someone has arrived whom I need to speak with privately."

Vladimir got up, took her coat from the closet, and wrapped it around her shoulders.

"You'll call me?" she asked, looking into his eyes.

Many years and a world of experience separated the two of them. "I will," Vladimir said, knowing he probably wouldn't. He escorted her into the hallway and pressed the button for the elevator.

When the door opened, Belarin and his two bodyguards were standing inside. Vladimir held the door open for Yelena, kissed her on the cheek. The door closed, leaving the men in the hallway.

"I didn't realize you had such charming company," Belarin said. "I suppose I should apologize for interrupting."

"Don't think twice about it, Maxim," Vladimir said, opening the door of his apartment. "But if you don't mind, can we speak without your associates?"

Belarin nodded at the two guards, who stepped back, their arms folded. Vladimir avoided making eye contact with them.

When they were inside, Belarin glanced around appreciatively. He stood stiff and rigid, his hands folded in front of him. He had the cold eye of the KGB officer he had once been combined with the petty greed and dogmatic shortsightedness of the classic *apparatchik*.

"A drink?" Vladimir asked.

"Whiskey," Belarin said, walking slowly around the edge of the room, as though gathering information.

"Please sit," Vladimir said. He motioned toward the pair of leather sofas arranged near the fireplace. He poured two short glasses of whiskey, gave one to Belarin, then sat across from him.

"How is political life?" Vladimir asked.

"Very well, thank you," Belarin replied in his deep, throaty voice. "Are there any listening devices in this apartment?"

"I have the place swept weekly," Vladimir replied.

"You can't be too careful," Belarin said, pursing his lips.

They looked at each other in heavy silence. The feeling between the two men had always verged on contempt; now it approximated hatred. Vladimir had never wanted to work with Belarin, never wanted to bring him into the deal with the Vatican and the Poles. But Belarin had discovered a dollars-to-rubles money-changing transfer

Vladimir had concocted in 1972 to bring cash through a Cyprus shell company into the USSR for Mikhail Gorbachev. He had done this several times in the past, but this time the KGB was monitoring his financial affairs. Belarin was the KGB officer who processed the information; instead of having Vladimir arrested, he came to Vladimir's apartment without warning.

At first he had used the leverage this information gave him to obtain money and favors from Vladimir, but after several months Belarin began to realize that Vladimir's operations involved more than mere money laundering. He insinuated himself into Vladimir's world by insisting on accompanying him to Poland, where he insisted on meeting Litwinski and Wojtyla. Vladimir had had no choice but to bring Belarin into his cabal. Belarin was a highly placed insider within the KGB, which helped Vladimir and Mikhail many times. But Belarin constantly demanded money, and his imagination was sparked more and more as he learned what Vladimir and Gorbachev were involved in. Belarin had always been a selfish, untrustworthy element. In time he knew everything about the Vatican, Poland, and Chicago. It was at that point that Vladimir had understood he would never be free of Maxim Belarin.

"To begin this conversation," Vladimir said, "I would like to declare that I have not made a final decision about MosElectric. But if I decide I want it, then I will make the highest bid. You and your cronies can go fuck yourselves."

Belarin smiled. He had a big head, a meaty slab. He sipped his whiskey, his large hands dwarfing the glass.

"I will not warn you again," Belarin said, his smile fixed on his face. "MosElectric is central to my plans. Do not stand in my way."

"Your plans," Vladimir said. "You mean becoming president. Do you really intend to ride on those criminals' backs?"

"Interesting." Belarin pointed at Vladimir with his glass. "You were once a criminal, weren't you? A black marketer if I remember correctly. And you were able to put a man in power."

Vladimir would have laughed out loud if it wouldn't have given Belarin satisfaction. The fool was right.

"But no matter," Belarin said with a shrug. "You have been warned. I cannot help it if you fail to heed this warning."

"Having Sokolov killed was unnecessary," Vladimir said. "I knew where you stood on MosElectric."

"Perhaps you didn't understand how serious I was," Belarin said. "In any case, the banker had stood in the way of some of my associates in the past on other matters. You should control your employees better."

Vladimir started to speak then stopped himself. He felt hot inside; his hands felt wet on his glass of whiskey. It was damnable and humiliating, this feeling, this fear. Belarin was an inferior man, limited in his thinking and in his heart. But he was also shrewd, cruel, and extremely dangerous. Vladimir fought to control his inner emotions, to show Belarin nothing but an icy exterior.

"We know each other's thoughts," Vladimir said. He took a cigarette from his jacket and lit it. "Perhaps there is nothing more to say."

"We are not finished," Belarin said in a flat voice. He tugged at his tie and smiled, showing his crooked teeth.

Vladimir smoked his cigarette. He fought off a burst of rage, the impulse to leap up from the couch. Belarin was talking to him like a subordinate, like someone he might have interrogated in the cells of Lubyanka. But there was nothing Vladimir could do, not if he wanted to learn more about what Belarin was planning.

"We did some interesting things together, didn't we?" Belarin said, almost wistfully.

"They were interesting times," Vladimir responded.

"How is Mikhail Sergeivich?"

"He is at his institute," Vladimir replied, feeling a surge of protectiveness for his old friend. "He is writing, promoting his ideas."

"His time is done," Belarin said. "He should have held on to power while he still possessed it. He had the right ideas and motivation. But he was weak."

"Unlike you," Vladimir spat back. "Now you want to have a nice office in the Kremlin. You think you can win the election."

"Elections are the reality of the day," Belarin mused. "But Russia needs a firm hand. We have been beaten down, humiliated. The world no longer fears us. That must change."

A very nice campaign speech, Vladimir thought. It might even work.

"Then good luck to you," Vladimir said. For a sickening moment he imagined the possible consequences of Belarin as president of Russia. He was a man who could start a war, who might think nothing of the slaughter of innocents—anything for his own power and glory.

"You want me to lose. You wish I would disappear," Belarin said evenly, looking into Vladimir's eyes. Vladimir fought off the urge to look away. Sheer will and heartless determination emanated from the man like a bottomless black void that nothing could fill. "But I won't. This is what I need to speak to you about. You are one of a handful of men left who are aware of our activities in the 1970s."

"That is true, Maxim," Vladimir replied, keeping his voice flat.

"I am sure there are a few in the Vatican," Belarin said. "But the remaining members of the Holy Fist will always remain silent. They cannot reveal that they were involved in a conspiracy with the man who became the last General Secretary of the Soviet Union. Imagine the scandal."

"Agreed," Vladimir said. He stubbed out his cigarette and burned with curiosity. What was in this man's mind?

"And they could never admit that this conspiracy led to the death of one of their own," Belarin continued. He raised his eyebrows and frowned, as though remembering something distasteful.

Vladimir said nothing. He never spoke about what had transpired within the Vatican in 1978. It was reckless of Belarin to talk about it at all, even in private.

"So I do not fear the Catholics," Belarin said. "The pope is sick now, but that does not concern me. It is their business."

Suddenly Vladimir understood.

"My main problem is at home," Belarin added. "Who knows that I arranged for my operative to travel to Rome? Mikhail Sergeivich does not—he would never have had the stomach to tarnish the reputation of Mikhail Gorbechev. In any case, Mikhail Gorbechev would never talk; it would destroy his place in history."

Belarin, with the backing of wealthy criminals, considered himself president already in spirit if not in fact. The subtext of Belarin's agenda became clear to Vladimir. Belarin knew that any kind of revelation of his own role in the deal that helped put Mikhail Sergeivich in power—along with his complicity in the conspiracy within the Vatican—would permanently ruin his political aspirations.

"Your reputation is safe, Maxim," Vladimir said. "No one in our cabal is going to reveal your role in an attempt to damage you. We all have too much to lose."

"Perhaps," Belarin said, nodding slightly to himself. "You know, it is a tricky thing, trying to win a democratic election. Power cannot be grabbed. It must be coaxed out of the people through persuasion. But it takes money, a lot of money."

"It's none of my business," Vladimir said, waving the cigarette. "I want nothing to do with your plans."

"And I can trust Mikhail Sergeivich?" Belarin asked.

"Please," Vladimir said dismissively. "Mikhail Sergeivich cares about few things more than the judgment of history. It would kill him if the world learned about the assistance he received throughout his career."

Belarin made a little humming noise, nodding, thinking. He had always reminded Vladimir of an industrial machine when he did this.

"What about the American?" Belarin asked, looking up at Vladimir. "What about David Olen? He is still a friend and associate of yours."

"We have an understanding," Vladimir said.

"Does he know about the Vatican conspiracy?"

"He doesn't know a thing about it," Vladimir told Belarin.

He took a drag on his cigarette, which bought a moment to think. Belarin had financial and media support for his campaign. He obviously saw the members of their old conspiracy as factors that might stand in his way.

Belarin and Vladimir hated each other; it was no secret. And now, in an attempt to intimidate Borchenko, Belarin had had Alexei Sokolov killed as a warning. But why not simply eliminate Vladimir himself?

"Is that so?" Belarin asked with a thin, contemptuous smile.

Belarin might have been hesitant to kill Vladimir because of the latter's power and influence. Or he may still have wanted something from Vladimir. For all his clout, Vladimir doubted whether anything could protect him once Belarin decided to end his life.

"You have always been a very good talker, Vladimir," Belarin added. "You have always been very intelligent, so sophisticated. Much more than me, that is certain."

Vladimir smoked his cigarette, said nothing. He felt a palpable danger in the air emanating from Belarin.

"So I wonder, always: Is Vladimir lying to me?" Belarin spread his hands in a gesture of openness. "Did he keep this secret from his good friend David Olen? Or is he protecting him now or maybe hoping that he can use him as an insurance policy?"

Vladimir wondered whether Belarin would take the risk of trying to kill a prominent American businessman. Perhaps he would if he thought it was absolutely necessary.

"Olen is meeting with you tomorrow," Belarin said, a flat statement of fact. "Perhaps you can raise this issue with him then."

"Fuck you," Vladimir said. "David Olen is a friend. He has nothing to do with your—"

"I am going to be president of Russia," Belarin said. His forehead turned red with anger. "Nothing will stand in my way. Not you with MosElectric, nor David Olen if he decides to share information to damage me."

"You're paranoid, Maxim," Vladimir said slowly, deliberately. "You're also a real prick."

Belarin stood up from the sofa. For a strange instant Vladimir feared he was about to be attacked.

"You have always overestimated yourself," Belarin said, putting on his overcoat. "You think you will always win. But now history is changing. My destiny and Russia's are converging."

"What a sickening thought," Vladimir said, pointedly not rising from his own sofa along with his guest.

Belarin looked down at Vladimir for nearly a full minute and didn't move; his eyes focused somewhere in the air in front of Vladimir's face. Finally Belarin shrugged, shook his head, and started for the door.

"You don't want to be warned; you do not want to hear how to save your own life. There is nothing more for me to say to you."

Vladimir finished his glass of whiskey as he listened to Belarin open the front door and let himself out without another word. He saw his own reflection in the window before him, his regal profile and the sharp cut of his suit. He had the look of a man fifteen years younger, a dynamic man of action and power.

But when he put down his empty glass, he recalled the look in Maxim Belarin's eyes. And his trembling hands dropped the glass onto the wooden floor, where it shattered.

# Part Three

# *The Holy Fist*

# Chapter Fifteen

IKHAIL SERGEIVICH GORBACHEV'S OFFICE was wide and sun-kissed, the windows looking out on a Moscow road that stretched long toward the outskirts of the city. On the walls were pictures of himself with Ronald Reagan, with Margaret Thatcher, with Helmut Kohl. One entire shelf of a bookcase featured a line of pristine copies of his memoirs. *Zhizn I Reformi—Life and Reforms.* He still stung from the reception the two-volume set had received in Russia. Sales had been paltry, public interest minimal. It was as though his countrymen expected Mikhail Gorbachev to silence himself and disappear, his historical moment having come and gone just a decade before but centuries past in the public mind.

Mikhail blew on the steaming cup of tea on his desk and waited until it was cool enough to drink. He took it Russian-style, with berry preserves added for sweetness. It was a cool, quiet morning; the day's business at his institute was yet to commence. He liked the institute, and he admired the vigor and spirit of the young people who had come to work with him. But in private moments such as this one, his mind wandered. He held no office now, wielded no real power for the first time since he was a young man. The events that made this come to pass were as vivid in his mind as the moment they occurred—time failed to blur their edges or to obscure their shapes into comfortable, half-remembered dreams.

The slide downward had come in 1991. First the ridiculous coup, from which Mikhail Sergeivich had to be rescued. Then the Ukrainian referendum in favor of independence from Moscow, a stinging loss. Less than a month later, a vote was taken among leaders of several Soviet Republics, and the Soviet Union was reduced to history. Mikhail was left adrift, without purpose. It wasn't as though he had seen it coming. After the failed coup, he had returned to Moscow and was humiliated by Yeltsin in front of the world. He had heard that Yeltsin was drunk during the meetings to eliminate the Soviet state, that his head was resting on the table and that from time to time he would snore.

This is the way in which the first and the last president of the Soviet Union, Mikhail Sergeivich, was stripped of his power. After his lifetime spent pursuing a single goal: to reform the state, to make the great ideals of Marxism come to life in a Soviet society cleansed of corruption and inequity.

Since he lost office, there had been stories in the disreputable corners of the press, rumors designed to humiliate Mikhail Sergeivich even further. Pernicious lies—that he had stolen money while in office and hidden it away in the West. That in a plot with the Americans, he had ruined Russia on purpose. Then a pop singer, a degenerate, had tricked Mikhail's mother into selling her house in Privolnoye; the bastard then ran to the press saying that Mikhail Sergeivich had abandoned his own mother, that he was a terrible person. Mikhail had been forced to beg the son of a bitch to sell the house back so that his sick mother would again have a place to live.

If he had stolen money, then why the hell would he have cared? He could have sent his mother to a spa in Switzerland. But Mikhail Sergeivich didn't have much money; he had never profited from his post, nor he had ever taken anything that didn't belong to him. But now few wanted to listen, and fewer still cared.

There was a stack of Moscow newspapers in Mikhail's desk. So many had come and gone since the communist state collapsed, along with the press controls that Mikhail had tried to mitigate. Today all the headlines were about Maxim Belarin, how his populist nationalism had propelled him from a little-known Duma member to a viable national candidate in a matter of weeks. Some of the papers said Belarin was a villain, an old-guard KGB *apparatchik* who would do nothing but solidify the corruption and stagnation that had gripped the Russian state and economy. Others described him in terms of heavy praise, calling him a man of vision and action, just the sort of leader wounded Mother Russia needed to regain her glory and stature.

Mikhail pushed the papers away and sipped his tea. Outside the winter sun was low on the horizon and struggled to shine through a sparse gathering of gray clouds.

*Maxim Belarin.* Mikhail knew him well, and he had never trusted him. When Mikhail was in the Politburo, then General Secretary, he had approved several of Belarin's promotions within the KGB hierarchy. He hadn't done it because he liked Belarin—in fact, he felt a deep distrust for the man from the moment he met him. Rather, he had sponsored Belarin's career at the request of Vladimir Borchenko, who said that Belarin had become an integral domestic player in their cabal and as a result was owed favors.

Mikhail hadn't come to rule the Soviet empire without dirty hands. He had made many deals; he had crushed his opposition when such action was necessary. But there was a darkness about Belarin, a core of violence and dispassionate ruthlessness that became apparent to anyone who was in his presence for more than a few minutes. He disturbed Mikhail Sergeivich and, moreover, Mikhail knew that Belarin had committed acts on his behalf that might have been immoral and wrong. As the KGB wing of their alliance, Belarin did dirty work on behalf of Mikhail, as well as Vladimir Borchenko.

Borchenko, typically, had shielded Mikhail from knowing precisely what these acts might have been. Even when he was ruling the largest country in the world, Mikhail had to accept that Vladimir Borchenko kept certain secrets from him. It had always been that way, ever since their plan emerged from pipe-dream conversations at Moscow University. In many ways their relationship never changed since those days, no matter how powerful they became or how much their actions shaped the world's destiny. In a sense, the shrewd diplomat's son was always more savvy than the country boy who ruled an empire and watched helplessly as it vanished.

*1950.*
*Moscow.*

ALL THE WAY FROM THE COUNTRYSIDE into the city, Mikhail Sergeivich gathered together his courage and confidence like a stash of treasure he kept deep inside himself. He had been a hard worker and an enthusiastic communist in Stavropol; he had distinguished himself and caught the eye of Oleg Karlov, a regional party secretary who had taken it upon himself to tutor young Mikhail in the ways of the Party and what was expected of its elite. Mikhail had been thrilled and flattered by Karlov's attentions and had heard that Karlov was associated with the NKVD and might one day hold a high post in Moscow. With a rich sense of excitement, Mikhail sensed that he had taken his tentative first steps into the sphere of the Party's influential circles. His acceptance into Moscow State University—unusual for a young man from his region—only deepened his sense of expectation.

On Mikhail Gorbachev's first day in Moscow, he hired a cab for ten kopecks from the Kievskaya Station. He gave an address to the driver and pressed his face to the car window. He marveled at the architecture of the city: the grand Stalinist architecture of the government buildings, the apartment blocks, the monuments to Russia's achievements in the Great War. He looked up startled when the cab came to a rough stop and realized that they had arrived at his destination.

Mikhail had fantasized that his dormitory would be a modern building, with landscaped lawns and trees, just like the pictures he had seen in newspapers and magazines. What he saw instead was a squat four-story concrete building tucked into a winding street. Its facade was dirty and worn away, making it look like a decrepit old hulk of a factory or warehouse rather than the home of the next generation of Soviet intellectuals.

Windows stared down at him like intrusive eyes. Metal doors opened to concrete landings, each covered with canopies of rusted sheet metal. Three young men were gathered in the nearest doorway and were staring at him. Mikhail was overcome with a feeling of self-consciousness, the knowledge that his clothes were plain and rough, his manner shy and provincial.

The driver went around to the back of the car and untied the trunk, which had been secured with a length of rope and was full of jars of preserves his mother had prepared for him. He wrestled out Mikhail's heavy trunk and let it drop to the pavement and let the canvas bag fall as well. Mikhail gave him a small handful of coins.

The driver counted them and looked up. "Two more," he said.

"But you—"

"Hauling luggage is extra."

Mikhail gave the driver the money, already worried about how long his meager supply of cash would last, and watched the car speed away. He hoisted the trunk onto his shoulder with a grunt, pulled up his other bag in his free hand, and walked slowly up the walk to the dormitory. He kept his eyes cast down to the crumbling cement and the weeds poking through. He felt the eyes of the three young men on him, their laconic curiosity.

Mikhail's father had always told him that a sense of humor won friends. So when he reached the final turn in the path, he cut a crisp ninety-degree turn in the military manner he had learned in Young Pioneer drills. He pivoted on one foot and kicked the other out in an exaggerated, comical manner. He hoped his small joke, a gentle parody of the martial training they'd all endured as Soviet youth, would ingratiate him with his new classmates.

Of the three men watching, only one responded. It was the tallest, the one in the dark overcoat. He threw back his head and laughed out loud, having apparently enjoyed Mikhail's little *shutka*. When Mikhail reached them, the tall young man stepped forward.

"Where did they find you?" he asked.

Mikhail could tell from the stranger's gentle, humorous tone that he meant no harm.

"A small village in the Stavropol area called Privolnoye," Mikhail said. "The land of early spring. How about you?"

The young man grinned, exposing his straight white teeth. His dark hair was rather long and uncombed, though it was clean. Beneath his overcoat he wore a bright-blue cotton shirt. His clothes fit well and looked new, almost as though they hadn't come from Soviet shops.

"I am from Moscow," the young man said. He reached into his pocket and produced a pack of cigarettes, knocked one out, and extending it to Mikhail, who shook his head. "But I have also traveled to various places."

Already Mikhail felt intimidated, though deeply fascinated. He fixed a good-natured grin on his face. "Various places," he repeated. "Anyplace I've heard of?"

"Prague, Warsaw," the young man said, lighting his cigarette with a show of nonchalance. "Vienna. Bucharest."

Mikhail simply stared at the young man and listened to this litany of exotic places. He had never met such a person before, so poised and sure of himself, even though he seemed to be the same age as Mikhail.

"My father is a diplomat. I get to travel." He shrugged, as though it was no big deal, then held out his hand. "The name is Vladimir Borchenko. Ignore these other two idiots who don't even have the common manners to make a newcomer feel at home."

Vladimir had an unusual face. His eyes were almost too wide, and his nose was asymmetrical at the end. But his overall impression was deeply sophisticated and refined, handsome in a distinctive way. His eyes sparkled with a ready reserve of ironic humor. Although Mikhail felt like a country bumpkin in Vladimir's urbane presence, Borchenko seemed genuinely interested in making friends.

Vladimir bent over to pick up Mikhail's smaller piece of luggage, an old bag held together with fraying leather straps.

"Let's find your room and get you settled," he said in a tone that indicated he was used to taking command. Vladimir led Mikhail up a flight of stairs, down another long hallway, then dropped Mikhail's bag in front of a door.

"Welcome to your home for the next four years," Vladimir said, gesturing grandly as he opened the door.

It was a large room by Stavropol standards. A small kitchen alcove, a couple of desks. The place was cluttered with chairs, books, clothes, bottles, papers, ashtrays. Mikhail put down his trunk into a small open space between a desk and a cot wedged against the wall.

He looked around, letting his mind grow used to the fact that this was now his home. There were electric light fixtures, hot-and-cold-water taps in the kitchen area. The paint was peeling from the walls, and the room was dirty, but it was luxurious by country standards.

Vladimir stood with his hands folded, his expression grave. "There is something important you must know."

Mikhail sensed his new friend might be joking, but he couldn't be sure. "What?" he asked.

"Come with me," Vladimir said, leaving the room.

Mikhail followed Vladimir down the hall, through a swinging door into a big tiled room that was even danker and mustier than the rest of the building. Little cubicles with wooden doors lined one wall. On the opposite side were wash basins, each with its own water tap. The shower area was in the corner and was separated from the rest of the room by flimsy, mildewed canvas curtains.

"This is crucial to your life in the city," Vladimir said. His expression was stone serious as he opened the wooden door to one of the cubicles. Inside was a toilet.

"We get people from the provinces who don't know what these are," Vladimir explained. "Now, listen. Don't be proud. Do you know what to do with this?"

Mikhail looked at the toilet, at the porcelain bowl filled with water, the long chain one pulled to flush it. For a moment he felt a confusing flush of anger mixed with shame. Vladimir took Mikhail for a country hick, a peasant who had never seen a flush toilet before. But then he looked up at Vladimir, who was barely restraining himself from laughing. Both young men began to laugh together, at Vladimir's joke and at Mikhail's earnest initial reaction to it.

"Look, I'll prove it," Mikhail said. He grabbed the chain, pulled it. A loud sound echoed in the room as water drained from the bowl.

Vladimir punched him lightly on the shoulder and continued to chuckle. "It's good to see you can take a joke, country boy," he said.

"Well, we live in the real world in Privolnoye," Mikhail offered. "You'd be surprised what filters down from the big cities."

Vladimir smiled at Mikhail's sarcastic tone. "Do tell," he said.

Mikhail fumbled for the right words. "I've worked hard to get here," he said. "And during holidays from class, I'll return home to work the combines and till the fields. I think people like us, young people with energy, can improve our society. We can . . ."

Mikhail fumbled, embarrassed. "Go on," Vladimir urged him expectantly.

"We can achieve the socialist ideals of our country," Mikhail said. He looked up into Vladimir's eyes and wondered whether the sophisticated diplomat's son would understand what he was saying or dismiss it as naiveté. "We can reach true justice through socialism. Just as we have been taught."

Vladimir laughed softly, his expression unreadable. "I have to go," he said. "I'll see you around the dormitory and on campus. Try not to embarrass yourself, country boy."

Mikhail heard Vladimir laughing softly to himself as he left. Life at the university was obviously going to be difficult, with many mysteries to unravel. And he sensed that Vladimir Borchenko would help him through.


*1953.*
**Moscow.**

THREE YEARS LATER, STALIN DIED after thirty years as General Secretary of the Soviet Union. Life at Moscow State University had been, for Mikhail Sergeivich Gorbachev, both intellectually invigorating and deeply disillusioning. He had become a Komsomol leader and started his law studies, although the influence of the NKVD intelligence service was everywhere, and words had to be chosen carefully even between friends. One exception was Vladimir, to whom Mikhail had grown closer.

Vladimir had connections to the underworld and ran a black-market business along with, Mikhail suspected, his diplomat father. Vladimir always had available cigarettes, liquor, fresh fruit, clothing. There had been whispers that interested parties could even obtain weapons from Borchenko, for the proper price. He was doing business with Chechens, a mercenary people of the Caucuses who ran elaborate supply networks in spite of—or perhaps alongside—Soviet military and civil police. Vladimir knew he was under NKVD surveillance, but he was protected by his father's status and was able to stay a step ahead of their agents and avoid being caught with contraband.

Vladimir had even managed to expand his operations beyond the confines of the University. In some quarters he became known as "Vladimir the fixer." If you wanted better phone service, Borchenko could help you. If you wanted a toaster that wouldn't burn down your apartment, Borchenko could make arrangements.

Mikhail Gorbachev was prominent in the Komsomol, and his patron Oleg Karlov had been promoted to a civil-intelligence post in Moscow. Mikhail sensed that he was poised to begin a successful career in the Party, and Vladimir agreed—and made sure never to involve Mikhail in his black-market business.

In private moments, Mikhail wondered where his career would lead him. He was acutely aware of the atmosphere of careerism and paranoia wrought by Stalin's regime. Other students in his law class were interested only in saying the right thing and finding the right factions with which to ally themselves. Socialist ideas were given lip service, but Soviet society had deteriorated to the point at which each person had become a Party of one, looking out only for his own interests in a cutthroat system rife with labor camps for "ideological undesirables" and psychiatric hospitals for "counterrevolutionaries."

The death of Stalin left the nation in a state of paralysis. Their leader had created a cult of personality around himself, a sense that he personified the USSR and that it existed only in concert with his own edicts. Immediately a sense of uncertainty and fear gripped the students; Mikhail even had to break up a dispute in his study group when one student accused the other of harboring anti-socialist ideas. It was as though Stalin's passing would, for a time, intensify the paranoiac mindset of the Russian people. Mikhail had gone to the library to be alone with his thoughts when, almost immediately, he felt a tap on his shoulder.

He turned around and looked up from his chair. "Vladimir."

"I haven't seen you in a couple weeks," Vladimir replied. "And I haven't been reading the papers. Has anything happened in the USSR that I should know about?"

Mikhail said nothing; instead, he looked around to see if anyone was listening. Leave it to Vladimir to joke about Stalin's death in public. At times his taste for living on the edge of propriety and good sense bordered on the irritating.

"Come on, walk with me," Vladimir said, nodding toward the door. "It's been too long."

Mikhail stood up, gathered his books, and looked across the study table at Arkady Okorokov, a fellow law student who was rumored to be a NKVD informant. The hell with it, Mikhail thought, if he was not allowed to talk with his friends, then he might as well not be alive.

Outside they turned down Gertsana Street. The few streetlights illumined the grime left by a recent thaw. Shop windows were streaked with dirt; the stores were closed for the day and empty of goods. Mikhail pulled his satchel of books over his shoulder.

"You have the look of a man deep in thought," Vladimir said as they walked. "Stalin's death has upset you?"

An unspoken understanding existed between the two friends. Vladimir was a pragmatist and a cynic. He would have worked on the margins of whatever system he might have lived in, manipulated it for his own gain. Mikhail, on the other hand, was a true believer. He was a student of Marx and a socialist idealist. Each appreciated the other as a sort of curiosity, almost as philosophical mirror images.

"Not Stalin's death," Mikhail said.

Vladimir lit a cigarette and looked at his friend with curiosity. "What, then?" he asked. "Is it Raisa? Is your girlfriend giving you trouble?"

"She's not my—" Mikhail said then stopped himself. Vladimir was ribbing him again, knowing that Mikhail was in love with a young girl at the university.

"Tell me," Vladimir said as they paused at a corner to let a trolley pass by.

"What would you say if I told you I was dreaming of the future?" Mikhail asked his friend.

"I would say you are like everyone else in the Soviet Union," Vladimir replied with a clipped laugh. "From the Politburo to that old lady sweeping the sidewalk."

They turned onto a side street where there was little traffic and no one could hear them talking.

"It is disgusting, the way this country is being run," Mikhail said softly.

"How do you mean?" Vladimir asked.

"Look around you. Our lives are full of corruption. Students informing on each other. This is not what Lenin intended."

Vladimir looked as though he was about to make a joke then stopped himself. He nodded instead.

"You should hear some of my father's stories," he said. "The camps, the disappearance of Stalin's rivals. I suppose I didn't realize you were harboring such thoughts."

"We don't speak enough these days," Mikhail said wistfully. "You think I walk in lockstep with the Party line. But I have my own mind."

"I don't underestimate you," Vladimir said.

Mikhail nodded, warmed by his friend's implicit compliment. Whatever their differences, they had always been able to talk about ideas. Mikhail had always respected the restless energy of Vladimir's ideas, the iconoclastic quality of his personality.

"What happened to communism?" Mikhail asked rhetorically. "It

212

was never meant to be a two-class system, with the Party officials enjoying special privileges and everyone else living in uncertain poverty."

Vladimir thought for a moment then said: "I agree. Differences between people are natural. But this system is based on patronage and corruption. I have benefited from it in my own life, but that does not make it correct."

They arrived at a small park, a patch of grass where two streets met at an odd angle. There was a fountain there, a couple of trees, some wooden benches. Mikhail sat down facing the fountain; Vladimir joined him and took an orange from his pocket, peeled it slowly, and placed the peel in a little stack between them.

"Look at that fountain," Mikhail said. "It's falling apart. Like our university. We have new buildings, but you know as well as I that they'll be falling apart in a couple of years. The walls will be crumbling; the lights will stop working."

Vladimir laughed softly as he handed half the orange to Mikhail. Such things were spoken about only in private, between trusted friends.

"Something is wrong with this system," Mikhail said, his voice grave, as though the sound of his own words shocked him. "The problem is deep, Vladimir. And it has to be corrected."

"Are you proposing another revolution?" Vladimir asked.

Mikhail bit into the orange, his taste buds coming to life with the tart sweetness of the fruit, its cool juice. He was only able to taste such good food because of his friend in the black market, he reminded himself.

"I am talking about changing things from within," he said. "Father Stalin's death has made me start to think. What is necessary is to reach a position of leadership. That is the only way things are done in our country. Orders are passed from the top down."

"That's all?" Vladimir asked, his eyes wide. "Just get a top Party position? Is it so easy? Remember Stalin—he got on top only after a bloodbath. That's the way the system works. That's what's going to happen now."

"It can be done," Mikhail said, looking into Vladimir's eyes. "It is a system; it can be mastered. As long as you believe that the end justifies the means. The system can be corrected from within; I am sure of it. I am willing to devote my life to it."

Vladimir swept up the orange peel, wrapped it in a handkerchief, and put it in his pocket. He was always fastidious about not leaving evidence of his contraband.

"That is a nice thought," he said to Mikhail. "But you should talk to my father. He *knows* the system. It's all rigged. Those at the top stay there until they die."

Vladimir shook his head and took out a pack of cigarettes. He lit one, not bothering to offer one to Mikhail after being refused countless times.

"Give me one of those." Mikhail nodded at the pack.

Vladimir, eyes wide with surprise, handed one over and lit it. "You must be upset," he said. "I've never seen you smoke before."

Mikhail took a puff and started to cough. He held the smoke down, though, and exhaled slowly. Never before had he felt so serious. Never before had he dared voice what he would say next.

"What if . . ." He paused, his voice fading into the rumbling of a big army truck shifting gears as it passed. "Oh, damn. I must be going crazy."

"All of Russia is insane," Vladimir said. "With the possible exception of you, Mikhail Sergeivich. What is on your mind?"

"I have an idea that I can't get out of my mind," Mikhail said. He got up from the bench. "Come on, let's walk. I want you to listen to what I've been thinking about."

Vladimir got up, pulled his collar tighter around his neck against the cool breeze. They walked back down Leningradsky Prospect.

"I know that I could change things if I was in the right position," Mikhail said to Vladimir, speaking fast in case he lost his nerve. "I could make this system function for the proletariat, for the honest worker. There is nothing wrong with socialism; it just needs reforming. I could loosen the grip of this damned police state we've all gotten used to."

Mikhail held his breath for a moment, unable to believe he had spoken such a radical notion. He was almost frightened to look at Vladimir and feared that he might have misjudged his friend. Such sentiments, reported to the NKVD, could ruin Mikhail's career.

"I . . . I understand," Vladimir said simply. As though reading his friend's mind, he reached out and put his arm around Mikhail's shoulder as a gesture of friendship and trust.

"So many changes need to be made," Mikhail whispered. "Take agriculture. The peasants on the farms need more input. I have seen this firsthand. And this repression of ideas . . . it is criminal. The intellectuals are being corrupted into cowardly yes-men."

Again Mikhail paused. He knew he could be labeled a counter-revolutionary for expressing these views. He might have been considered a dissident, thrown into prison. But didn't this prove his point? He felt like nothing more than a patriotic Soviet citizen, acutely concerned with the future of the USSR.

"What about the black market?" Vladimir asked with wide eyes.

Mikhail fought to keep a straight face. "Those who engage in the black market, we cut off their pricks and export them to China as aphrodisiacs."

Both men laughed hard together, the tension of the moment relieved. But when they stopped laughing, their eyes met. Suddenly each young man realized that the other had been very serious, that somehow their conversation had been more than idle dreaming. They started walking again in the direction of the university, each smoking a fresh cigarette.

"Maybe we could take steps," Vladimir said vaguely as they crossed a street.

"What?" Mikhail asked.

"Take steps," Vladimir said. "I have influence and connections, through my father. You said the ends justified the means, didn't you?"

Mikhail said nothing for almost a full minute, listening to the rhythm of their footsteps against the pavement.

"Tell me something," he finally said. "You have heard me out. But what is your interest, Vladimir? You are not an idealist. Pardon me if I am wrong, but you are not even much of a socialist."

Vladimir laughed, a loud, rich sound. He looked up at the sky as they walked, as though divining new constellations there.

"I will tell you the truth," he said. "What is good for the people is good for me."

"I don't follow," Mikhail replied.

"That is because you are a theorist while I am a pragmatist," Vladimir said. "Think about it. If the system were changed, if the people were granted small freedoms they don't enjoy now, who will they turn to?"

Mikhail didn't answer; he glanced over at Vladimir, at his striking profile in the moonlight. They were talking about an alliance, he realized. And for the first time he contemplated what compromises such a joining of forces might entail.

"Who?" Mikhail asked.

"Me. Of course." Vladimir smiled. "What's good for the people is good for the black market. You see a more just society. I see a country where I could do more business. Is there any reason why these two viewpoints are mutually exclusive?"

Mikhail thought hard, trying to fathom the full dimension of what Vladimir was suggesting. Vladimir sounded like a capitalist. Yet he was a trusted friend, a good ally, a man who had just the sort of craft and savvy that Mikhail needed to reach his goals.

"Perhaps not," Mikhail said softly.

Vladimir turned his head. "Already you sound like a politician. I always knew you were talented, Mikhail Sergeivich. Now all these things you say to me have got me thinking."

They had almost reached their dormitory. Other students were coming and going or milling in small groups and were still in a state of shock over Stalin's dying. Vladimir put his hand on Mikhail's shoulder to stop him.

"It takes courage to say the things you do," he said, his voice barely higher than a whisper. "But it will take a lot more courage in the future to turn your talk into action."

Mikhail took a deep breath. He felt drained inside, like he had just run ten kilometers.

"I know," he said.

"Good," Vladimir replied, apparently satisfied in his own mind. "Because I have a few ideas of my own."

## 1955.
### Moscow.

TWO YEARS LATER both young men were ready to turn idle talk into concrete reality. They walked together to the Lenin Hills to see the new University Building. It was built on a bluff overlooking the city, its square tower and ornate Stalinist architecture rising majestically toward the sky. The government claimed it was the largest and most impressive university building in the world—a testament to the success of Soviet socialism.

Mikhail Sergeivich had just returned to Moscow after several weeks in his village helping with the harvest. He was robust and tan, full of energy after longs days of honest work. Mikhail had chosen this spot to talk with Vladimir, in the shadow of the soaring monument to Soviet strength and education. They strode down a long walkway lined with busts of great Soviet scientists, thinkers, revolutionaries: Tsiolkovsky, Timiryasyev, Mendeleev. The walkway led to

217

a new road being cut through the Lenin Hills, where expensive dachas and embassy buildings were being constructed—a new enclave for the rich and powerful in a society ostensibly dedicated to equality and workers' power.

"I assume that you have been thinking over the summer holiday," Vladimir said. "You have that look."

"I saw a lot this summer," Mikhail replied. He spoke slowly, searching for the perfect words. "People in Moscow, they don't realize how things have gone wrong. The system cannot continue the way it is. There will be food shortages, crops will fail—and the government will have to become more repressive simply to maintain order."

"And we can change this?" Vladimir asked, his tone neutral.

"You think I am crazy," Mikhail said.

Vladimir shrugged. "I am not one to look down on a trusted friend because he has crazy thoughts."

Mikhail contemplated the city below. Some of the birch trees along the river were already showing yellow autumn leaves.

"We have been thinking small," Mikhail said. "We think only of the Soviet Union. We must expand our thinking."

Vladimir nodded. "I am listening."

"We need help," Mikhail said. There were other students all around, taking in the sun. He spoke softly, careful not to be heard. "The KGB protects the status quo, along with the military. Their power means we cannot succeed without outside assistance."

Vladimir puffed on a cigarette and looked down at the ground. He wore a Harris tweed sport coat over a black wide-collared shirt. Mikhail thought he looked like an American capitalist from a Communist Party propaganda poster.

"Where do we get help?" Mikhail asked. "Our system has too much built-in security."

Vladimir nodded impatiently. "You have an answer."

"Something happened this summer," Mikhail said, growing

excited. "One day the tractor I was driving wasn't running well. I figured the fuel pump was the problem, so I went to the maintenance shed and got a new one. As I was carrying it across the field, I looked down at the box it came in. It turned out it was manufactured in Poland. That's when it hit me—Poland. I stopped right there in the middle of the field, Vladimir."

"Go on," Vladimir said.

"Poland has been kicked around Europe for centuries," Mikhail said. He sensed he had his friend's attention. "And now it is under the rule of the Soviet Union. That is when I had my idea."

They stopped walking. Vladimir lit another cigarette.

"We have to look to the West," Mikhail explained. "To Poland. Its population is close to forty million."

"Keep your voice down," Vladimir said, looking around. "All right. Tell me. What does Poland have, besides fuel pumps and forty million people?"

"Catholics," Mikhail whispered. "Think about it. Who else has money, a system of communications and influence that transcends national boundaries, and a hierarchy that is, in its own way, as authoritarian as the Soviet Union's?"

"The Vatican." Vladimir frowned. "I see where you're going. But how in hell can you hope to influence the Vatican in any way—and what could the Vatican do for us here in the Soviet Union?"

"The Church controlled more than a hundred million Catholics in Central and Eastern Europe before the war," Mikhail explained. "Wouldn't the Vatican be interested in a plan that would return those millions back to the influence of the Church?"

Vladimir shrugged. "And how are you are going to do this?"

"If I am one day in a position to do so, I could simply let it happen," Mikhail said. "But I need support to help me one day reach the Politburo."

Deep in thought, Vladimir looked at the burning end of his cigarette.

"I have been doing some research at the library," Mikhail continued. "You have probably read about the Polish Cardinal Litwinski. He resisted the Nazis during the War. Now he is staunchly anti-Soviet."

"Of course," Vladimir said. "My father talks about him all the time. He is a troublemaker."

"Why is he a troublemaker?" Mikhail asked.

"Because he causes the *apparatchiks* and people like my father to lose sleep."

"Because he tells the Poles things no one else dares to say," Mikhail corrected. "He reminds them that they are living under the subjugation of the Soviet Union and the Communist system. Cardinal Litwinski sees room for reforming that system. And so do we. Do you follow?"

Vladimir was peering down river, where they could see the monuments of the Kremlin glittering in the sun.

"You're not saying this Litwinski can—" Vladimir began.

"Now you're thinking," Mikhail said. "We could get to the Vatican through someone such as Litwinski."

"He is a Catholic cardinal," Vladimir said. "We are Soviet citizens. How do we reach him?"

"Imagine that the Church is as political as the Politburo," Mikhail suggested. "There must be priests within the cardinal's circle who agree with his views. If we gain their ear, they lead us to the cardinal. That's where you come in."

"Me?" Vladimir asked.

"Your father is the COMECON attaché to Poland," Mikhail said, smiling. "You see, everything is falling into place for us. You could travel to Poland without arousing suspicion. You could get an audience with Litwinski."

Vladimir's already-pale face blanched further. "I understand," he said.

"I have thought about it from all sides," Mikhail added. "Think about a Soviet Union where the people would be free to buy all the goods they desired. You would do well, Vladimir."

Vladimir smiled and clapped his friend on the shoulder. "Believe me, Mikhail," he said, "I have already thought of that."

"Then you will talk to your father?"

"What should I tell him?" Vladimir asked.

Mikhail thought for a moment. "Tell him you have a vision of greater business opportunities. He will understand that."

Vladimir paused, looked around. It was as though he saw the world through new eyes, viewed the shape of the way things might be. Mikhail Gorbachev had come up with a brilliant idea, a scheme from which the Soviet Union, the Vatican, Poland, and other Central and Eastern European countries could all benefit. But was it really possible to implement it? All Vladimir knew was he wanted to be a part of this, to help make it happen.

"I will talk to him," he said. "I will see what can be done."

*February 19, 1998. 8:05 a.m.*
*Moscow.*

MIKHAIL SERGEIVICH GORBACHEV finished his cup of tea. In the office outside his door, he heard the sound of young people talking. The staff of his institute had arrived and was planning the events of the day.

He hadn't spoken with Vladimir Borchenko in almost a year. There was almost no need. So much had passed between them that idle conversation had gradually become almost impossible. And now that Vladimir was occupied with his financial empire while Mikhail provided a lone voice in the wilderness of post-Soviet Russia, there was little left between them to say.

For every idea that Mikhail had had, he and Vladimir had formed a plan. From Mikhail's first moment of insight came pragmatic possibilities. Mikhail had recognized that much Soviet corruption came

221

from the maintenance of the empire in Central Europe; he also saw that the millions of people living there under military occupation would one day become the key to the Soviet Union's future.

As soon as Mikhail had spoken these thoughts, Vladimir had started planning. He traveled often to Poland along with his diplomat father, and soon he came into contact with the Polish Cardinal Litwinski, a spirited dissenter against Soviet occupation who was indulged by the Polish puppet government only because of his popularity among the Poles. Vladimir had approached Litwinski delicately, with a cover story that he wished to speak with the cardinal to learn more about the grass-roots Polish citizenry; Vladimir was being groomed by his father for a position in COMECON, and he played the part of the eager son hungry for information. Vladimir was granted a brief interview with Litwinski, who seemed wary and suspicious and who abruptly ended the conversation after little more than fifteen minutes.

Vladimir accompanied his father to a COMECON symposium in 1955. It was there that Vladimir greeted Litwinski, who seemed warmer than the first time they met, and was introduced to Wojtyla, a driven and charismatic young priest who looked ahead into a future in which Poland's millions of Catholics would be free of Soviet atheism.

After a series of increasingly confidential talks during the coming months—and much convincing on Vladimir's part that he and Mikhail were very serious and weren't part of a KGB trap—a deal was made. Vladimir outlined the concepts he and Mikhail Gorbachev had developed and watched Litwinski and Wojtyla grow increasingly interested and excited. Litwinski agreed to use his sway with the Vatican to arrange to move money into the Soviet Union to support Mikhail Sergeivich Gorbachev's ambitions of power. Litwinski subsequently used his considerable powers of persuasion and motivation to organize the cabal in the Vatican that came to be called the Holy Fist. It was composed of a select few like-minded cardinals and bishops, as well as Cardinal Daniel O'Brien of Chicago—who became a prime source of cash and influence to fund the conspiracy.

In return, Mikhail would gain political influence toward a goal of lessening the Soviet Union's hold on Poland and eventually removing Russian control of the nation. It was a simple plan, and neither side could have conceived how complicated their conspiracy would one day become. In private, Vladimir and Mikhail Gorbachev observed an almost superstitious silence on the topic of whether they would succeed or fail. They knew their goals, if they came to pass, would change the world forever, a reality almost too vast and portentous to contemplate.

Neither side knew what the future might bring. It was an alliance of unlikely partners with different goals that somehow intersected perfectly throughout the '60s and '70s. No one could have predicted how well their cabal would succeed, that Wojtyla would one day become pope and that Mikhail Sergeivich would one day rise to the Politburo and then to the position of General Secretary. These developments came later, and the opportunities were seized as they appeared.

---

IN 1978 KAROL WOJTYLA became pope. His alliance with so-called anti-communist factions helped propel his rise. Few understood that his greatest ally was Mikhail Gorbachev in the Soviet Union, a staunch Communist whose primary concern was reforming his own country's stagnating political system.

Martial law was declared in Poland in 1981 because of the Solidarity uprisings. The world saw this as the Soviet Empire flexing its muscle once again. But there was a difference: This time there were no tanks, as there had been in Czechoslovakia and Hungary. Mikhail Gorbachev was at the center of this decision and was pushing for leniency. His policy had been based on more than living up to his end of the deal; it was a matter of conscience, of reforming the military excesses of the Soviet state.

Mikhail Sergeivich took a deep breath, let it out again. His body was tired, but his spirit was as strong as ever. When he remembered the past, and all that he had accomplished, for a moment he became again that young man at Moscow State University.

He looked down at the newspaper. Maxim Belarin was on the front page, pictured at a controlled rally of supporters.

Belarin had been like a cancer on something good and just. Vladimir had often called him a necessary evil. Mikhail had always wondered if this were true.

He stood up from his desk and straightened his tie. It was time to greet his staff for the day, try to fill them with the same spirit of optimism and reform that had guided his own life. They would never know his secret past, the deals he had made to steer history in the direction he thought it should go.

Perhaps it was for the best. He doubted they would understand. In his quest for reform, he had let the nation implode into fragments barely recognizable as the once-proud Soviet Union. Russia had been taken over by opportunists and gangsters, men who drained the country's wealth and stashed it in secret Swiss bank accounts. Men like his old friend Vladimir Borchenko.

It took a lifetime to understand Borchenko. It would take nearly as long to explain why a madman such as Maxim Belarin had been allowed to take part in the noble project that had started one evening at Moscow State in 1953. Compromises had been made; deals entered into that would be difficult for the uninitiated to comprehend.

Such were the secret pains endured by those who changed history.

# Chapter Sixteen

*February 19, 1998. 9:34 a.m.*
*Moscow.*

A CAR WAS WAITING FOR DAVID AND JASON outside the hectic chaos of Moscow's Sheremetyevo Airport; Olen Europe's Moscow driver, Pyotr, was waiting close to his Mercedes sedan and waved his arms in the air as David stepped out of the terminal. Pyotr was a short, thin, balding man in a faded leather bomber jacket. He cursed under his breath in Russian as he maneuvered through the heavy traffic in the direction of the city center.

David glanced at his watch. It was almost ten in the morning, about one a.m. in Washington. David might have had time to try Carl Becker again after checking in to the Hotel Metropol, to finish their conversation, but he thought better of it. Instead he would wait until it was a more reasonable hour in the States—and until he had spoken with Vladimir Borchenko.

David breathed heavily, trying to shake off the lethargy that always infected him after plane travel. He shook his head as he thought about what Carl had told him. Somewhere out there was a young, callow, apparently extremely ambitious CIA agent who wanted to resurrect some aspect of the international cabal in which David had been involved. The very idea made David want to laugh or cry out in anger—maybe both. So much had happened in the '70s and '80s: A Soviet General Secretary had come to power. A pope had been elected. An empire had fallen. It had all involved a delicate balance between factions that, on the surface, were so ideologically opposed that the world assumed they had nothing to do with one another. It wasn't the kind of arrangement that could be rekindled by an outsider to advance American interests—if that was all that Thomas Gleason had in mind.

"We need to set up a meeting this morning about the MosElectric proposal," Jason said.

David looked up, realized that his mind was everywhere but on his business. He nodded and forced himself to concentrate.

"You're right," David replied. "We need to get our final plan together before we go to the next stage."

"They have a requirement for 70,000 meters," Jason said, ruminating aloud. "Should be no problem."

David let out a burst of appreciative laughter over Jason's wry comment. If Olen Europe were hired to build the MosElectric corporation's new main office, it would be a huge building, a major addition to Moscow, and a major coup for an American company.

"First thing, I have to speak privately with Vladimir," David said.

"You're going to talk to him about GlobusBank trying to acquire the company we want to construct the building for?" Jason asked.

David looked at his young associate, hearing a trace of distrust in his voice. Jason surely thought Vladimir should have informed them that he wanted to purchase MosElectric. But David knew that simply wasn't the way Vladimir worked.

"Among other things," David replied. "Hopefully we can also get together with a couple of his top people and start talking about the financial structure on this thing. We need to pin down GlobusBank on what foreign investors they can get to commit."

It went without saying that Vladimir Borchenko would be a crucial factor in dealing with the politics of both the bid and, if it were successful, the subsequent construction. Doing ground-level business in Russia required an in-depth knowledge of the labyrinth of state and city agencies, laws, and regulations. It also required knowing who to deal with in the government and what they might ask in return. Vladimir and his organization had the necessary contacts and clout to make a large-scale deal happen in Moscow.

"I take it MosElectric's stance hasn't changed any," David said to Jason.

"Not lately," Jason said with a thin smile. "They don't want to put a *kopeck* of their own money into the building. We construct it, and they move into it."

"What's the ownership structure?" David asked.

"They're run by management elected by the workers council," Jason said. "A typical, Russian-style bureaucracy. They're hoping that getting a construction deal for their new headquarters will make them more attractive to investors."

"OK, so let's say we build the thing," David said. "Are we gonna be able to fill it? MosElectric isn't going to occupy all the space, is it?"

"I'm positive we'll fill it," Jason said. "A modern, attractive building with Western amenities in central Moscow? It'll be a score. I think we can fill it at more than the rates we're projecting right now."

David nodded slowly.

"All right," David said. "If we build it, they will come. Now, what's the latest on the financing?"

"We'll get one of the multi-laterals to finance it," Jason replied. "We'll need about forty percent of the project cost in equity; with the way things are in Moscow today, we think we can arrange that with one of the U.S. investment bank's London office."

David continued to nod, letting the proposed deal take shape in his mind like a cloud of vapor condensing into something solid and permanent. It would be a hell of a complicated deal, and he knew better than to bet on it—too many things could go wrong along the way. But the very idea of erecting a large-scale commercial property right in the heart of Moscow, an American-style tower done right, was enough to make David's heart beat a little faster.

He looked up. Jason was smiling at him.

"You're getting deal fever, aren't you?" he asked.

David smiled.

Pyotr was driving fast, weaving through traffic on a road leading into the city that had been built wide in order to move military equipment. David had heard that the roads were wide enough to take off and land airplanes. To either side were rows of ten-story crumbling concrete apartment buildings and plowed dirty snow piled high. It was a cold morning, though the sky was an azure blue and the weak wintertime sun cast long shadows.

"I assume you're going to talk to Borchenko about Sokolov," Jason said, looking out the window, his tone almost studied in its casualness.

"I plan to mention it," David replied.

The truth was, with all that was happening, David hadn't been thinking much about Alexei Sokolov. It depressed him for a heavy moment as he realized how quickly the banker had slipped from his memory.

David looked out the window at the traffic all around. It was mid-morning, but still the congestion was as bad as any city in Western Europe. There were the old Russian cars, and the Soviet-era trucks trailing black smoke. There were more and more European and Japanese cars every time he visited. A burst of motion caught David's eye, and he looked out the side window. Three BMWs with tinted windows were led by a Chevy Suburban and trailed by a Jeep Wagoneer, and were moving through the traffic as though it was standing still. They stuck close together in a sort of high-speed convoy. David wondered which Moscow gangster or oligarch was riding in the back seat of the middle car.

"What else are you talking to Borchenko about?" Jason asked, his eyes also locked onto the BMWs.

"Old business . . . things between the two of us," David replied carefully. "Look," David sighed. "I know what you're thinking."

"I'm not thinking anything," Jason said. He reflexively opened and snapped shut his briefcase. "Really. I understand there are things that predate my time with the company. Don't worry about it."

David sensed his young colleague's psychological defenses rising, a barrier that was impossible to break through once in place. Part of the reason David had succeeded in business was because he was able to intuitively understand people, what drove them, what they wanted, and what they would do to get it.

"It's not easy," David said, choosing his words carefully. "But look, after this trip . . ."

David probably knew Jason better than Jason's own family. David had met Jason's parents a few times, both of whom were still alive. His father was a retired bank officer, his mother a professor at Northwestern who still had an office though she rarely taught classes. Meeting the two of them had given David a lot of insight into Jason's character. He had grown up in an upper-middle-class family, the oldest of three children who had all grown up to be successful and prosperous. Yet there seemed to be no strong bond or connection in the family, no outward signs of closeness. Jason was smart, funny, ambitious, good-looking—but in a sense it was all on the surface. Underneath, he was out of touch with his feelings. As soon as a situation became difficult, he tended to retreat into moody silence. He had done all the right things in life; in fact, his background and his résumé were tributes to hard work and making the right choices. But somehow Jason had remained estranged from himself and his passions, as though the track of achievement he had always been on had saved him from the messy responsibility of becoming comfortable enough with himself to form deep bonds with others.

"Forget it, honestly," Jason said. He kept his eyes averted. "I don't mean to be a pain. It's your business."

Jason looked down at his briefcase, the awkwardness of the moment something he wanted to avoid.

"We'll be dealing with Nikolai Petrov and Natasha Alyeva at GlobusBank, I think," Jason said, as though they had been talking about nothing but business the entire time.

"What do you think of them?" David asked.

"Nikolai is no businessman," Jason said disdainfully. "I honestly don't understand why Vladimir keeps someone like that so close to him. He can't be trusted."

"I don't know," David admitted. "Maybe Vladimir sees something in him that reminds him of himself. What about Alyeva? I've only met her for a minute or two."

"I've dealt with her," Jason said. He paused. "Vladimir did the right thing in making her his head analyst. She's sharp as hell and on the level. She's really a pleasure to work with."

David knew Jason well enough that he could read his emotions even through Jason's mask of indifference. He saw Jason's eyes light up at the mention of Natasha Alyeva.

"What?" Jason asked, looking at David.

"Nothing much," David replied with a little smirk.

They had pulled off the main road and started into the tightly wound streets of the central city. Pedestrians filled the streets, and the architecture was a blend of czarist-era ornamentation and Soviet utilitarianism. GlobusBank's offices were less than a kilometer away, their hotel even closer.

---

JASON LOOKED OUT the car window and took a mental inventory of everything he wanted to accomplish while he was in Moscow. He liked to plan his time literally into fifteen-minute increments while he was traveling on business. First he would take a quick shower, change into a fresh suit. If there was time, he would try to book a massage for later in the day—provided he had time to squeeze in a workout in the hotel gym. Keeping the body strong and healthy was his secret to staying mentally fit.

He glanced over at David. David had sensed something when they were talking about Natasha Alyeva. It was vaguely irritating. Sure, Jason was attracted to Natasha. Any man would be. She was beautiful, smart, composed. But he could control his feelings.

He wasn't irritated at David because of Natasha Alyeva, he realized. It was because of the strange exchange they had had about Borchenko. David had secrets; anyone who became close to him understood that. It was something that everyone had to accept.

But Jason was tired of accepting it. He hated not knowing. And, deep down, it felt like a rejection. He and David were like family, and yet there was a secret core inside David that he refused to share with anyone. It reminded him . . . it reminded him of his own father, who had been a loving yet ultimately distant presence throughout his life.

*Put a lid on it,* Jason told himself. This was no time to think about these things. It was time to do business.

―――――――――――――――

DAVID WALKED INTO the gleaming lobby of the Gertsena Center, a modern, Western-style building that had gone up in the mid-'90s and had attracted some of the most prestigious tenants doing business in Moscow: financial-service companies, investment bankers, lawyers, Western accounting and consulting firms. Perched above them all, on the top three floors, was Vladimir Borchenko's GlobusBank.

Jason and Edward Preston followed close behind; they grouped together in front of the elevators and waited.

"Did you lose a few pounds?" Jason asked Edward.

David smiled. Jason was always giving Edward good-natured shit about his weight and recommending spas and health clubs throughout Moscow.

"Yeah, a few. You asshole." Edward laughed as he tugged at the waist of his trousers. "About ten pounds, in fact. If I lose any more, I'm going to have to invest in a new wardrobe."

"Finally," David teased. "We can donate your old ones to the Russian homeless."

"They can use them for tents in the summer," Jason offered.

Edward shook his head. "I can see I'm going to get it from all sides today," he said.

David often thought how little, in a sense, he had in common with most of the younger men who worked for him. David had lived his entire life based in Chicago, and he had never thought about living anywhere else. But Jason, Edward, Terry James, all of the expatriates, had willingly left America indefinitely. None of them had a firm timetable for ever returning. They were all successful businessmen, but in reality they were all running from something. A life as an expat might be exciting for a while, but it was a sure-fire way to avoid dealing with their fears and demons.

Jason was a rock, always keeping his life in perfect order. Edward Preston was another story. He had married in his mid-twenties, moving his wife and two children to Warsaw eight years before, before he had started working for David. He traveled all the time and lost himself in his work. The fact was he had been running away—from his home, his wife, and his family. Work was his excuse to be away from all of them. Predictably, his marriage had fallen apart, and his wife had taken the kids back to Milwaukee about two years before.

The elevator chimed. They got in, pressed the button for the top floor.

"Remember when Vladimir was in that old building?" Edward asked. "The one off Smolensky?"

"The one where the toilets didn't work," Jason added.

"That tells you something," David said. "He was the cream of the crop, one of the big players in the country, and he couldn't get a shitter in his office that flushed right."

All three men straightened their expressions when, a moment later, the door opened. They stepped out into a contemporary reception area with soft carpeting and mellow beige walls. A young woman wearing a headset telephone was working behind a long desk.

"*Zdrastvuite*," Jason said to the receptionist. "We are from Olen Europe, to see Mr. Borchenko."

"Of course," the young woman said in perfect English. She wore a tailored suit, her manner crisp and professional. "He is expecting you. Can I get you something to drink while you wait?"

"No, thanks," Jason said.

While the receptionist called Vladimir, the three Americans wandered over to the wall across from the desk; a single abstract painting hung there, accented by recessed lighting that played across its canvas of reds, blues, blacks.

"Patovsky," Jason said appreciatively. "One of the best post-Soviet painters. He died of a heart attack eighteen months ago. This thing is going to be worth a fortune in a couple of years."

"Is there anything he doesn't know?" Edward asked.

"Mr. Olen," said a woman's voice from behind them. All three men turned at once. Standing at the reception desk was a young woman in an elegant business suit, her black hair framing a delicate face with startling blue eyes. "Mr. Rudas, Mr. Preston. It's a pleasure to see you."

"Natasha," David said, shaking her hand. She had changed since David first met her. A year ago her hair had been long, tied into a ponytail. She had been beautiful before, though the new style lent her a deeper elegance and poise. "Congratulations on your promotion," he added.

"Thank you very much," Natasha replied. "I have been fortunate to work with Mr. Borchenko. Now, come with me. Vladimir is very eager to see you."

David and his colleagues followed Natasha down a long hallway lined with offices and cubicles. As they entered Vladimir's suite, the walls were adorned with contemporary art: Rothko, Jasper Johns, Warhol, together worth millions of dollars. He glanced into an empty meeting room, saw framed photographs on the walls of industrial sites and panoramic vistas, each a demonstration of a GlobusBank investment or holding. It never failed to amaze David how far Vladimir had come. Of all the men who had profited from the new Russia, Vladimir had been perhaps the most far-sighted.

They walked into the familiar luxurious confines of Vladimir's private office in the corner of the suite. David's eyes lingered on the plush leather sofas, the media center built into the wall, the halogen lighting system, the granite and wood inlaid bar. Vladimir himself sat talking on the phone behind a huge desk. He held up a hand by way of apology and spoke rapidly in Russian.

"It will be just a moment," Natasha said.

David caught Vladimir's eye; they exchanged a small nod. Vladimir raised his hand from behind the desk; he was holding a long squash racquet and gestured with it as he spoke. Finally Vladimir barked something in a dismissive tone, laughed, and hung up the phone.

"David," he said in his clipped, precise voice. He came around the desk and wrapped his arms around David in a brotherly embrace, patting him on the back. He then shook Jason's and Edward's hands.

"You made it here," Vladimir said. "Excellent. I trust your flight was pleasant? We will not have to buy Aeroflot in order to raise its standards of service?"

"Aeroflot's scary, but they're trying," David laughed. He pointed at the racquet, which Vladimir had dropped on his desk. "Is that yours? I didn't know you played squash."

"I've just taken it up. There is a club here in Moscow with a court. You have to try it."

"Maybe Jason will," David said. "I'll stick to basketball."

Vladimir clapped his hands together, his expression shifting. "We have a lot of work," he said. He nodded at Jason and Edward. "And I see you brought your best people to assist us. Excellent. You will be working with Natasha. She has my total trust. Anything you can say to me you can say to her."

"Great," Jason said. He met Natasha's glance. David watched the two hold their eye contact then glance away.

"Now you must forgive us," Vladimir said. "David and I must speak in private. Jason, I trust you and Edward can open discussions on the MosElectric project."

"Of course," Jason replied.

"I've reserved our main meeting room," Natasha said. "If you will come with me."

"Very good," Vladimir said. He pulled his coat from a rack behind the door. "Now there is something that I would like to show my old friend."

———————————

DAVID AND VLADIMIR sat alone in the back seat of Borchenko's black Mercedes 600 speeding along a heavily trafficked street away from the center of town. A tinted glass divider had been raised between the front and back seats and separated them from the driver.

"So you're not telling me where we're going?" David asked.

Vladimir smiled. "Indulge me. It is hard for old friends to have any surprises left. Rather like an old married couple, aren't we? Trust me, David. You will like it."

David leaned back in the plush, comfortable leather seat. There was no point arguing with Vladimir once he had a plan—there never had been. And it would be no use to tell him that David liked few things in the world less than a surprise.

"There are a number of things we need to discuss," Vladimir said.

"Where do we start?" David asked. "So much has happened."

"We will have a chance to walk and speak in a secure location,"

Vladimir said in a quiet voice. "But later. First I have something to share with you, and I don't want to ruin our fun."

"Fun?" David repeated. Despite himself, he was enjoying Vladimir's mischievous secrecy.

"Of course. Would you expect anything less?"

They pulled off the highway into a relatively desolate district of scrubby land and, in the near distance, rows of apartments. Vladimir's driver accelerated onto a long, straight road with little traffic.

"How is Annia?" Vladimir asked. "She is well?"

"Very well," David said. "She sends her greetings."

"And little Monica?"

"Fantastic," David replied.

"You brought pictures?" Vladimir asked.

"In my briefcase. I'll show you when we get back to the office."

Vladimir had met David's entire family during his trips to Chicago in the '80s and '90s; he had grown familiar with David's world and everything that mattered to him. It had brought the two old friends closer together. One evening the two had walked along the shore of Lake Michigan, and Vladimir had confided a secret pain that he had never shared with David before: the illness and death of his wife Sonia and his eternal regret that they hadn't been able to have children of their own.

Vladimir seemed to sink into a deep reverie for the moment, perhaps remembering the same evening the two spent together in America. But a few moments later his mood visibly brightened as the driver pulled the Mercedes onto a gravel track and stopped at a gate. The driver flashed a pass at a guard station and drove slowly forward.

"Here we are," Vladimir said.

David looked out the window. They had stopped alongside a flat stretch of concrete ringed in wire fencing. In the middle of the clearing was a helicopter, its rotor spinning. The driver got out of the car and opened the door for Vladimir.

"This is it?" David asked.

David stepped out of the car and fought off a surge of fear. The last thing he wanted to do was get in a Russian helicopter. It might have been unreasonable, but he was almost prepared to refuse.

"Nothing but the best for you," Vladimir said, clapping David on the back. "They offered me a Russian 'copter—I said: 'No way. My American friend will only be comfortable in a Bell model. American made.' It cost extra, but you cannot put a price on peace of mind."

Vladimir walked on ahead, his overcoat flapping in the wake of the craft's blades. David followed, one hand over his eyes to shield them from debris. He had been in helicopters many times before to survey building sites, but never before had he felt such a flash of fear as he had a moment before. But it was all right. It was as if Vladimir had read his mind—as he had so many times before.

———————

JASON SAT DOWN in the GlobusBank meeting room next to Edward. The tabletop was white Carrara marble; the Italian conference chairs were expensive and tasteful. Natasha closed the door behind them and nodded toward the carafes of tea and American coffee and the platter of cookies in the middle of the table.

"Please. Help yourself," she said.

Jason realized he was trying not to stare at her. The smooth skin of her face, the crystalline blue of her eyes. Her build was lean and athletic, her bearing upright and graceful. Though he had met her before, Jason couldn't remember ever feeling so awkward around a woman. It was almost as though something had changed inside him; he felt uncomfortably open, exposed.

"Your accent," he said to her, the words escaping before he could consider what he was saying. "I never noticed before."

"I know," she said with an enigmatic smile. "My English teacher was a Brit. Americans always say I speak like Mary Poppins. I even watched the movie, the one with Julie Andrews, so I could see what they were talking about."

"It's a lovely accent," Jason said, glancing at Edward who, he realized, was watching him. He quickly looked away, suddenly as self-conscious as a schoolboy.

"Thank you," Natasha said, looking down at her papers but still smiling.

Jason poured a cup of tea and opened his briefcase. He took a couple of deep breaths, focused his mind on business. He hoped he hadn't sounded silly commenting on Natasha's accent, like some kind of infatuated schoolboy.

"Edward was kind enough to send us a copy of your proposal for the MosElectric building," Natasha said. She opened her jacket, took out a pair of gold-rimmed reading glasses, perched them on her nose.

"We're close to getting a letter of commitment," Edward said. "They want follow-up documentation by the end of the week. What we can do today is firm up the projections—the more detailed the better."

"Vladimir is very interested in making this deal happen," Natasha said. To Jason's ears, her British-sounding voice using such an American colloquialism was for some reason unbearably attractive. He cleared his throat.

"We see this project as a potential steppingstone," he said. "We have the portfolio and the credentials throughout the United States and Central Europe. We've proved in Warsaw that we can put together an American-quality building in Eastern Europe."

"The Warsaw Commerce Center," Natasha said. "I have seen the plans. It is very impressive. But as you've surely learned in St. Petersburg, Russian bureaucracy is much more difficult than anywhere else. We need to stress your experience on the Nevsky site."

"I agree," Edward said, biting into a cookie.

Natasha nodded, looking through the documents in front of her place at the table.

"Here's the main thing," Jason said. "Vladimir has to play a role in coming up with the equity. We need commitments we can count on.

We'll have to arrange a debt structure with the multilateral lenders in a reasonable time frame. At the same time, we have to select architects who have high-rise as well as Central and Eastern European experience. Preferably one of the U.S. firms that has an office in Moscow."

Natasha looked up from the files and looked into Jason's eyes, her manner sharp, all business.

"I agree completely," she said. "We want to be a good partner in this deal. And, if I may be frank, I think that some of your concern might derive from GlobusBank's interest in obtaining MosElectric as it becomes privatized."

"Well, it has come up," Edward interjected.

"I'm sorry if you were surprised," Natasha said. She took off her glasses and rubbed her eyes. "As you know, Vladimir does not publicize his next move in advance."

"I know that," Jason agreed. "But in the interests of openness—"

"*Glasnost* in the business world?" Natasha asked.

Jason paused, unsure how to take her comment. But her thin lips curled into a smile, and he let himself relax.

"Of course, of course," Natasha said, smiling. "I led a team that performed a comprehensive analysis on MosElectric, and my recommendation was that it would be a good investment for GlobusBank."

"Why do I think there's a 'but' coming up?"

"But I honestly do not know for certain what Vladimir is going to do." A moment of perplexity played in her eyes. "He was interested, but I sense vacillation now. I do not know what other factors might be at play. So, for the moment, I cannot tell you what we are going to do."

Jason tried to read her tone, her expression; he decided that she was being completely candid. Strange, it wasn't like Vladimir to entertain uncertainty about a business decision once it was already made.

"If he buys a controlling interest in the company," Jason said, "then he would own a major stake in the building as well."

"It makes little difference," Natasha said briskly. "MosElectric would be a separate holding from the construction consortium."

"Separate entities," Jason said.

"For the time being," she replied. "Unless it becomes profitable to do otherwise."

"And you've been aware of this all along," Jason said.

Natasha looked down at her documents and seemed not to notice the hint of appreciation in Jason's voice.

"Naturally," she replied.

---

DAVID HELD TIGHT to his safety harness as the helicopter rose into the air and sent clouds of dust churning into the air until the craft banked over the neighboring apartment blocks. His stomach gave a lurch as the craft turned upright again and headed north, back toward the city.

"A beautiful, clear morning," Vladimir said. David heard Vladimir's voice through the headphones the pilot had given them before takeoff. He adjusted his small plastic microphone so he could talk as well.

"I've got to admit you surprised me," David said.

Vladimir grinned with satisfaction. Below them Moscow stretched far toward the horizon; David spotted the wedding-cake shape of Moscow University and the metallic roundness of the city sports coliseum. He leaned close to the window and looked down at the wide boulevards intersecting, at the series of rings that flowed out from the middle of the city like ripples in a pond: the Boulevard Ring, with its wooded park and old nineteenth-century buildings; the Garden Ring, which crossed the Moskva River near the grassy lawns of Gorky Park; the Outer Ring, encircling the outskirts of the city. He looked over at Vladimir, who was watching him with an expectant smile.

"We're going to check out the MosElectric site, right?" David asked. He calculated their position; within minutes they would be over the area that currently contained the Zaks Optical Institute and its grounds, the site where they wanted to build the MosElectric building.

"Yes, of course," Vladimir said. "But first, my surprise."

"There's more to it?" David asked.

Vladimir tapped the pilot on the shoulder and spoke to him over the intercom in Russian. The two seemed to argue about something for a few moments; David watched as Vladimir became more insistent and obviously won the debate. The pilot banked sharply over the Moskva River, and David looked down and saw the congested traffic below.

"Wait a minute," David said when he saw where they were headed. "We can't fly here."

"I made arrangements," Vladimir replied. "The hardest part was convincing this brick-headed pilot that it was permitted."

David's pulse quickened as they headed for a long canary-yellow building with a green roof, long and imposing. At regular intervals along the parapet were ornate spires rising toward the sky.

"We can't fly over the Kremlin," David said, anxiety coloring his voice. "It's against the law. It's dangerous."

"Normally." Vladimir smiled. "But I have my ways."

The helicopter slowed and hovered. To the left was the expanse of Red Square, the squat form of Lenin's Tomb nestled against the Kremlin wall.

"Now we go over the wall," Vladimir said. "You will be the first American to fly over restricted Kremlin airspace."

David leaned forward, his mouth feeling dry. He forgot his fear and anxiety as his spirit inclined toward the forbidden sights below.

"There is the Trinity Tower," Vladimir said, pointing down at a spire over Red Square that was topped with the imperial double-headed eagle. "It was built in the fifteenth century."

The workmanship was incredible. Delicate white vertical lines

241

created an upward movement that led the eye toward the tower's green point. David remembered that, just a few years before, the tower had been topped with a red Soviet star.

Vladimir pointed down at a series of huge structures, their yellow walls and white trim stark in the clear sunlight.

"Kremlin means 'citadel' in Russian," Vladimir said. "Down there, the building with the dome. That is the arsenal. There is the Presidium of the Supreme Soviet; it is the government center for Russia. And there, that Soviet-style structure in white marble, that is the Palace of Congresses. Today the Congress of People's Deputies meets inside."

They flew directly over the centuries-old seat of imperial Russian power, over halls that had been walked by Ivan the Terrible, Catherine, Peter, and then by Lenin and Stalin. David let his eyes feast on every nuance, every detail of this place that had been a symbol of secrecy and inscrutable power throughout modern history.

"Perhaps our old friend Mikhail Sergeivich would still be down there," Vladimir said wistfully, "if he had not miscalculated so badly."

David nodded his mute agreement. Vladimir rarely mentioned his old friend, one of the masterminds of their conspiracy. When he did, it was with this sort of vague disappointment and disapproval.

The helicopter banked to the right at Vladimir's direction. David caught a glimpse of St. Basil's Cathedral outside the Kremlin walls, the series of exquisite multicolored domes that symbolized Russia to the world.

"Down there," Vladimir said, pointing. "That is Cathedral Square."

David followed as Vladimir named each of the majestic structures below. The Cathedral of the Twelve Apostles, topped with five silver domes. The Cathedral of the Assumption, designed with five gold domes that glittered in the light. The Imperial Palace, with its dozens of window and regal yellow exterior. The Cathedral of St. Michael the Archangel, the patron of Russian warriors.

David took the moment and froze it in his memory like a photo-graph he knew he would want to look at again and again. The tow-ers and walls, the cathedrals, the walking paths, every detail of the center of the Russian empire.

"I do not want to take advantage of the favor I was granted. We should go," Vladimir said. He tapped the pilot on the shoulder. The craft hovered a second longer then banked and sharply accelerated over the outer Kremlin wall. They were gone as quickly as they had arrived.

"Well?" Vladimir asked with uncharacteristically boyish eager-ness. "What do you think?"

"Fantastic," David replied. "Thank you."

Vladimir beamed with satisfaction. "Well, it was a first for me as well," he said. "Flying over the Kremlin is forbidden. But for me, just this once, an exception was made."

David laughed at Vladimir's ironic, self-effacing expression.

"Now we get to work," Vladimir said. "We'll fly over the site."

Vladimir gave the order, and David felt himself pushed back in his seat as the helicopter accelerated over the city. When they reached the Zak Institute—potentially the future site for the MosElectric headquarters—the pilot lowered the craft and hovered. Vladimir and David leaned close to the window.

"This is it," Vladimir said.

The institute was an old Soviet-style rectangular building that served as a government center for training lens makers and optical technicians. It had shrunk over the years and fallen on hard times in the post-Soviet Russian economy, and its director had opened up four hectares of prime land for development. He planned to move the institute into a smaller building on an adjacent lot, opening up space for construction.

David looked down on the open land and imagined what he might be able to build there. The location was very good, close to the river, a few minutes by car from the central area around the Kremlin. Adjacent to the site, there was also a Moscow Metro station that could conceivably be incorporated into the building design.

"Looks like we could do it here," David said.

"I agree."

"All we need is the cooperation of the institute, MosElectric, and the Moscow city government—along with about fifty individual approvals from all the city agencies," David said. Vladimir laughed darkly; both men knew that getting all the approvals in line would be frustrating and difficult.

"We will make it happen," Vladimir said, as though resolving a debate in his own mind. He spoke to the pilot then added: "Now we will fly back to the landing site. We can talk nearby."

As they flew away from the city center, David glanced at his old friend. Vladimir seemed pensive, his expression distant. The flush of excitement that David had felt as they flew over the Kremlin had started to fade, replaced now by a gnawing anxiety. For a moment he had pushed the past out of his mind but, as always, it had returned along with all its repercussions.

They landed with a jolt on the concrete tarmac; Vladimir and David disembarked as the engine wound down and lowered their heads instinctively to avoid the still-spinning blade despite the fact that it was too high to injure them and posed no danger. David started to walk toward Vladimir's car, but Vladimir put a hand on his shoulder to stop him.

"If you don't mind," Vladimir said politely. He pointed toward a path on the far end of the open area, where the fence opened up to a shady wooded area. "We should take this opportunity to speak in private before we have to return."

"Of course," David said. For reasons he couldn't explain, the sight of the deserted woods made him feel hesitant. "Lead the way."

JASON STOOD UP from the conference table and stretched. He felt the tired, sore muscles of his back protest from sitting too long. Edward was in the adjoining office, on the phone to the Olen Europe Moscow office with a request for supplementary documents. Natasha sat across the table from Jason and reviewed the in-house GlobusBank attorney's reports on the MosElectric deal. Jason looked at her and tried not to stare.

He had to put his personal feelings aside for the moment. No matter what Natasha or Vladimir might say, Jason knew that GlobusBank's possible acquisition of MosElectric might screw up the construction deal. They had known for a long time that the company was in play, but Jason's instincts told him not to be reassured by the idea that GlobusBank could buy the utility company and keep its involvement in the construction project separate. The lease might not hold up, for one thing. And if Vladimir failed in his attempt to buy the company, the MosElectric directors might receive an unfavorable impression of the Olen Europe/GlobusBank alliance.

More than anything, Jason hated the fact that he and his associates had just learned about all of this little more than a day ago. Doing business in Russia was too often like this; everyone seemed to have important information that they were holding back. It was ingrained into the culture and way of conducting business.

There was a knock, and the door opened. Nikolai entered the room. Jason looked up and fixed a neutral smile on his face. He went around the table with his hand extended.

"Nikolai," Jason said. "Great to see you."

"Sorry to interrupt," Nikolai said in heavily accented English.

Nikolai shook Jason's hand, hard enough that Jason had to fight not to wince. The Russian's suit bulged at the shoulders and biceps. His neck seemed too big for his face, his thin lips, and widely set, dark eyes.

"How have you been?" Nikolai asked with a cold smile.

"Very well. And you?"

Nikolai looked down at Natasha, who seemed to be studiously avoiding any acknowledgment of Nikolai's presence.

"Fine," Nikolai replied. "We are discussing MosElectric today?"

"We are," Natasha said, not looking up from her documents. "I have discussed Vladimir's interest in buying the company. I think Jason is not happy about this. But he has not said anything yet."

Natasha flashed a small smile at Jason.

"There might be problems," Jason admitted. "We'll have to see how it plays out."

"There should be no problem," Nikolai said, his voice firm and commanding. It was almost as though he was trying to intimidate Jason from voicing any dissent. It was almost enough to make Jason laugh.

"We'll see," Jason said.

"I believe Olen Europe will get the commitment for the construction," Natasha said. "I will give you a report on our progress at the end of the day, Nikolai."

She still hadn't looked up. Her tone of voice was unmistakably intended to be a brush-off. Nikolai straightened his tie, cleared his throat. Anger flashed across his features.

"There are things I must attend to," he said, his face relaxing into a smile. "How long are you staying in Moscow, Jason?"

"A few days," Jason said.

"You will join me for dinner," Nikolai said. "There are new restaurants and clubs that I know you will like."

"Thanks," Jason said. "Let's do that."

He shook hands with Nikolai, thinking that there were few things he would rather do less than have dinner with the Russian. He didn't like or trust Nikolai Petrov. Nikolai left the room without saying anything to Natasha and closed the door loudly behind him. There was a moment of silence; finally, Natasha sighed, took off her reading glasses, and looked at Jason.

"You know the places he wants to take you," she said.

Jason was surprised by the brusque quality of her tone. "Where?" he asked, though he already knew.

"The men's clubs," she said. "You know what goes on there."

"I—" Jason paused, trying to adjust to this turn. "I was simply being polite to him. I have no interest in that kind of thing."

Natasha shook her head. "I'm sorry," he said. "It's none of my business. I am just irritated."

"Why?" Jason took a chair next to her.

"It's nothing," she said dismissively.

"Come on, tell me," Jason said. "Between you and me."

She looked up, seeming to try to gauge whether she could trust him. "I can't understand why Vladimir entrusts him with such authority. He is not a businessman."

"I don't know," Jason said.

"I am not complaining," she said quickly. "Don't misunderstand. Vladimir has given me great opportunities. I just can't see why he trusts someone who is one step removed from being a criminal on the streets. Nikolai has learned how to talk, how to act, but he hasn't changed. Do you understand?"

"I do." Jason agreed with her, though for an instant he wondered if her attitude was a form of snobbery. Jason could tell from her manner that she came from a privileged background.

Natasha's pale skin reddened. "I have said too much." She shook her head. "I should not talk this way. Forget that I ever brought up the subject."

"It's all right," Jason reassured her. "For what it's worth, I tend to agree with you. I don't know why Vladimir trusts Nikolai so much. But he also trusts you. Maybe he sees you as two ends of the spectrum."

Natasha raised her eyebrows. "What is the meaning of that?"

"Think about it," Jason replied. "Nikolai is from the streets. But he's also smart and motivated, no matter what else you think of him. He's spent his life in the underground economy, learning how to make things happen outside the law. At some level, I think Vladimir has a lot of respect for that."

Natasha put her elbows on the table and rested her chin in her hands. She said nothing, just listened.

"And you're the opposite," Jason continued. "You're educated, refined. Where did you grow up? Here in Moscow?"

"I have lived here my entire life."

"What about your family—if you don't mind my asking?"

"Not at all." She paused. "My father is retired. He was a captain in the Soviet Navy. My mother is a doctor. I know what you are driving at, and you are right. I had many advantages growing up."

"A good education. Connections." Jason sensed her pulling away and smiled, trying to keep the conversation friendly. "I don't mean to criticize you in any way. But maybe Vladimir likes to have both of you in trusted positions because of your differences. Maybe, in his mind, the two of you complement each other."

Natasha's lips tightened, and she looked away. "Perhaps you are right," she said.

"Don't get me wrong—"

"No, I understand." The lines of her face turned severe. "But you have to see how frustrating it can be. I know the kind of people Nikolai deals with, and I know that Vladimir needs these connections. I am not naive. But sometimes I think that because of my background, because I have not lived in their world, I am not included in making some crucial decisions. There are secrets that I am not permitted to know."

"I can imagine how you feel."

They both turned silent, glancing at the closed door.

She was fascinating. He tried to picture what she was like outside of the office. She was so proper, so self-contained. He tried to picture her throwing her head back with abandoned laughter, a glass of wine held in her manicured fingers.

A knock at the door broke the mood instantly. Edward bustled in, his tie loosened at his neck.

"I got everything but one page," he said. He gave a pile of papers to Jason. "I'm going to call back and have them re-fax the one that was screwed up."

"Thanks," Jason said, taking the papers and beginning to break them down into categories on the table. Edward left, leaving the door ajar a few inches. When Jason looked up, her eyes were on him.

"Look," he said haltingly. "This might seem forward, but I've enjoyed talking to you. Maybe we could talk some more in a less formal setting."

"That is very nice—"

"Maybe tonight?" Jason asked. "We could have dinner. I know a place where—"

"Thank you," she said, looking away. She seemed to think for a moment, until her features hardened. "No, I cannot. It is . . . I hope that you understand."

Jason returned to sorting the documents and hoped that his face wasn't turning too red. "Of course," he said. "I apologize if I made you uncomfortable."

Natasha sat down at the table without answering. Moments later Edward returned, complaining about the temperamental fax machine at the Olen Europe office. They worked on, Jason and Natasha pretending nothing had happened.

# Chapter Seventeen

*February 19, 1998. 12:16 p.m.*
*Moscow.*

AVID PUT HIS HANDS IN HIS POCKETS and shivered. He and Vladimir had walked to a wooded pathway that bisected an abandoned area between two huge apartment blocks. The land was rough and undeveloped, and cigarette butts and empty liquor bottles could occasionally be seen poking up from the dirty snow that covered the ground. Thin birch trees clustered close together; their trunks seemed like pale fingers rising up from the earth.

Vladimir lit a cigarette. David glanced at his old friend, marveled at how well he was aging. Vladimir's gait was still strong and upright, his face lined with age but his expression still sharp and strong. David could still easily see the younger man who he had met in Warsaw twenty-five years ago, the vital Russian who had explained the outlines of a conspiracy that seemed incredible but soon became the obsession of David's life.

"Are you ever going to give those things up?" David asked, motioning at Vladimir's cigarette. "They'll kill you, you know."

Vladimir held up the cigarette, inspected its burning end. "In some ways I am not as strong as you," he said. "When did you quit? Twenty years ago?"

"A little more."

Vladimir shook his head. "Such willpower," he said with genuine affection. "And you are still exercising?"

"Just about every day."

"Me, too," Vladimir said. "A man has to take care of himself in a country where the male life expectancy has fallen below sixty years."

They walked slowly, the sound of their footsteps absorbed by the snow. Vladimir sighed suddenly, a weary sound.

"What's on your mind?" David asked.

Vladimir looked down at the ground. "I'll tell you what, my old friend. You go first."

David laughed. It was vintage Vladimir: polite, a touch of humor. Beneath it a hard conviction not to give up information until he had received something in return.

"What do you know about Sokolov?" David asked.

Vladimir took a drag on his cigarette. "I know things," he said. He unknotted his scarf. Though it was cold, his face was flushed.

"Sokolov was honest," David said. "I hear that from everyone. I almost get the idea that he was killed because he wasn't playing ball with someone."

"That might have happened eventually," Vladimir said. "Sokolov was stubborn. I gave him much authority to make decisions. But, no, he wasn't killed because he wouldn't grant a favor or a concession. He was killed because I would not go along with someone else's plan."

Startled, David stopped walking. "Who?" he asked.

Vladimir pursed his lips. "Maxim Belarin."

David blinked, his mind raced. He opened his mouth but nothing came out, just a cloud of vapor as his breath condensed.

"Belarin has allied himself with Moscow gangsters," Vladimir explained. "They have put together money to bid for MosElectric, and they want to use Belarin as a front man because of his Duma membership and old Party connections. In return, they will assist him with his presidential campaign."

"They want MosElectric?" David asked.

Vladimir shrugged. "It is a good company," he said, his tone almost indicating sympathy for his opponents' wishes. "I want it, too. And there are not going to be many more privatizations. Right now there are too many competing political agendas. The result is inertia."

"Sokolov was in St. Petersburg," David said. "How did he—"

"You know how these people work," Vladimir said. "And you remember Belarin. One innocent life is nothing to him. Belarin has come to me more than once and told me not to bid for MosElectric. I told him to stuff it in his ass. And so—"

Vladimir reached out and, with a delicate gesture, pantomimed firing a gun in the air. He puffed on his cigarette and started to cough, cursing softly in Russian.

"Sokolov was killed as a warning to you?" David asked.

Vladimir nodded. "He died for nothing."

They started walking again until they reached a bend in the path. To either side was a chain-link fence topped with barbed wire. The ground beneath their feet was muddy where an open patch of trees had allowed in sunlight.

David shook his head, trying to come to terms with what he had heard. He remembered Belarin's stony smile on television, remembered the cold manner in which he conducted himself. Vladimir seemed weary and sad, which David could understand. They had come so far and accomplished so much, but Sokolov's dying for little reason seemed to taint it all with an unpleasant irrationality.

"When did the deal end for you?" David blurted out.

Vladimir dropped his cigarette to the ground, stamped it out. He looked around. They were alone.

"Precisely what do you mean?" Vladimir asked.

"Just what I said. When did you get out?"

Vladimir looked away, as though doing a math problem in his mind. "I stopped dealing with the Vatican shortly after our two associates were in power there and in the Kremlin. We had achieved goals we never dreamed of when we started."

"Mikhail Sergeivich came to power in 1985," David replied. "So that was the end for you?"

Vladimir looked deeply into David's eyes. "Essentially. Although not much money changed hands after the early '80s, you know that. Wojtyla was in the Vatican; Mikhail Sergeivich was in the Politburo. It was a matter of waiting for the old guard to die so that he could become General Secretary."

They walked slowly, each thinking silently. From somewhere far away was the sound of a machine, low and rumbling.

"My involvement with the Vatican ended almost simultaneously with yours," Vladimir said. "So why have you asked me this question?"

"What are you going to do about Belarin?" David asked.

"I am not sure yet." Vladimir frowned. "I think I want to buy the company and really fuck him. Then his friends will withdraw their support, I suspect, and he will not become the Russian president."

"He can't become president," David said. "God knows what he would do."

"Russia has had sadists and murderers in the Kremlin before," Vladimir mused. "But you are right. Heaven help us if Maxim Belarin takes charge of the Soviet military and its nuclear weapons."

"Do you think buying the company would effectively undercut him?" David asked.

"It might." Vladimir paused. "I am not sure what I will do."

David glanced at Vladimir, trying to read his expression. Sokolov had been killed over the MosElectric deal. David suddenly realized that Vladimir was afraid he might be killed as well. Somehow the very idea of Vladimir being scared was utterly terrifying. And if

Vladimir was scared, then how should David feel? He could just as easily be bumped off as Sokolv was. And now with the CIA wanting to pull him back into the thick of things—David's mouth felt dry, his palms clammy. Vladimir had always been calm, in control. Somehow Belarin had succeeded in breaking through Vladimir Borchenko's icy wall of confidence.

"I've been contacted by the CIA again," David said.

Vladimir looked at David, his eyes wide. "Who?"

"They came to me the same way they did in '74, through my old friend Carl Becker," David explained. "Apparently a young agent has gotten possession of Jim Allen's secret files."

Vladimir's mouth rounded into a surprised circle.

"As I understand it, Jim Allen was this agent's mentor," David added. "I really don't know whether or not Allen intended for the files to ever be seen. I didn't even know he kept files."

"It surprises me," Vladimir admitted. "Jim Allen was a formidable man. He also knew how to keep a secret. As far as I know, your own presidents never found out what we were doing."

"Well, I think Allen made a mistake this time," David said. "We just didn't find out about it until he'd been dead for almost ten years."

"A mistake? Why do you say that?"

"Because, from what little I know right now, it sounds like this agent wants to try to re-create the results of the deal we were involved in."

Vladimir winced, as though the very thought was painful. "Because Wojtyla is ailing?" he asked.

"That's my best guess," David said.

Vladimir laughed sarcastically. "How very American," he said. "If one is good, then two is better."

"What do you mean?" David asked.

Vladimir stopped walking. "Americans always want more," Vladimir said. "We were able to influence the Papal convention and put Wojtyla in power. It worked once, so why not try it again? What do the Americans want this time? An African pope? Perhaps they also want to put a liberal democrat in the Kremlin."

"I didn't hear anything about Russia," David said. "I think the idea might be to again influence the Papal election."

"Why stop there?" Vladimir asked, waving his hand in the air. "Why not the leadership of China while we're at it? Why set our sights so low?"

"I don't like it, either," David said. He found Vladimir's heavy sarcasm unaccountably abrasive. "It's a recipe for disaster."

"It is insanity," Vladimir said. "Are we suddenly the magicians of history, changing the world any time we like? Is this CIA agent unaware that our plan took decades of careful thought and action? No one can duplicate what we achieved. We can't make popes appear like some kind of magic trick."

"I'm not sure what any of it means," David said. "But I wanted to be candid with you."

Vladimir lit another cigarette and looked off into the distance.

"I'm supposed to see if there's any way to reestablish the old financial pipeline," David told him.

"Impossible," Vladimir said. "Majorski is dead, for one thing. We have no ties to the Vatican Bank."

"I know," David replied. "Look, I don't want any part of this. I want out. That's all I've wanted for years."

"We will never be done," Vladimir said. "Look at the present situation. Belarin has risen up like a bad dream of the past. It seems as though we will never be finished."

Vladimir started walking again. David followed, a few steps behind. He remembered the first time he had met Belarin. It had been 1978, the year Albino Luciani was elected to the papacy despite the efforts of David and Vladimir to aid Litwinski and Wojtyla, the Polish cardinals. They had been almost certain they could get Wojtyla elected, having called in decades of favors and energized a significant number of voting cardinals to the notion of a non-Italian pope who could fight for the millions of Catholics living under Soviet occupation in Eastern Europe. David had worked furiously that year and flew from Chicago to Warsaw, Rome, and Moscow more times than he could remember.

When he was in Moscow, he had come to the COMECON offices in the central city, to Vladimir's suite. Vladimir's secretary had led David to the innocuous institutional office, a perfect cover for Vladimir's international activities. There had been a man there in a military uniform and crew cut, powerfully built, his eyes cold, his spine straight as a rod. It had been Maxim Belarin.

"Belarin is concerned about more than MosElectric," Vladimir said suddenly, breaking the silence between them. In the near distance David could hear the sound of children's voices, yelling, playing some game.

"What else does he want?" David asked.

"He is worried about his role in our cabal becoming known," Vladimir said. "He cannot be the President of Russia if it became public that he was involved in a conspiracy with the CIA and the Vatican."

"The secret has been kept this long," David said. "Can't he see that we all would have something to lose if it got out?"

Vladimir balled his fist with frustration. "That would be the response of a rational man. But Belarin is not a thinker. Everything in his world is one a straight line, from one point to the next. No ambiguities, no shades of gray." Vladimir paused. He looked at David, but no words came out.

"He's afraid I'll let the secret out, isn't he?" David asked.

"When he contacted me, he was looking for assurances," Vladimir explained slowly. "He did mention you."

"That's fucking reassuring," David said. He sensed Vladimir was hiding something from him and suddenly flared with anger. He grabbed Vladimir's arm to make him stop walking, reached up and took hold of the Russian's lapel.

"I've never seen you like this before," David said. "I think you're scared."

"Get your hands off me," Vladimir hissed.

David did as he was asked, even smoothing the creased fabric as a gesture of reconciliation. Never before had he and Vladimir shared harsh words.

"I'm sorry, I lost control," David said. "But talk to me. Now."

Vladimir took a deep breath and exhaled loudly. "You do not know everything about Belarin," he said. "But some knowledge is dangerous. You must understand this, David."

David looked away. Of course he understood it. He had been making the same argument to himself for decades about not sharing his secret life with those closest to him.

Vladimir straightened his bearing, seeming to gather his strength. "I have dealt with him and his type before. There is nothing to worry about."

David weighed Vladimir's presence, his tone of voice. He concluded that there indeed was something to worry about. He didn't understand the Belarin situation. It would be so easy for Belarin to kill David and do away with one more piece of the secret—one less person to stand in his way. It was a realization that made him more frightened than he had ever been in his life.

---

"LET'S WALK BACK," Vladimir said.

David nodded, a sour expression on his face. "Fine. We'll sort this out later."

They walked in silence along the path through the woods. David seemed distant, disturbed. For the first time in years he craved a cigarette. His heart felt like it was about to jump out of his chest.

Vladimir was grateful that David hadn't pressed him for more information about Belarin. If he had, Vladimir wasn't sure what he would have said.

Vladimir put his hands in his pockets to keep them from trembling. More than anything, he had always feared David's reaction to the depth of the Vatican cover-up, the shocking aspects that he still didn't know. David had a strong moral sense. He would have been outraged, furious. There was no telling what he might have done.

"Sometimes it's all I think about," David said suddenly, breaking the silence.

"What do you mean?" Vladimir asked, grateful to be free of his thoughts for the moment.

"The deal," David said, looking straight ahead. "I read the paper, and there it is—the ramifications of what we did. I turn on the television, and it's there. It's been filling my mind ever since we first met in Warsaw."

"I understand," Vladimir said. He felt the same.

"I've kept the secret from my colleagues, from my friends, from my family," David said, sounding weary.

They reached a bend in the path. Vladimir could see his Mercedes parked close to the helicopter. The car's engine was running, expelling exhaust into the cold air.

"Tell me something," Vladimir said. "What if you were back at the beginning? What would you do?"

"You mean Warsaw?" David asked.

"All of it," Vladimir interrupted. "The deal. The conspiracy. Do you ever regret it? When you are alone at night, and there is quiet. Do you ever regret what we did?"

David was quiet for a long time and looked down as they slowly trudged to the car. Finally he looked up, his hair blowing off his high forehead in the wind.

"Never," David said. He paused and looked at the ground then back into Vladimir's eyes. "But I'm ready to be done with it. To get on with my life without secrets and lies."

Vladimir nodded in understanding.

*February 19, 1998. 5:06 p.m.*
*Moscow.*

"I . . . HOW DID this happen?"

David sat on the bed in his room at the Metropol Hotel and talked to his wife, Annia, on the phone. His shoes lay on the floor on the foot of the bed; his tie and jacket were tossed onto a chair.

"I was contacted first thing this morning," Annia replied.

"Who called you?" David asked. He stopped himself from adding, *Was it anyone I might know?*

"A Vatican secretary, a priest," Annia replied.

"They want you to come to Rome?" David was stunned. "Is his condition that bad?"

"They think he might be dying." Annia sighed. "*He* wants me to come to Rome immediately. He wants to see friends from his earlier days. The end might be near."

"And what about Andy Kapinski?" David asked.

"I called him right away," Annia explained. "They had already talked to him. We agreed to meet in Rome. Cynthia has already arranged my ticket and hotel."

"I guess you have to go," David said.

"What's wrong?" Annia asked. "Your voice sounds strange."

David rubbed his forehead. The pope had been sick many times in the past few years, but this time seemed more serious. David had seen Wojtyla's broad-chested figure grow smaller and more frail on television over the past few years.

"It's nothing," David said, trying to sound reassuring.

"I know you. What is it?" Annia insisted. "What's wrong over there?"

"I'm just busy," David said. "We're . . . we're all working hard on this new project."

"I wish you'd talk to me, Darling."

Thoughts flashed through David's mind. If Wojtyla was dying, that meant the CIA agent Carl Becker told him about might decide to take

260

immediate action. The CIA knew that the papacy was a politically powerful office in the right hands. An ambitious agent might see this as his chance for an intervention.

"It's nothing, Annia."

"I have to pack," Annia said with resignation. "This is such a surprise."

"He'll be very glad to see you again," David said. He tried to calculate: Could Annia possibly be in any danger if she were in the Vatican while the CIA was taking action? They would know she was David's wife; they would know her history. They might hurt her to try and silence David just as they killed Sokolov as a message to Vladimir.

"It's been so long," Annia said, her voice far away. "You take care of yourself," something she'd said to him time and again.

"That's exactly what I was going to say to you." David felt the phone against his ear, looked out at the fortress walls of the Kremlin outside the window. His memory wandered into a kind of infinite space at his wife's words, the moment telescoping into recollection.

# Part Four

# *Plausible Deniability*

# Chapter Eighteen

*1976.*
*Warsaw.*

BY 1976 DAVID HAD SPENT TWO LONG YEARS trying to balance his life and the new roles he was leading. He had begun developing industrial sites in Poland, with the cooperation of Vladimir Borchenko and COMECON. It was a laborious process of learning how to do business in a communist country, with the labyrinth of bureaucracy within the command economy and the disaffected attitude of the workers and managers. Simultaneously, David had become enmeshed in Borchenko's conspiracy and acted as a facilitator between parties that were supposed to have nothing to do with one another.

The contingent in the Vatican had been put together and groomed by Cardinal Litwinski, who was driving toward Cardinal Wojtyla's ascendance to the papacy and the eventual liberation of Poland. The two cardinals had the assistance of Cardinal Daniel O'Brien in

Chicago, who generated funds through his archdiocese that David channeled as directed. Also in the Vatican were three Bishops: Buenadona and Villetti, who worked to forward Wojtyla's interests in the closed world of the Curia, and Bishop Paul Majorski, the American head of the Vatican Bank.

Majorski was a central player, one that David grew to respect and feel irritation for in equal measure. Majorski was also from Chicago, from the infamous Cicero, and he was a hard-talking, hulking man who managed the intricacies of the Vatican's international holdings with shrewdness and supreme arrogance. In Wojtyla, he saw a talented young cardinal who, if he became pope, would grant Majorski many more years of running the bank with little oversight.

O'Brien generated money in Chicago, which Majorski laundered and placed in secret accounts. David moved money into Poland through his construction company, and Vladimir moved money from Poland into Russia through his black-market network and COMECON office. Some of the money went to Mikhail Sergeivich for his political efforts in Russia, and some of it Wojtyla used in helping the Solidarity Worker's Movement in Poland. Wojtyla also benefited from the connections and clout of the Vatican. In a sense there were two parallel systems, each working toward the rise to power of two very different men, each of which directly involved David Olen.

David was fixated on his role. It was heavy; it occupied all his waking thoughts. He found himself making up cover stories to friends, skipping out on important meetings, missing a planned ski trip, canceling dates with women. He became more introspective and somber, which made some friends worry about him. When they asked whether he was feeling all right, he inevitably would say: "I'm fine, fine. Just a lot on my mind with the business . . ."

But David was committed to what he was doing, and he believed in it, but still he was also anxious and frightened much of the time. He had no idea what would happen to him if he were caught. The CIA had begun to leave him alone after David briefed Jim Allen on his activities; Allen trusted David, also believed in what he was doing, and, probably, wanted to distance himself from it in case anything went horribly wrong.

David arrived in Warsaw in the middle of the summer. The Vistula River shone in the afternoon sun, and the Palace of Culture's imposing wedding-cake silhouette rose above the landscape as a reminder of Soviet domination. David spent the morning looking over the progress of an immense warehouse his company was building on the city's outskirts. The site had been dusty, the sun relentless, the cacophony of power tools and shouting voices had rung in his ears until his head started to throb. During the ride back into the city he had sat back, his window open all the way, and closed his eyes. Beads of perspiration had dripped from his forehead and his nose, but he was too exhausted to wipe them away.

When he reached his room in the Europejski Hotel, he peeled off his clothes and stepped into the shower. Hot water was by no means guaranteed even in the good hotels—and when it was available, there were no assurances that it would last for more than a couple of minutes. It didn't matter that day. David leaned against the tile and let cold water flow over his head until he was rejuvenated enough to read over the phone message slips he'd picked up at the front desk.

Fortunately, the desk clerk who had taken the messages spoke and wrote English. There was one slip from his secretary, Cynthia Barry, routine business. Another from Andy Kapinski, who was still working for Olen and Company in Chicago.

Andy Kapinski's message read: *Meeting this afternoon on Carlson project. Stage two discussed at four o'clock.*

Andy was working in David's structural engineering department and was also shuttling back and forth to Poland. He had been drawn into David's clandestine dealings with Vladimir Borchenko after Jim Allen at the CIA discovered that Andy had had personal contact with Wojtyla during his childhood in a Krakow orphanage—and also after Allen found a problem with his immigration status. Andy hadn't been drawn in as deeply as David, but he relished the chance to come back to Poland and leave freely again, and he knew enough about the Borchenko dealings to understand that the liberation of Poland was an item on the agenda.

David read the message again. There was no such thing as a Carlson project. It was a fictitious development Andy and David used as a secret code when they needed to convey messages to each other that might get intercepted by a desk clerk or phone operator who was reporting to the Polish intelligence service.

The code was very simple. Andy's message indicated that there was a meeting that needed to take place. There were code words for various parties: Vladimir was "Mr. Wolf," and Litwinski was "Mr. White." But because no code had been left in the message, David figured that he was supposed to meet someone new. The time given in the message was the real local time the meeting was supposed to take place. As for the "stage" of the project, this was a code for one of a few meeting sites. "Stage one" was the main entrance of the Palace of Culture. "Stage two" was the Barbican, the sixteenth-century fortress that marked the entrance of Warsaw's Stare Miasto, or Old City.

David put on jeans and a fresh polo shirt and emerged into the late-afternoon sun. He waved for his driver, who was waiting with the car across the street, reading a newspaper, and smoking a cigarette. The drive from the hotel to the Old City took only a few minutes, and David had the driver leave him a couple of blocks from the Barbican. As was his habit, he took an indirect path, doubled back once, and cut through a narrow alley leading into the part of the Old City that was being reconstructed after the ravages visited upon it during the war. David was never sure whether his darting around like a character in a spy story kept him from being followed. More than likely, Vladimir had used his local clout to keep the police from paying too much attention. Either way, David observed his cautions almost ritualistically.

He walked slowly up to the medieval brick fortress, the open square filled with tourists from other Eastern European countries who were walking through the heat and looking up at the landmarks. They were all dressed in unstylish, cheap-looking clothes that immediately marked them as residents of the Soviet Bloc. David wiped away a thin sheen of sweat from his forehead with a handkerchief.

He looked around. A family was gathered in front of the fortress gates, and they were speaking a language David didn't understand. David turned away from them. A few Soviet-model cars slowly made the turn around the square that led back to the central city. Pigeons fluttered all over the square and foraged on the brick for bits of bread that a pair of old ladies was scattering on the ground.

Any one of these people could be KGB, David reminded himself. At any time he could be tossed into a Polish jail. He willed himself to breathe calmly, to look as though he was just another foreigner spending the afternoon sightseeing.

"David Olen," said a woman's voice from behind him.

David turned. She was tall, almost as tall as he was. She was wearing a simple yet elegant designer blouse and pants. Her blond hair was long and full as it grazed her shoulders. She wore subtle makeup; her delicate features were perfect and beautiful in the heat, her skin pale white and flawless. This was a sophisticated, Western-looking woman, one who stood out in this stark setting. Certainly, not your average Polish woman, thought David.

"Yes, I'm David," he replied, looking around. She seemed to be alone.

"My name is Annia," she said. "I am a childhood friend of Andy Kapinski's. He told me a few things about you, and now he has suggested that we meet."

David glanced around again. Anyone could have been an agent. A man walking slowly toward them and smoking a cigar. The young couple holding hands looking at a city map. Even the old women feeding the birds. No one was looking at them, but David saw that

269

this woman knew the situation; she spoke quietly, her body language neutral.

"Well, you know about me," David said. "That's not really fair because I don't know anything about you."

Annia flashed a smile, showing perfect white teeth. She pointed toward the Old Town as though she were a local giving directions to a tourist.

"Let's walk this way," she said. "We can talk only when there is no one close enough to hear us. It should be all right."

Her self-assurance intrigued David, and he walked slowly beside her. "I know some of the things you are doing in Poland," Annia said quietly.

"What things?" David asked.

"Don't worry. You have to trust me," Annia said. "Andy does not tell me too much. Only what I need to know."

She spoke English with cool precision, a slight musicality in her accent. They walked under a brick arch and into the expanse of the Old City's main square, which was ringed on all sides by the restored remnants of handsome old burghers' houses first erected centuries before.

"Tell me more about yourself before we talk about those things," David said.

"I am a writer of children's books," she said plainly.

David must have revealed his surprise in his expression; Annia gave him a soft smile.

"How can I be a writer in a country dominated by communist propaganda?" she whispered to him. "Well, I am very effective. I write stories that make the Russians and Polish communists happy. Children all across Poland read my stories in school."

David listened for a note of sarcasm or cynicism in her voice, but none was there.

"Your books are successful?" he asked.

"Very," she replied with a note of pride.

They walked slowly across the square. Neither raised their voice above a soft utterance.

"I am one of the leading cultural figures in this country," she added. "You have not heard of me?"

"I don't read children's literature," David said.

She smiled. "Of course not. I am active in the Communist Party. I was the youngest in my class to attain full membership. I've been granted a five-room apartment, and I meet often with the country's Party leaders."

David tried to figure out how old she was. About thirty-three or -four, he decided. He wiped his forehead again, though she seemed cool and comfortable.

"I am not bragging," she said. "But you have to understand my position in Poland."

"All right, that's fine," David said. "But all I really know about you is that you say you know Andy Kapinski. Maybe that's true. But maybe you're also on some kind of fishing expedition for the—"

"Fishing expedition? What is this?"

David smiled, despite himself. "It means . . . it means when someone tries to get someone to talk about something they would rather not share."

"I see," she said. "Fishing. Like putting a hook in the water and seeing what is going to bite."

"Exactly," David replied.

"This is not a fishing expedition," Annia said. She steered them to the far side of the square and into a side street that led to an open pedestrian walkway overlooking the river.

"How do you know Andy?" David asked.

"I knew him in Krakow when we were children," she said. "We were at the same orphanage."

David recalled Andy speaking once or twice about his childhood in Poland; his father had died in the war, and his mother had died shortly after. He had ended up in an orphanage under the supervision of the state.

"Andy was five years older than me," she said. "He looked out for me, made sure I was all right. We stayed in contact even after he moved to America. And since he has started coming back here, we meet from time to time."

David listened in silence. Annia was beautiful, charming, smart—and she said she was a highly connected Party member in Communist Poland. His mind raced. What if this woman was working for the government? She might have drawn Andy in, based on their childhood bond. They stopped and looked out over the river. David stared at the water.

"Is there a message you want me to send to Andy?" David asked.

"Oh, no," She laughed. "You know, we can't meet in public much. It would be too dangerous. But we have a safe means for exchanging messages."

"How is that?"

She looked around. They were alone. "Through Wojtyla."

David folded his arms, looked down. He wondered what the hell Andy had gotten him into.

"Working within the system was my only choice," she whispered. "True, when I was young, I believed in the system with all my heart. But I grew out of my childishness. I realized that the system was robbing Polish culture of its very life. And now my books, my status, make it possible for me to fulfill my real mission."

"What is that?" David asked. He closed his eyes.

She paused, as though unsure whether she could trust him. "The real workers' movement," she finally said. "Solidarity. The liberation of Poland."

David blinked. He looked into her pale blue eyes, saw nothing there but sincerity.

"I know about the money you bring into Poland," she continued, speaking quicker now. "Wojtyla uses some of it to help the movement. I use my position to tell Wojtyla what the government is thinking; I find out as much as I can and pass it on to them."

David had heard that there was a homegrown anti-Soviet movement in Poland, but he had never been sure if it represented any kind of real threat to the Soviet puppet government.

"That is why I wanted to meet you," Annia continued. "Because you are doing so much for Poland."

David felt himself blush; Annia put her hand on David's arm for an instant then pulled it away, as though suddenly realizing that she had gotten too close, revealed too much. David fought against a sudden urge to pull her close to him, to smell the perfume of her hair. He suddenly realized that she was awakening a passion in him that had been dormant. It was more than her beauty; there was also some indefinable quality about her, some soulful depth.

But he had to be pragmatic. Annia was talking about things that David wasn't aware of. He knew that Cardinal Wojtyla was an activist, that he used money from Cardinal O'Brien's Chicago archdiocese for the Solidarity Movement. Now that he thought about it, the pieces began to fit together in his mind. Wojtyla was apparently engaged in a very worldly process of political opposition.

"I'm glad we met," he said to her.

"I am, too," she said softly, with a hint of shyness.

"Is there . . . can I do anything for you?"

"Are you sympathetic to the movement?" she asked. "We have American support in addition to the money you bring in. There is also the AFL-CIO, the American labor union."

"All right," David said. "I am sympathetic. I'm glad I'm helping."

"Good." She smiled. "Now I have something to report to the authorities in case they saw me with you today. I engaged the American in a political conversation. He is sympathetic to the opposition but not a threat to the Party."

He returned her smile. "Fine. Anything else?"

273

"One thing." She took out a slip of paper from her pocket and handed it to him. "Give me a number to contact you, please. And I will give you mine."

"Would you like to see me again?" he asked her.

"I would."

David felt light, buoyant. "I would, too," he said. "I would like that very much."

---

TWO MONTHS LATER, David contacted Annia again. She was going to Krakow to research one of her books; David arranged to meet her there, under the pretense of looking at a site COMECON was proposing for development for a state-owned meat-packing company.

They had spoken a couple of times since their first meeting, brief conversations in which what was unsaid seemed far more important than the light topics they discussed. David realized that he was inwardly counting the moments until he could see her again and, from her tone of voice, that she felt the same.

He met her on a quiet side street. He drove his own car because he had given his driver the week off. They drove into the countryside, on rutted highways and roads that deteriorated into little more than rough track. When they stopped, they posed as husband and wife, Annia doing all the talking. They ate river fish in a ramshackle public house and drank bitter wine together. They said little, not wanting to be overheard speaking English, instead staring into each other's eyes.

David realized that he was falling in love with this woman he barely knew. It seemed impossible; he had known her for such a short time yet he was so drawn to her.

In the eight weeks since he first met Annia, David thought back to his previous relationships. He had a few serious relationships with women back in Chicago but he had always been preoccupied with other things, with his career and his friends. Mostly he had simply been concerned first and foremost with himself. He had never been

274

able to commit himself to any of those women. But with Annia, he felt completely different.

He hoped he had grown. As he and Annia walked along a country stream and held hands, it was as though their pretense of being mates had dissolved. They were together. They were in the very first moments of mutual love.

David never was with another woman after he met Annia. He lived for the days he was able to spend with her. The carefully constructed meetings became all the more sensual and exciting by the secrecy and caution required. When they made love, he felt the barriers between them slip away, and when they rose together before dawn, he pulled her close so that he would remember the feel of her until he could steal another day in her presence.

He loved Annia in a way that he had never thought possible. It took almost five years, but David finally convinced her to leave Poland, to come to Chicago and marry him.

This was why, in 1998, when Vladimir Borchenko asked David if he had any regrets, he replied that he had none. Because without Vladimir, without the deal and all that it had wrought, he never would have met Annia.

# Chapter Nineteen

*February 19, 1998. 8:31 p.m.*
*Moscow.*

AVID PAUSED IN THE METROPOL RESTAURANT ENTRANCE and collected himself. He had spent the afternoon trying to concentrate on the details of the MosElectric project, all the while plagued by thoughts of Maxim Belarin, the CIA, Annia traveling to Rome, his discussion with Vladimir. All his life he had been a man who took decisive action, but for the moment he couldn't see a clear course that he could take to remedy the swirl of events that had erupted in the past week.

A waiter lightly touched his shoulder. "Mr. Olen?" he asked. David nodded. The waiter pointed toward a large circular table at the far end of the room. David looked across the expanse of diners seated in burgundy velvet armchairs and saw Jason giving him a discreet wave. The table was full of associates and friends.

David moved through the dining room. He thought of Annia, her bags packed and bound for Rome to see the former priest who had extended so much kindness to her when she was a lost little girl in a Krakow orphanage so many years ago—and who had introduced her to political activism when she had grown into a woman. He couldn't help feeling worried about her.

He thought of Wojtyla, the pope, once so vital and charismatic, now apparently confined to bed. David had tried to reach Carl Becker from his hotel room a half-hour before but had been able only to leave a message. David didn't really mind. Let this Thomas Gleason spin his wheels for a while. There was nothing more to be done. The twentieth century could go to rest clutching its secrets tightly.

"You look troubled," Jason said as David sat down, his voice low so the other people at the table couldn't hear.

"It's something with Annia," David said. "I can't really talk about it right now."

"Is she—"

"Don't worry," David reassured Jason. "She's fine. Something came up is all. She has to do a little traveling."

"Things are under control here," Jason said. "Maybe you should go join her."

"Maybe I will," David said. "I haven't decided yet. There's something else. Remember Belarin, the guy you saw on TV in my room? Turns out he's Vladimir's main competition in the MosElectric bidding."

Jason looked at David quizzically then motioned for a waiter. "You need a drink," he said.

"Good idea," David replied.

He looked around the table. In addition to him and Jason, there were Edward Preston and Jennifer Greene, a young woman who had worked for David in Chicago then gone out on her own as a Moscow real-estate broker. On the other side of the table was Dave Maynard, a project manager working in Olen Europe's Moscow office. And, to David's surprise, Nikolai Petrov.

"Sorry I'm late," David said. "I had to make a call before I came down."

David stood up and shook Nikolai's hand across the table. "I didn't know you were coming," he said. "It's good to see you."

"It is my pleasure," Nikolai replied in his deep voice. His huge hand completely encased David's.

"Jennifer, you look like you're doing well," David said.

He turned to Dave Maynard. "Glad you could make it," David said.

"Wouldn't miss a free meal," Maynard joked.

"Dave said things look good," Jason offered. "There's reasonable access to existing utilities."

"I'm liking the whole project," Edward interjected. "Providing there are no unforeseen complications." He adjusted his bulky frame in the relatively small armchair. Something in his phrasing and inflection sounded vaguely Russian; David had noticed many times how expatriates' voices and mannerisms tended to change the longer they spent working in foreign countries.

"Your employer had quite a surprise for me this afternoon," David said to Nikolai. "A helicopter ride and guided aerial tour of the Kremlin."

Nikolai smiled, an unexpected kindness gracing his coarse features. "So I heard," he said. "Vladimir was very excited. He made everyone in the office swear to secrecy."

"I'm jealous," Edward said. "That must have been incredible."

"The word 'incredible' barely does it justice," David said. "Part of me was scared to death. This might be hard for you to believe, Nikolai, but people my age grew up in America being taught to be wary of Russia. Now look where I am. This is what life is all about for me, these exciting new experiences."

"I understand." Nikolai lit a thin cigar. "We were also taught to fear you. And now we find we have so much in common."

"Sounds like a toast," David said. His drink arrived, straight vodka, which everyone else at the table was also drinking. "To friendship. To old friends and our new friends."

Everyone drank. The drink was cold and soothing to David's throat, the flavor empty yet refreshing in the manner of good Russian vodka.

"And where is Vladimir tonight?" David asked. "When I left him, he was making calls from his office."

"He has private business," Nikolai said.

"And Natasha?" David added.

"She went home," Nikolai said. "Her mother is ill. She spends many evenings at her parents' house and helps her father to care for her."

"I see," David replied. He glanced over at Jason. "Well, we'll try to get both of them out one evening before we leave."

"Of course," Nikolai said, taking a drag on his cigar.

"So what's the latest with MosElectric?" David asked.

"Edward, Natasha, and I put together a draft of the pre-development agreement," Jason said. "We're going to submit it in the morning and hopefully hear back by the end of the day."

"This could be a great deal," David mused. "I'll bet we're up all night negotiating. But we're not leaving Moscow until the letter of intent is signed with MosElectric."

"I will be available for all negotiations," Nikolai said.

"Glad to hear it," Jason said. He stared straight ahead, his tone cordial but somehow ironic. David wondered what was going on between these two.

"We'll all be in on it," David said. "I'll need all your expertise, believe me. And we'll have to keep Vladimir in the loop."

"That's right," Jason said to Nikolai after taking a drink. "We wouldn't want any surprises."

David gave a hollow grin. What the hell was wrong with Jason? It wasn't like him to make pissy comments like that. People at Olen Europe weren't happy Vladimir had kept them in the dark about his possible intention to acquire MosElectric, but that was simply the card they had been dealt.

"How's Annia?" Jennifer asked, sensing a shift in the mood at the table. "Did I overhear you saying she has to do some traveling?"

"She's fine," David replied, dodging the question. "I know she'll be happy to hear you're doing well."

"And how's Monica?"

"Great," David said. "The best kid in the world."

Nikolai stubbed out his cigar in a crystal ashtray. He cleared his throat and, with a hint of formality, squared his large body to face David.

"I have always wanted to ask you," Nikolai said. "Your name. Olen. You are aware this has a meaning in Russian?"

Everyone was silent, fascinated by the earnestness of Nikolai's tone. Normally he was quiet almost to the point of sullenness; now he seemed outgoing and interested.

"It means 'deer,'" David said. "Right?"

"Yes," Nikolai agreed. "A reindeer."

"I didn't know that," Jason said.

"Then you are Russian?" Nikolai continued.

"Ukrainian," David replied. "My father was from a village near Kiev. My mother was born in the States, but her parents were from Riga. I have a real Eastern European background."

Nikolai leaned forward. "I thought there was something Russian about you," he said.

David smiled at the obvious compliment. He knew his name helped him somewhat in doing business in Russia. No one could mistake him for anything but an American, but his name almost symbolically clicked with Russians and made them more comfortable dealing with him.

"Everyone in America is from someplace else if you go back far enough," David pointed out. "In my case you only have to go back one generation."

The waiter came and took everyone's orders.

"So if you don't mind my asking," Nikolai said, "why is it that you do not speak Russian? Didn't your parents teach it to you?"

"My father spoke Russian to his friends," David answered. "So I heard it around the house. But my parents wanted me to be an American. They wanted me to speak only English."

"I see," Vladimir said.

"My grandmother on my mother's side used to speak Italian," Jason said. "But she wouldn't let my mother speak it. It was almost like she was embarrassed about it."

"It's an immigrant thing," David said. "My father, you know, he was a smart guy. Sharp. But he didn't have the kind of perspective on life to draw me into his heritage, teach me Russian, show me about where my people came from. I guess there was never time. And I think he had no concept that knowing another language would be beneficial to me."

The maitre d' came to the table, folded his arms, and stood quietly until David had finished speaking.

"Yes?" David asked.

"Is there a Mr. Rudas at the table?"

"That's me," Jason said.

"There is a telephone call for you," the maitre d' replied. He wore a tuxedo and smiled politely. "I will take you to the phone."

Confusion flashed across Jason's face. "All right. Did the person say who was calling?"

"It was a woman," came the reply. "She did not give her name."

Jason stood up, dropped his linen napkin on the tablecloth. He finished his vodka with one motion and shrugged. "I'll be right back."

"I'm going to eat your dinner if you take too long," Edward said.

"I don't doubt that," Jason said with a friendly laugh.

David watched Jason walk with athletic strides through the dining room with the maitre d' and disappear around a corner.

"I see Jason hasn't changed," Jennifer said.

"How's that?" David asked.

"Getting calls from women in the middle of dinner," she replied. "I assume he still hasn't settled down."

"No, he hasn't," David replied.

Nikolai cleared his throat. "Could you tell me more about your childhood?" he asked, as though all other conversation was extraneous. Interesting, David thought. Nikolai obviously had little interest in anyone else at the table. His fascination with David was obviously related to David's status.

"The old formula," David said with a smile. "Hard work times opportunity. Divided by luck."

---

JASON TOOK THE PHONE from the maitre d'. He was in a little nook just off the restaurant's main entrance.

Before he picked up the line, he wondered briefly who might be calling him. Who knew he was staying at the Metropol? Probably Kendra, the woman he had recently been dating in London. She tended to be dramatic, as far as Jason was concerned. It was probably some minor thing that she had blown out of proportion.

"This is Jason."

Silence. An electronic pulse on the line.

"Hello?" he said, growing irritated. "This is Jason. Who—"

"Jason, this is Natasha." A pause. "Natasha Alyeva."

"Of course, I know who you are," Jason said. "Hey, did you change your mind? We have a table full of people, and the first course hasn't even been served yet. If you're nearby—"

"No, no, that's . . . that is not why I called."

Jason detected a strange note in her usually precise, clipped diction. Her voice was wavering.

"What is it?" he asked. "Is it about MosElectric?"

"It's Vladimir." A muffled noise, like choked-back tears.

"What about him?"

"His apartment, it . . ." She stopped.

"Just tell me," Jason said. "It's all right. Whatever it is, it's all right."

"I was watching television. A news report came on —. There was an explosion," Natasha said. "A bomb was planted in his apartment building. In Vladimir's home. It went off when he opened the door. The body was . . . he was almost completely destroyed."

Jason could hear the television on in Natasha's apartment in the background.

"It's on every channel."

"Jesus," Jason whispered. "Was anyone there with him?"

"No, I don't think so," she told him. "The apartment next door was empty at the time. They showed some film of it, after the explosion. Nothing is left. Just rubble. It's horrifying."

"You're sure it was Vladimir?"

"That's what the news is saying. He left the office with one of his bodyguards; I saw them leaving. Now the bodyguard is missing and so is the driver. We've tried to call them on the car phone, but there is no reply." She took a deep breath then continued, her words rushing out. "Something strange happened. The security guards at his building said they saw nothing, and the video camera over the door has malfunctioned."

Natasha spoke now in a stiff monotone, as though the shock of what she was saying was overwhelming her.

"Is Nikolai there?" she asked.

"Yes, he's at our table."

"I am about to call him on his pager," Natasha said. "I wanted to talk to you first. I . . . I am not sure why."

"I'm glad you did."

"Maybe it was unprofessional of me. I should have called Nikolai first." She sighed. "But I do not care."

"I'll meet you at the office," Jason said. "I want to see you."

"No, I don't want that," she snapped. "I . . . I can't deal with this. Nikolai is more suited to deal with this than I am."

"Then I'll meet you at your home," he said. He felt caught up in her escalating despair, felt that he could somehow help her.

"No," she said. "I don't want you there."

He pictured her blue eyes like water reflecting on ice, her short raven hair framing her face.

"I don't believe that," he said. "You keep pushing me away. But I know there's something between us."

"This isn't the time," she said in a small voice.

"I don't want you to be alone," he said. "I know we don't know each other very well, but . . . but this is a terrible thing that's happened, and you don't sound well. Let me take care of you."

He couldn't tell what she was thinking, whether she might hang up a moment later. He said nothing, frightened of shattering the delicacy of the moment.

"One hour," she said. She gave him her address.

"I'll be there," he replied.

"Please do not make me sorry." She hung up.

Jason put down the phone and leaned back against the wall and was overcome by a wave of dizziness. The impact of Vladimir's death washed over him like a delayed aftershock.

He walked slowly back to the table. There was a cloud over Nikolai as he smoked another cigar. David and Edward were talking across the table and were laughing loudly. A cart bearing their food was approaching the table.

"What is it?" David asked when he saw Jason.

Just then, Nikolai's beeper went off. He glanced down at it then quickly headed for the telephone.

"My God," Jason said.

"Jason," Edward said, starting to stand up.

"Vladimir's dead," Jason said.

Collective shock. David banged his knee against the table and recoiled physically.

"What the fuck happened?" David asked, his face colorless.

"That was Natasha Alyeva on the phone," Jason explained. "There was an explosion at Vladimir's apartment. They're reporting he was killed. It's all over the news."

"Was anyone else there?" Dave Maynard asked.

"I don't think so," Jason answered.

"God," David said. He dropped his napkin on the floor. His mouth moved without sound. Jason felt a rush of sympathy. Vladimir was more than a business associate to David; he was a friend. He saw him only hours ago. Did Belarin get to him that quickly? Was David or Annia next? He panicked.

Jason grabbed his refreshed drink and drained it in a single swallow. A waiter approached their table and started to serve them but stopped when he saw the pained expressions of the diners.

"Fucking assholes," David whispered to himself, too low for anyone but Jason to hear.

A second waiter appeared and, with hesitant expressions, they began lifting the silver covers off plates and placing them in front of each person at the table. The food was ignored, a sense of muted shock starting to replace initial surprise.

Suddenly Jason remembered what he had said on the phone, the way he had demanded to see Natasha. He wasn't even sure why he had been so insistent, but now he realized that he had to leave. He had to be with her. Jason put his hands on the table though he was uncomfortable with the idea of abandoning David and their colleagues. But he knew that he had to go. He looked around at the nearby tables, saw that the other diners were looking on with curiosity.

"I'm sorry," Jason said to David. "There's someplace I have to be."

"What?" David asked. "Where—"

"I'll contact you in the morning," Jason said. He moved away from the table and ignored the questioning looks of his colleagues. He

knew he was behaving completely out of character, but he was propelled by a pressing urgency that compelled him to move.

Jason brushed past Nikolai at the restaurant's entrance. The two
men stopped and stared at each other for a long moment. A vague
enmity had always existed between them and, in that moment, the
feeling seemed to surface. Nikolai frowned, rubbed his chin with a
meaty hand as though trying to control himself.

"She told you," Jason said.

"Yes," Nikolai said. He dropped his hands to his side and looked
away.

"Good . . . good luck dealing with everything," Jason said.

"Yes," Nikolai mumbled.

Jason stared for a moment longer at the Russian. He remembered
Natasha's misgivings about him, and the thought flashed through his
mind: *Could Nikolai have had anything to do with this?*

Nikolai patted his pants pocket and pulled out a set of keys. "I will
see you later," he barked to Jason as he bumped past him, through
the cavernous bright lobby of the Metropol Hotel and into the cold
night.

# Chapter Twenty

D AVID PUSHED AWAY HIS UNTOUCHED PLATE of food and looked around the table. He signaled for their waiter, who came immediately.

"There's been a . . . something's happened," David said, his own voice sounding strange to his ears. "Charge the meal to my room. I have to leave."

"Should I go back to the office?" Edward asked, folding his napkin neatly, his eyes round with emotion.

David felt for an instant as though he were falling. His chair felt flimsy and insubstantial beneath his weight, the floor hollow and ready to give way. Vladimir was dead, just hours after he had described to David the threat posed by Maxim Belarin.

"David?" Edward asked.

David moved pieces of information in his mind as if he were

289

assembling a complicated jigsaw puzzle. He realized that Belarin could come after him next. It would be rash to assassinate an American businessman on Russian soil. But it had happened before. No one would know the reason David or Annia might be killed or of his connection to Belarin. Their deaths would then be ascribed to an act of random violence, maybe a businessman's kidnapping gone wrong. David would vanish from the world just as Vladimir Borchenko had less than an hour before. The same could happen to Annia.

"David?" Jennifer Greene asked. "Are you all right?"

Something in her voice broke David out of his reverie. He cleared his throat and looked up. Everyone at the table was staring at him.

"Are you all right, David?" Jennifer repeated.

"Should I go to the office?" Edward asked.

"What for?"

"I don't know," Edward said. "Just to . . . in case we need to have someone there."

"Do what you need to do, Edward," David said. He got up from the table and glanced briefly from face to face.

"Where was Jason going?" Dave Maynard asked.

David didn't answer. He left the table without another word and walked quickly through the restaurant. When he got his coat and stepped out into the night, he had to put his hands in his pockets to keep them from shaking.

---

JASON SAT BACK in the company car and tried to slow his breath, feeling his heart race dangerously. The driver steered the car with swift confidence, maneuvering away from the Kremlin, through Theater Square, and into the city.

Jason shook his head, hoping he could settle the tumult in his mind. He had had a gut feeling back in the restaurant that Nikolai might have been involved in Vladimir's killing. Why? Because then Nikolai might be in a position to take over GlobusBank. He was

Vladimir's trusted aide, a young man in a position to take on great power.

The driver skirted past Tverskaya. Jason looked out the window and saw ten or fifteen women standing in the cold in front of the Moskva Hotel who were probably trying to supplement meager incomes. They turned onto Gertsena, a spoke in the wheel of one of Moscow's inner rings. Four-story apartment buildings loomed on either side of the street.

Jason blinked at the sights outside the window and suddenly realized what a scene he must have made in the restaurant by leaving so abruptly. The very idea made him feel adrift and uneasy. Olen Europe would be in a crisis mode with the death of Vladimir, one of the company's most important and influential friends.

You hardly know her, he said in an inner voice. You don't know who she really is.

The car slowed outside a five-story cement stucco building painted muted green; there were ornate iron bars over the windows on the ground level and a thin varnished wooden door at the main entrance. The driver turned around and motioned at the building, not caring to exercise his probably rudimentary English.

Jason had looked into Natasha's eyes, felt her grace and strength. It wasn't true that he didn't know her. Not at all. He understood everything he needed to know.

Jason heard the shrill tone of the security door unlocking, pushed it open and went inside. The foyer was gleaming white, with a brass fixture hanging overhead. This was one of the expensive renovated properties that had sprung up around Moscow and catered to the new class of professionals. Jason started up the spiral staircase to the third floor.

The staircase was solid, the only sound that of his feet impacting softly against spotless carpeting. When Jason reached the third story, he stepped out into the corridor. He glanced down at the slip of paper in his hand, found apartment 33, knocked on the door.

The corridor was silent. The building was old, with thick masonry walls. He knocked again, louder this time.

A stirring inside, then the sound of a lock clicking and a series of bolts being slid back. The door opened a crack then closed again. Jason heard the sound of a chain sliding in its track.

The door opened. Natasha was still in her business suit, buttoned up as though she were still at the office. Her eyes were red from tears, her makeup scrubbed away. Strands of loose hair spilled onto her forehead.

"Come in," she said impatiently.

Jason went inside and watched her locking the bolts, the chain. Her hands were shaking. They were in her living room, with parquet floors and Oriental rugs, a sofa arranged near the tall windows. The place was tasteful, well-furnished, immaculately neat. He stood breathing through his mouth, hearing his heart beat in his ears. He felt like he didn't know what to do, how to stand, what to say.

Natasha brushed past him without a word and disappeared around a corner. Jason was left alone, wondering what was happening.

"Natasha," he called out.

He heard a door opening, the rattle of wooden drawers being violently pulled open from somewhere inside the apartment. He walked slowly into the living room, saw the city at night through the windows. Along one wall there was a glassed-in antique bookcase full of hard-bound books. A rocking chair with a reading lamp was next to it, beside a small ceramic tile fireplace. Jason couldn't help but admire the place for a moment. It was warm and elegant.

He turned around. A small corridor led to a couple of closed doors, then a room at the end with the lights on. He heard a thump, a grunt.

He walked slow down the hall and felt like an intruder, but he went into her bedroom. The bed had a brass frame, luxurious blankets and pillows arranged in welcoming comfort. He looked away from it. On the wooden bureau were a series of framed photographs.

Natasha was on the floor and was pulling on a suitcase that was wedged under the bed. Her face was red, her expression furious.

"Can I help you with that?" he offered.

She looked up, blew her hair off her forehead. She shrugged, looked down at the suitcase, nodded.

Jason bent down and gripped the piece of luggage by the handle. He pulled hard, succeeded only in making the bed lurch several inches toward him. Then he saw the problem: A strap was wound round a piece of metal jutting from the frame. He loosened it, and the suitcase came out easily. He put it on the bed, opened it.

"Are . . . are you all right?" he asked. He hadn't expected this. She had barely acknowledged his presence since he came into the place. Now she was pulling open all her dresser drawers, grabbing clothes, and throwing them onto the bed. She went to the closet and started to take out blouses and slacks, not even bothering to remove them from the hangers.

"That's . . . that's not the best way to pack," he offered. "Everything's going to get wrinkled."

Ignoring him, Natasha went deeper into the closet and emerged with a few pairs of shoes, including a pair of Nike sneakers, which she dropped to the floor. The others went into the suitcase. She was breathing heavily, her body seeming electrically charged.

"Natasha," he said. She looked around, shaking her head slightly. He repeated her name.

Jason came around her side and reached for her. She tried to twist away, but he was too fast; he matched her movement and grabbed both her shoulders hard and held her there until she looked up at him.

"What is this?" he said. "What are you doing?"

She had clothes in her hands still, T-shirts that were wrinkling as her hands clenched into fists.

"What does it look like?" she said, her voice breaking. "I am leaving. I am going away."

"What? Why?"

"Don't be stupid," she hissed, her English still a precise British diction.

"I'm not being stupid," he insisted, still holding her. "Natasha, please. Talk to me."

She half-heartedly tried to twist out of his grip. "I am a business-woman," she said. "I do not fight against guns and bombs. I never thought it would come to this."

As she spoke her voice rose, the words coming in a torrent.

"Please," he said gently. "Sit with me."

He took her hand and led her to the bed. They sat down next to each other, sinking into the soft mattress.

"You're scared because Vladimir was killed?" he asked. "I understand. But don't worry. You haven't done anything wrong."

Her narrow shoulders hunched. She looked down at the floor.

"Is it Nikolai?" he asked. "Does this have anything to do with what we were talking about today?"

A single tear traced a path down her cheek. "I don't know," she said. "Nikolai might be capable of anything."

"I saw him at the Metropol," Jason offered. "He looked as shocked as any of us."

She nodded, brushed away the tear with an angry expression as though she hadn't wanted Jason to think she was weak.

"It is nice of you to come see me, but I am fine," she announced suddenly. She tossed the handful of clothes into the suitcase, stood up, slammed the luggage shut.

"Where are you going?" he asked.

She looked down at the suitcase as though seeing it for the first time. She blinked, her mouth open. Jason wondered if she was going into some kind of shock.

"You don't need to leave the city," Jason offered. He reached out and delicately took her hand, frightened that she might pull away.

294

She didn't. "A terrible thing happened to Vladimir, but you're safe. I'll look after you."

"Why are you doing this?" she asked.

He paused. "You know why."

For a second her hand grasped his. He felt her warmth, decided to pull her closer. But in that instant she pulled away.

"I have to speak to my father," she said.

"Where is he?"

"Just outside the city." Natasha looked into the mirror over the dresser and started to arrange her hair.

"I'm coming with you," Jason said, standing up. She looked at him in the mirror's reflection. "Don't say no. I want to be with you."

She sighed, folded her arms. Then she looked up at him and, almost imperceptibly, nodded.

He walked over to her; their eyes locked in the mirror. She stayed still as he put his arms around her waist, pressed his chest to her back. Her expression in the mirror was inscrutable, wary. Jason gently turned her to face him, not letting her slip away from his grasp for an instant.

She said his name, almost a whisper. He pulled her to him, felt the warmth of her body, the smell of her perfume. He kissed the soft skin where a tear had fallen and tasted the salt that remained on her flesh. She plunged one hand into his hair, pulled his face close to hers. Their mouths met, and Jason closed his eyes, felt the yearning of desire mingled with something stronger, more profound, like a spilling out of his soul into the moment.

For a second they stopped, both simultaneously remembering who they were, where they were, all that had happened. Their eyes met. Jason looked deep into the icy pool of Natasha's gaze, felt all the walls that fenced in his character begin to give way. The instant was suspended, almost timeless. Jason realized that they could stop now; they could tell each other it was a moment of madness and let it go forever.

He couldn't let that happen. He pulled her close again, kissing her, trying to communicate everything that was in his heart. They fell softly onto the bed again, with no words, just a new universe that the two of them were creating together.

*February 19, 1998. 10:31 p.m.*
*Moscow.*

DAVID RODE IN A CREAKY ELEVATOR inside a nondescript stone building just four blocks from the Kremlin. He had walked there himself, letting the cold soothe his senses and the exertion slow the rate of his heart. It had been only a half-hour since he heard of Vladimir's death, and already he felt empty, anxious, and vulnerable at the prospect of being in Russia without the familiar presence of his old comrade.

When the elevator stopped, David walked into the hallway. It was drab and ill-lit, with bad paneling and a threadbare, stained carpet under his feet. The long corridor was quiet, all the doors closed for the night. There were a lot of Western firms with branch offices in this building: consultants, telecommunications companies, even a couple of Olen Europe's competitors. But at the very end of the third-floor hallway was a door and a plaque reading "U.S. Consulate Special Affairs."

It had been more than three years since David had come here. David opened the door, which was unlocked twenty-four hours a day. A young man in civilian clothes stood up from behind a glassed-in cubicle and motioned toward an intercom box.

"Yeah?" he asked in a southern U.S. accent.

"I need to use a secure phone," David said. He took out his passport and a special I.D., put them in a tray carved into the Plexiglas. The young man slid the tray to the other side of the glass and examined the documents when they came through.

The secured telephone lines at this office were a secret known to very few Americans. David had had access arranged through the CIA since the early days of the deal, when the phones were located in the U.S. Embassy—David hadn't trusted those phones and had been proved right when it turned out that the new embassy in Moscow had been constructed with scores of built-in listening devices. Now these lines were available to a few high-level businessmen with sensitive matters to discuss that shouldn't be heard by a curious hotel operator or—although no one was supposed to say so—by an agent of the reconstructed Russian security services.

"All right," the young man said, turning the tray and sending David's documentation back to his side of the glass. "You know the drill, sir?"

"Sure," David said. "Which room is open?"

"Number two, right through there." He pointed at one of two doors at either end of the bare reception space.

"Thank you," David said.

David had once asked Vladimir to check out whether the secured lines at this consulate offshoot were indeed free from surveillance. David suppressed a chill when he realized that Vladimir had probably used Maxim Belarin to verify that the lines were indeed free of listening devices.

He opened the door and stepped into a small room. There was a U.S. map on the wall, a metal desk and swivel chair next to a large box with a phone receiver protruding from it. On the desk were pads of paper, pens, and a small American flag on a plastic base, like the kind sold back home for Fourth of July picnics.

David sat down at the desk and loosened his tie. The room was soundproofed, so quiet that he could hear the sound of the fluorescent lights buzzing over his head. He dialed a number from memory on the big phone after checking a series of red-and-green lights to indicate that the scrambling technology was activated.

"Representative Becker's office," said a woman's voice, as clear as if he were calling from across town.

"Coretta, this is David Olen," he said.

"Oh, Mr. Olen, Carl's been waiting for you," Becker's secretary said. "One moment. I'll put you right through."

David stared at the desk, pulled a sheet of paper, and started a nervous doodle.

"David, shit. Where have you been?"

"Carl." David paused. "I'm sorry I couldn't get back to you."

Carl said something, his voice muffled. A moment later he came back on the line. "I'm alone now," he said. "We can talk."

"I'm on the secured phone," David offered.

"Good."

"Borchenko's dead," David said.

"Borchenko—" David heard Carl inhale sharply. "Dead. How?"

"His apartment blew up," David replied. "They found his body in the wreckage."

"A hit?" Carl asked.

"One would assume."

A long pause. "Did you see him before it happened? You've been in Moscow all day, right?"

"Yeah, I saw him. I talked to him."

"What about this thing with the agency?" Carl asked. "Did you have a chance to—"

"Yes."

Carl sounded impatient, stressed. "What'd he say?"

"Basically he said the CIA could go fuck itself for all he cared."

"Sounds like the Borchenko you always told me about," Carl said. He had only met Vladimir once, and very briefly, in Chicago.

"It was in character," said David.

"How are you handling it?" Carl asked. "You sound weird. Maybe you should get out of there."

"I'm considering it," David said. "What else did you have to tell me?"

Silence. David sensed that Carl was choosing his words.

"Don't screw around with me, Carl." He closed his eyes and massaged them with his free hand. "Talk to me."

"Ah, shit," Carl said, sounding resigned. "This Gleason kid is raw, even I can see that. He worked with Jim Allen for a couple of years, and now he thinks he's a super spy."

"Vladimir wasn't going to help him," David said. "He wasn't stupid. There's nothing to gain from meddling in politics again, not the way he did, at least."

"Not from Gleason's point of view," Carl explained. "It turns out he told his superiors just enough to get approval for his plan. Turns out the agency likes the idea of having a friend in Rome for another twenty years or so. Wojtyla proved how much power can come from there."

"He was special," David said. "He's an extraordinary case."

"All I know is the activities you were involved in helped put him in power," Carl said. "Look what happened after that. Some people in Washington would like to have another go at it."

"Who?" David demanded. "Who's signed off on this?"

"He's not saying," Carl sighed. "And whoever it is, they probably don't know a tenth of the real story. You know how plausible deniability works. Don't ask; don't tell."

There was no window in the room—David had once been told that a KGB agent might sit across the street with binoculars and lip-read and take notes. As a result the little space might as well have been inside a submarine, deep underwater.

"There's no more Borchenko. Most of the Holy Fist in the Vatican is dead," David explained. "It's over. Gleason needs to realize this."

Silence on the line.

"Who killed Vladimir?" Carl asked suddenly.

Now it was David's turn to choose his words.

"You know, don't you?" asked Carl.

"It's someone you never met."

"Someone involved in the deal?" Carl asked.

"Yes." David leaned back, exhausted.

"Everything comes back to the fucking deal," Carl said. "You know, for twenty-five years now I've been waiting for the deal to come back and bite me in the ass. And now it's happening."

David didn't reply. He could only agree. He thought back to the long road from Japan to Warsaw to Moscow.

"It's dirty, all of it," Carl said. "It shouldn't have happened the way it did."

"What do you mean?"

"Are you saying you don't know?" Carl asked.

"Know what? I don't have time for—"

"Gleason told me about it," Carl said, his voice grave. "I didn't know until a couple of days ago. I was . . . I couldn't believe it. Borchenko knew; he arranged it. Are you saying you never—"

"What are you saying?" David asked quietly.

"It's about Albino Luciani," Carl said.

"Pope John Paul I."

"You remember what happened when he got elected instead of Wojtyla," Carl said. "I was out of the loop, but I remember you telling me."

"There was a lot of anger. It was like a betrayal," David said. His eyes were fixed on the nonsense scribble before him. He suddenly felt deeply afraid of what he might hear next.

*February 19, 1998. 9:08 p.m.*
*The Vatican.*

THE POPE LAY SUPINE in a hospital bed deep inside the Vatican. His eyes were closed, but he could almost feel the hand of God nearby. It was extended, almost touching him.

He had to hold on. The millennium was coming; he wanted to usher it in. But he wasn't sure whether he would survive this latest illness, and he had sent word that he wanted visitors. Those who remained from his youth in Katowice. Faces from his early days in Krakow, changed with age, eyes to see and voices to hear if it was indeed time for him to leave this earth.

His had been a long journey. When he was a young man, he thought he would be an actor or a playwright. He had even fantasized about becoming an athlete in the years when his strong young body had obeyed his every command. Then the Church had taken him, with its sublime mysteries and intellectual challenges. He had toiled to glorify God, and after decades under the tutelage of Cardinal Litwinski, he even dared to dream of becoming Pontiff. He remembered the elections of 1978, the hot summer in Rome, the bitter disappointment when his dreams seemed to be smashed.

Karol Wojtyla had arrived in Rome and been stunned by its beauty, by the awesome history of the home of the Church. He and his mentor, Cardinal Litwinski, had been taken directly to the Vatican.

First there had been the Mass of the Holy Spirit in the Basilica of St. Peter's then a procession of the 111 members of the College of Cardinals—all moving with slow gravity, their hands clasped together and their eyes lowered in memory of Pope Paul VI. Wojtyla had marched alongside Litwinski, his mentor and sponsor.

After the years of waiting, it was a relief to see the vestments of the cardinals undulating like a field of summertime flowers, to hear the Latin of opening prayers. The procession slowed at the entrance to the Sistine Chapel. Wojtyla gazed up at the exquisite arches and became transfixed by the beauty there.

It was summer, and the chapel was stifling as the cardinals searched for their places amid wooden desks and chairs. A working office for more than a hundred men had been created below Michaelangelo's immortal frescoes. The cardinals, wearing scarlet *mozettas*, shoulder capes, over their cassocks, began to fan themselves in the stuffy heat. Wojtyla gave a start when he heard a sharp sound. The doors were being chained and locked. The cardinals would be effectively imprisoned for the duration of the conclave.

301

Alongside the altar was a small stove. A metal flue rose almost to the ceiling, where it made a sharp angle to connect with a chimney. This would be the outside world's daily means of knowing whether the conclave was a success. Black smoke would rise from the chimney when the balloting failed to produce a new Pontiff. Only after a two-thirds majority had come to an agreement would white smoke be released.

For the duration of the conclave, the cardinals had been assigned makeshift living quarters carved out of the offices and private rooms in the Vatican offices adjoining the Sistine Chapel. The rooms were little more than cubicles, and inside them the air was even hotter and more close than in the chapel itself. There were concessions to seniority: The older the cardinal, the closer was his room to the chapel. When Wojtyla accompanied Litwinski inside his room, there was barely enough space for the two of them to stand together.

"This must be a broom closet," Litwinski said, his aged face creased into a tired smile. "My cell in seminary was palatial compared to this."

"Can we speak freely?" Wojtyla asked.

"Of course, Karol, within rational limits," Litwinski said. "Before each vote a great deal of conversation will take place. Favors will be collected—and future favors promised. There will be intense discussion about your qualifications for the papacy."

A knock at the door startled both of them; Wojtyla opened it.

Litwinski gave a warm greeting to Cardinal O'Brien of Chicago. A moment later they saw Bishop Majorski leaning on the doorway.

"What are you doing here?" Litwinski asked. No one but the cardinals were supposed to be in the convocation halls.

"It's all right," Majorski said. The head of the Vatican Bank smiled. "I happen to know my way around here. I went from the dining room in the Sala Borgia to here. They can't keep everyone out."

"I just talked to the Frenchman, Cardinal Lebard," O'Brien said. He was a short man with narrow shoulders. He had an intense, hawk-like manner that made him imposing despite his small size.

"Yes?" Litwinski asked expectantly.

Wojtyla stood looking down over O'Brien's shoulder. Suddenly this tiny room had become an impromptu meeting of the Holy Fist. Majorski was vital to their cause; although Wojtyla was cautious in his presence, the Vatican banker processed the money, with David Olen's help, that came from O'Brien's Chicago archdiocese.

"The Europeans will be voting for Poggioli," O'Brien said, rubbing his hands absently as he spoke. "I'm talking primarily about Schneider, Lebard, Jameson. They're going to be voting as one."

Litwinski shook his head bitterly, unable to accept such bad news for their cause so early in the conclave. "You must be mistaken," he said. "They've been made aware of the deal. They know how important it is for Karol to be elected during this session."

"It's not just them," O'Brien replied ruefully. "The squeeze is on."

"Pardon me," Wojtyla interrupted. "The squeeze?"

"Pardon the slang," O'Brien said. "What I mean is that the European Cardinals are getting pressure from their governments. There was a meeting recently, very quiet, between a group of cardinals and a top aide to the French president. They tried to keep it quiet, but I found out. The Western European politicians are afraid of the idea of a Polish pope. They see the potential liberation of Eastern Europe as a political and economic disaster in the making."

"How?" Wojtyla asked.

"Huge populations, suddenly freed, on their doorstep," Majorski said, his voice cold. "Immigrating to their countries, using their social services, disrupting their economies and their peace. Not to mention political fragmentation—in the Balkans, to name one obvious example."

"I see," Litwinski said, his voice cold.

"Europe mixes church and state," O'Brien said. "It's not like that in America."

"Not to the same degree," Majorski agreed.

The bishop, almost forgotten in the doorway, wore a grave expression. He was a big man with broad shoulders, strong arms, a large head with blockish features.

"This is terrible," Litwinski said.

"Perhaps it is not so bad," Wojtyla offered.

Wojtyla did not always know every detail of the Holy Fist's and Litwinski's dealings on his behalf in trying to raise him to the papacy. Money from the West had helped bring Wojtyla to prominence in the church, along with his own activism and intellectual activities. The same money flow had also gone to support Wojtyla's counterpart in the Soviet Union. There had been snags along the way, such as when Majorski opposed Wojtyla's using some of the funds to support the Solidarity worker's movement in Poland. But Wojtyla had eventually won that battle; in the end, he was the man who might become pope. Already a small degree of prestige enveloped him.

"We have the Third World cardinals," Litwinski said, almost to himself.

"Most of them," O'Brien countered. "Particularly the ones who are interested in keeping communism from taking over their countries."

"This will not be enough," Litwinski said. "We also need Europe."

"Agreed," O'Brien said. "We have to make it clear what Wojtyla represents. We have our work cut out for us."

The next day the murmured discussions in the chapel halls were replaced with intense silence as the cardinals awaited Cardinal Deacon Ambrotti's instructions. Wojtyla filled out his paper ballot and folded it as directed. The cardinals were called to the altar in order of seniority to place their ballots in an ornate wooden box.

Karol Wojtyla waited at his desk as three cardinals counted the ballots. He thought of the mysterious workings of God. The battle for souls between atheistic communism and the Church. He contemplated his own life lived between the evils of Nazism and the soul-crushing power of communism. He looked up from his contemplation when the results appeared.

The first name was Poggioli's: thirty votes. Then Wojtyla: twenty-eight. Vincenzo: twenty. Luciani: eighteen. Schneider: fifteen. The room erupted in noise when the tally was posted. Everyone headed for the doors. *Nero* smoke was soon released from the stove, indicating that the final decision had yet to be made.

"We didn't do badly for the first ballot," Litwinski said to Wojtyla as they sat together at the end of a long table in the dining room. Wojtyla smelled the baskets of sweet rolls placed on the table. He listened for the next hour as Litwinski cajoled the European cardinals and pleaded with them to vote for a non-Italian, for an intellectual, for new young blood in the Church. O'Brien watched from the next table, his gaze sharp as he slowly picked at his food.

After the second ballot Wojtyla realized that, if he were to become pope, it would only be after a mighty struggle. Litwinski's politicking had been successful, and Karol Wojtyla had led the balloting with thirty-five votes. Poggioli had thirty. Luciani had gained seven votes for a total of twenty-five. Vincenzo received sixteen while Schneider dropped to five.

A tide seemed to have turned in the dining room that afternoon. Wojtyla ate in silence, looked around. The curialists, Vatican insiders and traditionalists, looked preoccupied and disturbed. Third World cardinals, from the Philippines, Africa, and South America, gathered excitedly. They had started to truly believe that they had real power and influence in the election.

Wojtyla and Litwinski split up, each sitting with a group of Third World cardinals. Wojtyla sat with a group from Nigeria, Malaysia, and Argentina. He listened to their concerns, spoke genuinely of his hope for the Church taking on a new global focus and recognizing its brothers all around the world. He looked into their eyes and felt stirred by their compassion and earnestness.

305

The chapel was like an oven in the afternoon. The cardinals filed in and took now-familiar places at their desks. They filled out their ballots and slid them into the box. The smell of sweat filled the sacred air, sounds muffled in the thickness of the atmosphere.

Luciani had moved into the lead with fifty-eight votes. Wojtyla had forty-two. Vincenzo: fourteen. Poggioli: five.

Litwinski and Karol Wojtyla stood together in the hallway after the adjournment. There was another vote scheduled for a half-hour later, the last of the day. Some of the older cardinals walked heavily to their quarters; their sighs of misery could be heard in the hallway as the old men suffered in the intense heat.

"I don't like this," Litwinski said. "Who is this Luciani? He was never considered before the conclave."

"I suppose that's why he's gained so many votes," Wojtyla offered. In his mind was a picture of the Venetian Luciani: unimposing, his eyes behind black-framed glasses, a look of genuine humility on his face.

"I don't know that he even wants the papacy," Litwinski said. "Did you see how worried he looked when they posted the last vote?"

"I did," Wojtyla said. "But I can see why he's ahead. He's an Italian but neither a pastoralist nor a curialist. He's neither an insider nor an outsider. He can appeal to both sides."

"You've been paying attention to politics, Karol," Litwinski said, with a slight note of surprise.

Wojtyla smiled. It had been a long time since their first meeting with Borchenko. Now they stood at the defining moment of their plan. Their dream was about to be either fulfilled or destroyed.

Wojtyla went to his desk in the chapel. He was almost alone there; the other cardinals were taking advantage of the brief recess for rest, to eat, to drink water. Wojtyla leaned back and looked up at Michelangelo's work. His eyes paused on the panel depicting Adam resting on a cloud attended by angels. God extended His arm from heaven to the earthbound man. Their fingers nearly touched. The divine spark of creation gave Adam life, sealing the covenant between God and Man.

"Your Eminence."

Wojtyla, startled, jerked in his chair.

"Excuse me," said Cardinal Schneider.

"I'm sorry," Wojtyla said, embarrassed. "I was lost in the beauty of this artwork. It has been said many times before, but it is as though God himself was holding the brush."

The other cardinals began filing into the room. Soon it would be time for the final ballot of the day.

"I tried to convince the Europeans to take your side," Schneider said. His green eyes shone from under his lined forehead. "It is politics, a fear of what you represent. I made your priorities clear, but I was not successful. You must understand—there is political fear in Western Europe of the consequences of Eastern Europe's liberation. I am sorry, but I tried."

Wojtyla clasped the older man's hand, moved by his sincerity, and gave him deep thanks.

While the votes were being cast, Wojtyla experienced a deep sensation of peace. There was nothing more to be done. The Holy Fist had struggled, had put well-considered plans into action. The problem had come, he now understood from what Schneider had said, from an unexpected source. The political leaders of Western Europe were afraid of freeing Eastern Europe from communism. Now he saw that Majorski had been right. Western Europe feared the influence of huge populations suddenly freed from an oppression that had kept them under control and docile—as well as the ire of Russia should it lose its satellites.

Luciani received sixty-five votes, enough to win. Wojtyla received forty, followed by Vincenzo with six. A loud sigh seemed to echo through the high ceiling of the Sistine Chapel.

The cardinals rose as one to pay respect to the new pope. Albino Luciani, a small, frail-looking man, was led to the front of the chapel.

"Do you accept your canonical election as Supreme Pontiff?" asked Cardinal Ambrotti in a firm, clear voice.

"*Accepto*," said Luciani, tears welling in his eyes. A white Papal robe was slipped over his shoulders. Luciani sat on the magnificent throne beneath the Last Judgment as the cardinals formed a line to kiss the new pope's ring. Wojtyla stood stunned at the sight of Litwinski, his mentor, his surrogate father, bowing before the new Italian pope.

In that instant Karol Wojtyla thought that the deal—the confluence of the Holy Fist with Vladimir Borchenko and Mikhail Sergeivich in Russia—would never be consummated. The years of struggle were lost.

Wojtyla saw Bishop Majorski minutes later, moving through the crowd of cardinals that milled outside the chapel preparing for the aftermath of the conclave. Majorski shook his head angrily when he saw Wojtyla, the muscles in the Vatican banker's jaw working with tension and visible through his ruddy skin.

"I've come to pay respects to the new pope," Majorski said in a dry voice. "Just like everyone else."

"It is . . . it is a momentous day," Wojtyla said, keeping his voice low, aware that the cardinals would be watching him for his reaction after narrowly losing the papacy.

"When Luciani finds out what we've been up to, it's all over," Majorski said in a low voice, his lips close to Wojtyla's ear. "The Holy Fist, the money pipeline. The deal with the Russians. He's made no secret of his desire for reform. I understand that the Vatican Bank will be one of the first Church institutions to undergo a stringent review."

Cardinal Litwinski appeared at Wojtyla's other elbow, and the three men walked out to the steps overlooking St. Peter's Square. The sun was blinding; throngs of people sweated and cheered the election of the new pope. Wojtyla felt Litwinski sag by his side, as though this defeat was too much for him.

But on his other side Majorski was tense, radiating fear and anger. His fingers dug into Wojtyla's elbow.

"This is a disaster, unacceptable. I need to make a call," he said, turning away from the cheering throng. "What time is it in Moscow?"

---

ALBINO LUCIANI, POPE JOHN PAUL I, was dead within the month, felled by weak health and the stresses of a papacy that some claimed he never truly wanted. Wojtyla was elected pope during the next conclave, one that lacked the drama of the election just weeks before. This time Wojtyla ascended to the throne and watched the procession of cardinals approaching him with their heads bowed. He took the name John Paul II in honor of Luciani.

Now near the millennium's end, Wojtyla lay silent in his hospital bed, his eyes narrow slits, barely registering the objects around him and the medical staff that attended to his failing body.

The workings of God were magnificent and often unknowable. In quiet moments he had often wondered why Luciani had been raised to the papacy only to be taken away so quickly. It was like a puzzle that he was never able to solve to his satisfaction. But perhaps all that was important was that the Holy Fist succeeded. Poland was liberated. Communism fell. Hundreds of millions of Catholic believers were returned to the Church without bloodshed, trauma, or terror. The dreams of his life had come to pass, and perhaps now all that was left were these memories. He clung to life; he wanted nothing more than to see in the new millennium as the shepherd of the world's flock. But for now he was tired, his eyes heavy, the pull of sleep so strong . . .

*February 19, 1998. 11:02 p.m.*
*Moscow.*

DAVID SAT AT THE DESK in the U.S. Consulate special office, the drab environs an ironic counterpoint to what he was hearing. He glanced at his watch, saw that it was after ten.

"Albino Luciani's election seemed like a fatal blow to the conspiracy," David said to Carl Becker. "I remember that. Vladimir was distraught. Majorski was shitting in his pants. But it all worked out, didn't it? I mean, we got lucky. Luciani died in his sleep. He was one of the shortest reigning popes in history."

"That's not the whole story, David," Carl replied.

David took a deep breath. Of course it wasn't. He knew what his old friend was about to tell him; it was clear now. But he didn't want to hear it. He didn't want to speak the words. He didn't want to think that he had been even peripherally involved in such a thing.

"I had no idea until Gleason—" Carl began.

"He was killed, wasn't he?" David interrupted. "Pope John Paul I was assassinated."

Silence on the line, punctuated only by the sound of Carl breathing.

"Tell me it isn't true," David challenged him. "Tell me we weren't mixed up in something so . . . so heinous."

"Borchenko probably ordered it," Carl said. "When Albino Luciani was elected Pontiff in 1978, Maxim Belarin had dispatched a Chechen assassin to the Vatican. Albino Luciani had been poisoned, and Cardinal Beunadona, along with Bishops Majorski and Villetti, had known in advance that the assassination was to take place. The three men succeeded in a cover-up conspiracy to ensure that no autopsy was performed and that the pope's death was ruled the result of natural causes. I don't know how they got the assassin into the Vatican. It had to be someone with the Holy Fist. Majorski, probably. He was the one who had the most to lose."

"You didn't know?" David whispered.

"For God's sake, David. How long have we known each other?

They had a man killed. A man of God. I'm just . . . I'm just really relieved to hear that you didn't know about it, either."

"Jim Allen knew?" David asked.

"He knew," Carl replied. "He put the information in a sealed file. No one was supposed to have access to it until Allen was dead. I don't know why he did it. He wasn't involved in the killing, but he apparently picked up on it through a KGB contact."

The phone in David's hand felt sterile and cold. The room looked yellowed and insubstantial, like a stage set.

"We were part of it," David said.

Carl didn't reply.

"Did Wojtyla know?"

"I can't say," Carl answered. "Gleason didn't have anything to tell me one way or the other."

"You call this kid, Carl, and—"

"David. Calm down," Carl said. "I've heard this tone in your voice before. You know we're in no position to—"

"Never mind!" David barked. "I'll call that prick and tell him Borchenko's dead. And I'm not going to help him. It's over. I want out."

"This is the CIA, David. It's not like—"

"He has to stay away from the Vatican," David continued. "Annia's in Rome to visit Wojtyla. I'm going there to take her home. If she's approached because she's my wife, then I'm coming to Washington and getting restitution from Gleason and from the whole fucking CIA if that's what it comes to."

"David," Carl said quietly. A lifetime of friendship, confidences, and compromises were in his voice.

"I'm getting out of here," David said. "It's probably not even safe for me to be in Moscow right now."

"Do you think—"

"I'm sick and tired of living with all this. I'm taking Annia home. And then it's over. I'm out, Carl."

Before Carl Becker could reply, David slammed down the phone.

He sat staring at it for almost a full minute and tried to calm the shaking that racked his body before picking the phone back up and calling a number he hadn't dialed in years . . . but one he could never forget as much as he tried.

---

"I'M TRYING TO REACH a Thomas Gleason," David said into the phone.

"Who's calling please?" a female voice asked.

"Tell him it's David Olen and it's *urgent.*"

"One moment please."

The wait felt like hours to David. Adrenalin was coursing through his body. He'd never felt so angry. This was it—the moment he'd been waiting for, for years. He was getting out, no matter the consequences.

"David Olen, I've been looking forward to speaking with you. I didn't expect you to call me, though," said a male voice.

"Is this Gleason?" David spat.

"Yes, yes. I'm sorry. I'm Thomas Gleason. I assume you've spoken to Carl Becker."

"Listen. I'll say this once. I'm out. Borchenko is dead and I, no doubt, am lined up to be next. Or my wife. I've done my duty. Now I learn I was an accessory to an assassination. That's it. It's over. And stay away from the Vatican. My wife is there. I'm going to get her and take her home. Do you hear me? Do you understand?"

"Whoa, whoa, Mr. Olen. Hang on. Calm down. I know a lot has happened, but I think you're overreacting. I think we need to meet and discuss this calmly."

David shook his head. He took a deep breath. He spoke softly but with resolve. "Mr. Gleason. Thomas. You prick. I don't think you heard me. It's over. I'm out of it. No matter what you say or what you threaten me with. It is over." He placed the phone receiver back into its cradle and walked away.

# Chapter Twenty-One

B ACK AT HIS HOTEL ROOM, David let the phone ring a few more times before he shook his head and hung up. Jason still hadn't returned to his room. David began to pace from one end of his room to the other, the sound of his footsteps on the carpeting the only noise to break the silence.

He wished he could go to a gym, play some basketball, maybe take a run. He needed action to clear the riot in his mind.

He softly punched his open palm with his fist as he paced and enumerated everything he now knew. Vladimir was dead. Surely Maxim Belarin was responsible. Belarin had his old connections with the KGB; he had access to professional killers.

Like the killer who had assassinated Albino Luciani in 1978. The thought hit David's psyche like an echo, reverberating against his own sense of morality. Perhaps he should have guessed about

Luciani; maybe he had kept his own head in the sand and was unable to deal with the terrible reality of the act that brought their plans to fruition.

But no. He hadn't known; he hadn't suspected. He couldn't have been able to live with himself. And if Vladimir was responsible, David would have found it impossible to continue dealing with him. They had conspired; they had laundered money. They had committed any number of international crimes in pursuing their goals. But murder was something else entirely.

"Vladimir, you asshole," David whispered. He wished his old friend was in front of him right now. He would demand an answer, and he would tell Vladimir that they had sacrificed their decency.

The phone rang. David looked up, not recognizing the sound for a moment. He was on the other side of the room, and he rushed across to pick it up on the fourth ring.

"David Olen?" asked a deep, heavily accented voice.

David paused. "Yes."

"This is Maxim Belarin. It has been a long time. I hope that I am not disturbing you."

David felt a sense of lightness, a physical urge to run. Suddenly he realized that it was entirely possible that he might die that night, that he might never see Annia and Monica again. A sense of his own mortality came to him in a rush, almost incapacitating him.

"David?"

"Yes, yes, Maxim," David said. He hoped his fear wasn't detectable in his voice. But of course it was. Belarin was an interrogator, a torturer. He preyed on fear.

"I am not disturbing you?"

"No, of course not," David replied. "What can I do for you?"

"It is terrible what has happened to Vladimir Borchenko. You are probably as shocked as I am."

David didn't reply. He couldn't read Belarin's tone over the phone.

The Russian sounded sincere. But he also could have been speaking with a sadist's smile on his lips.

"I am shocked," David said. "Vladimir was a friend."

"I know the two of you had a relationship. He spoke highly of you."

There was a genuine warmth in Belarin's voice that broke David's concentration much more effectively than if the Russian had called and began making wild threats.

"It's late," David said.

"I understand," Belarin replied. "But I have one thing to ask of you. Would you do me the favor of meeting in the lobby of your hotel? I would like to speak in person."

"I don't—"

"Please don't think I am rude," Belarin broke in. "I would only require five minutes of your time."

David felt the phone slip against his ear. Sweat, he realized. The receiver was wet with his sweat.

"David—"

There was no point putting it off. He couldn't hide from Belarin. If Belarin wanted him dead, he might already be gone. There was no choice but to meet with him.

"All right," David said. "I can be down in the lobby in fifteen minutes."

"Perfect," Belarin said. "I am in my car. Please wait if I am a moment late."

"Of course," David said.

He hung up the phone and looked up into the mirror hanging behind the desk. His features were haunted with shadows, his eyes glassy with fear. And he had fifteen minutes in which to try to find a brave face.

---

"YOU HAVE A STRANGE EXPRESSION," Natasha said.

Jason looked up. She had changed into a pair of jeans and pulled on a black sweater. Her hair was combed back from her face. A half-hour ago they had made love with an intensity that now threatened to embarrass them both.

"I'm just thinking," Jason said.

He had subsumed his spirit into work, always thinking about the next deal and the next flight he had to catch. Now he was sitting up in Natasha's bed and was dressed in slacks and T-shirt. He felt totally exposed, almost helpless before her.

She came to him and put her hand on his. "I don't know—" she began.

"Wait," he said. "Don't say anything about what happened. Please don't say that it doesn't have to mean anything."

She looked at him strangely for a second, and then her expression softened. "That is not what I was going to say."

He took her hand and squeezed it. "Good," he said. "I want this to be a beginning for us, not an end."

She looked away then back at him. "There are things about me that you don't know," she said.

"I don't care."

She sighed. "I . . . I have to go."

"I'm coming with you." He got up from the bed, found his shirt and jacket, started putting on his socks.

"That would not be a good idea."

"It's a fact. I'm coming with you." He buttoned his shirt, ran his hands through his hair.

"I don't want you involved," she said. She picked up her purse from her dresser. "Look, Jason. You can stay here. I will only be gone for a couple of hours."

"You were terrified when I got here tonight," he told her. "I'm not going to allow you to be alone. Not right now."

She bit her lip, seemed to entertain some inner conflict. "I am going to see my parents," she said. "It is . . . it is delicate."

"I won't be offensive," Jason said. "I won't portray myself as your lover, just a friend. But I'm coming with you."

"You don't know . . ." Her voice trailed off. "Isn't there . . . someone in your life? Someone you will go back to?"

"No one," Jason said. He reached out and lightly touched her arm, felt the thick wool of her sweater.

"I don't know you," she said, looking into his eyes.

"You do," he said. "You know me."

She leaned toward him and grazed his lips with her own. "I suppose I do," she said quietly.

"Then we'll go together," he said, this time without receiving a reply.

Her BMW was parked underneath the building. She drove quickly and confidently, the headlights cutting through the darkness once they had driven past the Garden Ring. Jason watched her profile, sensed the conflict that was raging inside her. There was a lot he didn't know about her, but he knew everything that was important.

When they stopped at an intersection, she looked over at him. "We are crazy," she said, almost smiling.

"Tell me about your parents," he said.

Her expression hardened. "My mother is sick," she said. "We have a nurse to take care of her."

"Is that why we're going there?" Jason asked. "To check on her?"

She put the car in gear and stared at the road.

"Natasha?"

"My father probably will not be there," she said. "We do not get along. He was in the Soviet military and then in the intelligence services. Do you know what I mean?"

"KGB?" Jason asked.

"He was very prominent," Natasha said. Her jawline pulsed with tension. "He still thinks he is living in the Soviet Union. I received many privileges as his daughter. But he cannot understand my choices, the fact that I have gone into business. In his world he is the king. As his daughter I am supposed to obey his every command."

The venom in her tone surprised Jason. He looked out the window and saw that they were leaving the dense, populated parts of Moscow for the city's outskirts. Natasha steered the car off the highway and onto a two-lane road that branched off to the north. Jason realized that he was completely lost.

"Please be calm and quiet around my mother," Natasha said. "I don't want to upset her. She has been through enough already."

Jason watched her profile shift into light and out again. When she spoke of her family, she seemed to change, become conflicted and distant. He wanted to reach out to her, take her hand, caress her cheek. But this wasn't the time. She had receded into the deep emotions of her life, and it would take time before he could reach her there.

"I wonder if they've caught the people who killed Vladimir," Jason said. He was speaking aloud, changing the subject, but as soon as he spoke, he sensed that he had made a mistake. Natasha's grip tightened on the wheel. She winced, exhaled loudly.

The words formed on his lips: *What do you know?* But he stopped himself, feeling that he would drive her away from him in spirit. Natasha was harboring some information about Vladimir's death; Jason was almost sure of it—some shady deal in which Vladimir was involved, perhaps some kind of territorial war among the country's oligarchs that had contributed to his demise. He decided that he would wait until she was ready to tell him then deal with it however he could.

Another thought crossed his mind. David and his secrets. Could David be involved? After all, he was probably one of the last people to see Vladimir alive. It wasn't possible, was it? David was his mentor, his friend.

Then another thought hit him. Did it have to do with Nikolai? Was this why she had been so frightened, so prepared to leave the city? Because the man who was now her closest business associate was somehow connected to the killing? The thought gave Jason a burst of adrenaline. He pictured himself confronting Nikolai, hitting him, making him leave Natasha alone forever.

"Here," she whispered.

"This is it," she said. She glanced toward a small house set in a darkened grove. "My mother does not speak English, but she does not talk much to anyone. I . . . want to see her; then, we will leave."

"I understand," Jason said. He had never felt like this, trying to keep her near while she kept pulling away. It felt almost like desperation, but he didn't care. He imagined himself going to work tomorrow, talking about the MosElectric deal, and pretending nothing had happened. It seemed unacceptable, like letting the substance of his own life slip away.

The house was boxy and plain, constructed of brick with a huge chimney breathing smoke into the night sky. Natasha led Jason to a windowed wooden door at the side of his house then opened it with a key from her ring. It gave out a creak as she turned and gestured for Jason to follow. A moment later he was standing in a recently modernized kitchen. He had known that Natasha's family was well off, and the understated elegance of this room seemed to confirm it.

Natasha disappeared down a hallway and left him there. Jason put his hands in his pockets, unsure of what to do. From somewhere in the house, classical music was playing, soft strings. Tchaikovsky, Jason guessed, though he really wasn't sure.

He heard Natasha talking in a quiet voice and ventured into the hall. She was speaking in Russian. Jason took a couple of hesitant steps down the hall, his footsteps creaking on the wooden planks of the floor. He heard the voice of an old woman speaking softly and then a third woman's voice, probably the nurse that Natasha had mentioned.

Jason looked up and gasped involuntarily. Standing still just inside the doorway of a dark room, only a couple of feet from where Jason stood, was a man. He was about sixty, dressed in a simple shirt and slacks, with a mustache and piercing, angry eyes. He looked big and strong for his age, and he looked at Jason with a mixture of suspicion and contempt.

"*Dobre vyechyer,*" Jason said weakly.

The man stepped into the partial light of the hall; his body language was quick and aggressive. Jason fought off the impulse to flinch as the man began speaking to him in Russian. Jason couldn't understand what the man was saying, but he could tell that he was being interrogated.

"Jason?" Natasha called out.

"I'm right here," Jason said. "I'm with—"

Natasha came around the corner. Her eyes widened with shock when she saw the man. The moment Jason saw them together, he saw their similar noses, their raven black hair. The man was Natasha's father.

"Natasha," her father said, his voice cold, his eyes still fixed on Jason. He added something in Russian in a disdainful tone.

"Jason, please wait for me," Natasha said. She motioned angrily to her father and disappeared into another side room. Her father followed and closed the door behind them. A moment later they could be heard talking, their conversation turning heated after a few seconds. Natasha yelled at her father in Russian, and her father responded with the harsh voice of a man dressing down his daughter.

Jason turned the corner and found himself in the doorway of the house's main room. A masonry fireplace blazed at the far wall. He stood up straight when he saw a pair of eyes watching him suspiciously. A young woman in a simple dress stood close to the fire— the nurse. Next to her, in a wheelchair, was an old woman. She seemed old and frail, her hair wild and almost white. An oxygen tank was on a stand next to her, though for the moment the plastic mask was resting in her lap. She had Natasha's strong jaw and soft forehead, and she winced at the sound of her daughter and husband shouting at each other from the next room.

Jason gave a small bow and backed away, feeling terrible, like an intruder. He retreated down the hall and stopped. Natasha and her father were still arguing, the sound of their voices filling the house. He listened but couldn't understand a thing they were saying—until he heard the name of Vladimir Borchenko.

He paused, looked around in the shadowy nimbus cast by an electrical replica of an old Russian-style gaslight in the hall. Dozens of pictures were hanging there, each in an antique wooden frame.

There was a young couple, obviously Natasha's parents decades before. The man was wearing a Soviet military uniform, a red star on his cap. He stood up straight and unsmiling while the pretty woman next to him inclined her head slightly toward him.

Another picture, taken at a beach somewhere. Probably the Crimea. The father was wearing a bathing suit that showed off his powerful arms and broad chest. He was holding a little girl as a wave crashed around them. Their expressions conveyed almost identical joy. Natasha couldn't have been more then five or six years old.

The yelling had stopped. Now Jason heard their voices lowered, serious. Natasha was doing all the talking now, her anger detectable in her insistent tone.

Another photograph caught his eye. Natasha's father in another dress uniform, in another office, standing in front of a desk. The shadow in the hallway hit the picture and bisected it in half. Jason leaned closer. There was someone else in the picture.

Jason saw the broad brow, the deep-set eyes, the icy expression of superiority. He had seen this face on television in David's room just a couple of days before.

It was the presidential candidate, the ultra-nationalist that David knew. He had aged, but Jason was sure it was the same person.

What was his name? Jason closed his eyes for a moment and tried to remember.

Maxim Belarin. The man in the picture with Natasha's father was Maxim Belarin, the same man who was vying for the Russian presidency on a platform of militarism and anger.

The door down the hall opened. Natasha came out, her face an impenetrable mask. She went into the living room. Jason heard her speaking softly, saying goodbye to her mother. A moment later she stormed down the hall toward Jason.

She took Jason's arm and led him through the kitchen and back to the door. Jason opened it for her at the same moment as her father burst into the kitchen, his eyes blazing, his fists clenched.

He said something angry to Natasha, who waved him away. She shook her head and spoke in a tone of disappointment and regret then pushed open the door. Jason could see that she was fighting off tears.

"Jason," Natasha said from the doorway. "Come. There is nothing more for me here."

Jason felt the cold night air revive him and wake him up from the trance that the pictures had caused. As he jogged behind Natasha to her car, he glanced back one last time. Silhouetted by the lights inside, her father was watching from the window.

# Chapter Twenty-Two

THE ELEVATOR DOORS OPENED to the brightly lit lobby of Moscow's Metropol Hotel. Although it was nearly midnight, a few employees worked the desk, and a solitary woman was spraying and wiping the baseboards.

He stepped out of the elevator and adjusted the cuffs of the suit jacket he had put on for this meeting. He steeled himself, tried to convey an exterior of calm confidence. Come what may, he wouldn't let Belarin know that he was scared for his life.

Just as David walked across the carpet in the lobby, the glass doors at the far end of the room opened. Maxim Belarin walked quickly through the lobby and looked around. To his either side were bodyguards, big men with crew cuts wearing suits.

"David Olen," Belarin called out when he spotted David.

David nodded. He motioned toward a set of chairs close to the wall.

"Maxim," David said as Belarin extended his hand.

"It is so good of you to come down to see me so late," Belarin said. "I do apologize for the intrusion."

David nodded again.

Belarin glanced at his bodyguards, made a small gesture with one hand. The two men stepped away, toward opposite ends of the lobby. David followed them with his eyes, caught himself wondering where he would run if he had to, whether the desk staff would help him or even call the police if Belarin's men tried to drag him out of there.

"Please, please," Belarin said. He took a seat after David had.

Belarin was about the same age as Vladimir, although he hadn't aged as well. He had gotten fat, his wrists and neck straining against the fabric of his jacket. He still wore his hair in a military-style cut, although he had made concessions to his new incarnation as a civilian Duma member in the form of a bright necktie and matching pocket square. Despite the effort he was making to look modern, he reminded David of the old-style Soviet *apparatchiks* who had traveled to the West and looked hopelessly out of touch trying to mimic the styles they encountered.

"We haven't seen each other in so long," Belarin said. "You look well."

"Thank you."

"I apologize for not contacting you during your times doing business here in Moscow." Belarin gave a self-deprecating little shrug. "It is the politician's life. Always meetings. Always dinners. To tell you the truth, I am still adjusting."

David returned Belarin's smile. Out of the corner of his eye, he saw one of the bodyguards take his place next to a column.

"But I won't monopolize your time," Belarin said. "I wanted to see you because of the tragedy that took place this evening."

"It's a terrible thing," David said. He willed his hands to stay still, his gaze even and level. *No signs of weakness.*

"Vladimir Dmitrievich and I worked closely for many years,"

Belarin said, a note of regret in his voice. "We had our differences, true. But they were honest disagreements between two comrades. Always, *always*, there was respect. I was very fond of him."

Belarin gesticulated with his meaty index finger as he spoke. David felt a strong sense that he was being toyed with and that the terms of this dialogue could change in an instant.

"He was my friend," David said. "It . . . pains me to lose him."

"Vladimir spoke highly of you," Belarin said, leaning forward. "He said you were a man of integrity. And I am certain that is true." He paused then continued. "He might have told you that I am representing a group interested in acquiring MosElectric," he said.

David sat up a little straighter. "He mentioned it."

"It was a healthy competition between two old friends," Belarin said. "But now that Vladimir is gone, I expect that his bank will be in disarray. It is a sad, unfortunate consequence of this event."

"I haven't heard anything," David said. He felt a hot core of anger in his chest.

"Well, I still plan to obtain the company," Belarin said. "And this is the reason I wanted to speak with you tonight."

"About business?" David asked.

"Yes, business." Belarin smiled sadly. "I am sorry to lose Vladimir. We both are; I am sure. But life goes on, as they say. What I am suggesting is that we meet again in the morning. I will bring you to meet with key members of my consortium. I am also interested in the MosElectric construction project. It will be a major addition to the city, and I have contacted architects who I know would be very interested in meeting someone with your considerable reputation."

David almost laughed out loud. His spine felt like an electrical wire of tension; his hands were sweating in his lap. And Belarin was making him a business proposition. Somehow this turn chilled David more than if the Russian had come to make threats against his life.

"It's a considerate offer," David said slowly. "But I can't meet with anyone. I'm not going to be here."

"Oh?" Belarin tilted his head. "And why is that?"

"I have to get back to the States."

"So you are not interested in my offer?" Belarin asked with a hint of disappointment.

"I didn't say that," David replied. "I'd have to look at what your group is doing. But my involvement would have to wait until I can get back to Moscow. Why don't you have your people send some background material to my office? I can look at it while I'm—"

"Fine," Belarin interrupted. "I understand."

David stood up. He sensed he couldn't take much more of this tension. "I appreciate your consideration."

"It is a trying time," Belarin said, also standing. "I hope that you have a safe trip and that I will see you soon. Perhaps we could have dinner and speak of old times."

"Perhaps," David said. He shook Belarin's hand, felt the cool dryness of Belarin's palm and the hard certainty of his grip.

---

JASON GLANCED AT HIS WATCH. It was after midnight. He wadded up a few pieces of newspaper and stuck them under the logs he'd carefully arranged in the fireplace. He found a box of matches on the mantel and knelt down again and started a fire. The flue had a good updraft, and within a minute the kindling had started to ignite.

Natasha had excused herself almost a half-hour before, and Jason strained to hear sounds from the next room. They had driven back from her parents' house in almost total silence, Jason's one attempt at asking about her father deflected with a terse request that he wait until later. While Natasha drove, Jason could hear her breathing hard, and he saw her hands tremble whenever she released the wheel.

He looked out the window. The city lights still shone in this district, but the traffic had dwindled to almost nothing. A few scattered lights were on in apartments across the street.

"Jason," said a voice from behind him.

He turned. She was wearing a fresh sweater and pants, and her hair was wet. Her eyes were glassy from fatigue.

"You started a fire," she said.

"I hope you don't mind," he replied. "I was just looking for something to do."

"It's nice," she said. She drifted toward the kitchen. "I am going to have a glass of wine. Would you like something?"

"Wine would be fine," Jason said.

First Vladimir's death had put her into a state of near-panic. Jason could understand that because she worked so closely with Vladimir and must have felt his loss deeply. But she had been so frightened—whether of Nikolai or of something else—that Jason should have demanded an answer right away. But then he had held her in his arms, they had made love, and the power of her presence had overwhelmed him.

But now he needed answers. First her fiery yelling match with her father then the picture on the wall with the father and Belarin, Vladimir's competitor in the MosElectric bidding. It was too much. Jason realized that he was clinging to the hope that Natasha was innocent, that he had misinterpreted what he had seen.

But he needed to hear it from her.

"Here," she said. She handed him a glass of red wine. Jason took a sip.

"It's good," he said.

She sat down on a long, comfortable sofa and exhaled deeply. She leaned back and closed her eyes, her entire body seeming to slump from the weight of everything that had happened.

He sat down next to her. They both looked at the fire for almost a full minute before either of them spoke.

"I need you to be truthful with me," he said.

Her eyes remained on the fire. "It's too much," she whispered.

"You can talk to me."

Her eyes were hollow, distant. "Maybe I am sorry about what happened between us tonight."

"You're not," he said. "I . . . I want to make you happy. I don't want to be apart from you in any way. But you have to trust me."

She sipped the wine and thought.

"I saw a picture in your parents' house, your father with Maxim Belarin," he said. "You never mentioned that you had any family connection with him."

"My father knows many people," she said. "He was very prominent in the Soviet Union. His problem is that he doesn't seem to realize that those days are over."

"What's the problem between you and your father?" Jason asked.

She laughed bitterly. "What is not the problem?"

"Come on," he insisted. "Talk to me."

She glanced over at him. He could tell that she rarely dropped her guard or spoke frankly to anyone. It was obvious to him because he was the same way.

"I had privileges growing up," she said. "Good teachers, opportunities. It was all because of my father; I know that. I have thanked him many times."

"Does he feel you owe him something?" Jason asked.

"He thinks I owe him everything," Natasha said. "He cannot understand me at all. I went into a business career—this was his greatest disappointment in life. He called me a capitalist, an imperialist, an anti-revolutionary. I told him the revolution was over. His side lost."

"What did he say?"

"The same old thing." She stared into the fire. "I betrayed him; I was killing him. He even wanted me to marry the son of one of his friends, a colonel in the army. I told him I didn't want to be a military wife. I didn't want to become the wife of someone like him."

Jason listened quietly as her words began to come faster.

"My father is a product of the old system," Natasha said. "He only knows the old ways. Intimidation, corruption. He cannot even fathom my occupation. He said studying business was decadent and a waste of time. He thinks the medals the Soviets gave him allow him the right to do anything he wishes, even now."

"What do you mean?" Jason asked, sensing her opening up to him. He moved closer, took her hand. "Does this have to do with Belarin?"

She looked away shaking her head.

"Do you know Belarin?" he asked. "You've never said anything."

"I can't—" she began.

"You have to trust me now," Jason said, almost pleading. "I want to help you. Just tell me what's happened."

She looked up at him, a tear tracing down the curve of her cheek. "I knew Belarin since I was a child. My father had known Maxim through military intelligence channels; he had supplied information to Belarin during his tours of duty in occupied Eastern Europe. This eventually led my father to receive a KGB post and all the privileges afforded a high-ranking *apparatchik*. When my father retired, he remained in contact with Belarin."

Natasha paused. She nervously twisted the fabric of her sweater. Jason touched her hand and nodded for her to continue.

"Two months ago Belarin had contacted my father. Belarin knew that I worked for Vladimir. He suggested that my father approach me and ask for information on Borchenko's business dealings. It would clear the slate of all the favors Belarin had done for my father over the years, all the opportunities he had sent his way. The information Belarin required was not unreasonable, my father had thought: Vladimir's travel plans, his daily schedule, his intentions regarding the acquisition of MosElectric."

Natasha got up and paced the room, her voice becoming stronger. "I was furious with my father when he approached me with this proposition. I didn't care about any favors he owed Belarin. I hadn't seen him in years, and anyway, I disliked him since I was a child. I explained that Russia had changed. I would not betray Vladimir to the benefit of one of my father's old cronies. An argument erupted, one that is still unresolved. That's what you saw us fighting about at my parents' house."

"So what did you do?" Jason asked.

"I supplied no information. But I also didn't tell Vladimir about being approached. I didn't want to implicate my father. I had hoped that the matter would be dropped and simply disappear. I hadn't considered the implications of Belarin's interest in Vladimir, in his comings and goings and his business plans. I had no inkling that Belarin might resort to *murder* in order to attain his goals. How stupid I was!"

"Listen to me," Jason said. He moved behind her chair and softly rubbed at her knotted shoulders. "You couldn't have known."

"I should have known," she said. "I could have told Vladimir. He might have been more careful."

"You have to stop punishing yourself."

"No one needed to die," she said. She reached up and took his hands. He knelt and kissed one gently.

"You didn't kill anyone," he said to her.

"Maybe we can make it right," she said in a whisper.

"We have to try," he said. He caressed the soft skin of her neck and tried to communicate with a touch this newfound love he felt for her.

*February 20, 1998. 7:10 a.m.*
*Moscow.*

DAVID'S CAR WAS ON THE HIGHWAY early in the morning. He sat in the back seat with his GSM phone and listened to the extension in Jason's hotel room ring without an answer.

"Damn," he said as he hung up.

Somehow the feeling of motion made him feel safer, although he

330

knew that Belarin might come after him anywhere, any time. He had been awake all night. He slipped a couple of hundred-dollar bills to the clerk at the front desk, and she booked him a flight out of Russia. Still, he had to wait until seven in the morning, when the first streaks of the sun were appearing over the Kremlin. He had sat alone, watching the door, his packed bags on the floor beneath his feet.

Pyotr drove the Mercedes sedan with expert speed along the highway. David had ordered him to get to Sheremetyevo as quickly as possible with no stops.

David flipped open his electronic organizer and scanned through the telephone listings. He found the number he wanted and punched it in, hoping there would be a receptionist in the office despite the early hour.

"GlobusBank," said a voice with a Russian accent.

"Nikolai Petrov, please," he said. "David Olen calling."

The line clicked silent. David held the phone to his ear and watched the traffic. He had told his Moscow staff where he was going and at what time, and he had notified Cynthia in Chicago. At least he would be noticed missing if something happened.

"This is Nikolai, David," said the deep voice on the line. "Good morning."

"Nikolai, how are you?" David asked.

"Not well, to be honest," Nikolai said in a halting voice. "I was here all night."

"What about Vladimir?" David asked. "Have you found out anything?"

David considered telling Nikolai about Belarin and about everything Vladimir had told him. But he didn't. Vladimir would have told his young associate everything he wanted him to know. For now, David had bigger concerns.

"Not too much," Nikolai said. "Vladimir's bodyguard and driver are both missing. And so is his car. I don't know. Perhaps they were involved somehow. The security guards at Vladimir's building said they saw nothing, and the usual videotape evidence is not available."

"That sounds suspicious," David said.

"Very," Nikolai replied.

David paused. He heard the sorrow in the young Russian's voice, the deep sense of loss that mirrored his own. So much had happened in the last day, he realized, that he hadn't had time to properly mourn his old friend. David's own regret, however, had been tainted by the information he'd learned from Carl Becker. Albino Luciani's murder nagged at David's conscience, just beneath the surface of the fear he felt for his own life.

"You should know that Maxim Belarin contacted me last night." David said.

"Belarin?" Nikolai repeated. "Why?"

"He's aggressive on the MosElectric privatization. He wanted to offer me a chance to get involved."

"I see," Nikolai said.

"I put him off. I don't want to do business with him," David explained. *What an understatement.*

Nikolai didn't respond. "I just wanted you to know," David said. "To be honest, I don't know how the deal is going to play out now without Vladimir. His personality and influence were holding this thing together in a lot of ways."

"Of course," Nikolai said. "But we will try."

There was a click on the line. David thought it was his own phone but then realized it was an unfamiliar sound.

"Just one second, please," Nikolai said. "I have another call."

David leaned back. They were getting close to the airport. He was booked on a Luftansa flight to Stockholm and then connecting to Rome. If he could only get onto that plane and out of Russia.

"I am back," Nikolai said. "Please excuse the interruption."

"That's all right," David said. "I have to go, anyway."

"Are you coming to the office today?" Nikolai asked, sounding slightly surprised. "We need to work—"

"Edward will be there, and Jason," David said, although he wasn't even sure where Jason was. "I'm catching a flight. There's been an emergency."

"Nothing serious, I hope," Nikolai said.

David said nothing.

"Do you mind if I ask where you're going?" Nikolai asked.

"To Rome," David replied. "I'm going to Rome."

"I see." There was a noise in the background. "Then I will speak with you later. Thank you for calling me, David. I . . . this has been a terrible time."

"I know," David replied. "We'll all do our best."

"Certainly," Nikolai replied then hung up.

David put away the phone. Pyotr was driving up to Sheremetyevo's international terminal. He was almost there. He was almost safe from Maxim Belarin.

---

IRINA TURSAYEVA HAD WORKED in the Metropol office of Aeroflot Airlines since the mid-'80s and had served mostly foreign travelers by booking their flights and acting as an intermediary with the often capricious and labyrinthine airline bureaucracy. Much of the time the travelers were rude and imperious Westerners who automatically turned up their noses at everything Russian. But Irina suffered in silence. Her pay was good by Russian standards, and occasionally she was in a position to receive a gratuity that as much as doubled her monthly pay.

This morning had been a surprise. She had been awakened before dawn by a call from Igor on the night staff; he said that an American was in a panic and needed to book a flight out of Russia immediately. Irina had resisted until she was told that the American was offering $200 if the office could be opened early.

The American, David Olen, had barely been able to conceal his panic. Irina had dealt with him coolly and efficiently, managing to fight off her own curiosity as to why the American was so anxious. Igor had come in afterward and given Irina $100 of the gratuity—the conniving bastard had kept half for himself. Still, it was a respectable amount of money, and Irina planned to shop at GUM that night.

Now she was sitting at her computer and updating that day's reservation listings for travelers staying at the hotel. It was easy work, and her mind began to wander. Perhaps she would buy a new scarf.

"Excuse me, madam," said a man's voice. Irina looked up from her computer screen.

He was about thirty-five, dressed in a nice suit. He sat down at the chair opposite her desk.

"Can I help you?" she asked. He was speaking Russian; he obviously wasn't a tourist.

"I am looking for information on a guest here at the hotel," the man said. "I need to know where he is going and what flight he will be on."

"I can't give you that information," Irina said. "It is against the rules. You will have to ask him yourself."

"That is impossible," the man said. "He has already left."

"I'm sorry," Irina replied.

The man passed Irina a white envelope across her desk. She pulled it into her lap and looked around to make sure no one had seen. Inside it were three American hundred-dollar bills.

She could lose her job for giving out passenger information, but then she *was* the manager. No one else was around to tell the Aeroflot administration.

"What is the name?" she asked.

"David Olen," the man replied.

Irina typed the name into the computer. She could have told the man from memory, but for $300 she would give him a computer printout of the American's itinerary.

This was turning into a very profitable morning. And this time she wouldn't have to share the money with Igor or anyone else. She started to think about a new dress and a pair of shoes. She handed over Olen's itinerary and, a moment later, the man was gone, heading straight to Maxim Belarin's office.

# Part Five

# *Il Lupi*
## (The Wolves)

# Chapter Twenty-Three

*February 20, 1998. 10:20 a.m.*
*The Vatican.*

A NNIA OLEN WAITED IN THE CORRIDOR outside the pope's suite. Silence pervaded the place. She had waited for more than three hours alone, her vigil broken only by a nurse who had offered her coffee.

She hadn't seen Wojtyla in more than a decade, since a brief Papal audience she was granted once on a trip to Rome. The last time she had seen him, he had been his robust self—old but carrying himself with the force and energy that had always defined him. She was almost frightened to see him now and feared that he would be diminished and frail.

She checked her watch. She had spoken to Cynthia in David's Chicago office, found out that David was flying to Rome from Moscow as soon as he could. It was uncharacteristic of her husband because David was working on a large deal in Russia and typically wouldn't leave until it was completed. But Cynthia had said there was no arguing with him, that he had booked the flight himself.

Annia folded her hands. It had been a terrible week. She had learned from Cynthia that Vladimir Borchenko had been killed in Moscow. She had met Vladimir during the Russian's visits to Chicago, and she had liked him. Most of all, she had liked the way David came to life in Vladimir's presence, the way their mutual secrets—many of them not even shared with Annia—drew them close together. They had been friends for so long, and Annia knew that her husband had to be hurting from the loss.

"Annia."

She looked up. The man before her stood with his shoulders slumped, his graying hair swept across his forehead, his clothes so elegant compared to his humble appearance as a younger man.

"Andrzej," she said.

They embraced without a word. Nothing needed to be said, no matter how long it had been since they had seen each other. They had spent years together in the Krakow orphanage, had suffered under the communists, came to life in the radiance of the young priest Wojtyla. Time was incapable of weakening their bond.

"It is so good to see you," Andy said in Polish, still holding her in his arms like an older brother.

She looked up at him. How they had all changed. Andy's eyes were circled in purple, his cheeks lined with wrinkles. She remembered him out on the soccer field at the orphanage, where he would raise his arms with a boy's exuberance after scoring a goal.

"You've been working too hard," she said to him. "I can read it in your face."

Andy shrugged, gave a little smile. "Business," he said. "I have so many things going on at one time."

"You sound like David."

Andy laughed softly. "Is David here?"

"He's coming," Annia replied. "I didn't ask him to. He left important business in Moscow."

"There is no arguing with David Olen," Andy said.

The door behind them opened with a quiet click. Annia and Andy straightened like schoolchildren caught cutting up in the hall.

A nurse emerged; she walked quickly down the corridor without acknowledging their presence. After her was an older man in cardinal's robes, his stocky build and tight-set mouth belied by his compassionate eyes.

"I am Cardinal Spellano," he said to them.

"I am Andrzej Kapinski. This is—"

"I know," Spellano said. He pursed his lips. "The pope is weak. It requires effort for him to talk."

Annia nodded, unable to reply. She knew Wojtyla was sick and hadn't been able to contemplate the idea that he might really die. He was somehow more than human to her, beyond the reach of mortality.

"He wants to see you both," Spellano explained. "But we should not force him to talk for long. I hope you understand. When I motion toward the door, we must leave."

"Of course," Andy said.

Spellano looked from Andy to Annia, inspecting their faces, looking for something—perhaps a clue as to why they meant so much to His Eminence. He nodded toward the half-open door, and they walked through. Annia kept her eyes down, trying to control a surge of emotion that felt strong enough to overtake her.

His bed was by the window, the drapes closed. She saw a row of hospital monitors, a small antique stand with leather-bound books and framed photographs. A man in a dark suit sat quietly in the corner.

Andy walked around one side of the bed, Annia the other. He was waiting for them. His body seemed impossibly small beneath the blankets that covered him. But his eyes still shone. He was still the orphanage priest.

He took Andy's hand then Annia's. His grip was weak.

"My children," he said in Polish, his voice little more than a whisper.

*February 20, 1998. 3:40 p.m.*
*Rome.*

DAVID TOSSED HIS SUITCASE ON THE HOTEL BED and opened the curtains. The last light of the day was shining on the square below. Crowds moved slowly through the intersection of two roads. Lights outside a department store and a cafe were beginning to come on.

He had been lucky to get to Rome so quickly; he had made his connection in Stockholm with barely five minutes to spare. Now he was in Annia's hotel room on the fifth floor. He had tried to call her as soon as he landed at Fiumicino and tried twice more during the hectic cab ride into the city. She hadn't been at the hotel, and David assumed she must have been at the Vatican waiting to see Wojtyla.

First he would take care of a final piece of business. Then his goal was to find her, book a flight to Chicago, and take her home. He'd be finished. He would find a way to make peace with Belarin—and if he couldn't, then he would stay away from Russia until it was safe again. This would work, he told himself. It had to.

Cars crawled on the streets below and moved at a snail's pace in Rome's nonstop congested traffic. The Vatican was a short cab ride away, but it would probably be quicker to walk.

He opened his electronic organizer and flipped to an entry he hadn't used in years. The name was recorded only as initials, the telephone number a simple code. He knew he shouldn't have kept the number on him, that any CIA or KGB agent could have broken the code in fifteen minutes. But he had had a feeling that someday he would need the number again.

He picked up the phone, dialed a line out of the hotel, placed the call. A female voice answered in Italian, and David used a scripted reply that he hadn't uttered in more than a decade.

"*Buona sera*," David said. "*Parla lei inglese?*"

"*Un po'di, signor.*"

David exhaled. "Very good," he said. "I need to speak with Cardinal Villetti. It is an urgent matter."

"Cardinal Villetti is not available," the woman replied.

Villetti would be in the Vatican. Everyone in the Curia would be close to the pope and would be waiting to see what happened, ready if another conclave suddenly became necessary.

"Tell him it is a matter of *il lupi*," David said.

*Il lupi.* The wolves. It was an old code, left over from the earliest days of the cabal. Villetti had been the youngest member of the Holy Fist, the only conspirator still alive save for Wojtyla. He had been a Bishop in those early days and became a cardinal in the late '80s.

"*Il lupi*," the woman repeated with a note of confusion. David realized that she had no idea what he was talking about. Too much time had passed; the old codes weren't known anymore.

"Please," David said. "I am an old associate of Cardinal Villetti's. Please find him immediately and give him the message. It is extremely important."

"What is your name?"

David told her, spelled it twice. "Tell the cardinal I must talk to him right away."

David listened to the silence on the line. Hopefully the receptionist recognized the honesty and urgency in David's voice and would do as he asked.

Finally a voice came on the line that was still familiar, though deeper and rendered husky with age.

"Cardinal Villetti?" David asked. "Giovanni?"

"*Sí*, it is me," Villetti said. "It has been a long time, David."

"Too long. I almost wasn't able to reach you."

"I heard that you made reference to *il lupi*," Villetti said with a soft chuckle. "I haven't heard that in years."

"The affairs we worked on together have surfaced again," David replied. "I'm here in Rome. It seemed appropriate to use the old means of reaching you."

Villetti said nothing, but David knew he would understand. He gave Villetti a moment to reflect because he knew how shocked Villetti might be.

"I need to speak with you," David said.

"It is a difficult time. As you know, *Il Papa* is ill."

"I'm here because of that," David said. "My wife is with him right now. She was invited for an audience. I want to get her out of Rome as soon as that is concluded."

David and Giovanni Villetti had sat together many times in a Rome cafe just blocks from the Vatican. They discussed the flow of money from Chicago to Poland, as well as Wojtyla's progress. They had joked together, trying to hide their nervousness. They had never been friends, but they had forged a bond of mutual respect and familiarity. Now Villetti's voice was cold, suspicious.

"Would you like me to have someone locate your wife? She may be with *Il Papa*, but as soon as—"

"We have to talk in person," David interrupted. "I have information to share with you. Borchenko is dead. He was assassinated last night."

Villetti coughed. "I am sorry to hear that," he said. "I always enjoyed his company."

"It has to do with our work together—"

"Borchenko was involved in many things; we both know that. His affairs have nothing to do with me."

It was obvious that Villetti wanted nothing to do with David. Maybe he was trying to forget the past. Maybe decades of Curia politics had made their conspiracy something that he had tried to shed.

"Cardinal Villetti, I've contacted you in a spirit of candor and honesty." David took a deep breath. "I have information to share with you. As far as I am concerned, it will be the last time we ever speak to each other. Do you understand?"

Villetti waited before replying. "When?" he asked.

"Now. The sooner the better."

"My schedule—" Villetti began but stopped himself. "All right. Come now. How long will it take you to get here?"

"Twenty minutes," David said.

"And I will grant you twenty more to talk. No more."

"I won't need more." David hung up, buttoned his jacket. He was in the lobby two minutes later and walked quickly down the street in the direction of the Vatican.

If he had lingered a moment longer, he might have seen two men parked in a car across the street. They watched David with intense scrutiny. The driver started the car and began to drive slowly down the street. He kept David in clear sight at all times.

*February 20, 1998. 5:02 p.m.*
*Moscow.*

JASON STOOD NEXT TO THE FIREPLACE in Natasha's apartment and looked down at the city street below. The initial shock of what Natasha had told him had almost completely worn off, and he searched for calm in his mind so that he would have a clear idea what to do next.

Natasha came from the kitchen with a pot of coffee. Neither of them had slept. She kept her eyes averted as she poured. At first she had been almost paralyzed with guilt over what she had done, but the more she told Jason, the more she realized that the harm was done. She would have to live with her actions.

He still wouldn't abandon her.

"We need to call Nikolai," Jason said.

"But he . . . we can't be sure . . ."

345

The smell of the coffee was almost enough to make Jason feel as though he could go on for a few more hours. He sipped it slowly, feeling his confidence renewed.

"I know," he said. "But we have to deal with him sooner or later. Without you at GlobusBank, he'll be in charge for the moment. We both know that. We need to confront him."

"You're right," she said. She nodded slowly, as though shedding her fear and hesitancy. She went to the phone on her desk, dialed it, and asked for Nikolai.

"I am at home," she said after getting him on the line. "Jason Rudas is here with me."

Jason watched from beside the window and wondered how Nikolai would react. Natasha and Jason were united in their distrust for Nikolai Petrov. Now they would have to determine whether he was a threat to their lives. If he had been implicated in Vladimir's death, as a sort of palace coup, then he might not hesitate to attempt to eliminate all his opponents.

"May I put you on the speaker phone?" Natasha asked. A moment later she pressed a button, and Nikolai's voice emerged from the speaker.

"Hello, Jason," Nikolai said. "This is a surprise."

"Nikolai," Jason said. "The three of us need to meet."

Nikolai cleared his throat. "I should say so. Vladimir is gone, but we still have business. We have not completed documentation on the MosElectric bid."

"I've been thinking of other things," Natasha said.

"I understand," Nikolai replied. "But I need you here, Natasha. The atmosphere here at the bank is very unsettled."

"We need to have a discussion," Jason said. "And then we need to speak with Maxim Belarin. It's time to put everything on the table."

Nikolai didn't reply.

"We'll come there," Natasha said.

"Very good," Nikolai said. "Come, and we will talk."

He hung up. Natasha pressed a button to disconnect the line and came over to Jason.

"Is this the right idea?" she asked.

He embraced her. He had felt knotted and anxious while talking to Nikolai. He felt her tension dissolve in his arms.

"We'll see," Jason replied.


*February 20, 1998.*
*Rome.*

DAVID WALKED THROUGH the dense urban traffic in the city and jostled shoulders with other pedestrians in his rush to get to the Vatican on time. He was breathing heavily when he reached the regal expanse of St. Peter's Square. He felt himself dwarfed by the great piazza surrounded by Tuscan columns, the great hemisphere of the basilica dome.

He quickly found the main Curia administrative entrance at the foot of the Vatican palace, precisely the spot where he used to visit in decades past. He gave his name and was waved past a post of stone-faced Swiss guards in traditional chest plates and plumed helmets, each man holding a pointed staff upright. None of the guards even glanced at David as he was led past by a young woman dressed in a modern suit.

David and the young woman walked up a staircase, neither saying a word. The woman, her long dark hair pulled into a bun at the nape of her neck, maintained a neutral expression as she led David down a long tiled corridor. The ceilings were high with windows at each end of the hall that allowed in diffused sunlight.

David hadn't been to the Vatican in years, but he still remembered the way to the small, private reading room where he used to meet with members of the Holy Fist. Inside the door he recognized the old, long table, the leather armchairs. Casement windows were partially open to the cool air; to either side hung traditional Latin crosses. The young woman gestured to a chair, smiled, and retreated. David was left alone as she closed the door behind her.

David went to the window. He saw the Vatican Gardens, the slightly hunched back of a cardinal as he walked slowly along a path that bisected the trees and manicured spaces. David took a deep breath. The place was stultifying, oppressively quiet. It almost felt as though the Vatican was already in mourning.

The door opened with a creak. David turned as Giovanni Villetti shut it behind him and took a few steps across the polished wooden floor. He wore cardinal's robes and a skullcap, the fabric heavy and seeming faded with age.

"David," Villetti said with a wary smile.

David walked across the room and shook his hand, nodding his head slightly as a sign of respect for Villetti's office. The two men sat down across from each other.

Villetti had changed. He was in his mid-sixties. His hands shook slightly as he folded them against his abdomen. His eyes drooped at the sides, and his chiseled Italian features had begun to sag. Only his gaze was the same: focused, willful, acute. He straightened his vestment and cocked his head slightly at David.

"Thank you for seeing me," David said.

Villetti waved his hand vaguely, a gesture that was somehow characteristically Italian. Villetti was from Florence, and he had come to the Vatican Curia as a young man.

"This is not a good time," Villetti said. "You must understand this. The pope may die."

"I understand."

Villetti looked down at his folded hands. "This will be a time of tumult in the Vatican," he explained. "Old alliances will be brought to bear; new ones will be formed. Everyone is looking toward the next conclave. Perhaps that sounds callous. But it is the truth."

David fought off the urge to make a caustic reply. It was as though

Villetti had forgotten to whom he was addressing this condescending explanation.

"I don't have much time," Villetti added, looking up at David. "Please. Speak."

"I told you about Borchenko's assassination," David began.

Villetti nodded. "It is unfortunate. But a man like Vladimir develops enemies. Can you honestly say you never considered our friend meeting such a fate?"

"I spoke to Vladimir the day he died," David said, struggling to check his temper. "He suspected he might be in danger—from a former KGB official who was associated with our conspiracy."

Villetti registered no outward reaction. "This was a matter between Vladimir and this man," he said slowly. "I have no connection to anything that happens in Russia. I have not even spoken to Vladimir in more than ten years."

"The KGB official's name is Maxim Belarin," David added. "He's in the Russian Duma now. He has ambitions for the presidency."

Villetti arched an eyebrow. "I know of Belarin," he said. He winced slightly. "Do you think that you are also in danger?"

"I'm not sure," David replied. "I might be. But you need to understand—the consequences of our understanding, of our actions, haven't gone away. We're not free from the repercussions of what we've done."

"That is very dramatic and dire," Villetti said. "But let us be realistic. How many of us are left? Borchenko is dead now. I am the only remaining member of the Holy Fist, save for the pope. Gorbachev has faded into obscurity. Soon we will be little more than history. I think that the world will never know what we accomplished. Perhaps that is for the best."

David remembered dealing with Villetti, the way the Florentine possessed the ability to divert uncomfortable topics and steer the conversation on his own terms. Villetti was very smart, extremely shrewd, and equally evasive. This was why Cardinal Litwinski recruited Villetti into the Holy Fist.

"There's another matter," David said. "I've been contacted by an old friend in the American Congress. He's informed me that the CIA wants to reopen the activities we began in the '70s. An intelligence agent has gained access to files kept on our conspiracy and wishes to influence the next conclave—the same way we influenced Cardinal Wojtyla's."

Villetti's eyes widened. He seemed genuinely interested for the first time since sitting down.

"Who is this friend you speak of?" he asked.

"That doesn't matter," said David. "I trust him, and I know he's telling the truth. An agent, or agents, from the CIA will be coming to Rome for this purpose. I don't know precisely how they intend to further their goals, but I—"

"Does the CIA feel that it influenced Wojtyla's election?" Villetti broke in.

David paused, unsure what the cardinal was driving at.

"Of course it does," David said. "The CIA got me involved in the deal in the first place. I kept one of their agents aware of all my activities. You know that."

"And you were responsible for Cardinal Wojtyla's election?"

David looked into the cardinal's eyes, at his inscrutable expression, the flat line of his mouth.

"I didn't, not directly, of course not," David replied. "But Wojtyla and Gorbachev—"

"Wojtyla and Gorbachev made an arrangement through intermediaries," Villetti said. "But remember—Albino Luciani of Venice was elected pope in 1978. Not Wojtyla."

David shook his head. "You're not listening to me. I'm telling you that the CIA is coming to Rome. They might already be here. We're not talking about people we know and who understand the goals behind our actions. This is a young agent. He's not working under significant oversight, as far as I can determine. Are you familiar with the concept of plausible deniability?"

"Please educate me," Villetti said in a neutral voice.

"Many times a leader lays down general policy goals then leaves his subordinates to pursue these goals through any means necessary. The leader doesn't want to know how these goals are achieved, only the end result in broad terms. That way when the media, his conscience, or historians ask him what he knows, he can honestly claim he knew nothing of any immoral actions taken in his name. That's how the CIA works. And that's why I'm—"

"David, I have always respected you," Villetti said. He got up from his chair with a deep breath and walked to the window looking over the gardens. David remained seated.

"I will be honest with you," Villetti said, looking out the window. "It would probably be prudent to send you away with generalizations and half-truths, but it would not be right. We have done so much together, taken so many risks."

David listened intently.

"Wojtyla has expanded the number of cardinals eligible to vote in the next conclave to 122," Villetti explained. "When the conclave begins, he will have appointed all but sixteen of the Papal electors who will determine his successor."

David had heard this fact but never considered it.

"The next pope will share Wojtyla's passion for spiritual discipline, as well as his orthodoxy on Church teachings," said Villetti. "Much has been made of Wojtyla becoming the first non-Italian pope in almost five hundred years. Only a handful of us understand how this came to pass."

David resisted the urge to interrupt, to say that he was talking about something more concrete. He sensed that Villetti had an important point somewhere beneath his tangential speech.

"The next pope may be Italian, maybe not," Villetti explained. "It no longer matters. History required a pope who had lived under the

351

boot heel of communism—so that millions of Catholics could be freed from its atheistic, materialistic philosophy."

Villetti turned and looked at David.

"Wojtyla never stopped his crusade; he simply moved his attention elsewhere," said Villetti. "The pope has the power of belief and conviction. This is what has made him so powerful. Remember when he came to America, to Denver, several years ago? He was almost as excited then as when he visited communist Poland. Why?"

David found himself speechless.

"Because he wished to look into the face of the world's only remaining superpower and tell it what it had become." Villetti's voice rose. "To decry its materialism and godlessness. That is when I fully understood that his Eminence was never a political pragmatist. He is a philosopher, a great thinker of the spirit."

"What are you saying?" David asked. "That John Paul II is somehow anti-American? That's simply not true."

Villetti smiled. "David, we have looked behind the curtain of history. Let us not be simple-minded. In many ways *Il Papa* sees America as the hope of the world. He also mourns its sins. Either way, he will not be dictated to. He will not be influenced by its transitory agendas. Nor will those he has taught during his papacy."

"There are several candidates for pope; there always are," David said. "The CIA will try to reach them. And if—"

"Perhaps we have already reached the CIA," Villetti said.

David shook his head. "Now I'm confused."

Villetti let out a small, mirthful laugh. "There are several leading candidates for the next papacy. An African. A South American. Europeans. Italian Curialists and pastoralists. They all share one trait: They have learned from John Paul II's example. They know nothing of how he came to power, of course, but they have seen the way he has conducted himself. And they do not live in a vacuum. They see what is happening in the world: new confederations, the collapse of political orthodoxy in favor of global connection and economic interdependence."

"But this—"

"The Cold War is over, David. You won. But there is a trap waiting now—the possibility that the Vatican might become the tool of the United States or even another power. It could happen if we made shortsighted alliances for temporary agendas. But it will not, unless these are alliances that we form and control."

"The CIA can't influence you," David said, the substance of Villetti's point forming in his mind. "They've already been here. They've already tried."

"They try, they have tried, they will always try," Villetti said, his smile disappearing. "I have spoken to your CIA agent. My name is in his files. The United States acts to impose its power, to preserve its empire. This is understandable. But it is not the Vatican's interest."

"You talked to Gleason?" David asked.

Villetti's smile appeared again. "He is someone I can handle."

"What did he want?" asked David, feeling a flash of panic. He feared Gleason because of the CIA agent's potential for opening old connections, for putting into motion something that couldn't be controlled.

"What you might expect," Villetti said, a little disdainfully. "The usual range of concerns in these fragmented times. Financial markets. Trade. War and shattered societies. He wants a pope who will exert his influence to help the United States, to be its moral enforcer on human rights and its range of other interests."

"And what happened when you said you wouldn't help him?" David asked.

Villetti raised a hand to his cheek, blinking, looking at David as though he were a slow student.

"You mean . . . you made an arrangement with him?" David asked, incredulous. "You opened it up again? But there's no way of knowing how this might develop."

"You said it yourself, David. The echoes of our actions are with us still."

David stared at Villetti, trying to absorb the impact of what he'd heard. Villetti was even more manipulative, more canny, than David had ever guessed. It sounded as though he played Gleason like a violin.

"What about the conclave?" David asked.

"It will be different this time," Villetti said. "His Eminence has often spoken of the heat and the sweat of the conclave in the Sistine Chapel. He has built a hotel for the next Papal electors, with comfortable beds and air conditioning. They will be in a better frame of mind when they make their decision—a choice that will best benefit the Church in the new millennium."

"And only the Church?" David asked.

"The Church is ancient," Villetti explained. "Nations rise and fall. The Church has made many alliances throughout history. John Paul II's might have been the greatest, but perhaps there will be more."

David felt something welling up inside him, a spasm that moved up into his throat. He laughed as hard as he had in months, a deep roar that echoed in the high ceiling.

"You are amused," Villetti said, moving back to his chair.

David wiped his eyes. "I am amazed," he said. "I was worried about the CIA meddling with the Vatican. It turns out they should be worried about you."

Villetti patted David on the shoulder. "I have been truthful with you," he said. "And now I ask for your discretion. What we have discussed will remain between us."

"All right," David said. He started to stand, but the events of the past couple of days came back to him in a rush. He made another connection in his mind. Of course, it was so obvious.

"What is it?" Villetti asked. He obviously felt that this audience was over but saw David's change of expression.

"You said you knew Belarin," David whispered.

"I did," Villetti admitted.

David looked into the cardinal's brown eyes, and suddenly he knew. When Luciani was elected in 1978, it had been a dire blow to their cabal. He might have reigned for decades; their entire plan might have been ruined. But then Luciani died within weeks, and Wojtyla was subsequently elected.

They had murdered Luciani, all of them, whether they knew of it at the time or not. A KGB assassin had done the actual killing, probably ordered by Vladimir Borchenko and facilitated by Maxim Belarin.

But someone at the Vatican had to have helped. Someone within the Curia would have been necessary to grant the assassin entry and to cover up the murder afterward. David had suspected Majorski, the Vatican banker whose illegal financial dealings would have been exposed by Luciani's planned investigation. And Majorski might have been involved. But now David knew that he hadn't acted alone.

"You helped him," David said quietly.

Villetti gave a little nod, almost imperceptible, a lowering of his chin almost too slight to notice.

Now David knew.

He put his face in his hands as his body shuddered. He felt disgust running deep through him soul. They had killed a man to take what they wanted. Their lofty goals mattered for nothing in the face of this fact.

David rose and left the room without saying goodbye. He was finished. It was over. Although he knew the deal they made would haunt his thoughts until he died, he would try to walk away. And perhaps he would also spend the rest of his days trying to atone for the crime.

Villetti remained in his chair. He closed his eyes, alone with his thoughts. He heard the inner voice of his conscience speaking to him, and he answered it as he always did.

# Chapter Twenty-Four

*February 20, 1998. 8:10 p.m.*
*Moscow.*

JASON STOOD WAITING IN THE CORNER of Natasha's office. The room was comfortable and well-lit, with plush carpeting and a pair of leather sofas across from her stainless-steel glass-topped desk. But there was little in the office to indicate who occupied it, save for a small photograph of Natasha and her mother. Jason knew how fiercely Natasha guarded her private self, keeping it safely behind the walls of her professional veneer.

She was standing behind her desk and looking through a pile of yellow message slips. There was a funereal atmosphere in the GlobusBank office, as though Vladimir's death had taken with it the spirit of all its employees. Vladimir Borchenko and GlobusBank were one and the same, for all practical purposes. Jason had read the fear and uncertainty in the faces he passed when he came in.

There was a quick knock at the door; then, Nikolai Petrov came in.

He was in his shirtsleeves, his face looking haggard and tired. He glanced at Jason and met Natasha's gaze.

"Where have you been?" he asked in English, obviously for Jason's benefit. "It is chaos here. I've spent the day on the phone trying to reassure investors that we're proceeding with our projects."

"I needed time," Natasha said, her voice steely.

"Time for what?" Nikolai asked. "You know, I am grieving as well. It feels like I've lost my father."

Nikolai glanced at Jason, a flash of embarrassment playing on his features. He folded his arms and shook his head.

"And I suspect that we are not meeting to discuss work," Nikolai added. "Perhaps you can explain why you called me and talked to me as though I were some sort of stranger."

Natasha frowned, glared at Nikolai.

"I should have known that you would be eager to take over," she said. "Have you moved into Vladimir's office yet?"

"You were the one who disappeared," Nikolai said. "If I was not here, who would take control?"

"You play the part well," Natasha said.

"Perhaps you no longer wish to work at GlobusBank," Nikolai spat back. "That can be arranged."

Nikolai's muscular neck pulsed with tension. He looked at Jason. "So now the two of you are a team?" he asked.

"Leave Jason out of this," Natasha said.

Nikolai gave Jason a dismissive look. "I am sorry, but this is the business of GlobusBank," he said to Jason. "If you would leave us alone—"

"I don't want to be alone with you," Natasha said. "Perhaps I am all that stands in the way of your taking over the bank completely. Does that mean I am next?"

Nikolai pointed at her. "Be careful what you say. You don't know what you are talking about."

Natasha responded bitterly in Russian, her voice rising. Nikolai yelled back, their voices producing an unintelligible din.

Jason watched in silence, shocked by how these two business associates had immediately launched into such bitterness. He realized all at once that what he was witnessing was a result of intense competition between them, a deep antipathy that threatened to explode now that Vladimir was no longer around to temper their rivalry.

Natasha had suspected that Nikolai might have been involved in Vladimir's killing. He still had connections in the Moscow underworld, the kind of associations that might have led him to an agreement with Belarin's consortium. But now Jason looked at Nikolai, at the seeming earnestness with which he spoke. He didn't believe it. Nikolai wasn't helping Belarin. Jason realized that Natasha's own sense of guilt was driving her anger.

Doubt flashed across Jason's mind: *Did she tell me the whole story when she confessed in her apartment? Can I trust her?*

Of course he could. If she was lying, then nothing made sense. There was no saving any of them.

"Stop it, both of you," Jason yelled.

They looked at Jason, both seeming shocked out of a rage that had momentarily engulfed them both.

"Belarin is our problem," Jason said. "We all know that."

He could see Natasha breathing hard as she put her hands on her desk and dropped her head.

"What are we going to do about him?" Jason asked.

Nikolai was staring intently at Natasha with an expression that mixed surprise and disappointment. He shook his head slightly.

"You think I might have been involved in Vladimir's death?" he asked her.

She looked up, her face drained of emotion. "I do not know what to think," she said.

"You are right," Nikolai said to Jason. "Maxim Belarin is our true problem. But I can see that neither of you trusts me fully."

Nikolai walked over to Natasha and took her hand. He looked into her eyes and spoke from his heart. "Natasha, we have had our differences, but I ask you to set aside your fears. I ask you to trust me this once, and I promise—you will not regret it. We both loved and respected Vladimir. Please, trust me." He paused, looked at Jason and then back to Natasha. "I have a plan."

*February 20, 1998.*
*Rome.*

DAVID SAW ANNIA AND ANDY standing together quietly in the Vatican gardens. It was dark, and their faces were cast in shadow.

"Thank you," David said to the young priest who had led him there. The priest smiled politely and left, his footsteps echoing quietly.

Annia called out David's name when she saw him; they embraced deeply. David luxuriated in the smell of her hair, the familiar contours of her body in his arms.

"How is he?" David asked.

"He is sick," she said. "Almost too weak to talk. The doctor told us that there is little more that he can do."

Andy Kapinski approached without a word and warmly hugged David. Andy looked worn and fatigued; a lock of his hair hung lank over his forehead.

"It's good to see you," David said.

"And you," Andy replied. "I was surprised to hear that you were coming."

David shrugged, not acknowledging the note of suspicion in Andy's voice. Kapinski had always been very intuitive, and he probably sensed that something had gone wrong.

"I'll tell you later," David said softly, speaking close to Andy's ear. Andy nodded soberly.

360

"I've been to the hotel," David said to Annia. "I think we should get back there and pack. We might still be able to get a flight out of the country tonight."

"Tonight?" Annia asked, puzzled. "I don't understand."

"We need to get back to Chicago," David said. "Is that all right? Were you planning to visit him again?"

"No," Annia replied sadly. "We were told that he won't be able to see any more visitors. It might be the last time we ever see him."

David took her in his arms again, pulled her close. "I'm sorry," he said. "I know how much he means to you."

David felt the deepness of his love for Annia. He heard the suffering in her voice, as well as her soulful understanding of life that always impressed him and made him feel fortunate to have known her. Annia was the one he wanted to be with. No more secret deals with the CIA, no more hungry dogs like Belarin.

They walked together out of the gardens, past the Swiss Guards, back into St. Peter's Square. The lights had come on, illuminating the gentle night.

"I'm leaving for Warsaw in the morning," Andy said. "Are you sure you don't want to wait until then? We can have dinner."

"We're going to see if there's any way to get a flight out," David replied. He glanced at Annia and saw that she understood his determination. Andy looked as though he was about to argue, but then he nodded and stuck his hands in his pockets.

They hung together in the bustling crowds on the street and walked past cafes and restaurants. David's stomach growled, and he remembered that he hadn't eaten in almost a full day.

"Maybe you're right about dinner," David said, looking at his watch. "Let me call from the hotel and see if we can get a flight out. Then maybe there'll be time for—"

He stopped, his attention caught by something. He stopped walking, which caused a woman to bump into him.

"*Scusi*," David said to her. She ignored him and moved on

without a word. David took Annia's elbow in his hand, stopping her.

There were people all around. It was early evening, and a sense of relief at the end of the workday was palpable in the air. Traffic was moving slowly.

David looked into the open window of an automobile in the lane nearest the sidewalk. It was a black car, nondescript. If David hadn't happened to glance up at it, he never would have noticed it. Nor would he have seen the two men inside it looking straight at him.

"What's the matter?" Annia asked.

They were about thirty, both dressed in suits. Now that David had stopped, the car stopped as well. David looked into the eyes of the man in the passenger seat. The man blanched with surprise, said something to the driver. The car slowly started to move forward, but David could see that they were watching him in the side mirrors.

"David, what is it?" Andy asked. "Did you see something?"

"This way," David said. He took Annia's arm and led them back in the direction they had come. After a moment, Andy followed.

"Walk faster," David said to his wife. They wove through the crowd on the sidewalk, and when they came to an intersection, David veered to the left. He looked around. The car would probably be circling the block. But if they knew what they were doing, he might not see them again.

Until it was too late.

David tugged at Annia's sleeve and led her into the foyer of a cafe. It was dimly lit, off the street. Andy joined them, his eyes wide. David saw a flash of recognition in his old friend's features, an understanding that something had gone wrong.

"David, explain yourself," Annia said angrily.

He was being followed. He knew he would be a fool to pretend otherwise. It could have been the CIA wanting to talk with him—but then, why didn't they simply approach him in the open?

One possible answer: It hadn't been the CIA. Which left Belarin. Belarin had had Vladimir killed, and he surely saw David as a threat to his ambitions. He could have found out that David was going to Rome, sent those two men there to kill him. It would be perfect, in a sense. If David was killed in Italy, who would suspect that the architect of his death was a Russian?

"I'm sorry," David said to Annia. "But this is important. Stay inside here for a half-hour or so. Get something to eat."

"What—" Annia began.

David put his hand gently on her arm to silence her. "Andy, please stay with Annia," he said. He looked through the cafe window. He didn't see the car.

"Where are you going?" Andy asked.

"Just please stay with Annia," David said. "Do you promise me?"

"Of course," Andy replied.

In a flash David saw Andy as he had been in 1974, a frightened immigrant from Poland who was drawn into an intrigue that he desperately wanted to avoid. In the time since, Andy had found strength that he never guessed he possessed. David knew he could trust him to make sure nothing happened to Annia.

"This is ridiculous," Annia said. She followed David's gaze out the window with her eyes. "Did you see someone? What are you not telling me, David?"

"You have to trust me," David said. He grasped her hands. "Get out of Rome. Book a flight to Chicago. It's probably too late to get on a flight to America tonight, but take a flight to Paris or London and continue on in the morning. Call Cynthia when you get in, and I'll join you as soon as I can. Everything will be all right. I promise."

Annia's expression turned haunted. "You're scaring me," she said.

"I'll explain when we're home," David said. He kissed her cheek. "I love you."

"I love you, too," Annia replied. She started to say something, but David put his finger softly on her lips. He felt as though his heart was breaking when he left her there without an explanation. But he had to protect her.

David glanced at Andy and nodded. Then he stepped back out onto the sidewalk and looked around. He didn't see the car, but traffic was heavy on both the sidewalks and the street. David started walking fast, his mind racing. He had to think of some kind of a plan. His first impulse was to make a call, try to act first before the two men found him again. But he had forgotten his GSM phone at the hotel in his haste to meet with Villetti. He suddenly realized he was alone, cut off, and isolated. He began walking faster; his body tensed. He cast aside the fear that a shot would ring out on the crowded streets, that his life would be extinguished by men he had never met.

David felt his heart pounding in his chest, felt sweat trickle down his back. He glanced over his shoulder every few seconds as he walked, looking to see if anyone was following him. The car he had seen hadn't reappeared, and for an instant he wondered if he had been indulging in paranoia.

No, he told himself. He knew better. He had seen too much in his life to ignore his instincts at such a time. It felt as though everything that had happened in the past decades had collapsed into this one defining moment. He knew he had to be smart, and quick, to preserve his life.

He crossed a busy intersection and moved through a crowd milling outside a theater. A show was probably beginning soon. He overheard conversations, unable to understand Italian, but he recognized the calm, easy tones of couples out for a relaxing evening. He felt so far removed from them that they might as well have been another species.

*Think.* He didn't want to go to the airport or to the hotel. He needed to stay away from Annia. She wasn't implicated in any of this, and hopefully Andy would have her on a plane within the next couple of hours. If nothing else, he could keep her from harm.

*Then what?* He could hire a car, drive out of the city. No, that wouldn't work. If he was followed, the countryside would be even more dangerous than the city. He could go to the police, but what would he tell them? He searched his memory, trying to recall where the American Embassy was.

David looked up. A man was waving at him from about twenty feet away, rushing closer through the crowd on the sidewalk.

David froze. He looked at the man's face. It wasn't one of the men in the car who had been following him. Even if he had been, it was too late. The young man put his hand on David's shoulder and panted from the fatigue of his sprint.

"I'm so glad I found you," he said.

"Who are you?" David asked, twisting away from his grip.

"Don't run; don't be scared," the man said. He was in his late twenties, dressed in jeans and a sweater. His sandy hair was longish, almost like a surfer.

"Who the hell are you?" David asked, panicking, looking around.

"Please, I'm with the CIA. My name is Mike," the young man said. He held up his hands. "Don't be scared. We need to move fast. You're in serious danger. I've come to protect you."

David felt his legs vibrating beneath him.

"How do I know you're telling the truth?" he asked.

The young man pulled out an I.D. from his wallet. David studied the photo of the same young man, the CIA insignia he had seen before. The young man put his wallet back in his pocket and shook his head in exasperation. "Listen to me," he barked. "You're in real jeopardy. There are men here in Rome following you. We need to get you to the embassy, get you under protection. You aren't going to last another hour on the street."

Their animated conversation was attracting the attention of passersby. David knew they would soon be spotted.

"What do you want me to do?" David asked.

Mike relaxed, put his hand on David's shoulder. "Good," he said. "Just let me do my job. I have a car and a driver right around the corner."

They sprinted around the corner, where a Fiat was double-parked in front of a department store. The door was open, waiting for them. David slid inside, and Mike followed a moment later. As the car merged into traffic, David looked at the CIA agent's smiling face.

"Don't worry; we'll take care of you," he said. "I'm just glad we got to you before they did."

"Who are they?" David asked.

"Russians," Mike said. "I don't know who they're working for, but there's a price on your head."

David leaned back. For an instant he felt his body relaxing, his tension dissipating. He willed himself to stay sharp, focused. This wasn't over yet.

"Feeling all right?" Mike asked. "You look tired."

"I'm fine," David said. He wasn't familiar enough with Rome to know where they were going. The driver steered the vehicle with cool efficiency through the streets. David looked in the rearview mirror and caught his eye for an instant.

"Don't worry about a thing," Mike said. "You're lucky we were able to find you."

"What's your last name, Mike?" David asked.

"Parker, Mike Parker." Mike smiled calmly, looked out the back window. The young CIA agent had a competent, reassuring manner. He was younger than David would have expected. Now that he looked closer at him, he could have just been a few years out of his training.

"Is Gleason going to be where we're going?"

Mike paused for a moment then nodded. "We're going to rendezvous with him at the embassy. I guess you two have a lot to talk over."

"You can say that again," David replied. "Have you known Gleason long?"

"Not really," Mike said. "We trained in different areas."

David watched the driver make a sharp right turn. He was

searching to the left and the right as he drove, as though looking for something.

"How did you know where to find me?" David asked.

"We have our ways," Mike said with a sly grin.

The driver slowed down and pulled close to a public park. His eyes scanned the grass and fountain and looked over the people smoking and talking, gathered on benches. Then he accelerated again and made another sharp turn.

Mike leaned back in the seat next to David; the young man was only about a foot away from David. David smelled something from Mike Parker, a sweet odor of sweat.

They had turned onto a quiet street, with a couple of quaint storefronts and stucco office buildings. There were few people around; it must have been a business district that had closed for the day. The car slowed.

Mike reached under his sweater, felt around for something there. The driver looked in the mirror then up and down the street.

Something was wrong.

"What about Jim Allen?" David asked. "I assume that Jim will be there as well."

Mike nodded, his hand still under his sweater.

"Oh, yes," he said. "Jim Allen will also be there."

He pulled his hand out from under the sweater. David looked down in the dim light of the car and saw the shining shape of a glass syringe.

*February 20, 1998. 10:09 p.m.*
*Moscow.*

JASON STAYED A STEP behind Natasha, his hand pressed lightly to her back. Nikolai went first, through the doorway of the private Moscow club that occupied the top story of a renovated building just blocks from the Kremlin.

367

The place looked like an ordinary building from the street, an old masonry four-story structure that blended with the other offices and apartments on the block one street over from Old Arbat. The first three floors were a combination of private and commercial space. It took an armed security escort to ride the elevator to the top story. There the walls had been knocked down and a spacious club built, with lush red walls, leather chairs and glass tables, a long marble bar, and a dance floor with a small bandstand. Nikolai looked at home, as though he had been to this place before. Jason had never known it existed.

"I see him," Natasha said quietly. "There, at the other end of the room. At the big table."

Jason looked where she indicated. It was still early enough that the club was sparsely populated; at a big round table near the tall windows at the far side of the room, three men were drinking vodka and smoking. Two of the men were big, as big as Nikolai. They both stood up. The man in the center was older, and he remained sitting.

"Belarin," Nikolai whispered.

The three of them stood across from Belarin. Belarin smiled, his deep-set eyes shining in the darkness of the club.

"I am surprised that you arranged a meeting with me," he said in English.

"It is the new reality," Nikolai replied.

Belarin's expression froze. He looked from Nikolai to Jason, then at Natasha, with a deep inquisitiveness.

"We should not talk here," Belarin said. "There is a back room."

"After you," Nikolai said.

Belarin nodded to his two men. "I hope you will not be offended," he said. "These are difficult times. It is often hard to know who is truly one's friend."

Jason inhaled sharply as the two bodyguards came around the table. One came up behind Jason and patted down his back, under his arms, ran his hand inside his thighs. The other did the same to Nikolai.

Belarin watched the search with a neutral, almost glazed expression. One of the guards said something to Belarin in Russian and nodded at Natasha. Belarin shook his head, indicating that there was no need to search her.

They followed Belarin across the room to an unmarked door then into a small room equipped with a bar, a set of long leather sofas, antique lamps dimmed low. Belarin took a seat and motioned for Jason, Natasha, and Nikolai to join them.

Jason sat between Nikolai and Natasha and closely watched Belarin. The old KGB officer draped one arm over the back of the sofa and held a cigarette in his other hand. He nodded to his bodyguards, who left the room quietly and closed the door behind them.

"Now we can speak," Belarin said with a smile. "Please, help yourself to a drink if you like."

"That will not be necessary," Nikolai replied.

Belarin gave Nikolai a sardonic grin and said something in Russian. He tilted his head back and laughed.

"Please, in English," Nikolai said. "For Mr. Rudas' benefit."

"Of course. Where are my manners?" Belarin replied. He looked at Jason with an expression approximating warmth. "Mr. Rudas, this is a pleasure. I just spoke with David Olen last evening. I have offered him a business opportunity. Perhaps I will offer it to you as well."

Jason tried to read Belarin's features but couldn't. The light was too dim, and Belarin had the inscrutability of a Sphinx.

"There will be time for that," Natasha said. "For the moment, Nikolai and I wish to speak to you as representatives of GlobusBank."

"I see," Belarin said, exhaling smoke. "And Mr. Rudas would be here for . . . how do you say it—moral support?"

Belarin laughed loudly at his joke, a deep rumbling that filled the room. Jason realized that the man was far more imposing in person than any image on the television could have suggested. He seemed to be toying with them, all the while holding back his real agenda.

"Let me be frank," Nikolai began.

"Oh, yes, by all means," Belarin replied.

"Vladimir Borchenko is gone," Nikolai continued. "That is a fact that we cannot change. As a result, we have decided that GlobusBank will not bid for MosElectric. I wished to inform you of this in person."

Belarin puffed on his cigarette and suddenly became very interested.

"This is a decision that you made?" he asked Nikolai.

"It is a mutual decision made by myself and Miss Alyeva," Nikolai replied. "We were in direct competition with you for the company. I want to tell you that this is no longer the case."

Belarin nodded slightly, watching Nikolai carefully.

"There is more." Nikolai shifted on the sofa. "Natasha and I will be running GlobusBank from this day on. We are aware of your political aspirations and the likelihood that you will succeed."

Belarin leaned forward on his couch and cocked his head slightly.

"We are interested in the future, not the past," Nikolai said. "We feel we should make an arrangement."

"We are the new leadership of GlobusBank," Natasha agreed, her voice even and confident. "We want to make decisions that benefit the bank and us personally. There is no reason for us to continue to compete. We should cooperate."

Belarin glanced at the door then back at Jason.

"What do you think?" he asked.

"I think they're making the right decision," Jason said. He took a slow breath. "Being successful in business means having a clear view of the realities of any given situation. Olen Europe wants to build the MosElectric office tower, and GlobusBank would like to have a friend in the Kremlin."

"We would all benefit from an alliance," Natasha said.

Belarin pursed his lips and stroked his cheek. He nodded slowly. Jason realized that Belarin was flattered, and he could see Belarin already calculating the ways in which he could benefit from such an arrangement.

"You are young people of conviction," Belarin said. "I can see that. You have decided to be smart instead of acting on old rivalries."

"Whatever happened between you and Vladimir, it is over now," Nikolai said. "We have nothing to do with it."

Belarin locked eyes with Nikolai then with Natasha. Jason tensed, knowing he would be next. He leveled his gaze at Belarin and looked into the older man's eyes. He gave Belarin his best poker face.

Belarin broke into a big grin.

"You will have drinks with me," he said. "A toast. You don't mind, Mr. Rudas? I know you Americans do not know how to drink."

"I will have a vodka," Jason said, returning Belarin's smile. "The occasion warrants a celebration."

All four got up. Nikolai shook Belarin's hand and walked with him across the room to the bar. Jason put his hand over Natasha's, sure that Belarin couldn't see, and squeezed. He felt her warmth as she returned his touch.

Belarin opened a bottle of vodka and began pouring. He laughed and began speaking with Nikolai in Russian. He sounded relaxed, almost jubilant.

Jason didn't need a translation to know what Nikolai was saying. He was in the process of successfully learning from Belarin the precise dollar amount of his consortium's uncontested bid for MosElectric.

# Chapter Twenty-Five

*February 20, 1998. 8:10 p.m.*
*Rome.*

D AVID FELT A SURGE OF ADRENALINE as he saw the shape of the glass syringe, the long steel needle that poked out from its end. Mike Parker looked up into David's eyes, and the moment froze.

They weren't CIA agents. They didn't know that Jim Allen had been dead for ten years. David had been fooled, picked up on the street by a couple of men who were obviously trying to kill him.

It must have been Belarin. Belarin would have had access to intelligence agents who spoke perfect English, who would be able to lull David into relaxing in order to make their move. David wondered what might be in the syringe. A sedative, perhaps, so that they could take him elsewhere to murder him. Or it could have contained a chemical that would induce cardiac arrest—then they could drop him on this quiet street and leave him to be found.

These thoughts passed through David's mind in less than a second.

David had seen the syringe in the instant that Mike—or whatever his name was—had looked down to uncap it. This gave David an advantage of a fraction of a second.

Acting on instinct, David balled his hand into a fist and pushed straight out, in a martial-arts move that Jason Rudas had taught him at the gym years before. David contacted the younger man on the bridge of his nose and punched through his target. There was a sharp snap as Mike Parker's nose shattered, followed by a howl of surprise.

The driver looked into the mirror.

David lashed out again, knocking away the syringe as Mike Parker blindly tried to plunge it into David's skin. He reached down and opened his door and kicked himself out of the car and onto the pavement.

David rolled on the ground, the streetlights and the sidewalk a disorienting jumble. He raised himself to his feet in time to see the driver leaping from the front seat onto the street. Mike Parker also tumbled out, yelling in anger, one hand covering his face.

They were in the middle of the block. The car, and Belarin's two assassins, was between David and a busy street in the other direction. David turned and started running away from them as fast as he could.

His chest burned. His business shoes slapped hard against the pavement. He looked back and nearly fell, his mind registering the image of the driver pulling a gun from his coat and Mike following, yelling out in Russian.

"Christ," David barked when he looked ahead again. The street was dark in the direction he was heading. A big warehouse loomed at the end of the road. David suddenly realized why there was no traffic on the street. It was a dead end.

He heard the sound of a car's brakes squealing somewhere in the near distance, heard voices yelling in Russian. His thighs and ankles ached as he forced himself to run even faster. The voices were close, perhaps twenty yards behind him. David's blood roared in his ears; his head felt as though it was about to explode in a river of panic.

There was a fire-escape ladder in front of a narrow building to the left. David saw it blur as he ran, realized it was too high up for him to reach it. But just beyond, in the shadows, was an opening between two buildings. David headed straight for it, wincing, imagining the impact of a bullet in the back of his head.

It was an alley. David's brain cried out in a riot of joy. A possibility of escape. David turned into the alley, his feet sliding on damp pavement. He didn't dare look back, but he heard the noise of echoing footsteps coming close.

There was a loud sound, almost indistinguishable from the din in David's ears. But he realized it was something else. A car engine. In that same instant he heard a hiss close to his ear and saw a piece of brick shatter and chip away from the building to his right.

The bullet had missed his head by inches.

David's lungs protested, and his knees felt as though they would give way at any instant. He felt himself running slower, as though he had reached the limits of his body's capabilities. His foot hit hard on his next step, sending a shock running up his leg and into his hip. He knew he couldn't run any more.

He glanced back. The driver was in a firing stance, his pistol shining in the light from the street. Shining metal, David thought. It would be the last thing he would ever see.

But instead of firing, the driver glanced back and leapt to the side of the alley in a blind panic. Mike Parker, standing behind him, didn't move as quickly. The onrushing car, its headlights blazing, caught him from behind and propelled him into the air. He flipped over the vehicle and landed hard on the pavement.

David watched, stunned, as the car drove straight for him. He put up his hands to shield his eyes from the headlights and braced himself for impact.

But instead of running over him, the car slammed to a halt. The back door opened, a pair of hands reached out and pulled David hard. David hit his head against the door frame, but a moment later he was in the back seat.

He looked around, his senses lagging behind what was happening. They were suddenly moving fast, the engine complaining. David looked out the back window. Mike Parker lay broken on the cement, his partner pointing the gun but then letting it fall to his side.

David gasped when he saw a face inches from his own. It was a young man in glasses, a look of concern on his face that dissolved into a smile of pride.

"Thomas Gleason," he said, holding out his hand. "Pleased to meet you."

*February 23, 1998. 9:23 a.m.*
*Moscow.*

MAXIM BELARIN WALKED SLOWLY down the tiled hallway inside the Ministry of Finance. He straightened his spine and stuck out his chest, fixed his face with the expression of haughty condescension that had made grown men break into tears.

This would be one of the greatest moments of his life. Until, that is, the elections in 2000. Then he would have his greatest triumph.

The office was at the end of the hall. Belarin knew it from memory. It was spacious, having once housed the elite of the Soviet Union's command-economy financial bureaucracy. Today it was home to so-called planners and experts who struggled to keep the nation solvent from month to month.

He saw them standing outside the door and waiting for him. Palchikoff, the former army colonel who controlled the vast majority of the drug trade from Moscow to Volgograd. And Barinov, whose organization had taken hold of vast sectors of Russia's imports from Europe and had added arbitrary tariffs and blackmailed Moscow's government from behind the scenes whenever it needed a favor. Both men were continually expanding their businesses, and combined they possessed assets in excess of a billion dollars.

And they were backing Belarin. The man who would soon control the reigns of power in a new proud, powerful Russia.

"*Dobre dyen*," Belarin said to the two men stopping outside the door. Palchikoff was tall but stooped with bad posture, his white hair framing a narrow, distrustful face. Barinov, with his square jaw and bright blue eyes, could have passed for a movie star or, at the least, a player in a TV drama.

"Maxim," said Palchikoff, his arms folded. "You are late."

Belarin smiled. "Only a few minutes. I was speaking with the press on the stairs outside."

"It doesn't matter," Barinov said impatiently. "They are waiting for us. Let's go inside and get through the formalities."

"Then we will celebrate," Palchikoff said. His lined face creased into a grin. "There were times that I doubted this would ever happen."

Belarin opened the door and took the lead. Palchikoff and Barinov were there to represent the consortium as a verification of their financial structure for acquiring MosElectric. But Belarin was the key. He had the connections in the government; he had lent the gangsters credibility. He had also guaranteed their success.

As Belarin stepped into the meeting room and greeted the government officials there, a nagging thought crossed his mind. It irritated him. Just at the moment of his triumph, he was forced to think of one small failure.

He had been unable to kill David Olen. He had forged the plan to leave Olen for dead in the streets of Rome, the victim of a heart attack triggered by an injection. But somehow Olen had escaped from Belarin's handpicked men, had run through the streets, and was picked up by . . . someone. It could have been the Italian police or the CIA. It could have been any number of entities that spared David Olen's life.

No matter. Janovich and Elenkov, the two assassins, were in hiding in Rome, Elenkov nursing injuries after being hit by a car. Belarin had weighed the possibility that the two might panic and confess to someone what they had done and might have taken measures to deal with the situation. They would meet their own assassins within hours.

"*Dobre dyen*," Belarin said, smiling at the bureaucrats who rose from the meeting table in unison. He shook their hands. Their names were Palomov and Ostrov; both wore plain dark suits. Palomov wore glasses. As far as Belarin was concerned, they were faceless and inconsequential. Belarin had not even seen the need to bribe them.

The group sat down on opposite sides of the table; between them was a steaming pot of tea, a plate of pastries. Belarin smiled inside. Hundreds of millions of dollars were about to change hands over plates of *blini*.

"We have reviewed your bid for MosElectric," said Palomov. There was a bound copy of Belarin's bid in front of him. He put his hand on it lightly, his fingertips grazing its leather surface.

"I trust it is all in order," Belarin replied.

Palomov nodded slightly. "There was debate about your financing," he said slowly.

"Our financing is all in order," Barinov said, smiling, relaxed, and charming. Palchikoff sat silently, his face clouded with displeasure. The old *apparatchik*, Belarin knew, hated democratic formalities such as this open bidding.

"I will be honest with you," Palomov said. He took off his glasses and caressed the bridge of his nose. "We thought there would be more competing bids. We had hoped to get a better price for the utility company."

Belarin said nothing. Of course they had hoped to get more money.

"In any event," Ostrov said, clearing his throat. "We have your bid. All that is left is to compare it with one other bid."

"One other?" Palchikoff interrupted. He glowered over his beak-like nose.

"What is this, Maxim?" asked Barinov. "I thought—"

"Please," Belarin said, silencing his partner. He turned to Ostrov. "What other bid are you referring to? It is my understanding that ours is the only one."

Ostrov smiled politely. Belarin suddenly realized that the bastard was enjoying his little surprise.

There was a knock at the door. Belarin looked up, something inside his guts sinking, as though he was falling down an elevator shaft.

He saw Borchenko's associates enter the room. Nikolai Petrov was bright-faced, almost arrogant in his swagger. The woman, Natasha Alyeva, was carrying a leather-bound document. She approached Ostrov and placed it in front of him.

"I apologize for our tardiness," she said. "I hope this meeting is still in order."

"Of course, of course," Ostrov said.

Natasha handed a second copy of the document to Palomov.

"Wait," Belarin said. "This is a farce. I just spoke with these people earlier in the week. GlobusBank is in a state of disarray. They are in no position to make a competing bid."

Nikolai pointedly ignored Belarin. "We have provided ample documentation of our financing, and I trust you will find that our bid is higher than the competition's."

Belarin gripped the edge of the meeting table. His mouth dropped open. The meeting with Alyeva, Petrov, and the American, Rudas—they had made a deal; they had come to an understanding.

Belarin's mind flashed back to the meeting, the drinks, the good will. He suddenly remembered how, in a moment of boasting, he had revealed the terms of his consortium's bid to Nikolai Petrov. Now his head felt as though he was swimming in fluid; he pressed down hard on the table to keep his hands from shaking.

He looked up. Palchikoff and Barinov were glaring at him.

"This is ridiculous," Belarin said. "These two are trying some kind of double-cross. But you'll see—their bid is a joke, a house of cards.

GlobusBank is in no position to acquire anything without the backing of Vladimir Borchenko."

"That is correct," Natasha agreed.

"Vladimir is the glue that holds GlobusBank together," Nikolai said.

Belarin tried to control his expression. He realized he was baring his teeth, his instincts telling him to attack. But this was no place for violence. The stakes were too high. He tried to smile but knew it was coming out as a grimace.

There was a knock at the doorway. Each person in the room looked up one by one. Ostrov and Palomov shared inscrutable expressions of bemused surprise. Palchikoff and Barinov, a moment after the other, looked stunned, disbelieving. Belarin instinctively looked at Nikolai and, for an instant, saw the young Russian's amusement and triumph.

Through the open door came Vladimir Borchenko, dressed in a dark-blue suit and smoking a cigar. Borchenko nodded from face to face and paused when his eyes met Belarin's. He looked impossibly well; his face shone with robust health and rejuvenation. He was alive.

"I see I am the last to arrive," Vladimir said. "I do apologize. I trust my associates have submitted GlobusBank's bid."

For a moment the room was totally silent. Everyone had heard of Vladimir Borchenko's fiery death.

Belarin stood up. He fought off an urge to reach out, to touch Borchenko, to see if he had gone mad. But then Borchenko patted Belarin on the shoulder. Vladimir was real; he had substance.

He was alive.

"It's good to see you, too, old friend," Vladimir said to Belarin. "I'm sure you all know about the accident at my home. One of my trusted bodyguards was killed. It is a terrible thing."

Palchikoff got up from the table and looked around the room with an expression of disgust. A moment later Barinov did the same.

"Wait, wait," Belarin said. "This isn't over."

"I stand behind our bid for MosElectric," Vladimir said. "I will give you the appropriate time to review our financials. But I am extremely confident that our offer will be more appealing than Mr. Belarin's."

Palchikoff and Barinov moved away from the table, their chairs squeaking loudly. Belarin felt a tightness in his chest, a certainty that he had lost.

Vladimir smiled. "I apologize for the last-minute, unorthodox way in which our offer is being submitted," he said. "There have been a number of matters that required my attention."

"Understood," Ostrov said. He opened the binder and read over the first page.

"We will contact you within twenty-four hours," Palomov said. He looked at Belarin. "You will be notified within the same time period. I thank everyone for coming."

Palchikoff and Barinov left together without a word, without even a glance back at Belarin. Maxim Belarin was left alone with his enemies.

He looked at Natasha Alyeva, at Nikolai Petrov, at Vladimir Borchenko. They were all trying to hide their smiles. The meeting was concluded.

Belarin nodded at Vladimir. It was only sporting to acknowledge his defeat. He also knew he had to make amends to the consortium, to assuage Palchikoff and Barinov. Because their displeasure with him could be deadly.

Vladimir waited until the bureaucrats had left the room before he leaned close to Maxim Belarin's ear.

"By the way," he said. "David Olen sends his regards."

Belarin stayed in the room alone and stared out the window. He could see the Kremlin, the site of all his ambitions. Now it might as well have been a million miles away.

# Epilogue

I N AUGUST OF 1998, THE RUSSIAN ECONOMY collapsed. Eighteen of the country's twenty major banks essentially failed. The Russian stock market dropped to levels ninety percent below its high-water mark. The *ruble* became almost worthless, and citizens lined up outside the failing banks to try to withdraw currency that would soon have little value.

For David Olen, after August 1998, business in Russia was never the same. The MosElectric building project was shelved. David was forced to close down the Olen Moscow office. There wasn't much development activity in Russia although his business still continued to grow in Central Europe.

For David and the world, the crisis began when the Russian federal government defaulted on $40 billion of *ruble*-denominated bonds. The world's sixth-most populated country, a nuclear superpower, and a permanent member of the UN Security Council was in a position of defaulting on billions of dollars in debt payments that had come due.

At the same time, world oil prices fell precipitously, taking away one of Russia's main sources of trade and foreign exchange. Most public-sector workers had gone months without being paid, and the newly developed Russian middle class was financially destroyed.

Perhaps the most crushing loss was the faith of foreign investors, who had recently taken major losses in the collapse of Asian markets. Russia was now basically marked with a financial skull and crossbones; the enthusiasm and optimism of the past few years had almost totally vanished.

The so-called oligarchs, the wealthiest men in Russia, were not spared. Among the banks that collapsed was Vladimir Borchenko's GlobusBank, which existed in name only as it became apparent that it would never recover from its losses.

Foreign experts watched these events and wondered what possibly could be done. Money had been sent to Russia before. Much of it had been intercepted by corrupt officials who funneled it into numbered bank accounts before it could ever serve its purpose. And what was the point, many wondered, of lending more money to a country whose leaders could not manage to make even minimal reforms?

America looked at its former rival, the global power it had hoped to become a partner with, and felt a sense of foreboding. Russia's fate was being written anew every day, and the optimists were increasingly few in number.

At the Vatican, Pope John Paul II recovered from his illness. Although he remained weak and frail with his followers concerned about his health, he carried on with his work—traveling, speaking, and continuing to make a huge impact on the world.

*September 1998.*
*Washington, D.C.*

OUTSIDE THE CONGRESSIONAL CHAMBERS the summertime sun shone down on Washington with typically brutal force. Waves of heat emanated up from asphalt and pavement. The cloudless sky was a muddy overcast gray.

"How long have you known Maxim Belarin?" asked Michael Billings, a senior congressman from New York state.

"Since the '70s," David Olen replied.

Billings made a note on a piece of scrap paper in front of him. "What is the nature of your relationship?" he asked David.

"Pardon me if I'm mistaken, but I'm not here to answer questions about my life," David replied. "I'm here to issue a warning. Nothing more."

Billings frowned, leaned over, and whispered something to the congressman seated next to him.

David took a sip from his glass of water. He was seated at a table in front of a microphone. Arrayed in front of him was an impromptu, informal meeting of the House Subcommittee on Foreign Relations. Carl Becker's clout in Congress had made this hearing possible.

"Mr. Olen has made it clear that he doesn't want to get into his business dealings," Carl said. He was seated in the middle of the group.

"I don't mean to be disrespectful of the proceedings," David interjected. "I simply want to say my piece and then leave."

Virginia Hamilton, a congresswoman from California, tapped the table in front of her with a fingernail.

"Pardon me for being blunt, Mr. Olen," she said. "But I'm having a little trouble following your point. You're asking us to accept on faith that you have personal knowledge of Maxim Belarin's underground backing for the Russian presidency. And also that he is an extremely dangerous individual."

"Belarin underwent a recent setback," David said. "Before the financial crash of last August. But the very same economic breakdown might create a political environment in which an extremist such as Belarin might flourish."

"Belarin does represent the far right, nationalistic end of the spectrum," Billings agreed. "We've heard that."

"He's serious, and he has a number of connections," David said. "He is also a man capable of murder. He is someone our government would have a very difficult time dealing with—if we were able to deal with him at all."

"We can accept Mr. Olen's word as fact," Carl Becker said. "He's been doing business in Russia since the early '70s. He understands the inner workings of what's happening over there. What's more— I've known him all my life. I'll vouch for him."

Walter Lenard, a stern man in his seventies, was the ranking member of the panel. He cleared his throat, and everyone else stopped speaking.

"Let's say you're right," he said to David, his voice low and sonorous, his eyebrows and hair shocking white. "There will be an election in Russia in 2000. The people are desperate and disillusioned. They're fed up with the ten-year experiment they've had to live under. And God knows who they might vote for—perhaps even a violent extremist such as Belarin."

Lenard winced, as though the reality of what he was saying pained him. "Well, then, Mr. Olen," he continued. "What are we to do? You've come here; you have our ear. How do we stop this from happening?"

David looked up at Lenard, at each individual face on the panel. He leaned close to his microphone.

"I'm really not sure," he said. "Your committee needs to advise the president and the CIA of the dimensions of what we're dealing with. Even with that, it might not be enough."

---

AFTER THE HEARING, David and Carl walked together in the afternoon heat. David felt frustrated, irritable. He had gone to congress with his concerns, voiced them. But Walter Lenard had voiced the salient point: What could they do? The Russian economy had fallen apart; the people were tired and angry. Belarin stood poised to take power and live out his nationalistic, fanatical ambitions.

"Let's go get a drink," Carl said. "I'm buying."

"Fine," David muttered.

They heard footsteps coming from behind them and stopped. Thomas Gleason, his face dripping sweat, had been running to catch up with them.

"I'm glad I found you before you left town," Gleason said to David as he struggled to catch his breath.

"You shouldn't run in this heat, kid," Carl said, a little cruelly. "You'll have a coronary."

David shook Gleason's hand warmly. David didn't like Gleason's ambitions, but he owed the young man his life. Gleason had rescued him from certain death in Rome, a debt that David would never forget.

"How are you?" David asked.

"Fine, fine," Gleason said. "Look, I was listening in on the hearing on closed circuit. You did a pretty brave thing."

"What do you mean?" David asked.

Gleason took off his glasses and wiped them with a handkerchief. Here in the light of day, David saw Gleason for what he really was: an ambitious, ultimately well-meaning, patriotic kid. David hoped Gleason didn't get in over his head with the likes of Villetti.

"You took a stand and tried to get them to listen," Gleason said. "Most of those congressmen don't want to hear bad news. They think they've tried everything in Russia, and none of it worked. They just want to stick their heads in the sand and give up."

"How about you?" Carl asked. "What's your opinion?"

"Wait," David said. He held up his hand. "I don't want to hear this. I don't want to know anything."

"You're finished with it," Gleason said.

"Exactly. I'm out."

Gleason chuckled softly and looked around.

"All right," he said. "I can understand. I really could use your help, you understand, but—"

"He's out," Carl interrupted. "Come on. Give him some respect."

Gleason nodded and held out his hand again for David to shake.

"One more thing," Gleason said. "Everything I know about you from Jim Allen's files—it's all been destroyed. I shredded it all myself. And I give you my word that no one will ever find out about it from me."

David looked long and hard into Gleason's eyes. The kid was telling the truth.

"Thanks," David said softly.

"Congressman," Gleason said. "I'll be talking to you later."

Becker shook Gleason's hand and patted him on the shoulder before he walked away.

"What was that?" David asked. "You'll be talking to him later?"

Becker smiled. "You said you didn't want to know."

"You're right," David agreed. "Let's go get that drink."

They walked slowly down the avenue, not speaking, two old friends comfortable in each other's company.

David looked around. The world seemed different somehow, fresher. It was because it was finally over. He was finished with it. Forever.

———————

DAVID OLEN SAT under a beach umbrella in St. Barts and watched the waves gently caress the shore. Jason and Natasha were in the water up to their knees and were preparing to wind sail. Annia and Monica were also nearby; they were building a castle in the gleaming white sand.

"You never cease to amaze me, Vladimir," David said. He switched the cellular phone to his other ear.

"You know me, David," Vladimir replied. "I always find a way to ensure my survival."

"It's more than survival," said David. "You have a way of always coming out on top."

Vladimir laughed softly.

David shook his head. The explosion that was supposed to have killed Vladimir Borchenko had instead taken the life of one of his bodyguards, whom Vladimir had sent up to his apartment to retrieve some documents he needed for the next morning while he finished a business call in his limousine.

After the explosion, Vladimir had instantly devised a plan. He and his driver went into hiding and assumed that the blast was great enough that the body would have been difficult to identify. He immediately contacted Nikolai, his most trusted associate, who kept Vladimir informed of events and coordinated his business until Vladimir was ready to surface again.

David had heard the satisfaction in Vladimir's voice when he explained this a couple of days after David's return to America. The pleasure that Vladimir received from destroying Belarin's bid for MosElectric—and, hopefully, destroying Belarin's support in the coming Russian elections—seemed boundless.

"How long are you going to stay in London?" David asked.

"I don't know," Vladimir replied. "There isn't much for me in Russia. Perhaps I will see what opportunities the West holds. If nothing else, I will travel for a year or so."

GlobusBank was in ruins, and Vladimir had left Russia shortly after the August collapse. He had, over the years, moved tens of millions of dollars out of his enterprises into Swiss bank accounts. He also had large real-estate holdings in England, Germany, and the United States, held in offshore companies. Vladimir remained an extremely rich man, even as his country stared into the abyss.

"Jason and Natasha are here with us," David said.

David watched them in the surf. They were a beautiful couple, deeply in love. David smiled as Jason pretended to fall backward and dropped them both in the cool crystal ocean.

"You've forgiven her?" David asked.

"Please," Vladimir said dismissively. "I know she was never disloyal to me. She tried to honor her father without dishonoring me. I understand she was in a difficult position."

"I'm glad," David said. "She's a good person."

"She and Jason are still going to be married?" Vladimir asked.

"Early next year," David replied. "You'll come?"

"Of course. That will be enough to make me leave the considerable comforts of England in the winter."

David laughed.

"It's always good to hear your voice, my old friend," Vladimir said. "I will miss seeing you."

"I'm out of Russia, too," David said. "There's nothing going on anymore."

"We had good times, didn't we?" Vladimir asked. "Real experiences, the kind of things a man remembers all his life."

If David hadn't known better, he would have thought he detected a note of sentimentality in his old comrade's voice.

"We did," David agreed. "But then look what happened."

David didn't have to say anything more. Vladimir knew that David had been deeply shocked, even disgusted after he learned that their cabal had led to Albino Luciani's death and that Vladimir had known of Belarin's plans without taking action against them. He had assured David that John Paul II had never known of the assassination but the whole scheme had driven a wedge between the two men that could never be repaired.

"I know," Vladimir said softly.

"But it's over," David said.

A moment of silence passed between them, an instant in which both men felt the weight of the decades.

"What about Belarin?" David asked.

"He's still in the Duma," Vladimir replied. "I thought those gangsters would cut his throat for failing them, but it hasn't happened.

Perhaps he has a new plan. He is still in the news, you know, rattling his sword and talking about the defeated Russia rising from the ashes."

"That's not good," David mused. "You know he's capable of anything."

David had looked into Belarin's eyes and seen the soul of a killer. It was a vision he never wanted to look upon again.

"Well, look," David said. "My scuba instructor is waiting for me. I'll see you at the wedding?"

"If not before then," Vladimir said. "Please give my love to everyone."

David hung up the phone. He walked slowly to Annia and Monica, who had nearly finished their sand castle. David dropped to his knees and used the edge of his thumb to smooth the surface of one of the castle's turrets.

"That was Vladimir?" Annia asked.

"Yeah. He sends his love."

Annia looked down at the castle then up at David. "It's finally over, isn't it?"

"There's something I need to do first," David said, straightening. He paused to kiss his daughter's cheek. He smiled at Annia. "And I'm going to do it right now."

David walked to the water, let it wash the sand away from his feet. Natasha and Jason greeted him with exuberant hellos.

"I was just talking to Vladimir," David said.

"How is he?" Natasha asked. She seemed lighter somehow, truly happy, as though her new life with Jason had washed away the stern tension of her old existence.

"Good. I'm sure he's living like a king."

"I'm sure," Jason said, laughing.

"Look, I hate to interrupt, but can I talk to you alone for a little while?" David asked Jason.

Jason glanced at Natasha, momentarily confused. "Sure, David."

"I'll try not to keep him too long," David said.

"Take all the time you need," Natasha replied. "I am not going anywhere."

Jason met Natasha's eyes and smiled.

David and Jason walked slowly away from the waterline, up to the patio bar.

"Two beers, please," David said to the young man running the stand. He handed one to Jason, took a drink of the other. David and Jason stepped back down to the beach and walked slowly parallel to the water.

"What's the occasion?" Jason asked.

David looked at his young associate, his trusted friend.

"I want to talk for a while, and I want you to listen," David said.

"About what?" Jason asked. They walked slowly, keeping pace with each other.

"About everything." David looked out at the infinite expanse of ocean, took a deep breath. "It started in 1974. I got a phone call from my friend, the Congressman Carl Becker . . ."